CLOTHO

Author: Christopher Keith
Title: Clotho
www.christopherkeithauthor.com

ISBN: 9780648241416
ISBN: 0648241416

Published by Pagetrim Book Services
www.pagetrimservices.com
info@pagetrimservices.com

OTHER BOOKS
BY CHRISTOPHER KEITH

Balloon: Altitude
Balloon: Solitude
Balloon: Latitude
Lifeline
Clotho
Curse of the Travel Bug Vol. 1
Curse of the Travel Bug Vol. 2
By the Book

CLOTHO

CHRISTOPHER KEITH

PAGETRIM
BOOK EDIT &
DESIGN SERVICES

Thread of life, controller of fate

1

At the heart of the English capital, London City Station, the last stop on the purple line, was a hive of activity and noise as hundreds of protesters rampaged across the platform. A huge bonfire blazed at the centre, where a dozen people stood in a circle, hurling passports into the flames and igniting the crowd's fervour.

One of those was an older lady wearing a floral skirt and handcrafted jewellery. Her aquamarine bandana held back her long, white hair, which draped over her shoulders like a delicate spiderweb. She glanced up at the sky as though expecting rain and locked on a convoy of drones descending in synchronised formation, resembling a swarm of menacing, oversized locusts. Each drone was armed with a lethal arsenal of weapons, their dark, angular frames glinting in the bright morning sunlight. They moved as one, maintaining a tight, disciplined pattern as they hovered ominously above platform 2. The crowd barely noticed as the drones settled into a holding pattern with their cameras swivelled and locked onto the mass of people, their operators just a single click away from unleashing a cache of bombs.

The old lady turned her attention back to the bonfire. The maroon passport in her hand belonged to her late father and was thirty years past its expiry date. Why had he even owned a passport? He had always been fiercely patriotic, his loyalty to the nation bordering on obsession. A dyed-in-the-wool racist, his views were rigid and unyielding, shaped by a deep-seated intolerance that had hardened over many decades. Despite his strong opinions on the world, he'd never once set foot outside the country, his understanding of other cultures sadly limited to whatever he gleaned from the narrow boundaries of his own prejudices. She could still hear his hate-filled rants and bigoted opinions, venting at any person willing to stand and listen long enough.

She tossed the passport into the roaring bonfire, her hand lingering for a moment as the flames eagerly consumed it. The pages curled and blackened almost instantly, the ink melting away as the cover crumpled in the heat. She watched in silence as it dissolved into ash, joining the remains of countless other passports that had already met their same fiery fate. The fire crackled and spat, feeding hungrily on the symbols of identity and belonging, reducing them to indistinguishable fragments carried away by the wind. The lady glanced up at the drones and smiled in defiance, the sunlight glazing her wrinkled face as she cupped her hand around a self-rolled cigarette.

A man dropped a beer bottle at her feet and foam splashed onto her sandals and exposed skin. The liquid almost instantly evaporated from the hot concrete, but the old lady kept her focus upon the drones, watching as the first one circled above the crowd and dropped its payload. Much of the crowd was still oblivious to the drones above in attack formation.

Then came the explosion.

A burst of blue retardant chemical powder showered the fire and instantly put it out until all that remained was a charcoal swirl of floating ashes, like grey snow.

Two more drones closed in at either end of the platform, ready for phase two: *tear gas*. They emitted a chilling, unified voice that blasted across the platform, a cold and mechanical sound devoid of human warmth or emotion. "*Leave the station immediately!*"

One protester at the east end of the platform threw a beer bottle. It clipped the drone and sent it pirouetting down onto the magnetic levitation tracks, where it broke into pieces.

Noise swelled from the crowd, a raucous blend of anxious conversations and panicked shouts.

The old lady smiled, her eyes disappearing in her wrinkled face as she walked along the platform through the noisy crowd and stopped at the holographic train timetable. She studied the visuals, noting the trains were normally scheduled to arrive and depart every fifteen minutes, but low passenger numbers saw them running to a reduced timetable every hour.

The next train was due to arrive in five minutes.

On that eight-carriage, electro-magnetic train gliding smoothly above the tracks, turning the view outside the windows into a streaming yellow blur as it reached speeds of over two hundred and fifty miles per hour, was Nova and her father and a handful of other passengers, leaving most carriages completely empty.

The countryside was scorched and brittle, ravaged by the UK's most severe drought on record. Rivers had thinned to a trickle, leaving dry beds and feebly flapping fish right across the country. Farmers complained they had harvested the worst crop on record, labelling it a natural disaster. Wildfires burned across forests and heathland. The number of people suffering from heat stress, unable to survive unprotected in the open for more than a couple of hours, placed considerable pressure on the national welfare system. There were also reports of another Asian hornet invasion in the north.

"Where exactly are we going?" asked Nova.

Her father was in the middle of reading the e-book on his bionic contact lenses. He always had his eyes in a book, staring forward in a trance, detached from reality, almost unreachable in his own world. She was used to the spotlight of his attention turned away from her like the regular bright and darkness of a lighthouse lamp.

He blinked twice to close the e-book and turned his war-veteran eyes on her. "Did you say something?"

"Where are we going?"

He sat up and rubbed his hands together with a large grin. "Okay, are you ready for your big surprise?"

"I'm seventeen, Dad, not seven."

He passed her a graphene e-ticket with her name and citizen number printed on its screen.

She glanced at the ticket. "The New York State Women's Gymnastics?"

He smiled. "The finals. You've always wanted to go."

"Don't tell me we're teleporting there."

His grin faded. "I thought you'd be more excited."

She studied the ticket again. "Will it hurt?"

"Will what hurt? Teleportation?"

"No, cosmetic toe surgery."

"You may feel a little strange the moment you're teleported through, but there's no pain, I promise. It'll be over in just a few seconds."

She tied her long, brown hair into a bun and leaned back in her recliner. "How does it all work? Teleportation, not toe surgery."

"I dare say we'll find out at the orientation today. From my understanding, the teleportals are powered by a combination of solar energy, hydrogen-filled turbines, and electricity. Using gamma-ray radiation and the latest technology, the teleportals scan your body down to the sub-atomic level. That data is then transmitted to the reciprocal teleportal in New York."

The train swung in a wide arc and emerged alongside city buildings. Bands of hot sunlight rolled across Nova's lap as she stared at the countryside progressing into the high-rise skyline of London, leaving the scorched trees and parched orchards in their wake.

"Don't look so worried," he said.

"Me? Worried? I laugh in the face of danger."

"Well, teleportation isn't dangerous, Nova."

"Let's hope you're right."

At noon, London City Teleport filled the train windows. The terminal, which housed the teleportals, had convex solar glass walls leaning out from its base. Adjacent to the terminal was the auditorium, connected by a skywalk bridge, boasting a seating capacity of six thousand, and was equally photogenic.

Behind the modern terminal and auditorium, the airport's old runways had been converted into a field of solar panels, harnessing the sun's energy and converting it into power to run the teleportals, banking the excess so the teleport could remain energy efficient.

Newark Liberty Teleport in New York, the world's only other teleport, was set to have underwater cables installed that connected to the hundreds of thousands of solar panels in the Sahara Desert, intended to provide a new network of teleports being built across America with sufficient power.

The dome, doubling as the Museum of Teleportation and a warehouse for the data storage infrastructure, made up the teleport's three main structures, designed in a triangular layout. The dome logged the genetic code and neural information of every individual to have travelled in the teleportals, translating them into tiny bits of transferrable data that was transmitted to the corresponding data centre at Newark Liberty Teleport in New York.

The driverless train shuddered and crept into London City Teleport Station, coming to a halt at platform 4. As it arrived, thick plumes of white smoke obscured the station and blurred the windows with a ghostly haze. The acrid smoke carried the distant yet unmistakable roar of protesters' chants, creating a turbulent backdrop to the eerie scene. The muffled sounds of their slogans reverberated within the haze, merging with the mechanical whine of the train as it pulled up.

A figure appeared in the smoke outside Nova's window, his eyes blazing with the intensity of a madman. With a violent heave, he launched a flaming projectile at their carriage.

Nova instinctively ducked as her father, reacting with swift desperation, threw himself over her just as the solar-panelled glass window shattered into a rain of jagged fragments. Flames from the projectile ignited the upholstery on the adjacent seats. Within moments, a fierce fire materialised and spread rapidly through the carriage, engulfing everything within reach. Thick smoke billowed through the confined space, choking the air and obscuring visibility. The fire triggered alarms, their shrill wails penetrating the smoke as the carriage was consumed by the inferno.

For Nova, the terrifying incident marked the beginning of a catastrophic sequence of events that would forever change her life.

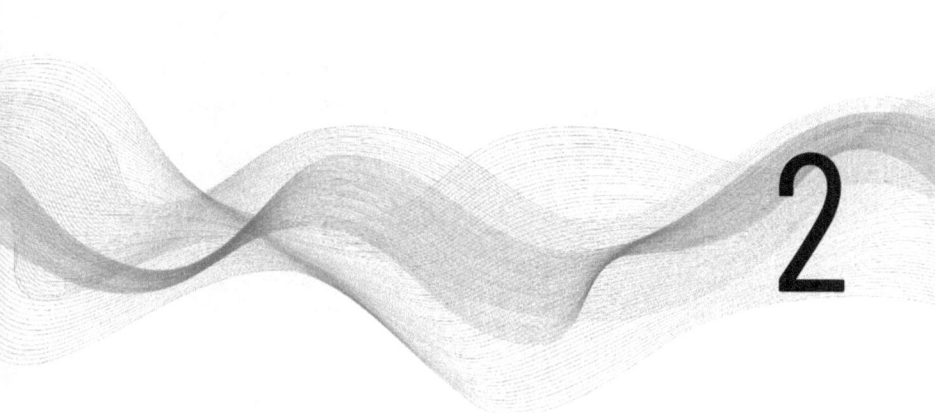

2

The train doors opened, expelling the smoke but fuelling the fire as fresh air poured in.

Nova coughed repeatedly as her father dragged her out of the train onto the platform. The fire raged through the carriage as the handful of passengers escaped onto the platform.

The smoke enveloping her on the platform was different to the smoke inside the train. It stung her eyes with a relentless burn and left her throat feeling as if it were filled with shards of glass.

"Tear gas!" said her father, grabbing Nova's hand. "Cover your eyes and hold your breath. Stay close to me!"

Squinting through the white smoke, Nova spotted a group of protesters leap down from the adjacent platform onto the tracks, then scramble up onto platform 4. Others had flocked to the underpass and rushed up the steps.

Nova froze as they streamed towards her, first in ones and twos, then in clusters, wild and crazed.

The unruly mob boarded the train and ran amok inside the carriages untouched by the fire, ripping the upholstery apart, smashing up the interior, setting more seats alight.

Navigating through the turmoil of civil unrest, Nova felt a deep sense of dread simmering in her stomach. She pulled her hood up, desperately wishing she could vanish into its shadow as she kept her eyes half-closed.

Local news stations had reporters and cameras poised at the scene. Even *they* looked frightened.

A man in tie-dyed shorts and no top streaked towards her and grabbed her shoulder forcefully. He had a pudding-basin haircut and was barefoot with an ankle bell on, waving a sign that read *Teleport to Hell*.

"The teleportals are dangerous!" he shouted, aggressively pointing at the words on his sign. "Stay away!"

Her father, small in stature but stronger than any man she knew, pulled her towards him as he pushed through the crowd. "Stay close to me!" He had been an infantry soldier who had spent years in dugouts, bunkers, trenches, and on battlefields, witnessing the atrocities inflicted on the innocent by dangerous enemies. His presence gave her some reassurance.

The man went on shouting long after she had pushed past him. "They don't fucking work!"

A voice in the sky drew Nova's attention to several drones. "*Leave the station immediately!*"

Hood up and face down, she kept moving, feeling like she had walked into a war zone. Voices overlapped, rising in pitch when the crowd grew and the noise intensified into a palpable wave of unrest.

An old lady wearing a light blue bandana, hippy style skirt, and sandals blocked her path.

Nova stopped, losing her father's hand in the crowd. The old lady held an acrylic banner, her thin, white hair blowing across her shoulders. When she leaned forward, Nova saw her deep, rheumy eyes were different colours. One eye was brown, the other sky-blue. She was a tall lady, late sixties or older, with a small scar on her brow. She tutted and shook her head slowly. "Have a nice day!" she said.

Rooted to the spot, spooked by the intimidating lady, she stared into her spooky eyes until her father's hand reached out of the human mass and grabbed her bicep. "I told you to stay close!" His voice was laced with anger as he wrenched her away from the old lady.

She disliked busy public places, especially when filled with raucous and menacing people. She wondered if it qualified as claustrophobia.

The protest was boiling over into a riot. A sudden crackling sound, sharp and explosive like gunfire, erupted, illuminating the smoke in flickering light. It made Nova flinch and left her momentarily deafened, stunning her senses.

After a few minutes of stop-start progress from the train, they eventually reached the travellators just as the ear-splitting firecrackers burned out and the drones unleashed their second wave of tear gas across the platform.

Reaching the terminal, where everything became normal and quiet once more, Nova's tension and adrenaline started to finally wane.

"Bloody Luddites!" said her father, stopping to check on Nova. "Eyes okay?"

"Stinging. That was awful. I'm still shaking."

"For someone who laughs in the face of danger, that's a bit melodramatic. Tell me, what should you do in situations like that?"

Nova pulled her hood down. "Hide?"

"I've told you before. Stand tall, stay calm. Look at those making you feel unsettled, tell yourself: how dare you risk my life, what gives you the right?"

"Should I do that now? To you?"

He frowned and stepped back. "What do you mean?"

She'd never been to America. New York was supposed to be grand and exciting. She wasn't excited, not at all. Cities were horrible places. She was a country girl and preferred the rural lifestyle. "I didn't want to come here. I'm really frightened of teleportation."

"You were the one who wanted to watch the New York State Women's Gymnastics."

Going abroad for the first time was a daunting prospect to Nova, and the thought of putting her life into the hands of a teleportation machine... teleportal... whatever it was called, seemed like madness. "It just sounds dangerous."

"Nonsense! Do not pay attention to those technophobic nut jobs outside. They like to spread fear and generate hatred. Today's society was built using technology. Either they learn to embrace it, or they bog off back to their silent caves with their bibles. Now, come on!"

Taking in the majestic interior, admiring the imaginative visual elements, they arrived at the lifts, taking them up to self-processing on the second floor. They underwent the biometric iris, facial, and fingerprint recognition, followed by a mandatory health-screening test. The passport and visa checks were each efficiently conducted through the biometric scanning process.

Advancing along the skywalk towards the auditorium, they passed a young couple, arms linked, clearly together and not afraid to show it.

"Careful out there!" said Nova. "It's kicking off big time!"

The couple pretended not to hear her and walked on with lowered heads, clearly thinking she'd exaggerated or was mad.

Nova and her father scanned through the floor-to-ceiling turnstiles by placing a finger on the authentication pad to enter the auditorium. Their names and holographic faces projected from a wall-mounted rover.

Inside, they navigated the crisscrossing aisles, searching for a decent place to sit, with plenty of choice. The amphitheatre-like arena had a seating capacity of six thousand people. Nova counted forty-five attendees.

"What's a Luddite?" she asked, once seated.

"It describes people who are willing to destroy machinery because they believe it'll threaten their lives and replace them in their jobs. Basically, they fight against the future, well, their perceptions of the future."

"What kind of machinery?"

"The automation of factories has already decimated careers in traditional manufacturing. Automated cars and trains have killed the livelihoods of commercial drivers and chauffeurs. In recent years, prisons and hospitals and other businesses that manage large volumes of people have become computerised, herding people from one station to the next, processing their data and categorising them by injuries, crimes, or whatever the nature of the business, like what we did here with the biometric processing. The rise of AI will continue to wipe out jobs in many industries."

"Why call them Luddites?"

"The term originates from Ned Ludd, from the eighteenth century. He was the instigator of a famous rebellion and the first to express his concerned views. Since then, his name has become synonymous with those who disagree with technology. The ATM is full of these ruffians."

"ATM?"

"The Anti-Tech Movement. That's who we ran into on the platform. They were protesting against teleportation."

"Are they only in this country?"

"They operate in several countries but are most active in Europe. They are a growing demographic, gaining popularity worldwide, and are becoming more aggressive. The worst ones are in America."

"They get worse?"

"Washington often faces ATM demonstrations, especially since the arrival of teleportation. They've vandalised buildings, attacked police officers, set cars alight, you name it. They're a populist group and will only grow bigger and more powerful. Right now, teleportation is still new and only operates between London and New York. Just you wait until it's fully operational in every major city."

"Hmm, I can't wait."

Nova admired her father. He had short, silver hair and a weather-beaten face through years of outdoor combat. His two main ideologies were freedom and scientific progress, shaped by over twenty-five years of military service. New technologies not only provided a tactical edge, but they had also liberated entire countries, saving millions of people. How many lives he had *taken*, he could only estimate. Throughout his career, at the behest of one prime minister after another, he had fulfilled his duty, completed every mission, and served his country to the highest standard. The mere fact he was still alive he attributed to technology.

"It's about to start," he said.

The lights dimmed over the empty auditorium.

It was obvious, just by looking around, that the potential for tele-travel was still largely untapped. Nova's father blamed it on anti-commercialism and a generation unwilling to let go of the Jet Age.

Outside the terminal, a heavy police presence moved in on the platform to establish order, the drones having failed to have the desired effect with the tear gas. The officers made several arrests and ushered the remaining protesters towards the exit travellator using their batons and whistles, blowing long blasts.

Some escaped the police by jumping down onto the tracks and climbing over the barriers.

The old lady cast her eyes on the terminal and threw down her banner. For months, she had studied the layout of London City Teleport, learning about its procedures and protocols, and exposing its security flaws. She lit another hand-rolled cigarette and blew smoke rings into the air.

Behind her, a ruckus broke out between a group of men and heavy-handed police officers. She was still focussed on the teleport as she bent down and lifted her banner, reading: *Have a Nice Doomsday.*

3

The Chalkhill Estate in London was undergoing further urban expansion. The old tower blocks, painted in an unappealing shade of lilac, were set to be replaced with new homes, densely packed into the limited available space. Some road extensions lagged behind planned developments, resulting in unfinished construction sites and idle heavy machinery scattered around the area. Protests against the project had been disregarded by the local council.

Arthur strolled along the dog-fouled footpath through the construction site, one hand tucked into his pocket. He spat his chewing gum into a commercial skip brimming with rubble and scrap iron. After he turned right, the forty-nine-year-old headed towards a row of shops set back from the main road.

Inside a large wine store, selling everything from rare wines to boutique bottles, Arthur passed the staff sitting behind the counter, who eyed him with a disinterested gaze as he breezed by towards the back of the store, where a private staircase led down to a steel door, beyond which was a long, dark corridor. His presence triggered a bank of bright fluorescent bulbs.

He punched the pin number into the security panel at the end of the corridor, giving him access through a door to the wine cellar. As he entered, he saw three men gathered around a table in the centre of the room, studying a building blueprint.

One was Travis, owner of the wine store, a man with an enormous gut and an orange beard down to his chest. The two other men he didn't recognise.

Travis threw Arthur a can of beer.

He snapped it open and drank some.

"You look like shite!" said Travis.

Arthur had spent another night on his boat. Marital stress. Long story and not particularly interesting.

"Who are these grockles, then?" he asked.

Travis held out his palm. "Meet Theo, and this is my old friend, Nate. Our newest recruits."

"Where's everyone else?"

"Marching on Parliament."

Arthur sized up the newbies and folded his arms. "What's your story, then?"

The shorter of the two, Nate, had an unsettling presence that could easily unnerve anyone who took a closer look at him. His features were sharp and angular, with a pale, almost sallow complexion that made him seem as if he spent little time in the daylight. His oily, jet-black hair hung limply around his face, often falling into his eyes, which were a piercing shade of mahogany brown, almost black. His grey coat, worn and frayed at the edges, hung to his knees, adding to his shady appearance.

The coat looked like it had seen better days, much like the man who wore it.

Theo was a full head taller, broad-shouldered, fiftyish, and wore a designer-label polo jumper and skinny jeans. He looked like an elegant man, though something about him did not sit right with Arthur.

Nate brushed a lock of hair off his face. "It's offensive to me that our politicians have allowed technology to take over and govern our lives. I've lost family because of technology. It's beyond human control, and it's time for things to change. I joined the ATM to make a difference."

"Ark at he!" said Arthur, glancing at Travis and raising his can in a mocking salute. "How do you intend to do that, then? Bring change?"

Nate struggled to lift a large drum filled with a pale liquid inside onto the table. The strong smell of gasoline, extremely scarce nowadays *and* illegal, piqued Arthur's curiosity when he unscrewed the cap.

"Where did you get that?" he asked.

"Friend of ours, he's well connected. There's plenty more where this came from. I can also get my hands on some bomb-grade chemicals, enough to bring down Teletron, Parliament, a small city block, you name it. One call and we could own a device capable of levelling any location simply at the touch of a button."

Travis laughed into his beard, which covered the majority of his face. "You couldn't put a battery in a toothbrush without dropping it. How the fuck will you handle explosives without getting caught or blowing yourself to smithereens?"

Nate buried his hands in his coat pockets, the sure sign of a man on guard. "Piss off, Travis!"

Travis put a hand on Arthur's shoulder. "I've known Nate for years; I've never seen him finish a drink without spilling it."

Nate punched Travis in the upper arm. "Don't listen to this dickhead. Our contact also has unlimited access to some of the most toxic pesticides in the country. Might even be able to get our hands on some anthrax."

Travis smiled. "And that's why I brought these two guys in. They can bring something a little different to the table, spice things up a bit. What do you reckon?"

Arthur shook his head, which could have been interpreted as marvel or despair. "That ain't who we are, terrorists. Since when did we become them?"

"You think I'm a terrorist?" asked Nate.

"It don't matter what I think. We take down Teletron, or any building for that matter, and we'll *all* be labelled terrorists. Teletron is a government-funded organisation. Any attack on Teletron is an attack on the government."

Nate shrugged like he had just proved a point. "And?"

Something in Nate's eyes Arthur did not like. There had to be a better way to halt teleportation in its tracks. He thought about it clearly and deliberately, and above all, logically.

"This here connection of yours. Anyone we know and can trust?"

"Goes by the name the Merchant," said Theo. "Needs to stay protected."

"Never heard of him."

"Exactly," said Theo.

"If you ask me, it sounds too risky," said Arthur.

"No one's *asking* you," said Nate.

"Come on, Arthur," said Travis. "We need this, you know it. I thought you'd be more receptive."

"We've tried everything, we have," said Arthur. "Petitions ain't effective; any oaf can set up a phoney online account or add fake names to a petition. We've tried picket lines, lectures, campaigns. We've made political statements, even published jokes and satirical cartoons. We've had pop idols endorse our views. Two weeks ago, a thousand ATM members staged a passport-burning event at London City Teleport to draw public attention."

"Why passports?" asked Nate. "They were replaced years ago by biometric security."

"To make a statement," said Travis. "By burning our old passports, we demonstrated our opposition to travel and what it's become."

"Did it have any effect?"

Arthur narrowed his eyes. "The institutions that we protest against just wait it out, and everyone loses interest, as do them media. We've made a name for ourselves. Everyone's heard of the ATM, and they know what we stand for, but we ain't never taken seriously. We're considered a stain on modern society. Truth is, we're a minority group. We ain't big enough yet. We need to change the way people think. Make people understand how lethal technology is and the risks it poses to our humanity, security, and the world's survival. Teleportation is priority. It's dangerous, and if we don't wake up soon, we ain't got no hope as a human race."

Travis frowned. "All what you just said makes what Nate said even more credible. As you say, we have tried just about everything. Except we haven't, and it's high time we *were* taken seriously."

Arthur decided to take the next few days to get to know these new recruits. Building a rapport with them was essential not only to understand their strengths and weaknesses but also to establish their intentions. He would observe them closely, noting their interactions and how they handled the challenges ahead. He would take a patient approach, engaging with those who were willing to talk and giving space to those who were more reserved. By creating an atmosphere of openness, Arthur hoped to learn what motivated them, identify potential issues early on, and ensure they didn't sabotage all they had worked towards.

He looked directly into their eyes, sizing them up. Nate was all mouth, but Theo was harder to read.

"I've been around long enough to know what works and what don't. I've seen lots happen, and not a lot of change. It's about managing expectations and encouraging people to fight with the ATM. You ask me, we wait until we've got enough bodies with enough social support."

"Who put you in charge?" asked Nate.

"Actually, me and Travis here are the founding members."

Nate looked sheepish all of a sudden.

"Most people think the ATM is full of troublemakers. That all we want to do is make trouble. We're policymakers. We ain't going to make new policies with pesticides and bloody petrol, only trouble."

Arthur turned to his partner. "Travis, a word. In private."

Travis glanced at Nate and Theo. "Sure."

Just then, the door blasted open and crashed into the wall. Half a dozen people piled in.

"Did you hear the news?" Claire, Travis' sister, shouted.

Travis put his hands on his hips. "What news?"

"The government's just announced London City Teleport will be shut down immediately."

The news stunned everyone into silence.

The closure was attributed to low travel demand and heavy financial losses. Despite attempts to cut costs and streamline its operations, the lack of travellers meant revenue fell short of covering the most basic expenses. Newark Liberty Teleport in America also planned to close.

It remained unclear whether the ATM had influenced the decision or if the government had closed the teleport under the guise of its own political agenda. Some voiced fears it was strategic, rhetorical appeasement.

Once the commotion died down and Arthur finished his beer, he faced Nate and Theo. "Guess that there concludes our discussion."

4

The summer had yielded record hot temperatures. Today, the first day of winter, was twenty-three degrees, but the humidity made it feel warmer. The unusual spell wasn't set to last, with storms predicted the following week, plummeting temperatures across the country.

Nova watched her father from her bedroom window, bent over a sack of leaves and unloading them onto a fire. He was incredibly productive when nobody was around to disturb him as the tranquil surroundings contrasted with his wartime past and soothed a mind filled with battlefield trauma. He liked to potter about, fixing things that needed fixing, keeping himself to himself with little in the way of a social life.

Standing in the space between the end of her bed and the wall, she ran her hands down the sides of her figure-hugging leotard. She looped her silver medal around her neck, awarded for second place on the vault in the Artistic Gymnastics British Championships. Next year, she hoped to win first prize at the IAIGC World Championships, inspired by the performances she'd seen in New York five months ago. She'd be mentally prepared and physically at her best.

The time on her bedside clock showed 09:10. Her father wanted to leave for London no later than half-past. When she glanced out of her window, she caught him wandering to the back gate, which opened onto a vista of orchards and forest divided into smaller plots by low stone walls. Countryside she considered so English. She watched him push through the gate and walk away from the cottage.

Nova ran down the stairs and into the garden, stopping at the rear gate. "Dad?"

His head turned, but he continued walking deeper into the orchard. He was a hundred metres from the cottage when she caught up to him.

"Dad? Where are you going?"

"I have to see… what's his name? The man in black."

"Who?"

"There's a message for me at the barracks. From the man in black."

"What are you talking about?"

"The man in black!"

"Come on," she said, taking his arm. "Let's go back."

He put up no resistance and allowed himself to be guided back to their cottage.

"What time is it?" he asked.

"Almost nine-thirty."

He stopped with a surprised look on his face. "We need to leave if we want to be there by noon."

"Maybe we shouldn't go today. Why don't we stay home?"

"What about the exposition? I don't want to miss it."

She gave him a faint smile. "Okay, let me quickly change. I'll meet you out the front."

Their old car was a rare model, one of the earliest electric-powered cars with more than six hundred batteries and four electric motors, one powering each wheel. The seats were made of bio-leather, the interior finished in chrome.

An antique, he called it. A *fossil*, more like.

She had begged him to upgrade to a newer model since he idealised latest technologies and invested in top-of-the-range gadgets and appliances. By his own admission, he preferred the spartan functionality and the soothing whir of the old batteries, the sense of rustic charm that suited his driving desires. Nova believed her father believed the car held precious memories of her late mother, as if her scent was still baked into the fabric, and parting with the car felt like losing a piece of her memory. That with his own memory fading, he was determined to hold onto that connection to her.

Nova's father wasn't himself that day, somewhat guarded and preoccupied. He fastened his seat belt and adjusted the rear-view mirror. Before engaging first gear, he used his hands to flatten his red beret.

"You look dashing," said Nova.

"Gracias," he said, tipping his beret.

As soon as they left the cottage and drove into the narrow lane that wound through the countryside for a few miles before merging with the main road, he switched on the local radio and pushed up the volume to discourage conversation. The news coverage concerned the reopening of London City Teleport in mid-February next year, with the ATM already in deep strife for conducting destructive protests outside Teletron's HQ, the birthplace of teleportation.

Nova studied her father behind the steering wheel, her toes habitually pointing in the footwell and her mind automatically choreographing moves to the music now playing on the radio.

"Out with it!" said her father, turning down the volume.

"Out with what?"

"What's eating you?"

She looked down at her lap. "I can't go through it again, like what happened with Mum."

"What are you talking about?"

"Are you okay? You've been acting... weird."

"Don't worry about this old fool."

"You'd tell me if something was wrong, wouldn't you?"

"Of course. We promised to tell each other everything."

"I know."

"So? Out with it!"

"I can't believe I let you convince me to go back to London City Teleport."

"You're not worried, are you?"

"I will be if the ATM's there again."

A glider high in the sky caught Nova's eye. She watched it vanish into the white clouds. "What was flying on a jumbo jet like?"

"Taking off and landing were the most exciting. The stuff in between was just killing time in the sky. Did you know, more than a hundred thousand planes used to fly around the world daily, and you know what, Nova? Very few ever experienced calamities."

"I'm not sure which is scarier: flying or teleporting. That many flights? The sky must've been constantly full of planes."

"Not really. Around airports in big cities, yes, but generally, you would rarely see a plane flying overhead unless you lived near an airport. It's a big old sky."

"Do you think jumbo jets will ever come back?"

He shook his head. "Approximately ninety per cent of all our transportation used to be fuelled by oil. All land, sea, and air transport. The world used to consume around one hundred and ten million barrels of oil a day. When oil supplies started to run dry, prices skyrocketed. So, countries around the world began using hydrogen fuel, biofuels, and fuel cells. Still, none of these could cater to the aviation industry as we all knew it, with so many millions of people travelling afar every day. The replacement fuels just couldn't keep pace with the demand. Hydrogen fuel was the only worthy replacement to jet fuel and a cleaner fuel source, but the planes needed much larger tanks to accommodate the fuel as it burned off quickly. Long-haul flights were the first to go. Tragically, the number of flights decreased, prices kept going up, and the number of travellers rapidly declined until one day, the aviation industry was shut down forever, and the Jet Age finally came to its inevitable end. Fortunately, tele-travel had been in construction for over two decades, and before long it went commercial."

"Before you took me out of school, we learned about fossil fuels and the end of oil production."

"I remember. And what did you learn?"

"The world reached its peak point of oil production in the summer, about twenty-two years ago."

"That's right. A sweltering summer from memory, and it's now referred to as Peak Oil Day. In fact, it was many months during the year that the world reached its maximum oil output. After the plateau, there was a progressive decline in oil. There may be oil reserves out there still to be discovered, but we just don't have the right technology to extract it. Even if we did, it would never reach the levels needed to restart aviation."

Pleased with the traffic flow and making good time, they passed a few cars and eased into the middle lane.

"I'm excited about the exposition today," he said.

"I'm glad someone is. If I never went to that teleport again, it would be way too soon."

"Come on. The Luddites were harmless, really. You know the story of Charlie and the Chocolate Factory, right?"

Nova frowned. "How's that relevant?"

"That's what today will be like. You'll get exclusive access behind the scenes of one of the technological wonders of the world."

"Will there be a chocolate river?"

He gave her a more generous laugh than it deserved and explained that about five thousand invitations – golden tickets he called them – had been sent to UK citizens through random selection by a corporate lottery system. Nova and her father had been two lucky winners. The exposition would kick off with a presentation inside the auditorium, promptly followed by the opportunity to meet with the self-proclaimed *intergalactic* physicist engineers. They would talk about the teleportation experience and answer questions. A free buffet lunch would be followed by free time inside the Museum of Teleportation, and a guided tour of the data storage dome would conclude the visit. All lottery winners, including Nova and her father, would then be eligible for a seventy-five-per cent discount on their next five return journeys. The exposition, entitled *The Era of Technological Change,* aimed to boost passenger confidence by promoting the modern technology and encouraging tele-travel.

The government hoped to demonstrate teleportation was safe, convenient, and cost-effective.

"*Turn left at the next junction,*" said Cass, her holographic face superimposed on the windscreen.

"This next one coming up?" asked her father.

"*Correct. Please consider recharging soon. Battery is at twenty-five per cent. Range one hundred and ten miles.*"

The battery icon flashed on the windscreen.

He pinched the bridge of his nose. "I forgot to charge her overnight. Actually, that's not entirely true. I plugged the EV charger into the lawnmower."

"That's not like you," said Nova.

He shrugged. "First time for everything."

"*The nearest EV charging station is four miles from here. Would you like directions?*"

"We're fine for now, Cass."

The warmth of the winter sun upon the windows and the rhythm of the wheels running across the asphalt made Nova sleepy.

Later that morning, something startled her awake, and she lifted her head off the window. The time was still before noon. It was as if someone had scissored out a ninety-minute slice of her day.

Her father had claimed a parking space in lot 41 inside the multi-storey car park. The teleport loomed in the foreground, a staggering fortress of steel and glass.

She felt her blood pumping at her temples. Her mind was overloaded with worry. Was she worrying unduly? Her previous encounter with the ATM had left her emotionally fragile. She quickly pulled herself together. Spending a day out with her father would be a welcome change, and something they both needed. For her father, it would be a rare opportunity to step outside the cottage and enjoy a simple pleasure.

Little did she know that this day, and the events that would soon unfold, would put her life in constant danger.

5

Portable fences erected in front of the auditorium were angled to funnel the crowds into six lines, making the approach easier but turning back impossible.

Stewards checking and collecting the e-tickets wore white T-shirts with the tagline *The Era of Technological Change* printed on the front. Admission was only granted through fingerprint verification, automatically comparing people's identities against the guest list and the national biometric database before letting anyone through.

"You notice something strange?" asked her father as they shuffled down the far-left line. "There are no protesters here."

"You sound disappointed," said Nova.

"It's strange, that's all. Today is the day the government is attempting to change public opinion and get teleportation up and running again."

"Do you really think this Expo thing is going to work? You think people will start using tele-travel?"

Her father shrugged. "You can lead horses to water, you can't make them drink."

"What on Earth does *that* mean?"

"They may come to see what the Expo is about, but there's no guarantee they'll feel any more comfortable with the idea of teleportation. The concept remains the same, and I don't see how giving people scientific knowledge will change that. I'm hoping that's not the case with you."

"Don't get your hopes up."

"Come on, Nova. Approach it with an open mind. Soon teleportation will be global, and we'll see the world together." He pointed at a dome-shaped building to their right. "Look! That's where all the data is stored. We'll get a tour inside there later."

Tired and nauseous, Nova couldn't summon the energy to care. "Woo?"

"Every detail about your anatomy at the molecular level is stored in there so you can be put back together just the way you were. Your body is made up of atoms. Every atom is a set of unique data, including the type of atom and energy state. It's translated into computer petabytes. And that's why they need such large data storage facilities, all very carefully monitored and managed by quantum supercomputers."

Nova made a bored face. "Fascinating, professor. Do go on."

A disturbance within the crowd made Nova flinch. Was it another orchestrated protest? Two beefy security staff argued with a cameraman stood behind his tripod. They grabbed him by his arms and forcibly escorted him and his camera away.

"Not here," said one of the officers.

The cameraman protested, listed his rights, but the officers ignored his plea as they led him off the premises.

"Keep moving forward, please!" the stewards called out at the entrance.

Nova and her father reached the front of the line, flashed their e-tickets, and took turns pressing their fingers against the authentication pads connected to vertical turnstiles.

"Proceed," said the steward, handing them an electronic pamphlet outlining the schedule.

On the other side of the turnstiles, stewards upon pedestals wearing identical T-shirts drove everyone along the corridors. "Keep moving, please!"

Nova continued bravely, enduring a few shoves and a curse when personal space was breached.

"Stay close to me," said her father.

She shared an anxious look with him, recalling the last time he said that to her when circumstances were not too dissimilar. A pandemonium of laughter and conversations in raised voices raised her anxiety. Sweating and struggling to stave off what felt like an impending panic attack, she desperately wished for everyone around her to clear a path.

Passing through a set of double doors, they walked into the familiar auditorium. Rows of plush, red velvet seats fanned out before them, but unlike before, when they'd had the freedom to choose any seat, this time they found themselves assigned to seats in Row C. Nova's eyes roamed over the crowd, seeing that most seats in the central seating area, if not all, were taken. The lower stands filled up, too, with crowds channelling along every aisle. The stewards circulated, politely asking people to take their seats.

Consulting the schedule, Nova noted that the intergalactic physicist engineers were to open the Expo with a presentation about the history and evolution of teleportation, explaining the principles of atomic structure and the way energy and matter interacted. As part of the occasion, the engineers planned to showcase a live teleportation demonstration on stage, offering the audience a visual display of the technology in action and a glimpse into the future of interstellar travel.

Nova dabbed the sweat on her forehead with her purple handkerchief and brushed her wet fringe from her eyes.

She stood abruptly, and with a strained expression, said, "I'm going to the bathroom."

"You want me to come with you?" asked her father.

"I know how to use the toilet, Dad."

Every eye turned on her as she shuffled along the aisle. She repeatedly apologised as people tucked their legs in to allow her through. She had to fight against the human flow until she reached the corridor, where she could suddenly breathe.

Clinging to the wall like a sailor on rough seas, she found her way to the bathroom, ignoring the *Staff Only* sign on the door. She locked the cubicle, gently pressing the button, and sat on the toilet, needing a moment to regulate her breathing and slow her heart.

She could still hear voices in the corridors, but they started to fade as the queues to get inside the auditorium shortened until there was no sound at all. Twisting her hair and securing it in a bun, she wiped her face on her handkerchief one more time.

The moment she stood, her eyes rolled, and her legs gave out. She dropped like a brick, striking her forehead against the cistern, which robbed her of consciousness.

When she came around, she couldn't tell if she'd been out for a few seconds, minutes, or longer. A sharp pain radiated through her skull. Her forehead was slick with blood, marked by a large, swollen lump.

She staggered to the row of sinks and mirrors, desperately splashing water onto her pale face. Pressing her finger lightly against the swelling lump on her forehead, she winced at the sharp, pulsating pain. She felt desperately parched and cupped water in her hand, drinking several gulps to ease the sudden dryness.

Leaving the bathroom, she stumbled into the corridor and found herself panting heavily. She pressed her forearm against her nose to filter out the overpowering smell of gas in the air. Her eyes began to sting and water, adding to her discomfort as she struggled to steady herself and find a way back to her father in the auditorium.

"Can anyone help me?" she called out. "Is anybody there?"

Her words echoed along the silent corridor, alerting her to the panic in her voice. The building was eerily silent, devoid of the stewards and security. It was clear an evacuation had likely been underway due to the gas leak. She realised her father had to be outside, frantic with worry, searching for her among the spectators. She imagined him pacing anxiously, his mind racing with concern for her safety. It spurred her on, fuelling her urgency to find her way out and reunite with him as quickly as possible. She expected a lecture during the drive home for her disappearing act, the severity likely to bring tears to her eyes, especially with his tirade of angry hand gestures that could direct four-way traffic on a busy Monday morning.

"Can anyone help me?" she shouted again. "Anyone there? I need to get out."

She bent over and retched violently, her body heaving as she vomited. Some of it splattered on her purple dress, staining the fabric with an unsightly mark.

Rebounding off the walls and swaying unsteadily down the corridor, fatigue and the overpowering presence of the leaking gas quickly took their toll. Her strength waned as she struggled to stay upright, and her vision blurred. She sank to her knees, a brief respite from the disorienting haze enveloping her, making it difficult to focus or think clearly.

After a minute, she regained her feet, holding onto the wall as she stood. She tried to exit through a set of double doors, but they were padlocked shut with a thick chain looped around the handles. So she moved from one room to the next, trying random doors, finding some locked and others opening into dark, empty spaces.

She gagged, fighting the urge to throw up once more. Her dizziness and her heavily impaired vision made it difficult to make any progress, as if the ground beneath her kept shifting. In her disoriented state, she began to hallucinate, seeing giant insects with enormous, round snouts and wide, menacing eyes crawling across the floor. She screamed, no words, just a high-pitched, frightened shriek.

A fire exit sign was at the end of the corridor. She headed towards it, pushed down on the lever, and fled the building. Unsteady on her feet, she crossed the stone paving until she reached the grass.

Far from the auditorium, she inhaled deep breaths, feeling her lungs gradually recover from the suffocating atmosphere from which she had escaped. But the fall and blow to her head had affected her balance reflexes. As soon as she straightened, her stomach churned, and she doubled over, her body heaving as she threw up again. She clutched her sides as the force of her retching wracked her already weakened frame. The taste of bile burned in her throat, but the act of purging left her feeling slightly more clear-headed, even while she remained hunched over, waiting for the dizziness to subside.

Lifting her head, she saw she had come out at the side of the auditorium. And then it exploded, forming a perfect sphere of white fire that flashed like a miniature sun.

6

Traffic on the main road encircling the teleport had come to a standstill. The oncoming lane was completely bare. Up ahead, drivers pulled their vehicles out of the queue, made U-turns, and headed back the way they came to avoid the gridlock.

Owen, a young boy with skinny legs that had outgrown his trousers, exposing his ankles, held onto the back of a bus that jerked with gear changes to a sudden stop, joining the traffic jam. When the bus driver disengaged the electric motor, Owen climbed onto the roof to find out what was causing the hold-up. A long line of vehicles stretched out before the bus, halted by a police blockade, their vehicles running lights and sirens. He went onto his tiptoes, expecting to spot a road accident.

Instead, something else caught his eye. Thick, black smoke rose over the residential rooftops on his left where a red-hot mountain of flames tore out of London City Teleport.

He lay on his stomach and shimmied over the edge of the roof. Hanging from the rim, exposing his stomach tattoos to the passengers inside the bus, he dropped to the asphalt and crossed the road, sprinting along the footpath until he cleared the terrace of houses behind small gardens and box hedges, reaching the teleport's perimeter. Scrambling up the wrought-iron fence, he lowered himself down the other side and headed towards the mayhem, observing the palls of smoke forming an impossibly dark ceiling over the teleport.

The whole circus was present—police, paramedics, press. Several firefighter divisions battled the blaze, their unreeled hoses shooting water over the destroyed auditorium and the terminal, where enormous, orange tongues licked through the broken windows. Unlike the flattened auditorium, the terminal still stood, but the firefighters with their blackened faces and helmets covered in soot had their work cut out keeping it that way. They already had their hands full restraining people from going anywhere near the blaze.

The solar farm surrounding the auditorium was in ruins. Owen had to step between the glass and scattered debris as he crept towards the teleport. The fire seemed to suddenly roar in his ears, a snarling, monstrous sound, a dragon's breath.

Approaching from the side, he watched the terminal walls cave in, pouring fresh air into the fire, hitting him with the heatwave. A cloud of black smoke driven deeply into his lungs made him cough profusely.

With his Ventolin inhaler in hand, he took two quick puffs and inhaled deep breaths to open his airways. As he turned his head away from the fire, he glimpsed a girl lying between the trees. Her legs were twisted unnaturally, and her arms were stretched above her head as if in surrender. The sight was so jarring he had to look twice to believe what he was seeing. Was she dead? She looked dead from this distance.

He ran over, weaving between the trees until he reached her lifeless form. Her torn purple dress was covered in blood. Her legs and arms and face were cut and badly bruised. The bracelet on her left wrist looked made of chrome. Little value in that, but her gold necklace had to be worth something. He reached behind her neck to undo the clip. She moved. She was still *alive*. Should he help her? The fact she looked middle-class clinched it.

"Hey, you okay?"

Her face was bloody and filthy, but he could tell she had the white skin of someone who preferred the shade to the sun. A sprinkling of freckles covered the bridge of her nose, and she had very brown brows and hair, worn bobbed.

He lifted her slack hand and shook it, trying to bring her back to life. "Hey, wake up!"

A small explosion made him swing round. It had come from the terminal, and the inferno doubled in size.

His attention was pulled to the right of the terminal where a line of people in business suits sprinted towards them.

He gently tapped the girl's face and shook her, rousing her from unconsciousness. "Can you stand?"

She looked as though she had trouble hearing and barely moved.

He eased her into a sitting position.

"You need to stand up."

She stared at him in confusion.

"It's okay. I will help you."

She closed her eyes again, collapsing into his arms, losing consciousness.

The men drew nearer.

He took off his cardigan, covered in stains that mottled the fabric as though it were brown tie-dye, and draped it over her shoulders.

Her eyelids rose, and her eyes rolled back into position.

"You have to get up!"

He hoisted her onto her feet.

She was weak and clung to him.

Owen cleared his throat, still sore from smoke inhalation, and spat out what he had summoned.

He guided her through a gap in the fence where exploding fragments had turned into flying lethal weapons, ripping open the wire mesh.

The approaching men, now fewer than a hundred metres away, were probably police officers. It wasn't the first time he had played cops and robbers. He imagined himself leading a mission into enemy territory but was spotted trespassing along the border. Foiling an ambush and forced to retreat with his wounded subordinate. Escaping a hero and declaring the failed mission to save London City Teleport in his report to HQ a waste of time, effort, and lives.

Snapping out of the daydream, he hoisted the girl higher on her feet to stop her legs from dragging.

"C'mon, walk!"

He hustled her down an embankment towards the road, one arm around her shoulder, the other flagging down passing vehicles.

When a green minivan approached, Owen stepped into the road and held up his palm, using the young girl's limp state as a sympathy-gaining ploy. The minivan stopped.

"Room for two?" he asked through the passenger window.

"I'm heading into Central London," the female driver said, raising her sunglasses to her hairline.

Owen nodded, and when the automatic side door rolled open, he lifted the girl up onto the middle row of seats.

The driver pulled away and craned her neck. "She okay?"

The girl had blacked out. Her fringe covered some of her blood-smeared face, and his cardigan concealed her dirty dress. "She fainted."

"You want me to drop you at the hospital?"

Hospital administrators would alert the police, and she'd be on her own.

"No."

"This doesn't have anything to do with the explosion at London City Teleport?" asked the driver.

He glanced out the window towards the trunks of black smoke billowing into the sky. "No. What happened?"

"It's all over the news. They're saying a gas leak caused it. The teleportals use large gas turbines, and one of them might have leaked."

"Anyone die?"

"They're saying five thousand people."

7

Nova's central nervous system misfired like a short-circuited transistor. She propped herself against a wall, feeling as though the ground had been pulled out from under her. The air was tainted with the stench of urine and bin juice, causing bile to rise in her throat.

"C'mon," said a voice, drowned out by a high-pitched trill that rang in her ears, making it hard to hear anything.

Spots bloomed in her vision, and the young boy seemed to fracture into several clones. Even through the haze, his striking blue eyes stood out against his fair hair and the faint shadow of a budding moustache. His cheeks bore acne scars beneath the grime covering his face. Dirt clung to his fingernails, and intricate tattoo sleeves wrapped around his thin arms.

Barely clinging to consciousness, Nova registered the high-ceilinged corridor in which she stood. Her footfalls echoed in the space as they lumbered along the subterranean labyrinth. The concrete walls showed cracks in some places, allowing in rainwater that had formed puddles, and the ceiling sagged from structural failure and gravity's pull.

Her hold of his arm grew tighter when she swayed on her feet, almost colliding with the wall.

The long corridor led to half a dozen rooms with darkened doorways, their metal frames glimmering under a small, wall-mounted lantern.

"This way," said the boy.

She wanted to stop and rest, but he kept her moving until he opened a door and guided her to a wicker mat, easing her down and lying her on her back.

"Home sweet home."

The room measured six by six metres, with walls that felt oppressively close. It had the atmosphere of a sealed tomb: airless and stifling, with no windows to let in light or fresh air. The door was the only exit, its presence adding to the sense of confinement.

"You're safe in here."

When she closed her eyes, the room swayed. When she opened them, it became still. She kept them open, trying to process what had happened, finding gaps in her memory. She closed her eyes. The swaying started again.

Sometime later, Nova jumped up from the mat and ran out of the room. There was a drain hole near the wall that she had seen earlier. She arched over and threw up. Little came up.

Someone rubbed her back.

Nova slowly turned, gasping when she saw a young boy. "Who are you?"

"I'm Owen."

"Do I know you?"

"We met, remember?"

She shook her head, unable to recall. She couldn't hear him well, as if someone had cupped her ears.

"Where am I?"

"Used to be a war bunker." He pointed at the ceiling. "Was a demolition up there years ago, caused some of the tunnels to cave in. Been completely forgot now."

"Where is this place?"

"London."

Her father had once told her that London was a city with ancient roots, steeped in both history and mystery. Beneath its bustling streets and towering skyscrapers lay a web of hidden tunnels and secret passages, some dating back centuries. He'd spoken about forgotten catacombs, abandoned underground stations, and secret routes used by smugglers, spies, and even royalty in times of war. These hidden pathways crisscrossed beneath the city and few people knew they existed. His stories had always fascinated her, imagining the layers of history and secrets buried beneath the surface of modern life.

"What happened to me?" she asked.

"That explosion."

She tried to piece together something tangible from her vague memories. She still had painful ringing in her ears and simmering nausea, threatening to come to the boil again. She had been concussed before and knew the tell-tale signs, having suffered for twelve days after a series of backflips ended with a brutal headfirst landing on the gymnasium floor. She was rushed to hospital with concussion and experienced splitting headaches, blackouts, and continuous sickness. One morning, she completely forgot who she was, waking up in hospital with a worried father by her side. The darkness made the space seem smaller, and Nova had difficulty breathing, as though her lungs were too atrophied to function independently. She put her hand on her chest, suddenly struggling for air.

"Panic attack," said Owen. "I've had those." He took her back to the mat inside the room, where a candle burned. "Try and get some more kip."

She sat and drew the tatty blankets across her legs. She let Owen tuck her in and stalked him with her eyes as he moved to a rattan armchair. As her breathing settled, she studied this boy in his magisterial perch.

"My thinking chair," he said. "Where I daydream."

Nova faded into unconsciousness, and this time, she never expected to come back. Fortunately, she didn't die during the night. Or slip into a coma. When she finally fought her way back to wakefulness, though, she wished she had. She felt like she had just gone three rounds with a heavyweight boxer, with crippling weakness in her limbs. She woke hungry and covered with sweat. It was so dark she couldn't tell if her eyes were still closed or open. She saw a bright orange light blossoming and crackling like a red-hot piece of coal. It illuminated crooked, callused fingers, like splayed branches, as if they were ghosting out of the darkness. Was she hallucinating again? She realised the boy had his fingers wrapped around a cigarette, and each time he drew in the smoke, the orange embers illuminated his eyes and longish fair hair with an oily, yellow glow. His teeth, against all odds, were clean and perfectly straight, but one was missing at the front. He looked content, smoking in his rattan throne as he contemplated the world from his secret cave.

"How long was I out?" she asked.

He exhaled a stream of smoke. "Two days."

His lips moved, but she barely heard his words through the buzzing in her ears. "Did you say two days?"

He nodded.

Something had happened to her. She didn't know what and whether her mind could salvage anything.

Owen dropped the cigarette on the stone floor and pressed his thumb into the hot ash.

"What's smoking like?"

He pondered the question for a moment before he replied, "So good."

"I've never smoked before."

"Next time I find a fag, you can try."

"Did you say *find*?"

He nodded. "Floor, bins, donations."

He took out his Ventolin and pressed it into his mouth.

A troubled expression crossed Nova's face. "You have asthma, but you smoke?"

He shrugged.

She sat up. "You haven't told me your name."

"Owen, remember?"

"What happened to me?"

"You survived that explosion."

All recent events had been cut out of her memory. "What explosion?"

"At the teleport."

She couldn't recall ever going to the teleport. She merely remembered... nothing. She struggled to articulate anything, confused by the situation she found herself in. Her cognition and senses were too impaired to consider leaving this place, putting her at the mercy of this street kid. She was too tired and just wanted this experience over with. As soon as she had her memory back and felt strong enough to walk unaided, she would leave.

"Welcome back," said Owen, still perched on his rattan throne and smoking.

"Was I sleeping again?"

"Out like a light. For like, three hours."

"Who are you again?"

"Owen, remember?"

He watched her as she studied the room with a pained look on her face, trying to figure out who she was, where she was, and why she was there. "You live here?"

With his cute, gap-toothed smile, he nodded proudly.

"Tell me about yourself."

He shrugged. "What do you want to know?"

"Anything."

"Like what?"

"Just... speak."

"I don't know what to say."

"Tell me about your childhood."

If Owen was supposed to say something profound and interesting, he didn't know what. He didn't want to tell this stranger he was six the year he had learned the truth about his mother's death. He had been born prematurely in a car park between a row of parked coaches, triggered by his mother's drunken fall at thirty-three weeks. The emergency crews had arrived to find a deceased woman propped up against a bus wheel cradling her bloodied baby, his cord uncut, his naked body exposed to the cold night. Owen had no recollection of his earliest beginnings, only that his father was unknown and his mother had been a hopeless drunk. Born deaf, he had spent his first four years inside a soundless cocoon until he received crucial cochlear implants, and a nano-hearing device was fitted, bringing adequate sound into his life for the first time.

"You still awake?"

Nova changed position on the wicker mat but kept her eyes closed. "I'm waiting for you to talk."

What did she want to know? He didn't know what to say about his childhood, or lack of one, or how he had spent his early teens living in an orphanage with staff who always strived to make him feel unwelcome, located in an area of London where you had to know how to look after yourself to get by. He soon learned the only way to survive was to abandon pride and avoid confrontation at all costs, even if this meant losing face. Knowing how to get out of sticky situations, working out escape routes, and outrunning pursuers was what had kept him alive. He also spared any details of his upbringing, how he had never learned to read or write, never played sports, and was never taught good manners or what was socially acceptable. That homelessness and survival were his only education, and where he had learned how to manipulate the thoroughfares, get by on limited resources, and stay safe. Or how grateful he was for small mercies, learning to appreciate what little he had and to deal with whatever life threw at him.

When he checked, Nova was asleep again.

He tucked her inside the blanket and settled back on his throne. He had lots of time to think. And lots to think about. With Nova's presence, he experienced a feeling he had never known before: a profound sense of companionship. For the first time ever, he had someone at his home who wasn't only his cousin, breaking the isolation he had always felt. Not just someone. A girl. She was pretty, but unlike him, brought up by a middle-class family in a decent home surrounded by loving people. She probably had hundreds of boys dying to be her partner. He would never live up to her high standards and meet her expectations as a friend or otherwise. She was out of his league.

What had she been doing at London City Teleport?

Was she feigning her concussion? Had she really lost her memory or was it just an act?

Had she taken what she remembered and twisted it?

Taken as a whole, her story could be true, and he had no reason to question it. Chewing his fingernail and staring at the brick wall, he ran through his options, deciding how she might best suit his interests.

8

Something pricked at her brain, but she couldn't catch hold of it right away. She came from somewhere deep and black and finally her eyes flickered open. It was dark all around, like the bottom of some river far from the sparkle of sunshine on the surface. Her eyes were open, but she couldn't see or breathe, as though submerged in deep water with some force weighing her down.

A deep voice punctured her subconsciousness. Her eyes adjusted, and she saw a tall man with a torch kicking Owen's ankles as he slept in his chair. He was so far gone he didn't move at first.

Nova's eyes roved up the man's long legs, lingering on his skinny waist before making a slow path towards his heavily tattooed arms, which trailed up his neck behind ears full of piercings. His straggly, black hair with greying temples hung in greasy waves to his shoulders, and his pockmarked face was covered in black and white stubble.

The man deliberately dropped a brown paper bag on top of Owen's head. "Wake up, cretin!"

Owen stretched his arms above his head and rolled his shoulders. In doing so, a bread roll tumbled out of the bag and fell down the side of his chair.

"Breakfast, snotbag!" said the man, his head jerking like he was trying to fend off a mosquito.

He turned the torch on Nova, sniffing and snorting loudly. "I don't bite." He snapped his teeth at her in a menacing way, and his smug smile never wavered, as if welded on.

She looked at the floor, away from the bright light.

With a loud sniff, he turned and passed Owen a new sealed Ventolin. "Outside. Now!"

Nova heard a harsh whispered exchange between them in the corridor, talk obviously not for her ears.

Owen returned with the man now gone and dropped back into his chair. He reached down his side for the bread roll and bit off a large piece. Looking up at Nova, he offered her a second roll from the paper bag.

"You must be Hank Marvin."

"What?"

"Starving."

Nova sat cross-legged and nibbled on the roll with quick bites. She *was* starving.

Owen scoffed down the bread, chewing with his mouth open, his lips smacking loudly.

Coming from a family strict on table manners, she couldn't help thinking her father would have certainly disapproved.

Owen was still chewing when he spoke. "Good grub?"

She nodded.

"You talked in your sleep last night," said Owen.

Nova said nothing and continued eating in silence.

Packets of mini wet tissues from fast-food joints were piled in the corner of the room. Nova ripped one open and wiped her hands clean. She used two more to remove the blood and dirt off her face, still feeling tender around her forehead.

She saw a tin cup beside a stack of cardboard signs.

Help a homeless out, the top one read.

The second sign read: *Play me at coin toss or toss me a coin.*

She flicked through the pile.

Don't drink or drugs, just need a feed.

Wanna be an actor but need to pay for acting classes first.

Hungry and cold. Please help me. Good Bless.

"You spelled God wrong."

He shrugged.

The last on the pile made her unsure whether to laugh or cry.

Mum delivered me on the street and asked me to wait there, that was sixteen years ago.

Nova wiped the breadcrumbs from her lips. "Did you write these?"

"Friend of mine. I can't read or write."

"Which has the most success?"

"Depends on where I am."

She straightened her legs and stretched her arms. She had lost track of time but was thinking more clearly, even though the details of what had happened to her remained murky. "I need to go."

"Where?"

"Home."

"Where's that?"

She hesitated before responding. "Not here."

He stared at her as if he could discover all her secrets.

"Why are you looking at me like that?"

"Just wondering where you live."

"Local, okay?"

She felt uneasy making up lies so quickly and smoothly just to be convincing. He was a stranger, and that justified the lie. He didn't need to know where she lived. In any case, she only had a vague idea of her address. All she knew was the name of her village, which had only just come back to her.

"I need to go home and get back to my dad. He'll be so worried about me."

Owen sniffed sharply. "Where is he?"

"You ask a lot of questions."

"Sorry."

"I have to go now."

She turned to leave, but he stopped her. "Let me tag along. Got nothing better to do."

Nova shook her head. "Look, thanks a lot for helping me. You're very kind. But I don't belong here, wherever *here* is. We probably won't see each other again."

He took off his cardigan and hung it over her shoulders. "It's cold outside."

It fitted perfectly.

"You have more for yourself?"

"Don't worry about me." He paused and looked her in the eye. "Hold out your hand."

She slowly stretched out her palm.

"Here." He handed her a greasy rabbit's foot.

She frowned.

His smile was contagious. "For luck."

Revived, recovered, and ready to return home to where she belonged, she said goodbye, hoping she never had a reason to come back.

9

"This is definitely it," said Nova, frustrated by the time and money she had wasted. Computer-automated taxi pilots were designed to be flawless in their efficiency, free from human traits like impatience or temper. Emotional intelligence wasn't hardwired into their circuits. Their systems operated purely on logic and data, devoid of the ability to understand or respond to human emotions. They were incapable of empathising with people suffering from a concussion and experiencing random memory lapses, like forgetting where one lived.

"I'll get out here," she said, finally recognising the single-lane track enshrouded in darkness. She paid by fingerprint and climbed out.

The taxi vanished behind the trees, leaving Nova standing alone on the gravel. Her mouth felt revolting. She needed a wash. Her skin and hair needed urgent attention. She needed to reunite with her father, so she sprinted towards her cottage and into the driveway, stopping with dread when she saw only blackness behind the windows.

She pounded on the sea-green front door and waited for a light to pop on or the sound of locks disengaging.

Giving up, she sat on the doorstep, realising her father's car wasn't in the driveway. He must have been out looking for her. In a society where women had traditionally borne the duty of care for young children, her father had been her primary carer after her mother passed away following a long battle with dementia. He was a superhero, and her parents had been the perfect couple. After her mother's death, her father became a shadow of the man she remembered. He retired early from the military to devote himself to caring for Nova, committing his time and energy to ensure she grew up to be capable and self-reliant. He firmly believed in the value of maturity and personal responsibility, emphasising the need for her to grow up quickly and take ownership of her emotions and actions. Adopting a military approach to parenting, he instilled in her a sense of discipline and accountability from an early age. His methods were strict, but they were designed to prepare her for life's challenges, shaping her into someone who could face adversity with resilience and independence. Their time spent together had forged an unbreakable bond between them, strengthened by their shared experiences and a mutual understanding. He cherished exploring diverse cultures and studying geography, finding deep satisfaction in the richness and variety of world beliefs and behaviours. He also harboured growing frustration with the impact of globalisation. He thought the homogenising forces of global interconnectedness eroded the uniqueness of cultural traditions, replacing them with a more uniform and less varied global culture. Tension between his love for cultural diversity and concerns about its erosion became a significant topic of conversation, reflecting his passion for preserving the heritage and culture of individual countries while grappling with the realities of a rapidly changing world.

"Fifty years and everywhere will look the same," he told her. "See as much of the world as you can before it's too late."

The irony was he wanted her to see the world but hardly ever let her leave the village. The older she got, the more she learned and understood his overprotective nature, blaming it on his wartime past and loss of his life partner. The only times she left the village were to attend the Academy of Gymnastics in Birmingham. She had stopped going to school because the cyber-bullying had got so bad. Name-calling and death threats to her social portals occurred daily. The other girls didn't like that she was an elite gymnast. Given she was a country girl and lived in a cottage, it was an easy hook for her tormentors. They called her pretentious and pig-headed. Many close friendships had deteriorated into gossip, recriminations, and bullying. She still didn't understand why. She had never provoked any of the tormenting or played someone off against anyone else. She never bragged or bickered. At her father's insistence, she had agreed to home-schooling. She'd also agreed, with reluctance, to delete her online accounts. As a result, she was headed into college life next year a dolt with digital interaction. Her father had opted for safety over technological convenience, another striking irony given his strong advocacy for technology.

Home-schooling had its advantages. No rigid routines. No overbearing discipline. No having to sit through boring lessons in regimented classrooms. More importantly, it also meant no cyber-bullying. The downside was it resulted in no friends, no flirting, no exploring the opposite sex. She wanted a sister and had always dreamed of having one, someone to confide in and disclose secrets with, filling the void left by having no friends. She wanted someone who would always stick by her no matter what. Someone to practice her gym moves with, sharing both the highs and lows. Instead, her father had become her best friend. And she had accepted his restrictive brand of parenting years ago.

"Just going out for a walk," she would say.

"Not too far. You know the boundaries."

She would tell him she was popping next door to see Mrs. Cooper.

"Come straight home after, no dillydallying. How long will you be?"

"An hour. Maybe two."

"Is it an hour? Or is it two? Can't be both."

Mrs. Cooper!

Nova darted to the hedge and peered into her neighbour's garden. The upstairs lights inside her cottage were still on, and she saw more lights when she went round to the front. Mrs. Cooper kept a spare macro key to Nova's rear door in case of emergency. She and Mrs. Cooper had a lot in common. They were sentimental about wildlife, protective of all animals and insects. Both had turned vegetarian at an early age. Nova had lost her mother, and Mrs. Cooper was not on speaking terms with her son, so they had found comfort in each other. They had enjoyed taking long walks together through the orchards, inhaling the fresh, dewy air, watering the garden flowers during summer, and making iced lemon tea.

She went up to the door and rang the bell. There was no answer, so she gave it five seconds and rang it again until her finger grew numb. She knocked on the window, issuing eight raps with her knuckles. She cupped her hands around her eyes and pressed her face against the windowpane. The glass was so old that some of the diamond-patterned sections had become warped, creating a distorted effect.

She raced up the side path to the back of the cottage. The rear door was open ajar. She applied a little pressure with her fingertips and felt it give. She shook her head. How many times had she warned Mrs. Cooper about being too trusting, even though the village had no history of crime? And how many times had she talked about upgrading her locks to electronic security? She walked into the kitchen. "Mrs. Cooper?"

Nova found the tap running cold water onto a plate inside the sink. She switched it off. She saw half a glass of red wine on the kitchen counter. Next to it was a graphene e-ticket for London City Expo. The electronically lit text across its digital face transitioned between paragraphs:

Dear Mrs. Cooper. We are delighted to inform you that you have been selected in our corporate lottery to attend an exclusive exposition titled The Era of Technological Change.

This highly anticipated event will be held inside the auditorium at the prestigious London City Teleport, a hub of innovation and cutting-edge technology.

The exposition promises to offer an immersive experience into the latest advancements and future trends in technology, featuring keynote speakers, interactive demonstrations, and a glimpse into the transformative changes shaping our world.

Please ensure you present this e-ticket upon arrival to gain access to the event. We look forward to your participation and hope you find the exposition both inspiring and enlightening.

The screen then transitioned to the date and time before looping back to repeat the original message.

Nova peered into the lounge. "Hello? It's Nova."

It was cold around the cottage. And quiet. The hollow kind that normally arrived after midnight.

She saw Mrs. Cooper lying on the floor, her body sprawled in a way that suggested she had collapsed suddenly.

Nova rushed over. She wanted to find her alive.

Instead, she found her dead.

10

Mrs. Cooper's mouth hung wide open, as if frozen in mid-speech or gasping for breath. One arm was awkwardly raised above her head, the fingers slightly curled as though reaching for something unseen. The other arm lay squarely across her stomach, its position unnaturally stiff. Her eyes were partially closed, giving her an eerie, lifeless appearance. The scene was unsettling, her usually composed, dignified presence replaced by this jarring image of vulnerability and distress.

At first, in the darkness, Nova couldn't make out the knife wounds slashed across her wrists, where the arteries had bled out. She didn't notice the red stains spread across her blouse or the folded suicide note resting on the arm of the sofa. Her focus was on trying to revive her, shaking her by the shoulders and feebly attempting the CPR techniques her father had once taught her. When she spotted the bloody wrists, she recoiled, slamming her back against the wall and cupping her mouth with her hand to stop herself from screaming. Every muscle in her body tensed as shock hit her square in the chest. She'd never seen a dead body before, much less the gruesome corpse of a loved one.

She didn't dare breathe until she had switched a light on. That's when she saw the note on the sofa. She unfolded it.

Enough is enough.

Collecting the spare macro key to her cottage from the rack in the kitchen, Nova ran home. She pressed her thumb to the screen. The electronic key, paired to sensors within the door, signalled the locking mechanism to open.

Once inside, she closed the door, leaned back against the frame, and then, decision made, pressed the computer icon on the key. A glass monitor rose out of the low table in the living room.

"*Hello Nova,*" said Cass. "*Welcome back.*"

Her essay on the pros and cons of nuclear energy set by her father flashed in the top right-hand corner of the glass.

"Close homework," said Nova.

A weather bubble showed the temperature would drop overnight to five degrees. A memo bubble floated across the glass: a reminder of the gymnastic trial coming up next week.

Pursing her lips, she blew the digital bubbles off the screen.

To report the death next door, Nova nervously tapped the emergency services icon in the top right corner. A computer-automated operator appeared on the screen, its mechanical voice cold and efficient. Struggling to find her words, Nova's explanation came out in fits and starts as her voice trembled with shock. She fumbled through the details, her mind still reeling from what she had just witnessed. Once she managed to convey the situation, the operator's response was calm but firm, instructing her to remain where she was until the police arrived.

Next, she called her father on his bionic lenses by tapping the retina icon on the macro key. She sighed when it passed directly to voicemail. Growing increasingly worried, she hit the shutdown button on the key, and the monitor slipped back into the table.

She collapsed to the sofa, her face crumpled with sadness, shock, and confusion. She stared at the dark rooms behind the open doors with a creepy feeling someone might be watching her. Her ears strained for sounds, and when her mind started playing tricks on her, adding to her paranoia and fear, she used the macro key and activated the lounge lamps for reassurance.

Before paramedics and first response units arrived at the cottage, she went from room to room, hoping to find signs her father had recently been home. She searched for his beret and boots but found neither. She sprinted up the stairs and peered into his bedroom, tripping the lights. She sadly ran her fingers over his dressing gown hanging on the back of the door. She had left her bed unmade the day they left for the teleport. She dashed to her room to check, finding the bed still unmade. She moved over to the window, hoping to find him outside raking leaves, stoking a bonfire, or just admiring the stars from the comfort of the swing chair on the patio. He wasn't there. She stared out across the dark, undulating orchards, then twisted, looking over her shoulder at her bed once more. She pictured the daily arguments when she struggled to wake up early in the morning to begin home study. It began with her father shaking her gently, her pretending to be asleep, and with his repeated attempts, her burying her head under the pillows.

She wanted a hot shower, so she removed Owen's cardigan and shrugged herself out of her dirty, torn dress. It felt good to shed her clothes. Stepping over the high rim of the bath, she closed her eyes, letting the low-pressure spray hit the back of her neck. Her hair was a mosaic of dust, mud, and blood. Black water streamed down her legs and pooled around the plughole. Sobbing, unable to get Mrs. Cooper's death out of her mind, wondering if she could have done more at the time, she traced the bump on her head with her fingertip, struggling to recall how she had got it.

After the shower, she looked herself up and down in the mirror. She had a cut and large bruise under her hairline that spanned three fingers, and scratches on her nose and cheeks. A deep graze was on her elbow and a series of yellow and grey bruises dotted her legs. She put on a pair of deep brown jeans and a plain T-shirt before slipping into her favourite purple hoodie. She felt safe in this outfit. Zipping her purple trainers, she took her dress and Owen's cardigan to the washing basket. As she let go, she felt something in the pocket. She pulled out the rabbit's foot. She turned the furry limb in her fingers before putting it in her jeans pocket. She could do with the luck.

Thinking she might have to spend the night at the police station, she put together a small backpack, keeping it light and sticking to the essentials: two hundred pounds in cash from her father's emergency stash in the pantry, two spare T-shirts, underwear and socks, a hairclip, and a toothbrush. If only she owned a pair of bionic lenses in case her father tried to reach her, and she wasn't home.

Everyone her age owned the wearable bionic lenses, both phone and web-enabled through a stretchy mix of graphene and nanowires. Linked to a transmitting earpiece, the lenses projected a virtual retinal display directly onto the eye with a 45-degree field of view, leaving the peripheral vision free so the user could maintain situational awareness. Because of the cyber-bullying she'd faced at school, her father had confiscated her electronic devices.

Downstairs, she threw her backpack on the armchair and looked at the macro key. A list of orange figures on the black interface displayed the air temperature readings of each room, water temperatures inside the boilers, and kept track of energy consumption.

Nova went to the security monitor on the wall. "When was the front door last opened?"

"Thursday morning, nine thirty-three," said Cass with robotic calm.

"The day we went to the Expo."

"Correct."

"How about the side door?"

"Saturday evening, seven twenty-five."

"Me earlier."

"Correct."

Staring at the floor, thinking, working things out, taking control of the situation, she selected the car icon on the macro key. It split into two new icons: car readouts and GPS tracker. Choosing the tracker, a map formed around a flashing orange dot labelled *London City Teleport Car Park*. According to the transponder, her father's car was parked in lot 41.

The knot in her stomach unravelled and became hollow. She should have asked the police about her father. *Stupid.*

She had been so absorbed by Mrs. Cooper's death that she hadn't thought to report her own sorry state of affairs. Once the police arrived, she would tell them everything.

Using the macro key, she closed the automated window screens and went to the fridge. The interior light illuminated the entire kitchen. Not a great deal decked the shelves. Friday was grocery shopping day. That was yesterday. She sniffed a carton of gone-off milk and poured it in the sink. She wanted to chuck her father's sausages. They were close to expiring, anyway, and she was gradually weaning him off meat. To throw them away now would be to accept a reality she could not yet comprehend, so she left them in there. The lower shelf was lightly stocked with fruits and a variety of organic vegetables.

In a square tub with a green lid was leftover risotto. She ate it cold, spooning it into her mouth. *Delicious.* As always, her father had cooked it to near perfection. A tear rolled down her cheek as she washed the bowl in the sink.

To keep her mind off her turmoil, she busied herself by doing a general tidy-up. She returned a discarded tea towel to its rack. She parked the automated vacuum cleaner inside the pantry under the stairs. A basket of clean washing was on the sofa. She carted it upstairs and folded the clothes away in the cupboards and drawers. She made her bed and sat on it, almost bouncing from the softness of the mattress. The room needed some colour. Her mother used to buy them flowers. Her father never bought flowers, but he tended to them regularly in the garden.

With a deep sigh, Nova wrapped the thick duvet around her shoulders, closed it at her neck to keep the chill at bay, and waited for the police.

The cottage was momentarily bathed in a bright flash of light that swept across the walls. They were here.

She ran to the front bedroom and peered out the window onto the driveway below. A sedan with mud-spattered number plates had pulled up. It had no official markings or light bars on the roof. It must have been an unmarked police car.

One man, then another, climbed out of the sedan. They headed for the side door and not the front, confusing Nova.

She ran downstairs to the living room to open the door for them, but instinct stopped her. She switched to home security on the macro key instead. The hidden camera at the side of the cottage tilted on the men. Nova watched them on the macro key's tiny screen. One was an enormous, bald man with a gun. He rattled the handle, finding the door locked. Then he broke the glass with his elbow and reached his hand through.

It was electronically locked from the inside. So he broke the door down with his shoulder.

Cass made a series of beeping sounds before activating into full alarm mode.

Nova pressed her back against the wall as the men burst into the kitchen.

She grabbed her backpack from the sofa and slipped her arms through the straps. She ducked under the brick arch of the fireplace. Standing upright, she glanced up inside the dark chimney shaft. The stars, framed by a brick square, sprinkled out at the top. She had never reached the top before, only high enough that her legs could not be seen dangling. It used to be her favourite hiding place until she once refused to answer her father's increasingly frantic efforts to locate her, landing her in trouble.

Her father had once explained how hiding was a skill that had kept countless soldiers alive during battles. The ability to find the perfect hideout wasn't just a tactic; it was a matter of survival. In the mayhem of combat, knowing where to conceal oneself could mean the difference between life and death. A decent hiding place provided the crucial seconds necessary to evade detection, regroup, or plan a counterattack. It was a skill honed through experience and instinct; one he believed could be applied to more than just the battlefield; it was a lesson in survival for any situation where danger lurked, just like now.

The chimney prank had backfired last time when her father called the police, fearing she'd gone missing. After the lecture she received when she climbed down from the chimney, she never went back inside. Tonight, though, she would go all the way. She had scaled many steep walls before, so this was not a stretch for her.

Still, she had to approach the climb with confidence as the next few minutes could prove crucial to her survival.

11

A cold draft spiralled up the chimney, sending a shiver down her spine as cobwebs brushed against her, clinging like dusty silk. Dirt and soot dislodged from the bricks, cascading down over the fireplace in a fine, gritty shower.

Nova froze with her arms and legs fully stretched out in a star position, convinced the intruders had picked up on her movement inside the chimney. But they hadn't, probably due to the noisy alarm.

Reaching the top with the physical ease of a gymnast, she levered herself out. Her hands were black. Feet on either side of the chimney, she hopped down onto the roof, landing on the six-inch-wide ridge tiles. Balancing precariously, her arms extended, she made small, careful steps like she was crossing a balancing beam. A tumble from this height with no safety net would certainly end in death or severe injury, but it was no less nerve-racking than standing on a beam waiting to be scored by a panel of judges.

She cast another sorrowful glance down at Mrs. Cooper's cottage. Soon it would be sealed off and overrun with several SOC officers, paramedics, and a pathologist investigating her death. It upset her she hadn't spent any quality time with Mrs. Cooper in over a year. She couldn't even recall the last time they had been together. Something had driven her to suicide. What? Loneliness? Depression? The deteriorating relationship with her only son, who had moved to Boston with his wife and started a family, had left her heartbroken. She hadn't spoken to him in eight years and had never even seen a picture of her granddaughter.

A shadow moved at the front of the cottage.

She dropped into a crouching position. The police would soon arrive and save her from these dangerous men. Who were they? What did they want? Had they killed Mrs. Cooper?

She had two choices. She could stay on the roof and wait for the police to arrive, risking that the men might spot her and shoot her down before help came. Or she could climb down and make a dash for the forest, hoping to disappear into the darkness before they noticed her. Option two appealed to her common sense. The police could be delayed. She *did* live in the middle of nowhere.

First, she used the macro key to activate her bedroom light, hoping to draw the men upstairs. Then she slowly descended the sloping roof tiles. Peering over the edge of the gutter, she spotted the trellis fastened to the wall, thick with ivy that clung to it like cladding. She began her descent by carefully stepping onto the rungs. Her foot faltered when one snapped under her weight, but she quickly shifted to another, her heart racing as she regained her balance. Halfway down, she jumped onto the grass, landing on two feet with perfect execution.

She moved on tiptoes along the side of the cottage to the rear garden. From the patio, she peered up at her bedroom and searched for the men. Now it became a tactical game. Hide and seek and tag combined, played with guns and battle strategy.

She saw a shadow flash by her bedroom window, and it was her cue to bolt through the garden and vault the rear gate into the orchard. She slipped seamlessly into the cover of the forest, moving fast in her purple trainers. She moved from tree to tree, weaving between them with a fluid, almost sensual rhythm of twists and turns. As she ran down a steep hill, she clung to the trees for balance. Her foot slipped, and she almost fell, but she managed to stay upright.

She saw the farmhouse, located on the same plot of land as Brookfield Riding School. Terry, who owned the land, was an old school friend of her father's. For years, he had been her riding instructor. He'd always given her preferential treatment, allowing only her and his youngest daughter, Geraldine, to ride the return journey bareback. Nova couldn't remember a time when she hadn't known Geraldine. They were the same age, born the same month of the same year. As kids, they had been inseparable until they enrolled in different high schools, and their lives took different paths.

Even from this distance, she could tell the farmhouse lights were all off. Terry was holidaying in the Cotswolds with the family, she recalled, her memory returning incrementally.

A twig snapped.

She froze, holding her breath.

She glanced back at the dark forest, scanning for any sign of movement. When nothing happened, she turned and raced down the rest of the hill. She hurdled the farmhouse gate but swung left towards the riding school instead of the farmhouse.

A bale of hay wrapped in green and white plastic blocked the stable entrance. Rolling it aside, she frantically opened the door. She went from stall to stall, looking for Winifred, a dark brown Exmoor with a white patch shaped like a diamond on her neck. She found her corralled in the fourth of eight stalls, her familiar patch a comforting sight.

"Hello, beautiful," she whispered. "It's Nova." She stroked the horse's neck and pressed her face against its coat. "I missed you."

Strapping on a bridle, she quickly led Winifred out of the stall and climbed onto her back.

"Let's go!"

She pulled on the reins, urging Winifred out of the stable, digging her heels into the horse's flanks.

Winifred, seeming to sense the danger Nova now faced, exploded into life, leaped over the locked gate, and bucked and swerved up the embankment rising to the road. Breaking back into the forest, the rhythmic *clip-clop* of Winifred's noisy hooves disturbed the silence. She feared it would give her away.

The footpath branched off in three directions, forcing her to slow to a canter. She strained to recall the way to the train station as the lack of light and lingering concussion muddled her memory.

Catching unsettling noises among the trees, she attempted to guide the horse away from the track, but Winifred panicked and bolted back into the forest.

Fifteen minutes later, she came across the train tracks at last. The bus depot was approximately a mile away, connected to the train station. Her best hope of escape was the first bus out of there, no matter where it took her, so she could find a police station and report the break-in. The tracks stretched out before her, a narrow path cutting through the wilderness and guiding her towards safety.

She hopped down and gave Winifred a quick slap on the thigh, unwilling to take her into populated areas. "Go!"

Winifred blew the air out of her nostrils, sidestepped into Nova's arm, and brushed her soft nose against her skin.

"Go!"

Winifred paused a moment longer before running off into the trees. Nova was reassured that Winifred would easily find her way home.

An electro-magnetic train came out of nowhere, forcing Nova to step back from the tracks as it passed at frightening speed. As the sound of the train died away, the peace of the countryside rolled back in, and she thought she saw a dark figure on the other side of the tracks near a wall of trees.

As she paced along the train tracks, she glanced over her shoulder, her instincts informing someone was following her. She could feel it, the hairs on the back of her neck prickling with dread. Without a second thought, she darted back into the forest, pushing herself into the fastest sprint of her life. Frightened animals scampered in different directions as she tore through the undergrowth.

Finally, she skidded to a halt, breathless, and threw out her hands in front of her, ready to defend herself, even though she could barely see her hands, but she was prepared to fight.

Hearing no movements, she turned and found her way into a rocky enclave where she hid behind a boulder. One would need to be lost to find such a secluded place. As she waited, she heard footsteps pounding past.

A sliver of moonlight filtered through a gap in the trees, glinting off the bare scalp of a man in a dark duffle coat, bigger than any human had any business being. The moonlight slowly intensified as the clouds parted, washing out the stars, casting the trees in varying shades of silver. It also lit up the man's features, and she realised she had seen him at her cottage.

As he moved away, she slipped in the opposite direction, hoping to avoid detection. The forest became a ploughed-up field with a dormant tractor in the middle, and when she got there, she found the door was unlocked. The interior reeked of damp leather and dry mud. She could still smell Winifred's horsey scent on her skin and clothes.

Crouched in the tractor's narrow footwell, she pulled her hood over her head, grateful for the darkness to hide in. She stifled tears that built up in her eyes. Her father had never worn his emotions on his sleeve. Even when his wife of thirty years slipped away. He'd taught her the importance of always staying calm and in control of her emotions as it raised the odds of survival.

12

The bus rolled into Central London as the first light of dawn broke. It slowed and pulled into a layby alongside a towering multi-storey bicycle parking lot.

Nova stretched and walked along the aisle with the other bedraggled passengers. Hands still black with chimney soot, she wiped her fingertip on her trousers and tapped the pay-pad device before stepping off the bus. The nine other passengers reclaimed their luggage and slowly drifted away, leaving Nova standing alone on the footpath.

Crossing a square bustling with the early stirrings of city life, she saw a homeless man huddled in the doorway of a small furniture shop surrounded by a dishevelled array of paper bags and discarded polystyrene cups. The scene reminded her of Owen and the difficult life he no doubt led, filled with the kind of struggles she could scarcely imagine. The man was slumped forward, staring at the ground and muttering to himself in a disjointed, incoherent stream of words. The air around him carried the heavy, unpleasant stench of urine-soaked fabric.

"Excuse me, where can I find a police station?" she asked.

The homeless man lifted his eyes slowly from his lap. Dark, sagging bags hung under his bloodshot, glassy eyes. His mouth, hidden beneath his greying beard, revealed itself as he spoke, causing the hair on either side of his lips to part. "They take you, lock you up. It's a desecration of the human body."

"Thank you."

She moved quickly along the footpath and passed an open window where she could hear voices inside. At the end of an alley, people shouted in a heated exchange, and further along, a dog barked at her from a set of concrete steps, startling her. She hated London. The imposing skyscrapers. Drunk, noisy strangers. Relentless traffic. The swollen electronic walkways where people charged instead of walked. You couldn't stand still on one. Flow was essential. People didn't want to negotiate obstacles on the busy travellators.

Despite the city's earnest efforts to present itself as an eco-friendly oasis with its innovative sky farms and lush vertical gardens climbing up the sides of gleaming skyscrapers, it could not match the tranquil beauty and harmony of the countryside. The city's green spaces felt like mere patches within sprawling concrete. Sky farms and lush vertical gardens offered glimpses of nature but ultimately lacked the raw, unspoiled essence of the countryside. These urban attempts were just sophisticated simulations, unable to capture the true, unrefined beauty and peace of rural landscapes. Nova appreciated the deep, earthy aroma of the forest, the gentle rustle of leaves in the breeze, the sky and its array of stars not dulled by city lights.

A pack of dogs prowled the footpath, barking, growling at passersby until they turned a corner and moved out of sight. Abandoned, homeless dogs roamed most major cities, sniffing around bins in search of food, dashing across busy roads, and barking at invisible targets.

London was now a megacity, with gardens growing smaller and tower blocks reaching ever higher into the sky. As a result, homeowners couldn't provide their pets with sufficient space, and landlords grew more finicky about their tenants keeping animals. The situation had spiralled out of control, leading to a surge of stray dogs that had escaped from their owners and proliferated at alarming velocity. The streets teemed with these feral animals, their numbers growing like an epidemic. Animal impound facilities were overwhelmed and struggled to cope with the ever-increasing influx of homeless dogs. News reports frequently highlighted the growing number of vicious attacks on civilians, a troubling sign of the escalating crisis. And the resurgence of rabies, a disease that had long been eradicated, had reemerged with a vengeance, spreading rapidly among the growing stray population and reaching unprecedented levels. In response to the crisis, the UK government was compelled to implement an emergency sterilisation program, intended to curb the out-of-control breeding rates and manage the swelling numbers of strays. When the program rolled out, it sought to address not only the immediate public health concerns but also to restore some semblance of order to a situation dangerously out of hand.

Nova found a newspaper on the footpath. The front page was missing, so the first page was actually page three.

Black Thursday, the media had headlined the article detailing the explosion at London City Teleport a few days ago.

No sooner had she read the first line than the bald man who had broken into her home and pursued her through the forest punched her in the stomach, knocking her over. All the air in her lungs was expelled in one coughing gasp.

She was lifted off the footpath by arms like gigantic pillars of muscle and flung over the man's shoulder like a ragdoll.

Too weak to struggle, she tried to scream but had no air in her lungs. She tossed her head about furiously before she was thrown into the back of a vehicle.

13

No one had spoken to Nova since her abduction. Not a word from the driver, the skinhead who had snatched her off the footpath, or the person who had injected a drug into her bicep on the back seat, rendering her unconscious for hours. Now she was awake.

The tight hood was yanked off her head with a sudden jerk, snapping her head back, leaving her momentarily disoriented. The gag in her mouth remained. Her knees hurt from taking up the uncomfortable kneeling position she found herself in. She blinked rapidly, squinting against a harsh spotlight flooding her vision. Her mouth was dry from the nasty tasting gag. Her hands were bound by zip ties and anchored to a burning hot pipe running vertically along the wall into the ceiling. It scalded her wrists whenever they strayed too close. Apart from a dull ache in her stomach, she had no other injuries.

As her eyes gradually adjusted, she began to scan the room, taking in her surroundings with a mix of apprehension and curiosity. The bright spotlight revealed an austere, empty room with a low ceiling propped up by thin, unadorned beams that seemed almost too delicate to support the structure above. Her eyes were drawn to the deep crimson stains spread in irregular patterns on an otherwise clean floor. The sight of it unsettled her. Was it blood? The sheer size and intensity of the stains suggested something serious had occurred here.

In its design, the dank brick walls gave the room a medieval prison look. Old candle brackets mounted high on the walls were stained by waxy residue. A fruity smell dominated the air, one she recognised well but could not place. Several deep holes punctured the wall in even alignment. At first, she thought they might be bullet holes, and then it clicked. The familiar sweet aroma in the air combined with the red stains across the floor suggested the room had once functioned as a wine cellar. The room was reminiscent of the cellar beneath her cottage, where her father sometimes brewed his own wine, and where she used to play as a child. The small holes in the wall had probably held bolts for the wine racks that had once stood there.

Nova turned her head and saw three people in the dark corner of the room where the spotlight did not reach. She slid her wrists vertically along the pipe to chest height until they reached a mounting bracket. Someone had to have witnessed her abduction. There must have been at least one eyewitness who saw what happened. It was almost certain a police drone, ever vigilant in the city's surveillance network, had captured her abduction from above on camera. She imagined the frantic coordination of officers outside, full of concentration as they devised their tactical plan for her rescue. The thought of their rapid response, combing through footage and piecing together evidence, provided a slim thread of hope.

A full ten minutes elapsed before someone approached.

Before any words were exchanged, they grabbed her by the throat. Nova let out a half-strangled gasp as the hand squeezed the breath out of her. Her vision turned white, and her mind was consumed by paroxysms of fear.

They grabbed her hair and pulled it so hard it forced her to stand, her bound wrists still clipped to the pipe, now at waist height, forcing her to arch over. The hand manoeuvred with lightning speed across her gagged mouth to silence her noisy whimpering. One hand became two that clamped around her ears like a vice and shook her head back and forth violently before letting go.

Through her tears, Nova saw the hands belonged to a lady. In appearance, she could have been a fairy-tale witch, only older and without the black costume. She had a large, pointed nose, a sharp, carved jawline, and a tight mouth. Her hair, tied back military-style, was white and thin. Her face was a cache of wrinkles, and her eyes showed different colours: one blue, one brown. They looked capable of anything.

Nova's own eyes widened when she recognised her as the scary lady who had blocked her path on the train platform the day she went to New York. At first glance, she looked like any other lady her age—friendly and full of life experience, perhaps a grandmother to young children.

She studied Nova up and down with an unblinking stare, as dispassionate as a bird. "Telling us the truth is your only option right now."

Nova nodded.

"Good." She removed the gag from Nova's mouth.

Nova opened her mouth as wide as it would go to stretch her jaw muscles before swallowing a large gulp of fear.

"Tell us why you think you're here, Nova?"

Oh God, they knew her name.

She slowly shook her head to say she didn't know, looking contrite suddenly. Her face screwed up and tears spilled down her cheeks.

"Stop that!"

Nova sobbed loudly before taking a deep breath.

"London City Teleport, what happened to it?"

"Who are you?" asked Nova.

"I'm the one asking the questions, and I asked you what happened at London City Teleport."

With a snivelling voice, Nova repeated the question. "Who are you?"

"God's advocate. The teleport, tell me what happened!"

Nova lowered her head. She had only a vague memory of finding her seat in the auditorium and getting up to use the bathroom, but little else. "I don't know anything. I had nothing to do with it."

"Nothing to do with what?"

"The explosion."

"What explosion?"

"What?"

"You said there was an explosion."

"Wasn't there?"

"You tell me."

Nova paused, wondering if she had somehow got her wires crossed. Owen had told her about the explosion. Had he got his information mixed up? No, because she'd seen the headline in the newspaper on the street: *Black Thursday*.

"I saw it in the newspaper, and I heard from someone."

"Who?"

Nova hesitated, wondering what to say and what not to. "Was there an explosion or not?"

The old lady crossed her arms. "There was."

"Then why ask me?"

"I want to know who caused it?"

"How would *I* know? I'm seventeen."

"What did I just say? About telling us the truth?"

She had never coped well with confrontation, despite her father's best attempts to raise her tough. She was never shy about expressing her emotions at home around her father, but not in public, in front of strangers. She gave the old lady a face meant to show she was harmless, but the little girl act didn't seem to be working.

"No one's leaving here until you tell us what you know."

"What, you think it was me?"

The old lady glared at her a moment longer, then slipped away to the dark corner.

When she returned, she signalled to her companions. At her signal, they emerged into the light.

The small man next to her holding the needle would find the vein in her arm to inject the truth serum.

The enormous skinhead with a flattened nose that looked like it had been broken one too many times, giving him a brutal look, came from behind, holding a metal pole.

The old lady watched with clinical calm.

When the needle pierced her vein, she looked down at the syringe sticking out of her arm as the plunger was pushed in to release whatever chemical was about to flood her system. They then waited a few minutes before resuming.

"Right," said the old lady. "Let's start again."

Nova's mind relaxed, the serum obliterating her anxiety and her inhibition as it manipulated her synapses, channelling electric pulses along several million different pathways.

She was asked the same questions over and over.

Who was she?

How had she survived the explosion?

Who was responsible for it?

Who else knew what she knew?

It went on for hours.

What did you see?

What do you know?

Who have you told?

She didn't have any answers. Despite multiple top ups, the truth-telling serum eventually wore off. Hours had passed, and reality returned as if waking from a terrible dream.

Nova was given a glass of water and some bread.

Later, when the old lady returned, she put her hands on her hips and gave Nova a nudge, waking her from her slumber against the wall. Her wrists ached inside the cuffs, and she had multiple burn marks on her skin where her arms kept touching the hot pipe.

"When can I go?" she asked wearily, her heavy head unable to remain still on her shoulders.

"Are you ready to give me answers?"

"Please, I've told you everything I know."

"You've told me nothing."

"Which is everything I know."

"You're a clever girl, Nova. I see that. Did you really suffer a head injury from the explosion? Or are you simply playing games with us?"

"Where's my dad?" asked Nova.

But she just stared at Nova with those witch-like eyes. She had called herself God's advocate, a religious fanatic maybe, but Nova wondered if she even had a soul.

Exhausted from all the questions, shivering and sweating at one and the same time, she feared worse to come.

"I understand you're scared, Nova. You should be. Do you think faking memory loss is going to save you? Think again."

She turned to her colleagues and confirmed with a tiny nod that their ears had not deceived them.

The skinhead stepped forward, tapping the pole against his palm.

Nova's shoulders shook as she silently sobbed.

The old lady snapped. "Stop crying!"

Nova felt her face turn red as rage took hold. Anger usually drove her to stamp her feet, scream, throw tantrums, or throw objects. Her mind was like a cauldron of swirling potions that formed into destructive thoughts and, if unleashed, could be turned into raw force. Then she let it vent. "What do you want from me? You broke into my home, chased me through the forest. You keep asking me all these questions. I don't know anything! Let me go home and leave me alone! I had nothing to do with what happened at the teleport. I just want to go home. You can't keep me here. It's illegal!"

The old lady pulled out a Ruger and pointed it at Nova's head. "Last chance!"

Nova had never seen a gun so close before. Her father had kept his weaponry sealed in a safe in the cottage. Relics from the war. Worth a fortune someday.

She felt the cold muzzle push against her skull. She tried to raise her head, but the gun held it in its place.

"I'm going to count to three."

"I don't know anything!"

"One."

"Please, I don't know anything."

"Two."

"I don't know anything. Please! I don't know anything. All I know is there was an explosion. That's all I know."

"One."

"*Please!*"

14

A knock at the door in the next room had the old lady retreat the gun from her head and turn to the men. "Get that!"

They ducked out of the room.

Nova lowered her head, letting her chin rest against her chest as she squeezed her eyes shut, trying to block out the overwhelming stress. She exhaled slowly, releasing a long and shaky breath. Her arms felt like lead, the muscles strained and aching from the relentless pressure of bracing against the metal pipe. She was utterly exhausted, her body drained from the constant tension and desperate effort to hold herself steady. She knew she couldn't continue in this vein for much longer; something had to give, but she wasn't sure if it would be the situation or herself.

She heard voices outside.

Then a drawn-out silence.

A gun was fired. Three consecutive shots.

There was shouting, a cascade of foul language.

Another gunshot rattled throughout the room.

A spooked rat scuttled out from a gap within the wall. The creature's sleek, grey body moved in a blur of frantic motion, its tiny claws scratching against the floor as it scuttled across the room.

The old lady dashed out of the door, gun up and out.

A fifth shot was fired.

Then a sixth.

Nova's entire body trembled uncontrollably. She clenched her jaw to stop her teeth chattering. How had she ended up here? Her mind raced in a desperate attempt to piece together the series of events leading her to this utter nightmare, but the memories were a blur. She felt this tightness in her chest and wondered if she was experiencing another panic attack.

Out of the corner of her vision, she glimpsed movement outside the room. A figure passed the door. Was it the police? Had they finally come to rescue her? She strained to see more, leaning slightly towards the door, her breath catching in her throat. But the figure moved too quickly, vanishing from sight before she could make out any details.

She teetered between hope and despair. Was help finally here, or was it just another threat lurking outside the door? Her body remained tense, her nerves stretched to breaking point as she climbed to her feet, sliding her wrists up the hot pipe.

Owen causally strolled into the room, sniffing and smiling as if nothing had happened. "Hi, Nova." He cut her hands free using a flick knife. He took her hand. "Come."

Shocked and frightened, Nova grabbed her backpack from a hook on the wall and slipped it over her shoulders.

In the next room, the skinhead was out cold on the floor. Blood gushed from the gunshot wound in his shoulder, but he was still breathing.

Another two bodies were lined up next to him. The man who'd administered the truth serum, still holding the syringe. He had been shot twice: once in the chest, once in the head.

A bullet had tunnelled through the old lady's brain, killing her instantly.

When Nova looked up from the bodies, she saw a skinny man holding a gun and standing with his foot on the dead man's stomach. She recognised his tattooed arms and long, greasy hair.

"My cousin," said Owen. "Spider."

With what looked like some kind of nervous twitch, Spider acknowledged her with a slight bow. "Okay, sometimes I bite."

Nova ran her hand over her head. "How did you find me?"

"You got my rabbit's foot?" asked Owen.

She frowned and reached into her pocket. She pulled out the rabbit's foot and handed it back to Owen.

Owen turned it in his fingers. "Got a tracker inside."

Nova looked at the dead bodies again, then at Owen, her mouth hanging open, unsure what to think or say.

Owen touched her shoulder. "Everything's okay."

She shook her head. "No, it's not." She left the room in a hurry.

Owen chased after her, but Spider snatched his arm. "Do not let her out of your sight this time."

Owen nodded and ran out of the room, catching up with Nova in the corridor. They emerged from the underground room into a large wine store. The lights were off, and the store was closed. They quietly slipped out of the front door into the stillness of the day. As soon as they were outside, Nova bolted. She didn't dare look behind her, focussing on the path ahead and nothing else. Her feet pounded on the pavement, fuelled by adrenaline and the urgent need to escape.

A few blocks away, after passing a cluster of construction machinery, Owen pulled back on her arm to slow her down. They stopped beside a yellow skip brimming with rubble.

"You're safe now," said Owen.

She wiped away the tears running down her cheeks. She hated crying. She had always felt uneasy whenever she allowed herself a moment of weakness, as if her father always had his eyes on her, ready should she break.

The sun sank behind the concrete horizon, planting Owen in shade, but she saw him clearly for the first time. There was a quiet strength in the way he stood, his posture relaxed yet ready, as though prepared to face whatever might come his way. His eyes held a steady resolve that reassured her. In that moment, she realised he was someone she could count on and trust, someone who had already proven himself in ways that mattered. His help meant more than she could articulate into words. His actions spoke about his selflessness, his unwavering decency, and his willingness to step up when others might have turned away.

As the last rays of the sun disappeared, leaving them in the deepening dusk, she knew she wasn't alone. If she needed a reason to stay strong and not give up, she had one right in front of her.

15

Nova struggled to fall asleep, fearing what might lurk within her dreams, so there was always a sliver of light between her eyelids. Every time she did doze off, she jerked awake in a sweat, convinced she was in a nightmare and had to find a way out.

Now she was wide awake. She sat upright, pulled her hair back from her face, and secured it with her tortoise-shell clip. She was under such stress, what with her missing father and a dead neighbour, the break-in at her cottage, the cross-country pursuit, the abduction, the lack of memory, and of course, the psychological torture. It had taken its toll. Her abductors could have dumped her by the road with multiple injuries or bleeding out across the ground. They could have killed her in that god-forsaken basement. The interrogations could have lasted days, weeks, months, or even longer.

At any moment, she felt her head could implode. All she wanted was to be reunited with her father and for this to be behind her. But she was too frightened to go home. She had to rely on her father to track her down. To fling the door open and charge in, holding out his arms. She prayed this terrifying ordeal was not actually happening, that she was dreaming the nightmare and the only way to abandon it was to wake herself up.

"Hold out your hand," said Owen.

Nova dried her eyes and extended her palm. "You're not giving me another piece of animal, are you?"

He laughed, then opened his fingers and dropped a purple plastic flower into her hand.

"What's this for?"

He grinned. "You like purple things."

Now her lips curled, just a little, into a smile. "Purple is my favourite colour."

"I've got something else," he said, pulling out a pristine cigarette from his pocket.

He lit it, took a long drag to ignite the tip, and passed it to her.

"How do I... do I just suck?"

He nodded.

She drew in a small amount and blew the smoke out before it reached her throat. She filled her lungs on the second draw. The nicotine rushed to her brain, making her dizzy. The harsh tobacco taste made her almost retch.

Owen couldn't help laughing at the face she pulled.

"How long have you smoked?" she asked, flapping a hand in front of her face.

"Since eight."

"Eight? That's so young."

She passed the cigarette back to him, and as he leaned over to accept it, she saw the hearing device in his ear.

He inhaled a lungful and blew a series of smoke rings up at the ceiling.

She watched them float off and dissolve in the damp air.

He straightened his legs and accidentally kicked Nova's left foot.

She flinched and let out a sharp breath of irritation.

"Sorry."

"It's okay. My feet have blisters. I spent last night running for my life."

He went to rub her foot, but she hugged her knees to her chest, wishing to protect her modesty, unaccustomed to male attention.

"I'm chuffed you're here," he said.

To his credit, she was only there because he had saved her life, thanks to the rabbit's foot.

"I never said thank you for getting me out of that horrid place."

He waved it off like it was nothing.

He had a dignity about him, a closed-in quality, like a box taped shut around its contents, but it made him hard to read. Yes, he was gentle-natured and such easy company. But he no doubt had a shady past.

"I wonder why you were adopted."

"Adopted?" She frowned. "You mean abducted?"

Owen bit his bottom lip, a little embarrassed. "Yeah."

"They kept asking me what I knew about the explosion at London City Teleport."

"Why?"

She shrugged. "No idea. Am I a suspect? Do they think I did it?"

"They?"

"I recognised one of them. The old lady. I ran into her on the train platform at London City Teleport about five months ago during a pro..."

"What?"

"The ATM!"

"Huh?"

"She belonged to the ATM."

"The who?"

"The Anti-Tech Movement."

"What's that?"

"My dad told me about them. And I saw them with my own eyes. Dangerous people. They don't like technology. They think it will replace them in their jobs and harm the planet." She stood and brushed herself down. "I need to find out why they took me."

"Now?"

"I have to go to the police and tell them everything."

Owen stood, too. "Bad idea that. Can't trust the pigs."

"What should I do, then?"

"My cousin will know what to do. He'll help us."

"Us? You want to help me?"

Owen smiled. "I'll take you to his shop."

16

Spider's shop was actually a tattoo parlour in a double-storey terrace on the corner of where the road forked. The building was worn and unsightly, its brick façade marred by cracks and weathered into a bleak eyesore.

Spider had first picked up the needle at fourteen years of age, dropping out of school to learn the trade, and by twenty had opened his own business. He was the eldest of three, each one blessed with creative abilities. While Spider remained loyal to the tattooing industry, one brother had become an interior designer, the other a graffitist in constant strife with the law.

"Mind the high step," said Owen, opening the door to the parlour, inviting Nova in. Brain-piercing heavy metal blasted from a radio in the back room.

"Here's trouble!" Spider yelled over the loud music as he came through a curtain into the front room.

Under bright spotlights, Nova finally saw Spider in vivid detail. His eyes, though framed by dark circles, held a certain charm, a mischievous sparkle that belied the roughness of his appearance. Yet, the more she looked, the more she noticed the wear and tear that life had carved into his features. Eczema flared up on both sides of his nose, the inflamed, scaly patches of skin giving his face a raw, uneven texture that added to his rugged, unkempt appearance. As he yawned, she saw his teeth, stained a dull yellow from years of neglect, were crooked and badly chipped.

"Can you help her?" Owen shouted, competing with the music.

Spider looked her up and down, snorting loudly. "I already saved your life! What more do you want? A tummy rub?"

"Please!" she shouted.

He cupped his ear with his hand. "What's that? You want a tummy rub?"

"I need your help!"

"Now that daddy's gone?"

"My father isn't gone! He's out looking for me!"

"Then why do you need *my* help?"

"I'm trying to find out who abducted me! I'm worried they will come to my home again! It has something to do with the explosion at the teleport! Owen seems to think you know what to do!" She cocked an eyebrow. "I'm not convinced!"

He crooked his finger like summoning a naughty child to receive punishment. "Follow me!"

He drew aside the curtain that separated the front and back rooms. The music was louder in the back until Spider reduced the volume.

Nova followed Owen into the next room.

Bound to a reclining leather chair by coils of old telephone cord was the skinhead from the wine cellar, the same man who had been inside her house. The cords dug into his flesh, taut against the chair's worn leather, restricting his movements but doing little to diminish the aura of raw strength that emanated from him. His left shoulder was tightly bandaged to stem the bleeding from the gunshot wound he had sustained earlier. Despite the serious injury, his posture was resolute, leaning forward purposefully with an imposing intensity as he studied his reflection in an operable mirror mounted on the wall in front. He scrutinised his features with a mix of frustration and disbelief, his jaw clenched tightly, making the muscles in his neck bulge.

"Why is he here?" asked Nova, unable to hide her shock.

"I brought him here," said Spider. "You want to know why he abducted you. Ask him. He's telling me shit."

Her hands shook as she approached this repulsively violent man. "Who are you?"

"Speak louder!" said Spider. "His ears are still sore from me screaming down them."

She took a deep breath. "Why did you abduct me?"

The skinhead didn't take his eyes off his reflection in the mirror and continued to breathe loudly through his nose.

Spider marched up to him. "Man, you have one of those faces people just want to slap. Answer the question!"

The skinhead slowly turned to face them.

Nova gasped and stumbled backward.

His eyes were as black as a shark's—dark voids where the iris and pupil had dissolved into blackness. Not a single trace of white remained, making his eye sockets seem hollowed out. And tattooed across his forehead were six letters: *CLOTHO*.

"I kill you all!" he said.

Spider laughed. "Hey, Jesus loves you, but everyone else thinks you're a big tit."

He switched on the ceiling fan, an industrial model with enormous paddles, as Nova ran out of the room, holding her hand over her mouth.

Spider and Owen joined her in the front room.

"You okay?" asked Owen.

She shook her head, removing her hand from her mouth. "What's wrong with his eyes? Why are they so black?"

"Nothing's wrong with them. I just injected ink under the conjunctiva. It's called corneal tattooing."

"Can it be removed?"

"It's irreversible."

"Isn't it dangerous?"

He shrugged indifferently. "It could result in blindness or infection, damage to blood vessels, possible haemorrhaging. Who cares?"

"What's Clotho?" she asked.

"No idea. A Serbian swear word?"

"Serbian?"

"He has an old Serbian identification card in his wallet. His name is Gagan. After I'd pumped him full of drugs, I asked him if he got off abducting young girls. I asked him why, and he said *Clotho*. I asked him to speak English. He found it funny and shouted *fucking Clotho*. So I punched him on the nose. And as he seemed so fond of the word, I thought he could wear it permanently."

Nova didn't know what to say, so she said nothing.

Spider smiled. "If you want answers, you've got to do what it takes to get them."

Nova looked up from the floor. "What?"

He picked up his tattoo needle. "Round two. You ready?"

She shook her head.

"You want to find out why you were abducted, right?"

She looked at Owen, then at Spider. "Yes, but–"

"We don't care for this big cow's cock, right?"

"But..."

Owen beamed. "Do it!"

"What are you going to do?" she asked.

"He's bald. That's a whole lot of canvas up there."

Nova and Owen followed Spider through the curtain into the next room, only to discover the Serbian had escaped, the cord binding him to the chair now scattered on the floor. The back door was wide open.

Spider threw the needle on the floor in a fit of rage. "Fuck! There goes my fucking reward!"

"What reward?" asked Owen.

"I know he was the prick who bombed the teleport. The police will find out soon enough when they search the ruins, and no one will get the fucking reward."

Nova shot a look at Spider. "What did you say?"

"The police are offering a large reward for information."

"No, you said bombed. It was an accident, right? A gas leak."

"It was no accident."

"How do you know that?"

"The teleport in New York exploded the same day."

17

The shockwave surged through the auditorium with a sickening roar, rippling across the space like a tidal wave of sound and force. Hot, white light exploded outward, searing through the darkness with blinding intensity. The brilliant flash illuminated men and women of all ages in their seats, their faces contorted in terror and pain. Nova was thrown to the ground, her body hitting the floor with a jarring impact. She had only a moment to gasp for air before the crowd's panicked movements led to a torrent of bodies collapsing on top of her, making it difficult for her to move or even breathe. The acrid stench of smoke and burning flesh filled the air, stinging her eyes and throat. All around, the scene was apocalyptic. Bodies lay sprawled across the floor, charred and smouldering fiercely. The intense heat from the explosion seared through clothing and skin alike, turning the auditorium into a grim furnace of destruction.

Looking around in horror, Nova saw the burned remains of people begin to disintegrate, breaking apart into flakes that fluttered through the air like ashes caught in a fierce wind.

Nova screamed and gasped in a single motion. Unsettled by the sudden silence, she heard someone call her name. She tried to head towards the voice as it summoned her, but she couldn't tell from which direction it came.

"Nova!"

It took repeated attempts for the voice to pull her back to reality, away from the haunting vision.

"Nova!"

Someone stood beside her. "Dad?"

"Come on," said Owen, holding her arm while he led her back to the room, lit by candlelight. "In here."

She flinched at every faint sound, her nerves on edge, only able to settle when Owen reassured her it was safe.

"You had a nightmare. You walked off."

"Some air fresheners," she said, standing in the middle of the room. "That's what this place needs."

Owen's face was expressionless, his silence unbroken.

"And plants. Lillies, or some daffodils."

He lowered her onto the wicker mat. "Try and get some more kip."

She spread herself across the mat and stared at the ceiling. Everyone inside the auditorium had perished, according to Spider. There had been no survivors, except her. But the police didn't know that. Neither did the staff at the teleport. Neither did the media. It wasn't on the Internet. There weren't people out looking for her. Apart from the thugs who had abducted her. And two of those were dead. The only people who knew of her existence were Spider, Owen, and the Serbian.

She tried to convince herself everything was normal and forget that nothing would ever be normal again. Was it easier to accept her father was gone so she didn't have to live with empty hope? No, he was more than just a man caught in the crossfire; he was a survivor, a seasoned soldier who had honed his skills through countless battles. His entire career was built on the art of evading bullets and dodging bombs. Each near-miss and narrow escape had sharpened his senses, making him a master at staying one step ahead of danger. His survival was not a matter of chance but the result of years of training and experience, mastering the volatile world of combat.

He was alive. She had to believe it. Because not believing it could only mean one thing—she would never see his face again.

The only place Nova felt reasonably safe was with Owen, hidden away below the ground, but the crushing walls and low ceiling made her feel like she was trapped inside a mausoleum. How long could she tolerate the isolation? How long before she started losing her mind?

The candle had melted and snuffed itself out. Owen lit a new one. With the room once again visible, Nova thought it would be good for her psyche to exercise. She stretched her body in a range of sculptures, touched her toes, then reached in front of them with her palms flat to the floor. She stood on the points of her toes, her legs and back as straight as a tree trunk, as graceful as a sunflower. She held the pose for several seconds, then practiced some moves, including the scorpion and candlestick.

"You some kind of athletic?" asked Owen.

"You mean athlete? I'm a gymnast."

"Yeah? Can you–"

"Do the splits? Do backflips? Touch my nose with my feet? All the above."

"Show me."

She launched into some energetic aerobics. "Maybe later."

Owen stood and started to mimic her actions, following her stretches with awkward grace, trying hard to keep up with her rigorous pace. It made her smile.

After five minutes, she stopped. "Okay, that's enough." She took off her left shoe and massaged her foot.

"Feet hurting?"

"Sore feet, painful knees, twisted ankles. You name it, I've probably injured it."

"Why do it?"

"I walked around my home on my hands from when I was five years old. Since then, I practically ate, slept, and breathed gymnastics."

"Cool."

She glanced at the door. "I need to get out of here."

"Do you do competitions?"

"I've competed in a few."

"Have you ever won?"

"I came second. That's my best result so far."

"Still good."

She paused, looking at the door again. "I need to get out of here before I go crazy."

"And go where?"

"I need to find out."

"About what happened?"

"No, if we really landed on the moon."

"The moon?"

Nova laughed. "You say daft things sometimes."

He stifled a yawn.

"I can't sit here doing nothing. I need to know why."

Owen frowned.

"Why the teleport was bombed. Why I was abducted. Why me? I need to find my father. He must think I'm dead."

"I'll come with you."

"Why?"

"Better than staying here."

She glanced around the sterile enclosure with a question that had been bothering her for some time. "Why don't you live with your cousin?"

"He don't want me there."

"But you're family."

"He brings me grub and that."

"And money?"

"He ain't got none."

She paused. "Why are *you* helping me?"

He shrugged.

Nova sighed. "I need to get out of here. Seriously."

"Where you gonna go?"

"I should go to the police. They might be able to give me some answers. They might know where I can find my father."

"Never trust the pigs," said Owen, shaking his head.

London City Teleport had exploded first, she had learned from Spider. And then came the encore in New York. A matter of minutes separated the explosions. Both had been successful in their objective destruction. The news had filled her with dread, but also with a more pressing desire to seek the truth.

It had been a number of days since the explosion at the teleport. Her concussion had waned. The bruises on her body were going down, and the cuts had almost healed. Her memory had not fully returned, but time would see to that. Either she risked her life trying to find the truth, or she risked her sanity trying to stay hidden.

"Your cousin said the police will find the answers at the teleport. What do you think he meant by that?"

"He often talks shit."

Nova headed for the door. "I think that's where I'm going to go. Seems like the best place to start."

18

A half-moon hung over the teleport exclusion zone, which was surrounded by enormous concrete walls. The towering barriers formed an imposing square, extending half a mile out from the epicentre of the zone, enclosing it like a fortress. It was a place no one dared to enter and where the rules of the natural world no longer applied. The very atmosphere seemed charged with a strange energy from the unknown forces that had wrought destruction there.

Owen stood up by the cold, grey wall stretching endlessly into the distance, just as the urge to release his bladder became unbearable.

"What are you doing?" asked Nova, watching as hot steam drifted around him as if his spirit was leaving his body.

"Dying for a leak."

"Here?"

He stepped back from his steamy deposit, smiling at Nova. "Much better." When he looked back at the wall, he spotted an abandoned fire hose, coiled up like a snake. He lifted it over his shoulder and showed it to Nova. "Why don't we climb over this wall?"

"We're not climbing over the wall."

It was in the range of twelve to fourteen feet, far too high to reach even standing on each other's shoulders. The smooth exterior made climbing impossible, anyway, and the hose in Owen's hand was useless without something to latch it to.

Nova put her hands on her hips. "If I had known it was surrounded by walls, I wouldn't have bothered coming."

"You're gymnastic...er. Jump over."

"I'm not superhuman. Or stupid. There's a reason these walls were built."

Before they made any further decisions, they agreed to do a lap of the site to see what they were up against. They walked along the perimeter, turned the corner, and followed the wall all the way to the end. They were at the back of the teleport now, among the field of broken solar panels, each one burned or smashed to pieces, leaving a sea of debris receding into the dark grounds.

A variety of graffiti tributes and comments filled the wall. Nova read some:

May God rest their souls in peace.

The luckless lottery.

Never forgotten.

Here lies Martin Hu, loving brother and pro kitesurfer.

Official signs showing the international radiation symbol were nailed to the wall, warning that prolonged exposure could prove detrimental to health.

Owen pointed to the top of the wall, where two vertical metal bars stood with a single horizontal bar connecting them, forming an H shape. "Look, a ladder!"

Nova narrowed her eyes to see it. "What's a ladder doing on the inside?"

"Maybe firefighters left it. Like this hose."

"How can we get it on this side of the wall?"

Owen made windmills with the end of the fire hose and grinned. Legs apart, he launched the nozzle towards the ladder. It flopped over the wall. He pulled it back and tried again. The second attempt was just as feeble. The third was also off-target. The fourth try resulted in the nozzle getting stuck between the ladder's leg and the wall. Playing a tug of war, he pulled hard, and the hose sailed back to the ground.

On his sixteenth attempt, by which time Nova had noticed her fingers were purple with cold, the hose looped between the top and second rungs. He let out some slack, allowing it to feed through until the heavy nozzle landed in his waiting hand. He tied a slip knot in the hose and pulled hard, watching as the knot slid upward until it reached the top rung and tightened securely in place. With the hose connected to the ladder, he pulled and dragged it over to their side. The ladder balanced tentatively at the top of the wall, reached tipping point, and dropped, hitting the ground with a clunk.

Owen set the ladder against the wall. "You want me to go first?"

Nova looked up. "I'm not sure about this."

Owen chased up the ladder and stopped at the summit, peering down inside the enclosure where the teleport used to operate.

"What do you see?" asked Nova.

"See for yourself."

"But what's it like?"

"Messed up."

A few minutes passed before Nova, her face hidden in the shadows of her purple hood, gripped the ladder so tightly her hands felt soldered to the cold metal.

Reaching the top, she peered across the black, empty void below. She climbed into a seated position on the wall, facing Owen, and blew warm air onto her cold hands. She scanned the vast, darkened landscape, black and grey like a charcoal sketch, illuminated by the half-moon appearing periodically between the clouds. A cool breeze blew through the remains, unsettling flakes of charred ash. Burned foundations, twisted, and fragmented, rose out of the radioactive rubble where the auditorium and terminal once stood.

Together, they heaved the ladder onto the wall and lowered it down the other side, leaving the hose swinging at the wall's exterior.

Owen descended the ladder first.

Nova followed him. She leaped from the last three rungs and spun to face the ruins.

She clicked on her torch, glad that she had heeded Owen's advice and purchased one. He was proving to be a great asset, and she was thankful he had accompanied her. She shuddered at the thought of going there alone.

They combed through the wreckage, sifting through the twisted metal and shattered debris in search of answers, hoping to uncover a clue that might explain what had happened. The air was thick with the scent of charred materials. The silence between them was occasionally interrupted by creaking ruins or structures collapsing deeper within the wreckage. The task was daunting, but they pressed on, driven by a determination to understand the tragedy that had unfolded there. One thing was certain. The victims had been vaporised by the blast. There one minute, gone the next. No one could have survived. All those people, all those children. Search parties in their hazmat suits would have come and gone, leaving with empty body bags and hearts full of despair.

Nova deconstructed how that day had gone so wrong. If only she had convinced her father not to attend the Expo after his unexplained jaunt into the orchard. If she had allowed him to accompany her to the bathroom. If he'd left the auditorium of his own accord before it exploded.

If, if...

Owen saw Nova kneeling with her head in her hands. He touched her shoulder.

"I miss... him," she said, only able to speak a few words at a time.

Owen rubbed her neck.

She needed a minute. She bowed her head, reluctant to face a terrible truth. Her stomach writhed, and it made her retch up what little she had inside, pulpy blobs of half-digested bread.

"He might still be alive, you know."

She dried her eyes and stood slowly, nodding with what looked like hope. "You're right."

Swinging the torch from side to side, she headed deeper into the ruins, mindful of every step and the dangers around them as she climbed over a large mound of shifting steel and concrete. Some of the terminal walls remained standing, and rows of blackened, broken chairs were still attached to their steel frames.

Nova stopped. "This is crazy. There's nothing here."

Owen shrugged and held out his palms. "Go back?"

Nova saw a flash of movement.

Owen also saw something from the corner of his eye.

She swung the torch beam to her left. It landed on a man crawling over the rubble.

"Dad?"

19

Nova shook the torch when the light faded, strengthening its beam. When she swung it back towards the man, her heartbeat quickened. He was no longer there.

Then he was.

"Dad?"

He wore a dark green coat, military in both style and cut. He squinted when she shone the light on his face.

"What's a young girl like you doing here, then?" he asked.

Disappointment set in hard and fast. It was not her father. She lowered her head. "Looking for answers."

"Answers to what?"

"I'm not sure. I just think… I don't know."

"That there makes two of us."

Nova took backward steps when he closed the gap, fearing a confrontation.

"But I'm curious, and I repeat, what's a young girl like you doing in here?"

She didn't have an answer. It was clear nothing at the site would help her understand. She had no rational reasons, no one to take her by the hand, look her in the eye, and make her believe her presence there made any kind of sense.

"I think my father may have… in the explosion. I want to find out why."

"I can tell you why."

Nova glanced at Owen when she spoke. "We know it was caused by a bomb."

When she looked back in the man's direction, he was gone. She ran the torch sideways but couldn't find him.

"Suitcase nuke, it was," he said, circling back into the beam, lighting up his ageing face and grey hair combed neatly to one side. He had long sideburns touched with black. But he was not old, the right side of fifty. He had a short button nose, a tight mouth, and was tall and trim with a runner's physique. He looked the type who could consume five hamburgers in a single sitting and not gain an ounce.

"Between two and four kilotons, weighing around thirty kilos. Small enough to fit inside a suitcase and large enough to destroy the auditorium and spread enough radiation to deter people from probing these here ruins."

In fact, he explained, there had been two suitcase nukes. One had been placed in the auditorium and had detonated successfully. The other had been found buried underneath the terminal. For some reason, it hadn't exploded, providing an opportunity for the investigators to track down its maker. On their own, each bomb could take down large buildings. But in tandem, they would have destroyed whole suburbs.

"How do you know all this?" she asked.

The man grinned. "I read the news, I do. Obviously, you don't. Instead, you come down here, playing detective when you ain't got no clue."

"Why are *you* here, then?"

"Good question. I suspect my answer ain't no different to yours. I don't believe what I'm reading in the news. You ask me, I think them in the media are covering up a larger story. I hoped by coming here, I could find out what that is."

"Why?"

"Why what? Why don't I believe the news? Or why am I down here, in this here war zone?"

"Both."

"More good questions. Neither is exclusive. Many people in this country don't believe them news reports, but they ain't here, like us, risking their lives for answers. We're down here because we've both lost loved ones. And we both want justice, or at the very least, to understand why this has happened."

"You lost family here?"

"Wife and daughter."

His tone carried a hollow ache.

"I'm sorry to hear that," said Nova.

"Likewise. How does a girl your age deal with the loss of her father? My daughter was a bit younger than you. I couldn't imagine her being orphaned, it don't bear thinking about."

"I'm not an orphan until I know he's… you know."

He looked at Owen. "What's your story, then?"

Owen's eyes widened. "I *am* an orphan."

"Lost your parents here, too?"

"He's not dead!" Nova said with tears in her eyes.

"When I was a nipper," said Owen.

"Well, you're both wasting your time. You ain't going to find squat here but ash. That's what happens when you set off a nuke under the feet of five thousand people."

"Who did it?" asked Owen.

"I've got my suspicions."

"It was the ATM," said Nova, drying her eyes.

"What makes you say that, then?"

"I was at London City Teleport five months ago, and I ran into one of the protesters from the ATM, this old lady. Two nights ago, I was abducted. She was one of them. I believe they were involved."

"How can you be sure all them protesters you saw were ATM?"

"Because the ATM is full of nasty people."

"That's a sweeping statement, and an act of defamation. Who told you that, then?"

"My father."

"Some see them as fanatic zealots who consider technology as an abomination. Others will argue we've got innovators and scientists who lost sight of humanity years ago. Our brains are constantly being influenced by new technologies, and we just ain't keeping up. It's been proven electronic devices impact the micro-cellular structure and the biochemistry of our brains. Technology's blurring the line between humans and machines, and between our bodies and the outside world."

"People depend on technology," said Nova. "We need it."

"We don't *need* it! You ask me, unless people wake up to the damage it's doing to our minds, we could be heading for a future in which technology governs us and not the other way around."

"They hate all technology?" asked Owen.

"Not all. Only them that cross ethical boundaries such as teleportation, genetic engineering, biometric databases, nuclear energy, neurochips, cloning. You know how many lives got destroyed since the advent of the Internet all them years ago? You can understand why the ATM opposes it so much."

"Why do they have to be so vocal and... violent?" asked Nova.

"They're a minority group, but they represent a whole lot of people. They see technology evolving beyond the pace of putting proper regulations upon their use. New and existing technologies are unstoppable. That's obvious. But someone's got to stand up to the impact it's having on humankind. We are on an escalator to disaster, and technology will be the root cause."

To Nova, the conversation was pointless. Why were they debating technology amid a fallout zone?

A beeping sound interrupted their discussion, and white dots of light blinked in the man's eyes.

"Anyway, Nova, my time in here's up. I need to get out of this here pit before I receive too much radiation."

She brushed her hair behind her ear nervously. "How do you know my name?"

The man breathed out long and hard.

She looked over her shoulder at Owen, then back at the man.

"You're wise to be suspicious, but don't fret. I heard you talking when you came in."

She was exhausted. Ground down by the grisly scene and struggling to come to terms with her father's possible death, she decided she had also seen enough and wanted to leave. Staying there perpetuated suffering and prolonged her grief.

Though running into this man had raised her hopes, showing her that others had been swept into this quest for answers, helping her to not feel so alone, the failed visit had dampened her fading morale.

"We're going, too. Can we leave with you?"

He flicked on his torch. "Let's be off, then."

They scaled a mountain of unstable rubble, heads down, following the torch beams, watching every step, careful not to trip or tread on a sharp object.

"Where do you live?" the man asked.

Nova was reluctant to reveal too much, so she said, "In the West Midlands, but right now, I'm staying with Owen. How about you?"

"Got me a boat on the Thames. I live on that now. I can't face going home."

"Why not?"

"Too hard, seeing their pictures on the wall, the smell of their clothes and that."

"What's the name of your boat, you know, in case I want to contact you?"

"The *Anna Belle*. Named after my daughter, Annabelle. It was also my mother's middle name. It's big and red with a double mast. You'll find it down at the new marina at the Docklands. You can't miss it."

She committed the details to memory.

"I never asked you your name," said Nova.

He extended his hand. "Arthur."

Nova shook his meaty, rough hand, suggesting he was no stranger to hard, physical labour.

He faced the wall. "Where's my ladder?"

"That was your ladder?" asked Owen.

Nova frowned. "We left it in the same place you did."
"Well, it ain't here now."

20

The young Labrador trotted miserably along the footpath, as if the weight of the world pressed down on its small, muscular frame. Its tail was drooping low, its ears flattened as it padded through the damp evening air. The pavement was slick beneath its paws, the remnants of this afternoon's rain still lingering in the air. As the dog approached a lamppost, it paused, lifting its back leg to relieve itself, the small stream splashing against the post with a faint hiss. It looked up at the sky. Hovering above the street, a police drone drifted silently, its mechanical hum barely audible over the distant sounds of the city. The drone's blue and red strobes flashed rhythmically, lighting up houses in an eerie glow. The Labrador, sensing its presence, let out a sharp bark.

The drone, unaffected by the dog's protest, continued its surveillance, swivelling its cameras to capture every angle of the street below. The dog, perhaps expecting some response, stood frozen for a moment with its eyes locked on the drone before finally lowering its head with a resigned sigh, just as a dozen police officers in protective clothing and carrying some serious artillery crept by it, stopping at the front door of a terraced house.

Beneath that house, three men and two women gathered around a table inlaid with an interactive map of London. The radio was on, and the host introduced the next track, drowning out the sound of the front door breaking open.

The tactical commander steered the first of many assault rifles around the wall at the foot of the basement stairs, fixing on the targets. Tonight would see one of the most significant operations in anti-terrorism history, aimed at dismantling the ATM, limitless with its resources and waging a crusade against the country. At the commander's signal, the officers moved silently and swiftly, forming a semi-circle around the suspects.

Four raised their hands, surrendering immediately.

One of the men reached beneath the table.

He was shot by an officer near the door.

Hearing the gunshots, two more officers opened fire, their bullets hitting the man's chest, killing him instantly.

"What part of no shooting did we misunderstand?" yelled the tactical commander.

Elsewhere, in a quiet suburb eighteen miles away, Travis lay awake in bed, his eyes fixed on the ceiling. The room was dimly lit by the soft glow of streetlamps filtering through the curtains. Despite the late hour, sleep eluded him. His mind was filled with thoughts of the public committee he had to address in the morning. He had rehearsed his speech countless times, yet his doubts kept him awake. What if he stumbled over his words? What if they questioned him on something he wasn't prepared for?

The ceiling was suddenly bathed in red and blue flashing lights, followed by the sound of drones hovering outside his house, buzzing like blood-thirsty mosquitoes. He leaped out of bed and ran to the window. Pulling back the curtain, he saw the police drones with their lights ablaze. Several officers were lining up on his front lawn.

He fingered his long, orange beard. "Fuck!"

Police enforcement laws had been revised in recent years, providing authorities with more leverage and less red tape in the perpetual fight against crime and terrorism, arming law enforcement officers of all ranks with firearms and allowing them to break into any property where criminal evidence was suspected, meaning no time was wasted applying for a search warrant. The controversial law had not been well-received, and complaints about human rights violations were filed daily, with police hunches most often tenuous, at best. Even without solid evidence, the police department could hold suspects for weeks without laying charges.

Travis slipped in his earpiece, activating his bionic lenses. When he said *Nate*, his friend's profile picture beamed from the transparent graphene onto his retina.

"The police are at my house," said Travis.

"*And here*," said Nate. "*What the fuck?*"

Travis didn't know how long he could hold out under siege in his own house. Not long, judging by the stream of officers lining up outside, pulverising his front door. It brought many residents out into the street or to their windows behind the safety of the glass.

Nate's breathing turned heavy through the earpiece as he was confronted by several police officers. After the gunshots, the silence ended with his profile picture shrinking into a tiny dot.

Travis knew now this heavily armed raid was one of many, intent on undoing the ATM.

What sounded like a herd of elephants charged up his stairs and rushed in through his door with raised guns.

Travis flipped the window latch and pushed it open.

"Hands up, right now!"

Travis raised his hands. He dropped his chin to his chest, creasing his beard.

The officers would find the toxic chemicals in his kitchen. They would find the unlicensed firearm under his bed. And they would find the illegal gasoline in his garage.

Two officers pushed Travis to the floor. He hit his face, and one of his bionic lenses fell out, leaving a blurry wheel of icons in his left eye. Cuffs were snapped over his wrists.

An officer stuck his rifle in the back of his neck. "You're under arrest for the bombing of London City Teleport and the murder of two people found in the basement beneath your wine shop."

"Wait, what?"

"You have the right to remain silent, and anything you say won't be believed, as frankly, no one gives a shit."

"I want my—"

A punch to his jaw stopped him mid-sentence.

"Careful!" said one of the officers. "Don't draw blood."

Coordinated raids swept across the country as crime squads driving armoured personnel carriers descended upon targeted locations. With force, they stormed buildings and broke down doors, making multiple arrests.

Two Caucasian men and a Russian woman were detained inside a hotel in Windsor on suspicion of terrorist intent and playing a role in the downing of London City Teleport.

Seven homes were overturned in the northeast with just as many arrests. During the raids, police discovered ammonium nitrate, a raw material found in explosives, several submachine guns, and a hundred thousand pounds in cash.

The contraband was traced back to a man named Theo, now in police custody on suspicion of espionage and accused of national security crimes.

21

Nova's torch flashed a line of light up the wall and circled back, running across a heap of blackened scrap. She aimed the beam at Owen. He had his back against a charred slab of concrete with his arms folded.

"Stack the broken bricks and climb up?" he suggested.

Arthur scanned the ruins using his torch and night-vision bionic lenses. "And how do we get down the other side? We need that ladder. Someone's taken it." The timer on his lenses continued its countdown. "I'm dangerously over the limit, I am." Becoming frantic, he pulled two long, metal poles out of the rubble and stood them side by side, clearly thinking how he might use them to aid in their escape.

Nova and Owen watched him.

Finding no use for the poles, he threw them onto a pile of debris. "Got any bright ideas, then? You're at risk here, too."

After a helpless shrug, Owen rubbed his nose.

Nova shook her head and looked around the wall. "Are we standing in the right place? Is this where we came in?"

"It's the right place," said Arthur.

The sound of someone whistling a brief tune halted their conversation. They turned towards the sound, but it suddenly stopped, and they couldn't see anyone lurking within the ruins or near the wall.

Then the whistling resumed.

Nova glanced up at the wall and saw a silhouette at the top. Someone's head goose-necked just above the summit.

"Who's there?" asked Arthur.

Whoever it was continued to whistle mockingly, heralding some unfamiliar tune. "Good job I came."

"Who are you?" asked Arthur.

"It's my cousin," said Owen.

Nova turned to Owen. "Did you tell him we were here?"

Owen removed the rabbit's foot from his pocket and held it up, smiling.

Spider climbed onto the wall, hauled the ladder over, and lowered it down inside the ruins.

The moment it met the ground, Arthur charged up it. He stopped near the top and faced Spider, now sitting astride the wall with his hands clasped together, looking smug.

"Who are you?"

Spider laughed. "Who are *you*?"

"This is my ladder. What are you playing at?"

"Playing? I just saved your life, mate."

"Why did you take my ladder?"

Spider folded his arms. "I found it over in the trees by the fence."

Arthur shook his head. "What grockle did that, then?"

"Pranksters, perhaps? Either that or someone wants you dead. I can't think why, you seem lovely."

Arthur spotted a knot around the top rung and peered over the edge, tracing the hose hanging down the wall. He looked at Spider, then down at Owen and Nova on the ground. "No wonder it got pinched. You left a hosepipe tied to it."

Spider laughed. "I always said Owen was a genius."

Arthur gave Spider a long, cold stare. "Bloody Einstein, is he? Hold this ladder steady for me so I can climb down this here hosepipe."

"Say please!"

"I ain't in the mood for games!"

Switching places, Arthur climbed on the wall while Spider stepped onto the ladder, six rungs down, using his weight to keep the ladder stable.

Arthur clung to the hosepipe and abseiled down the wall, dropping the final few feet and landing with a roll. He stepped back from the wall and put his hands on his hips.

Spider looked down at Nova and Owen. "Well, what you waiting for? Get the fuck up here!"

Once everyone was safely out and Arthur had left with his ladder tucked under his arm, Spider belted Owen across the face.

"What have I told you about hanging about with strangers, huh?"

Owen rubbed his cheek. "He knows about the ATM, the people–"

"I know who the ATM is!"

He turned to Nova, his head jerking and eyelids flickering. "Trouble just seems to follow you everywhere, hey?"

"It was my idea," she said, almost apologetically.

"Course it was."

Owen was quiet and standoffish. His chin dipped slightly, the weight of his unspoken thoughts pulling it down before he finally muttered an apology. The words were barely audible. As he finished, his hands moved almost reflexively, his fingers intertwining with one another in a nervous, fidgety motion. The tell-tale sign of fear.

Nova opened her mouth, about to voice her objection until she saw the obedient response from Owen, so she pressed her lips tightly together. She didn't know Spider well but was well aware of the damage he could inflict. She had seen what he had done to the Serbian's eyes, not to mention the execution of his colleagues. The thought of pushing his buttons and provoking that same brutality sent a shiver down her spine. The last thing she wanted was to end up blind, or even dead.

Owen gave her a sidelong glance before lifting his head and straightening his posture, trying to project an air of toughness, but it came across more sullen than threatening, as with most teenagers. His resentment towards Spider took her by surprise, and she wondered how deep it extended.

A dangerous calm settled in Spider's dark, sunken eyes. "Got something to say, snotbag?"

He had the air of a hooligan. A hooligan capable of taking lives and unashamed about doing it.

She could see Owen racking his brains for something to say.

"Leave him alone!" said Nova.

Spider turned his cold eyes on her. "Excuse me?"

Now at this man's mercy, the unusual situation became a terrifying one. She looked at Owen, who had lowered his eyes again. She looked across the field of scattered debris, seeing if Arthur was still around. He wasn't. She was careful of what she might say because he could turn on her if she didn't handle him properly.

"It's my fault he's here, okay? He was just trying to help me. I accept full responsibility. We won't come here again."

Spider struck Owen's face with the back of his hand. There was no closed fist this time but a vicious slap, leaving a rose handprint on his cheek. "Look at you two! If you're gonna run around playing Scooby-Doo, try and be smart about it. Now, off you jolly well piss!"

They walked away, but Spider held Owen back by his bicep and whispered, "Get me her address, or no food for a week."

22

Nova and Owen arrived at the Thames, now sitting at low tide, churning up the smell of shellfish and decaying river matter, and leaving several boats stranded upon the pockmarked tidal mud, dotted with the tracks of wading birds.

Nova looked downriver and saw a cluster of boats in the new marina. "It must be that one," she said, pointing to the only red boat with a double mast bobbing in one of the many berths, surrounded by modern-looking vessels. It was a tatty-looking boat, its worn exterior showing signs of many years spent battling the elements. Its red paint had faded to a dull, patchy hue, chipped away in places to reveal the weathered wood beneath. At forty-three feet long, the boat had a certain rugged charm, like a forgotten relic of a bygone era, stubbornly clinging to life. *Anna Belle* was stencilled in blue letters across its starboard side. As they approached the marina, they heard the battery-operated motor quietly running, the boat swaying lightly on old ropes that looked as though they could snap at any moment.

A woman on the jetty repaired her fishing net. Behind her was the contents of her tackle box, strewn across the wooden platform.

Sidestepping the scattered gear, Nova and Owen greeted the woman and jogged to the end of the jetty. Nova hesitated halfway across the boarding ramp, fearing she was making a mistake going there.

She boarded the boat anyway.

Later, she would conclude it had been a huge mistake.

The wheelhouse, its wood rotted to a softness no wood should be, was situated midway between the bow and stern and surrounded by a mostly flat deck, littered with remnants of past voyages—a tangle of old nets, rusting tools, and a few forgotten pieces of equipment that had long since outlived their usefulness.

"Hello?" Nova called out.

Owen peered inside the empty wheelhouse.

Nova saw a red vinyl sheet covering some equipment at the stern, held down on each corner by brick pavers.

"Hello? Arthur?"

They descended the steps leading down into the cabin.

Nova knocked and got no answer. She knocked again as a courtesy, received the same result, so she entered the cabin and was immediately struck by the smell of cigarette smoke. She ran her eyes around the dark and gloomy interior. The compact cabin was devoid of any luxury, unsurprisingly. A tiny galley in the corner was equipped with a marine fridge, a gimballed two-burner gas stove, and a tiny sink. A small, mahogany table was situated nearby, and in the corner was a hammock close to a single fold-down bed in an upright position against the wall. Shelves on one wall were crammed with books. Built into the old mahogany joinery were art deco lights, with none switched on. A candle was aflame on the table, and an unlit oil lantern was suspended from the support beam. Clothes were spread across the floor or deposited on the backs of chairs. Empty tobacco pouches also littered the cabin, and a plate on the table brimmed with fag ends.

"Hello?"

And then she saw him, hunched over in the shape of prayer on the floor. He shifted onto his knees and stood slowly, fixing his white hair and straightening his shirt collar. He picked up a half-smoked cigarette and bent over the candle flame to light it. He took consecutive drags, tilted his head back, and blew smoke out through his nose. "You came. Like my boat?"

Nova frowned. "Very... nice."

"Stripped her down, I did, and rebuilt the upper deck. Still needs a few structural repairs and a repaint, but she's as strong as a warship, built of the finest oak. Apologies for this here mess. Never was one for keeping tidy. Come in, don't be shy. Please, sit."

They took seats at the table.

Arthur held out five pre-rolled cigarettes. "Fag?"

Owen helped himself and lit it on the candle.

Nova raised her hand. "Not for me."

"Drink?" He held out a bottle of rum. "Wait, how old are you two?"

"Seventeen," said Nova.

Owen shrugged. "Fifteen or sixteen, not sure."

"Either way, you ain't old enough. Tea?"

Nova politely refused.

"It's no bother," he said.

"I don't like tea."

"You'll like mine. Make it a special way, I do."

She wrinkled her nose to say *no*. "Do you have any Coke or anything?"

Arthur filled two glasses with semi-cold Coke and poured a small amount in his rum, stirring it through with his finger. Then he launched into a monologue about the Thames, home to anything from houseboats and submersibles to ambulances and luxury solar cruisers. Most modern boats ran on solar cells, he explained, giving them infinite range. Arthur wanted solar cells installed on his boat, but they cost a fortune.

A ginger cat sprang out from under the table. It pawed at a rubber ball, playfully rolling it under its claws.

Nova clicked her fingers, summoning the cat onto her lap. It mewled and closed its eyes as she ran her fingers along its spine.

"He or she?"

"She," said Arthur. "Name's Bebop."

"Hello, Bebop." She kissed the top of her head. "She must love all the homeless dogs everywhere."

"She's had a few scuffles and picked up a few scars."

Arthur put his elbows on the table. "Annabelle found her in the garden one day when she was still a kitten. She had no tracking device or tag, so my wife took her in, worried she would get mauled and pick up rabies. I had no interest in cats. But after they died in that explosion, I went home to collect a few belongings, and I saw Bebop. So I brought her back here. You ask me, she's the closest thing I've got now to family." Arthur talked more about Heather, his wife. During marriage, there'd been heated arguments, and Arthur blamed himself for putting all his time into his work over a happy home life. Now his family was gone, and he had to face life alone. He spoke of fishing and hydroponics, his hobbies, but his true passion was brewing his own ale and was an avid collector of beer glasses. Since their deaths, he'd lost interest in everything, trapped in a frighteningly downward spiral.

Nova wasn't paying much attention. Her head swung one way, then the other. Where were they? Had she left them by the cabin door? On the welcome mat?

"What are you looking for?" asked Arthur.

"My purple trainers."

He glanced at her feet. "You're wearing them."

She looked down, confused, and when she looked up, she spotted a laceration on Arthur's right wrist.

Arthur rolled down his sleeve, covering the deep scratch. "Caught it on a nail. Bloody hurt, too."

Nova arched her eyebrows. "I'm wearing them."

Arthur and Owen traded confused looks.

"Your shoes?" asked Arthur.

She nodded. "They're on my feet."

"Yeah, I just told you that."

Owen put his hand on top of hers.

"Why are you both looking at me weird?" she asked.

Owen said nothing.

Arthur stubbed out his cigarette and immediately lit a new one. "Let's talk."

Nova frowned. "About what?"

"The reason we're all sitting around this here table right now."

Nova went along with the change of topic. "Okay."

He released a steady stream of smoke from the corner of his mouth. "Why don't you start at the beginning?"

23

Nova exhaled sharply, unsure where to begin. Chronologically made the most sense, so she started with her trip to New York.

"How was that, then?" Arthur asked. He grabbed an old notebook and a pen from the shelf and slipped on a pair of reading glasses.

"Like all cities: too noisy, too busy. My father enjoyed it more than—"

"I mean getting there, teleportation. How did it feel?"

"Strange, like when you're dozing, close to falling asleep, but still conscious. It just feels like you're floating, or falling, but you come out of the doze almost straight away. I hated it. I'll never do it again."

"Your clothes go?" asked Owen.

"Nothing goes with you. Only physical human matter can pass through the teleportals."

You couldn't take a suitcase. You couldn't take clothes or shoes. You could hire everything on arrival, but you couldn't pre-order. You couldn't take electronics or jewellery into the teleportals, but you could leave them behind in a locker. You couldn't bring back souvenirs or purchased shopping items, but you could ship them home.

"So you go naked?" asked Owen.

"It ain't neither here nor there," said Arthur, impatience in his voice. "Continue."

She talked about the demonstrators on the platform that day. And about the old lady with different coloured eyes, the same lady who had abducted her. She belonged to the ATM, in a senior position if not top, and it wouldn't be long before it got out the attack was the ATM's work.

"No!" said Arthur. "Ain't no old ladies at the ATM."

"But I saw her there with—"

"She may have been there, protesting and that, but it don't mean nothing. And you said she abducted you? Do you know why?"

"About the explosion at London City Teleport. It went on for hours. I would have died if Owen hadn't found me locked up in an underground basement."

"Underground?"

"It was under a wine store."

Arthur stroked his chin and slid his chair back from the table. "Anyone else know about this basement?"

"Only Owen and his cousin. The old lady kept asking me who was responsible for the attack, like I knew, as though I was responsible. The more I think about it, the more I know she was involved and wanted to find out if I knew about what she and the ATM had done."

"You ask me, I'd say she was some homegrown radical or offshoot, maybe even an undercover cop. But not ATM."

"Why do you think that?"

"I belonged to the ATM."

It threw her, and her eyes bulged in shock. Now she saw Arthur for who he was—a terrorist. Or a man with close links to a terrorist organisation. She didn't speak. She didn't know what to say.

"I quit a few months ago," he said.

She threw a dagger look at Owen.

Owen hadn't paid much attention and traced his fingers in the wood grain patterns of the table.

Arthur finished his smoke. "She may have been working independently of the ATM, a sub-group perhaps. Anyway, let's continue."

Continue? How could she after learning that? She wanted to bolt for the door, run away, and never come back.

The increasing silence made the situation worse.

"Listen, I could be wrong," said Arthur. "She could have been a new recruit. You ask me, the most important thing we need to ask here is why you were abducted. Tell me about them other abductors."

"Why did you quit the ATM?" she asked.

"Long story. In a nutshell, we lost our way, had a few rogue elements join us. Them abductors, tell me more."

She hesitated, then gave a sketchy description because the old lady had run the show single-handedly. Of the Serbian, she revealed all she remembered, including what had happened to him at Spider's tattoo parlour: the awful eye procedure and the Serbian word, *Clotho*, inked onto his forehead. The man with the needle may as well have been a shadow on the wall. Other than that, all she could tell Arthur was they wanted to find out what she knew about the explosion.

Arthur nodded. "And what *do* you know?"

Impatience crept into his tone again.

Her eyes brimmed with tears. "Nothing."

Arthur rubbed her arm. "Must've been tough on you, this whole ordeal. I can't imagine the toll it would take on a girl so young."

Nova opened her mouth, wanting to say she didn't need sympathy thank you very much, but the words wouldn't come out, so she turned her back on him.

"Maybe now's a good time to make that tea." He rose and headed to the kitchen. "Sure you don't want one?"

Owen stuck his thumb up and indicated one for Nova, too.

With the kettle boiling on the gas stove, Arthur prepared three mugs and milk. He unwrapped a foil package containing dumplings and held them out on a tray for his guests. "These are proper job."

Owen took two. "What are they?"

"We call them doughboys in the West Country."

He returned to the galley as the kettle began to whistle.

Nova ran her eyes around the cabin. It was a lounge cum bedroom cum galley all in one, about twice the size of Owen's underground room but without the gross drain smells. Though the cabin was sparsely furnished, it... she inhaled a deep breath through her nose. "I smell gas!"

Arthur checked the valve on the portable propane bottle. It was undone slightly, so he tightened it back up and wafted the air. "My mistake."

Nova stood slowly and put her hands flat on the table. "I smelled gas at the teleport. The day it blew up."

Arthur walked quickly to the table, balancing two mugs of tea for Nova and Owen. He pulled out a chair and picked up his pen. "Go on."

She sat down. "It was so strong, my eyes started watering, and my nose was running. It made me throw up, but I think that was because I hit my head when I fainted."

"Fainted?"

One step in her memory led to the next. "I'd left my father to use the bathroom while people were still taking their seats inside the auditorium. I wasn't feeling well. I sometimes get claustrophobic and anxious when I'm around too many people. Gives me panic attacks. I fainted and hit my head on the toilet. When I woke up, with concussion, I could smell gas. At least I think that's what it was. Like I said, I was concussed."

Arthur continued to take down her statements inside his old notebook. "They use hydrogen gas to create energy, them teleportals."

"It must have been hydrogen, then."

"Hydrogen ain't got no odour."

"Smell is added to gas, though. So you can detect if there's a leak."

Owen stuck out his bottom lip. "Never knew that."

"If there'd been a hydrogen leak, you wouldn't have known about it. You can't see, smell, or feel it. It's invisible, just like air. You could suffocate if the air was filled with one hundred per cent hydrogen. But a hydrogen leak from them teleportals, which were in the terminal, not in the auditorium, would've floated up and disappeared quickly. It don't travel horizontally, hydrogen. It just ain't possible."

"Well, there was something in the air, and trust me, it was not pleasant. It made me feel really dizzy and sick."

"It sounds symptomatic of concussion. You said you were concussed. You sure there was a gas leak?"

She shook her head. "I don't know."

"Did you actually smell gas?"

"I think so. Maybe. I don't know."

She continued to describe the hazy details of her escape. Remembering everything took some doing, and her voice was close to breaking. Rewinding, she remembered experiencing a hallucination of giant insects with big eyes and noses crawling across the floor. It had freaked her out. She also recalled seeing exit doors chain locked.

Arthur was quick to point out it was against fire regulations and asked her if they had been fire exit doors.

She couldn't recall.

Arthur shoved his chair back and left the cabin, climbing the stairs up to the deck.

Nova shook her head and looked at Owen. "Drink up! We are going after this. I don't trust this guy one bit."

She had seen the volatility in his eyes—*the windows of the soul*, her father had once told her. It was one of those old sayings that had always stuck with her, passed down like an heirloom of wisdom. "You can tell a lot about a person from their eyes," he would say.

She had a few sips of the tea and, to her surprise, liked it. Hungry as she was, she drank more of the tea, working out her next move. She ate a couple of doughboys. Remarkably tasty they were, too. She sat quietly, thinking about the conversation with Arthur, frustrated by her leaky memory.

Taking her empty mug to the sink, she stopped and turned her head to one side. "We're moving!" She looked out of the porthole, then at Owen. "The boat's moving!"

24

The Anna Belle cruised along the Thames, sturdy in the water but sluggish on the turns. The sky had turned dark and murky like a polluted body of water, and the wind had picked up.

Arthur obeyed the speed limit as he drove beyond Cricklade Bridge and Teddington Lock and accelerated out past the Port of London Authority's boundary towards the North Sea. With a hand on the helm and the other wrapped around a cigarette, he mulled over the conversation with Nova. She needed to straighten out her story, start telling some truths. He knew he had to push her harder, to dig until she finally cracked and revealed everything she knew. Until he got the information he needed, she wasn't going anywhere. He'd failed the ATM and had to make amends. He was determined to protect its legacy, no matter what it took or how high the cost, because letting the organisation falter was not an option.

The ATM, conceived a decade earlier, had grown beyond anyone's imagination. In its early days, he and Travis had been the ATM's sole members. To provide a safe place for hatching plans and discussing tactics, Travis had converted the cellar beneath his wine store into a secure basement, where only the privileged members knew the door's combination pin. Wine stock had dwindled after the brutal murders of his parents in one of their vineyards in Belgium. Strangled with wire, their hands had been severed, and the criminals had used them and their fingerprints to withdraw their entire life savings before dumping the dismembered limbs in a fishpond. Such crimes soon became commonplace in the new world, with people forced to implant nanochips in their hands that set off alarms at the bank if blood flow was drastically altered, locking down accounts and alerting police of a possible attack. It was what had drawn many people, including Travis, to the ATM.

In the space of fifteen months, the movement had spread to eight countries in Europe, with over 100,000 members and growing. And the year after that, a whole new ATM mob had popped up in North America. They were independent of each other, with no affiliation and no shared strategy or intel. Yet, when one group staged a new protest or advocated for change, the groups overseas followed in their footsteps. The ATM's mission was simple: revolt against technological growth and a global culture dependent on artificial intelligence to prevent the disruption to human social systems.

As a founding member, it was Arthur's duty to ensure the organisation did not fade and vanish into history. There was still time to free ATM members, realign its values, and pledge allegiance to a common cause. They still had targets to meet, work to do, minds to change.

Owen approached the wheelhouse with a pale face and lost his balance when a large wave rolled under the boat.

"Steady on there!" said Arthur. "Bit choppy out."

White crests topped the waves on the open sea.

"Where are we going?" asked Owen.

"An excursion. It don't do no one no good, all that city smog."

"Can we go back?"

"Don't worry, we ain't going far."

The boat rose on a high wave and plunged down the other side.

"I can't swim," said Owen.

"Then don't fall in."

"But we—"

"Look, if you can survive on the streets, you can survive a night on my boat." Arthur was aware of the tone in his voice. He thought he'd make amends by saying something nice. But he couldn't think of anything nice to say.

"We're staying the night?"

"Got somewhere else to be?"

"No, but—"

"Then you go and check on that there girlfriend of yours. I'll be down later."

The smell of the sea hung in the air, of fish and seaweed and of danger so pungent, Nova could almost taste it. She folded her arms at the cabin door when Owen appeared at the top of the steps. "Where's he taking us?"

Owen raised his shoulders. "Looks like we have to stay the night."

"What did he say?"

"We're staying the night."

"Why?"

Owen came down the steps and sat on the last one. He put his head between his legs. "Something about smog."

Nova's stomach took a turn with the rocking motion of the boat, but she was nowhere near as seasick as Owen. She assumed he had always been good at adapting, but his senses would need time to adjust to the immediacy of boat life. It was apparent he was no seafarer. His pale face had a sheen of sweat that made him look only slightly healthier than a dead body. She sat beside him, rubbing his back.

Every metre separating them from the mainland put Nova further on edge. Had Arthur showing up at the teleport been by chance? Or had he made it happen? That she'd been duped and this was a trap seemed likely. If so, with the trap set and the bait taken, what happened next? She had not even thought this could lead to a hostage situation. She wasn't sure she could endure another round of physical and psychological torture.

"You two must be hungry," said Arthur at the top of the steps. "How do egg sarnies sound?"

Owen almost threw up over the threshold.

Nova helped him up and led him to the table inside.

Arthur went to the galley to fry up some eggs. "Talk among yourselves."

Owen raised his head off the table momentarily. "Looks like you were worried over nothing," he whispered.

Nova watched Arthur tying an apron around his waist, still unconvinced. "We'll see."

Owen lowered his head back onto the table but remained talkative. "So you arrive in New York all naked. Then what?"

"Stop picturing me naked!"

He smiled. "I'm just curious."

"If you must know, you step out of the teleportal into a small changing cubicle where you select the clothes and shoes you want to hire from a screen. You also get bags, toiletries, and general stuff like that. The items are then delivered to you through the floor, and you get dressed, pack the bags, and go."

"What about dosh?"

"Unlike this country, America is now a completely cashless society, so all payments are made by fingerprint."

Arthur turned, waving a spatula in his hand. "By the way, police arrested several members of the ATM for the attack on London City Teleport."

Owen raised his head off the table slightly, but lowered it just as quickly, his face still pale with green hues.

"I don't want to say I told you so," said Nova.

"No point, it weren't the ATM."

"Then why were they arrested?"

"*Mistakenly* arrested. Let's be clear. They're activists, they are, not mass murderers. Trust me, the police got the wrong people."

25

While Owen lay on the fold-down bed battling his seasickness, Arthur continued with the questions, forcing Nova to answer everything again as he cross-examined her story.

What time had they arrived at Expo?

How long had she spent in the bathroom?

What had happened after she woke up?

How about that gas?

What did she see?

Who did she see?

What was said during her abduction?

Who was this Serbian bloke?

She had difficulty remembering, blaming her concussion. Every time she tried to recall what had happened, she was met with a frustrating haze, the details just out of reach, her brow furrowed as she tried to force clarity out of the fog, but it was no use. The concussion had scrambled her mind, leaving her with only disjointed and unreliable flashes of the past.

"Clotho!" said Arthur.

"What?"

"You said Clotho got tattooed on his face."

"Yes, a Serbian swear word."

"Is it? In Greek mythology, Clotho was the youngest sister of three."

"And?"

"She was the sister of fate, a young maiden spinning the threads of lives and fate, deciding who lived and who would be killed. Sounds like this Serbian bloke thinks he's some kind of fate master."

"That's just stupid."

"Know any Serbians? Might be worth finding out if Clotho means something."

"No, I don't know any."

He made a note to translate the word Clotho from Serbian to English.

"Right, let's start over, figure this out."

She started at the beginning, *again*, with the transfer to New York, and described in some detail how the day had unfolded. When she rewound each scenario and conversation inside her head, something came to her from nowhere. The hippy on the platform warning her teleportation was dangerous and didn't work. He had explicitly warned her not to travel through them. Nova thought little of it, but Arthur seemed intrigued by this warning.

"I wonder what he meant by that."

Nova shrugged with disinterest. "He was drunk. I guess he was just trying to scare me. He did a good job."

"Wait up, let's not dismiss this completely. Teleportation worked well, right? Your physical mass got teleported from London to New York. You arrived safely. You ain't got an arm missing or a kneecap where your elbow used to be. Obviously, it worked, at least it appears that way on the outside. You feel okay?"

"I feel fine. Why?"

"Your body got destroyed and recreated. I wonder if you got recreated properly, or if you got jumbled up along the way. Your organs, they all in the right place? Got any strange lumps anywhere?"

"Stop it! You're scaring me."

"What about that mind of yours? Working as it should be? Having any weird visions or impairments?"

Reluctant to share her chilling dreams, fearing it would fuel a line of questioning that was as futile as it was exhausting, she said, "I told you, I'm fine, just concussed still. I keep forgetting things, and sometimes I get these sharp headaches."

She continued to deconstruct the day of the explosion at the teleport, piece by piece, mindful of every detail, however inconsequential it seemed.

But Arthur had a hook, and he wouldn't let go. "Something happened to you!"

"Nothing happened to me!"

Arthur stood, slapping his palm against the table, causing Nova to flinch. Owen reared up on the bed.

"Never trusted Teletron. We should pay them a visit, let them know we're onto them. Stir the pot. I'd give my right arm to see them capitulate." He sat down again. "In the meantime, you should get some tests done."

"What tests?"

"At the hospital. Scans, blood tests, get a full psychological examination. We might find something."

"What?"

"Complications. Clues."

She pressed her lips firmly together. She tried to keep a handle on the discussion. She wasn't doing a good job. Arthur spoke with such assertiveness and persuasion, she wondered why he hadn't exploited this talent in sales or politics.

"There's nothing wrong with me, okay? Please, stop!" She convinced no one, and that included herself.

Arthur topped up his glass with rum and knocked it back in one gulp. "What do we really know? What have we learned about teleportation? Or rather, what have we been told? Yes, we get transported from one place to another. Yes, we arrive quickly. It's convenient and instantaneous and hassle-free. But what happens to our minds and bodies? We get destroyed and recreated. Our anatomy is deconstructed, no, it's disintegrated, and after all them tiny pieces are threaded through to the other side, we're reintegrated. Atom by atom. That there teleportal machine is responsible for putting us back, one piece at a time, as its microprocessor got programmed to do by the so-called tech experts. But what does a computer really know about the human anatomy?"

Nova wasn't sure if he was actually asking a question or not. Others had been rhetorical.

Owen returned to the table with a little more natural colour in his cheeks. He brushed his fingers through the candle flame, causing the light in the room to flicker.

Arthur slid the candle away from him. "Stop that! It's like being with a bloody child."

Owen was met with Arthur's trenchant stare.

Arthur's jaw muscles bunched as he turned to Nova and ground his teeth together. "Well?"

"I don't know," said Nova.

She stole a glance at Owen.

His face remained unreadable.

"Them computers only know what us humans teach them. Humans make mistakes. That's what makes us fundamentally human. But they don't make mistakes, them computers. They do what they're programmed to do, or experience a technical malfunction, but their integrity and efficiency are complete at the level at which they got programmed. But they can only be taught by humans. What if them super computers were taught human biology with only ninety-nine per cent accuracy? What about the one per cent? Huh? What's the result? A reintegrated human who ain't quite complete."

Arthur insisted once more she undergo a series of hospital tests, including a toxicology screening and a brain scan. Then pressed on with his questioning, but most of his enquiries were met with her blank stares and silence; she had no answers to give. Eventually, she sat cross-legged on the floor, sobbing and rocking back and forth.

Bebop sauntered over, and Nova wrapped her arms gently around her, pressing her cheek into her soft fur. Bebop licked the tears off Nova's face.

Arthur sat back in his chair and sparked a cigarette. With his empty glass, he walked to the galley for a refill of rum and let out a loud, frustrated sigh. Kicking off his boots, he relit the lantern and shook the match to extinguish the flame. He adjusted the oil flow to the maximum output, and the flame grew tall, brightening up the room as dusk began to settle over the North Sea.

Nova dried her eyes. Since the incident at the teleport, she had not been herself. She was nervous and panicky, and her dreams seriously scared her. It must have been what victims of trauma experienced. Still, this interrogation had dragged on for long enough. She wanted Arthur to take them back to London immediately.

She was about to insist Arthur turn the boat around when he spun and inserted ammunition into a black gun, gripping it between his thumb and forefinger. He smacked the magazine into the grip. "One bullet left."

Nova and Owen glanced fearfully at each other.

Arthur finished the last of his rum and walked over with the gun tight in his grip. "I'm a dangerous man right now."

To seize any opportunity that might present itself, Nova scanned the room, seeking an escape route or some weapon she might use in self-defence if called for. Near the table were his tools, some in the toolbox, some strewn about the floor. They looked old and greasy. Years of use and abuse. A rusty box cutter was in one of the shelf compartments. That would work. If a stab wound didn't kill him, the infection would. That would take time, though. Time she didn't have. Neither did she have the stomach to inflict such harm on another human being if it came to the crunch.

Arthur leaned aggressively towards her.

She could smell the tobacco in his clothes and the rum on his breath.

"What do we do now, hey?" he asked.

Silence filled the room like the pungent fumes he emitted.

Nova breathed out slowly, frozen in fear.

"Hey?"

"I don't know," she said.

"She doesn't know," said Owen, his face ashen. "Leave her alone!"

Arthur walked to the wall and pulled the blind. It shot up, stopping with a clunk.

It startled Owen and Nova.

He bent down so his face was level with the tiny porthole. "A boat's coming!"

26

"Who is it?" asked Owen.

Arthur shrugged. "Coastguard? They often check on boats out here, routine and that, but after–"

Before he could finish his sentence, Nova bolted for the door, sprinted up the steps to the deck, and started jumping and waving her arms at the approaching boat.

Owen was left staring across the room at Arthur. He kept his mouth shut, allowing the uncomfortable silence to stretch.

Arthur held out his palms and shrugged, and Owen took that as a free pass. He slipped out the door and ran up the steps to join Nova on the deck.

Two circular lights in the dark bobbed towards them.

In her mind, Nova went over what the conversation with the coastguard would sound like. First, she would tell them she was a survivor of the bombing at London City Teleport. They would take her and Owen back to land, far away from this self-destructive terrorist, and safely escort her to the doorstep of a police station. She wished she had ignored Owen's advice and gone to the police earlier. She should have known better than to expect a street kid having any trust or interest in the police. The very idea of involving them would have set off alarm bells in his mind, triggering a deep-seated instinct to avoid them at all costs. His life had likely been a series of run-ins, reinforcing a profound mistrust woven into his mind. To him, the police weren't a source of protection or help; they were the enemy.

The lights grew closer and belonged to an old speedboat that looked like it could take on water at any moment. As it neared, the lamps on deck provided enough light to illuminate two men, both wearing black jackets with standing collars, one with a cap, one without.

Nova's mouth dropped when she saw the machine guns strapped over their shoulders. This was no coastguard. These were Arthur's men, reinforcements from his destructive ATM operation. They had arrived with a purpose, and it wasn't to offer protection or aid. No, they had come here to continue the interrogations, picking up where the old lady had left off before she was murdered. Arthur had orchestrated everything, ensuring his men would be there at the right moment to take control. She realised with a sinking heart she was now caught up in something far more dangerous than she had imagined.

She breathed deeply as the speedboat nosed over to the bow, colliding lightly against the portside, causing a scraping sound. She saw the men's heads through the guard rail, slightly higher than the deck.

"Do you have permission to be out here?" the boat driver called out from behind the wheel.

Nova looked at Owen with a hint of confusion, thrown by the question. "I don't know. Do we need permission?"

The man paused. "Identify yourselves, please."

At that moment, Arthur struggled out of a hatch at the stern. He crouched behind whatever equipment lay covered by the red vinyl sheet. A faint glow appeared in his eyes. He had activated his bionic lenses. Why? The only reason she could fathom was to utilise his night-vision lenses, which explained the way he was scanning the speedboat from his vantage point.

"Why?" asked Owen.

"Identify yourselves now!" said the driver.

Nova's stomach was hideously alive with nerves. She stood tall, her courage shaken but not broken. She thought about her father. By an act of sheer will, she kept calm and composed.

There was hesitation and indecision as they lapsed into a silent and tense standoff.

Nova glanced towards the stern at Arthur, cowering out of sight, perfectly calm. He held a finger to his lips, urging her to stay quiet. It struck her then these men weren't affiliated after all. The machine guns over the men's shoulders, their stern demands for identification, and Arthur's desperate efforts to remain hidden and keep her quiet all pointed to something far more serious. They definitely did not belong to the coastguard, but maybe they were part of some undercover anti-terrorism unit. That would explain their intimidating presence and why Arthur was so intent on staying out of their line of sight. They were on her side, and could bring an end to all this madness, arresting Arthur and bringing him to justice for the attack on London City Teleport.

"Please help us!" she screamed. "We've been taken hostage by the owner of this boat, Arthur, who works for the ATM."

The man asking the questions hesitated. "Who are you?"

"I'm Nova, and this is—"

All hell broke loose.

Shots were fired, and at first, Nova didn't know where they had been fired from. Bullets zipped through the air, chewing away at the soft wood of the wheelhouse.

Owen pulled Nova down flat on the deck.

They crawled up behind the wheelhouse as more bullets flowed in their direction. Nova's legs shook. She tried to hold them still by pressing her hands on her knees but couldn't stop them. She balled up to avoid the flurry of bullets ricocheting off the wheelhouse, shattering the windows.

The shooting terminated with the sound of smashing glass on the deck.

The pause enabled Nova to look in Arthur's direction. She couldn't see him. He appeared at the side of the wheelhouse, holding a couple of gas canisters. Nova was about to scream when he put his finger over his lips to silence her. He made a series of gestures, pointing in the direction of the speedboat, informing them to stay low.

Owen stole a glance at the speedboat and looked back at Nova gravely, whispering, "They're trying to get on our boat."

Nova also peered around the wheelhouse and saw one of the men reloading his machine gun. At any moment, the firing could resume.

Nova looked at Arthur again. He'd crawled back over to the stern. He had his gun in hand. What was he up to? She remembered him saying he only had one bullet. One bullet against two men, who had machine guns.

Arthur's face was one of calm but stern determination. He looked excited by the challenge. Perhaps his involvement with the ATM had sharpened more than just his wits. Membership in such a secretive organisation likely demanded more than just strategic thinking; it required the ability to act decisively and defend oneself under pressure. Maybe it was through the ATM that Arthur had honed his self-defence skills, turning him into someone who could face danger without flinching.

A fresh burst of gunfire disturbed the evening stillness.

Owen and Nova pressed themselves flat to the deck.

If Arthur had a plan, he needed to execute it now.

The deck was twice the height of the speedboat, and once the men had worked out the only way aboard was the ladder at the stern, they would be within killing range.

Nova turned towards the stern once more and saw Arthur unscrewing the caps on the gas bottles. He then launched them underarm onto the speedboat. Dropping to a crouch position, he pointed his gun two-handed and made the close-range shot. Even to untrained eyes, one could tell he knew his way around a firearm. The bullet struck the gas bottle. It wasn't intended to puncture the high-strength steel exterior. It wasn't possible. But the strike generated the fine spark needed to ignite the gas clouds looming around the speedboat.

When it failed, the men offloaded a stream of bullets that crossed the small gap between the boats.

Arthur ducked as the bullets flew over his head, striking the guard rail and equipment blocking him from view. Arthur raised the vinyl sheet, reached underneath it, and pulled out a rag. He wrapped it around one of the brick pavers, took out his lighter, and thumbed the striker. The chemical-soaked rag caught fire in an instant. It burned Arthur's fingertips until he launched it like a shotput, watching it sail over the water and land on the speedboat.

The gas lit up in flames instantaneously and funnelled all the way down to the source. A ten-foot blast of fire erupted from the gas bottle, shooting it fifty feet high. One of the men was catapulted into the air. He landed on his head. Engulfed in flames, his face a mask of blood, he pitched forward into the sea, disappearing beneath the waves.

The explosion threw Arthur's boat sideways.

Nova's head lurched forward, then back, slamming against the wheelhouse wall. After the pain subsided, shock set in.

Owen stood and glanced at the speedboat. It was fatally holed at the waterline, the blast having punched through the inner and outer walls. It began to list. Fire consumed the deck, and black smoke rose into the sky.

The driver stood defiantly. His arm was alight, but he looked too stunned to notice.

Arthur climbed over the guard rail and jumped down onto the speedboat, even as it began to sink.

The driver collapsed to the deck, writhing from a shrapnel wound in his throat. Seeing the size of the shrapnel and the severity of the injury, Arthur knew he had little time to get some answers.

"Who are you?" asked Arthur.

He couldn't, or wouldn't, answer. He just stared up at the stars, bleeding out on the deck.

"Tell me who you are!"

He turned his eyes slowly towards Arthur. "No one," he said with an eastern European accent.

"Who are you working for? Who sent you? Why are you out here?"

He raised his shoulder to relieve the pain in his neck, but it didn't stop the blood pouring out in thick rivulets. His eyes turned red, and blood gurgled in his throat as he lay helplessly on the deck. "Clo...tho."

The hair on Arthur's arms crackled, the heat from the fire burning his skin.

"What is Clotho?"

The driver closed his eyes and passed away.

Arthur tucked the gun into his belt. He jumped to reach the ladder on his boat and hauled himself back on board just as the speedboat went under, extinguishing the flames.

The driver drifted away, his buoyant arms rising like wings.

Arthur charged across the deck and came heavily around the wheelhouse, his boots grinding against the glass fragments. Slamming the peppered door shut, he started the motor and swung the boat around in a tight circle. He was so caught up in what he considered a triumph, he failed to notice the smoke seeping from the cabin and spreading across the deck behind him.

As soon as he cut the motor, Owen appeared at the door. "Fire!"

27

The gap at the bottom of the cabin door revealed flickering orange light that bathed the foot of the steps, and thick, black smoke that poured out, swirling like a ghost escaping capture. The smell hit Arthur's nose, snapping him out of his confused state. He bolted down the stairs, his feet barely touching the steps in his frantic rush. He crashed through the door, the heat slamming into him with physical force. His eyes widened in horror at the sight before him. His bed was engulfed in flames that crackled and burned with such ferocious intensity. Smoke tendrils rose in torrent spirals, as if a massive vacuum sucked the air out of the room. The cabin was a whirling vortex of heat, smoke, and destruction, creating an otherworldly glow in the compact space. Arthur could barely breathe, his lungs filling with the choking smoke, and his eyes stung from the intensity of the char-filled air.

As he assessed the scene, the cause of the disaster became painfully clear. The explosion had shaken the boat, sending a violent tremor through Anna Belle. The force had knocked a candle off the table, causing it to roll across the floor towards the foot of the bed, leaving a waxy trail in its wake. Its flame had quickly ignited the duvet and bedsheets, and the fire had spread rapidly across the fabric. Nearby, the lantern hanging securely from its hook now lay shattered in pieces on the floor. The explosion had torn it free, and the impact had caused its glass casing to splinter, spilling oil across the wooden boards. The oil had pooled and spread in a wide arc, feeding the hungry flames and turning a small fire into a raging inferno.

Black smoke plumed in thick clouds, filling the air with the smell of charred wood and burning fabric. Arthur covered his mouth and nose and ran to the galley, pulling the extinguisher from its wall clamps. The flames were as tall as him now and hot as hell. He aimed the extinguisher at the base of the flames, unleashing a powerful blast of foam that momentarily dulled its intensity. The flames sputtered and receded, as if retreating from the attack, and for a brief moment, it seemed he might gain the upper hand. But as soon as he cut the spray, the fire roared back to life, finding flammable materials as it ventured from one piece of furniture to the next.

"What's taking him so long?" asked Nova.

He had been gone for almost five minutes. Even from the safety of the deck, it was clear the fire was a serious one. The amount of smoke pouring through the cabin door and tinged a bright orange obscured the entire staircase. No one could survive in such thick smoke for very long without protective gear.

The cabin door suddenly flew open, and Arthur charged up the steps, coughing loudly into his hand. His face was black and sweating. "She can't be saved. Time to abandon ship."

Owen shook his head. "But I can't swim."

"Now's a good time to learn."

Owen held all the air he could in his lungs and shoved past Nova and Arthur. He disappeared down the steps, snatching the fire extinguisher from Arthur on his way.

Nova was frantic and called after him.

Arthur struggled to hold her back, his hands gripping her shoulders firmly as she wriggled and fought against him.

"No, we can't leave him down there!" she cried out, her voice breaking with emotion. She yanked against his hold, her breath coming in ragged gasps as she struggled to break free.

"He's gone!"

"No!"

"We need to go before she explodes or sinks."

Arthur dragged her towards the guard rail. He let her go, but she ran back to the steps as a large pall of smoke erupted from the cabin door, forcing her back.

"Owen! Owen!" But he was gone. Taking backward steps until she reached Arthur standing at the guard rail, she turned and leaned out over the dark water. She looked for the horizon but couldn't see it.

"We need to hurry. There's a storm coming in later. Can't risk getting caught in that."

Arthur climbed up the guard rail and jumped in, making a small splash. His head broke the surface, and he treaded water, looking around him. He shook his head like a wet dog, flinging droplets everywhere. He looked up at Nova. "Come on, then, we ain't that far from land, about a mile tops."

The whole night had been packed with drama. It was as if she had been on trial with Arthur hounding her on the witness stand. Now she faced the death penalty in the cold waters of the North Sea. If hypothermia didn't kill her, then drowning certainly would. Decision-making had never been so tough. She had choices, difficult choices, and very little time to make them.

She placed a foot on the first rail and stepped up, her thighs pressing against the cold steel. The breeze carried thick, black smoke in her direction, and for a moment she lost sight of Arthur.

She heard a whine and twisted round, hoping to see Owen.

Bebop sat on the deck, whimpering and licking her nose.

The sound of someone coughing drew her attention to the cabin steps. She jumped down from the guard rail. "Owen!"

He collapsed onto the deck, his body succumbing to the overwhelming exhaustion. He could barely move, his strength drained by the relentless smoke and intense heat that radiated from the spreading flames.

She emitted joy and relief at seeing him alive.

Owen cleared his lungs and pulled out his inhaler, taking several puffs. His lips moved, but no sound escaped.

"We need to get off this boat," she said. "I'll hold onto you in the water. I won't let go, I promise."

Nova helped him into a seated position and whacked his back, helping him cough up the smoke. His face was black, and his eyes looked like glass globes.

"It's out!" He coughed repeatedly and took one more hit on the inhaler. "The fire's out!"

28

The scent of charred wood clung to the cabin's interior. The bed was destroyed, its mattress reduced to a brittle husk that crumbled with the slightest touch. The ceiling bore the dark imprints of flames, like phantoms etched into the mahogany.

Arthur inspected the wall, rubbing his fingertips against the blackened surface. "Superficial burns." His voice was muffled behind the wet towel wrapped around his mouth to blunt the awful smell. His grey hair lay plastered to his scalp, damp from his earlier plunge. "Paint restores a burned wooden surface as long as it ain't damaged. You ask me, it don't look damaged. Some tack cloths and a new coat of paint should fix that." He turned and faced Owen. "Thought she was doomed."

Nova removed the towel from her mouth. "Can you take us back now?"

"In the morning. I ain't got no energy right now."

She sighed to show her frustration. Why had he brought them out there in the first place? What was he truly trying to accomplish? By isolating her from the mainland, he'd ensured she had no escape, no chance of fleeing back to the safety of society. Here, he could pressure her for information tirelessly with no interference. But maybe there was more to it than that. Perhaps he craved something beyond control or answers. The emptiness caused by his family's death had left him stranded in a loneliness that ate away at his sanity. Perhaps, in his twisted logic, he believed by dragging her into his solitude, he could stave off his own despair. Whatever his reason, she didn't want to spend another minute on his godforsaken boat. The cabin reeked of smoke. Owen stank, too. It was hard to tell when he had last bathed, but it wasn't in the last week, and probably not in the last month. His lack of hygiene bothered her and was exacerbated by his firefighting capers.

She finally found the courage to ask Arthur the question on her mind. "Why did you bring us out here?"

Arthur turned from the wall. "After what happened at the teleport with my ladder, I thought it was safer to talk far away from the city. You ask me, the safest place for you right now is anywhere but land."

Nova folded her arms. "For a start, that's not true. Or did you not see those men shooting at us?"

He placed his hands on his hips. "Don't give me lip, young lady! It's clear we've stirred up a hornet's nest, and people out there want us dead."

"Who were they?" asked Owen.

"I don't know, but we need to be extra vigilant, make sure we don't have a repeat of what happened this evening. I'll keep watch tonight."

"How are you supposed to keep watch if you've got *no energy?*" She even lifted her fingers to make air quotes.

"Don't mock me, Nova!"

He sounded like her father.

Nova was too exhausted for any more conversation. She couldn't stand up for much longer. She reapplied the towel to her face and climbed inside the hammock.

Owen found a corner on the floor and curled up, bending his knees slightly to squeeze into the tight space. One shot on his inhaler and he instantly fell asleep.

Arthur bid them both goodnight with abrupt formality and went up to the deck.

Nova experienced another night unable to settle and sleep well. Yet another night filled with fear and speculation with dreams haunted by memories and visions. She attempted to roll over, a complicated manoeuvre that caused the hammock to swing perilously.

Giving up, she rolled out of the hammock and tightened the towel around her mouth and nose.

Arthur was asleep on his bed, having flipped his toasted mattress over. So much for keeping watch.

Owen was still on the floor in the same position, having not moved once.

She visited the tiny galley for a glass of water, ignoring the grunts and snores coming from her fellow inhabitants. On her way back to the hammock, she paused to look at the shelves overflowing with volumes spanning a wide range of subjects. She ran her fingers along the different coloured spines. There was a well-worn book on farming and irrigation, its pages dog-eared from frequent use. Next to it, cookery books of all kinds, from basic recipes to more intricate culinary techniques. A thick tome on anatomy caught her eye, a subject she herself was interested in. Nearby, a book about European history was nestled between a guide to medicinal herbs and a volume on astronomy. As she continued to scan the shelves, she noticed works on philosophy, classical literature, and even saw a dusty manual on wilderness survival. The eclectic collection hinted at a mind that was both curious and resourceful, someone who sought knowledge in every corner of life.

Arthur's notebook was tucked in among the books. It had a ragged spine held together by tape. She had no clue what she expected to find inside it, but she hoped it would shed some light on this enigmatic man and remove some of the mystery. The notebook's inside cover contained numerous doodles, and random lines and shapes were scribbled in the margins. He had underlined various words throughout the pages, including the name Peter Huxley. One entry described a meeting held at the ATM's safe house, detailing plans for an attack on Teletron HQ using anthrax, gasoline, or bombs. This alone was enough to raise serious alarm. Her testimony was scrawled across two pages without any clear order or system, just messy thoughts and observations. The notebook also contained a list of work contacts in relation to his trades as a technician, electrician, plumber, and general handyman. But it was the sketch on the second-to-last page that truly unsettled her: a crude drawing of a mass grave with bodies piled high in a gruesome display. The level of detail suggested he'd invested significant mental energy on this disturbing image.

Flipping back and forth through the notebook, she saw it was almost full except for a few blank pages. And she saw that name again: *Peter Huxley.*

Her eyes narrowed as she shut the book and stepped across the room to search the drawers in the galley.

"What are you looking for?" came a weary voice.

She turned to find Arthur's eyes were wide open, though he remained in a sleeping position on the bed.

She had to think quickly. "Can I use your bionic lenses?"

"For what?"

She paused. "To check the news."

"They ain't connected to the web. Go to sleep, please."

Exhausted and weak, she returned to the hammock. Her balance was still compromised by the headaches, nausea, and light-headedness. She shut her eyes, feeling the cabin sway. She couldn't tell whether it was the lurking concussion or the boat rocking. Either way, it eventually rocked her into some kind of sleepy contentment.

29

Seventy-five-knot offshore gales roared across the sea as storm clouds dumped heavy rain and jagged pitchforks of lightning illuminated the sky.

She crossed the deck slowly, tiptoeing across the wet wood barefoot with unseeing eyes. She was incarcerated in her own mind, incapable of thinking about... anything. Strong winds whipped her soaked hair across her face as though they might tear it straight from her scalp, but she remained oblivious until a violent flash of light and deafening crash jolted her out of her trance. She returned from nothing more than just a momentary phantom of herself. She blinked, and as awareness dawned, she noticed the cold in her joints. Her fingers and toes were numb, her legs so stiff she barely had any bend in them. She suddenly became conscious of the cacophony around her: the howling wind, the breaking waves, the booming thunder, and relentless pounding of the rain. Whichever direction she turned, she saw darkness stretching off into the distance.

Arthur appeared in front of her, lit by the close lightning. Nothing at all was friendly or engaging about the way he stared at her. She stared back, her eyes wide with fear. "Help!"

He just stared at her with his neck crooked against the wind and rain. "You're gonna need it!" He suddenly grabbed her by the shoulders with both hands.

Was he planning to kill her in some horrific way and then toss her overboard to become fish food? The thought sent a surge of panic through her, and she instinctively tried to break free from his tight grasp, turning her head to shield her face against the stinging horizontal rain. But Arthur's grip on her shoulders remained unyielding. Then, with a forceful twist, he spun her around and steered her past the wheelhouse, guiding her towards the stern. When they reached the staircase, he led her down the steps, one at a time, until they were back inside the warm, dry cabin.

He let go and grabbed a towel and a toiletry bag, passing them to her. "Take a hot shower," he said. "It'll do you good."

She froze, confused and scared as she accepted the towel and toiletries.

She leaned back against the door, needing a moment to collect herself in the solitude of the tiny shower room. Scum had formed in the tiles, and the damp stench was more than just residue. The boat rocked. Nova had to keep adjusting her balance as she undressed and hung her clothes on the door rail. It took time for the water to heat up, and even then, it barely reached lukewarm. Her hair was tangled like seaweed from the salty sea spray, but when she massaged the grime out of her scalp with shampoo, she became more relaxed, the warm water soothing against her skin. She stared down at her soapy hands, noticing something tangled between her fingers. *Hair.* The wet, dark strands clung to her skin, a sight that had her suddenly breathing faster. She rinsed them under the shower spray, but as she raked her fingers across her scalp, more strands came loose, slipping free in unsettling clumps. It accumulated at her feet, clogging the plughole.

Stepping out of the shower, she dried herself with a towel and wiped away a patch of condensation from the mirror. Her reflection revealed bald patches scattered across her scalp. Her hands started shaking. She tried to keep them steady but not successfully. She stared at her reflection, trying to find a logical reason for the hair loss. She thought she might know why.

When she finally emerged from the bathroom with a towel wrapped around her head, an hour had passed. The sun started to rise, but the wind went on howling and the boat continued to rock on the choppy waves.

Arthur was on the other side of the room. He had his nose inside his notebook. He placed it back on the shelf when he saw Nova.

"Better?"

"No."

"What happened? Up there on deck?"

She paused, trying to recall, but had no recollection. "Must have been sleepwalking."

Arthur went to the galley and put the kettle on the gas hob. "Tea?"

"Yes, please."

He turned, holding a teaspoon. "You ask me, I think it's high time we paid Teletron a visit. It's where them teleportals got manufactured."

Though it seemed like a harebrained idea, Nova considered it with all seriousness, if only for a moment. "You can count me out, but no one's stopping you."

In a seamless motion, Owen shifted from the floor to a chair, propped his legs up on the table, and drifted back to sleep, all within five seconds.

Nova envied the fact he could fall asleep anywhere, on any surface, and sleep so deeply and undisturbed.

When Arthur joined them, carrying two mugs of tea, which he placed on mats, he slapped Owen's feet, forcing them off the table.

Owen jerked awake. He sat up, momentarily startled. He wiped his nose on his sleeve, then sagged back in his chair and closed his eyes.

Nova removed the towel from her head and brushed her dishevelled hair back.

"What's with your bonce?" asked Owen, now holding one eye open.

"My hair? It came out in the shower."

Arthur folded his arms and studied her scalp, bending his knees to peer at either side. "Probably stress-related, that is. It can cause hair to fall out."

Tears hung from her eyelashes. "Not radiation?"

"Radiation? Nah. You ain't exhibiting no other symptoms like vomiting, fever, blistering skin, major internal pain. Look, I ain't no doctor, but Owen and I ain't losing our hair, and I was in that exclusion zone much longer than you."

"But you weren't near the explosion at the teleport. I was right beside it."

"I can clean you up if you want. Got my own clippers."

She agreed.

Nova let him guide her to a chair positioned in front of an oval mirror. Gently, he draped a towel around her shoulders, securing the ends snugly under her chin. As he prepared the shaver, he ran it delicately behind her ears, sweeping it across her scalp, trailing down the back of her head to her neck. His careful strokes ensured an even trim, and the buzz of the shaver created a calming hum as he worked his way around her head before adding the finishing touches along her hairline.

"There."

In less than three minutes, he had reduced her head to a smooth, bare surface. The lustrous length of her hair was now gone, vanished in a flurry of clippings that lay scattered around her feet. The transformation was swift and left her with a new appearance that felt foreign and strangely liberating. She ran her hand over her shaved head, bristling under her palm, the strangest sensation.

Arthur tapped the hair out of his grooming supplies before packing them away.

Nova examined her reflection, struggling to recognise her face in the mirror. Her eyes and nose still looked familiar, but her lips appeared thinner than she remembered, and her ears seemed more pointed. The bruise along her hairline had faded to a yellowish hue. Sitting so close to the mirror, she could see every detail, including the anxious movement of her throat as she swallowed nervously.

30

Arthur steered Anna Belle through the murky brown waters of the Thames, drifting past the low-lying marshlands, mudflats, and salt marshes that lined either side of the estuary. The boat carved a gentle wake through the water, and the river began to narrow, its sodden banks creeping closer together with each passing mile. The air was thick with the briny scent of the sea, mingling with the earthy aroma of the marshes and thick mud, a sensory reminder of the ancient gateway to London on which they cruised.

Nova ran through a series of leg exercises at the portside guard rail and twisted her arms behind her back, stretching out the curved posture the hammock had shaped her into. The weather had turned bleak and miserable since the storm. The temperature had plummeted, and a thin mist enveloped them. For the first time in her life, Nova was desperate to see the high-rise buildings of London, those towering structures that had always seemed so imposing but now symbolised safety and escape. They'd be a sign she was finally back on solid ground, far away from the nightmare she'd endured. The past few days had been a harrowing blur, steeped in danger and fear. Arthur's relentless interrogation had stripped away her defences, those piercing questions leaving her emotionally raw and on edge. Then there were the ruthless men who had sprayed bullets in her direction, the deafening sound of gunfire still haunting her fragile mind. No wonder her hair had started to fall out. Stress manifested in the most visceral of ways. All she wanted now was to see those familiar skyscrapers, informing her this ordeal was finally over. They were near. Boats emerged from the mist, and marinas and buildings appeared on the banks.

Nova ran her hand over her shaved head, the smoothness of her scalp still unfamiliar to her touch. It felt strange, almost as if a part of her identity had been stripped away with her hair. She felt exposed, naked in a way that went beyond the physical. Though it brought vulnerability, there was a small comfort in the change. No more tangled knots to comb through in the mornings, no more fussing with the unruly strands that never seemed to cooperate. It was one less thing to worry about, a minor relief in the grand scheme.

Arthur joined Nova on the deck. He angled a mug of tea her way. It was a peace offering of sorts. She enjoyed a long sip, letting the tea's warmth combat the chill in her bones. She did like his tea, made with just the right balance of long-soaked teabag and a splash of sweetened coconut milk.

Arthur slipped his hands in his pockets. "Have my ups and downs, I do. I needed to vent last night. Sorry you were on the receiving end."

CHRISTOPHER KEITH

Apology accepted. Trust denied. Yesterday was suddenly a blur to her. Everything had unfolded so quickly. If he had set out to trap them, he had spun his web perfectly. But the mug of tea, the apology, and the fact he was taking her back to the mainland planted seeds of doubt about his true intentions.

Was he a terrorist?

Or just another grieving parent?

She offered him a half-hearted smile, a mere curve of her lips that lacked any real warmth or sincerity. It was more of a reflex than an expression of genuine emotion. She wasn't good at disguising her true feelings, and the effort showed.

Arthur crossed the deck, stepping carefully over the broken glass. At the wheelhouse, he stopped, glanced back over his shoulder, and said, "But get yourself examined at the hospital, if not to get some general tests done, at least to find out why that hair of yours has fallen out."

She nodded and looked past him, out across the river.

Arthur ducked inside the wheelhouse.

Sometime later, Nova felt the boat's speed descend a notch and spotted the marina ahead. More boats were docked there than before, some tied up with rotting ropes or plastic cords, the majority clearly owned by rich people.

It came as such a relief to finally return to land. Too much had happened over the past few days. What she wouldn't give to have this all behind her. What would it take? She needed a distraction, something to spirit her away from all this drama. She needed to be with her father, not with someone who might turn on her at any moment.

Arthur manoeuvred the Anna Belle in a designated berth, launched a rope over the mooring post, and cut the motor. He hopped across the gap onto the jetty and wheeled the boarding ramp into place, positioning it on the starboard side so Nova and Owen could disembark safely.

Nova was free to leave. She had made it through the night. Somehow, she sensed it was just the beginning of more trials ahead.

31

Nova hadn't managed much sleep, and the few hours she did get were fitful and broken, leaving her more exhausted than before. Whenever she shut her eyes, the darkness was invaded by vivid, haunting visions of death—scenes that played out in excruciating detail. Faces of people she knew flashed before her, twisted in agony. These visions had become disturbingly frequent, creeping into her mind with increasing regularity, and each time they did, they gripped her with fear, not just of the visions themselves, but what they might indicate. Were they a sign, a warning of something yet to come?

Bicycling her legs to push the white sheets off, she sat on the edge of the bed, leaving her feet swinging above the floor. Her hand stroked her almost bald scalp on autopilot. It would take some getting used to.

"Morning."

She shot round and put her hand against her chest. "You scared me half to death. How long have you been here?"

Owen smiled.

She passed him a snarky look. "You're going get me into trouble. Visiting hours don't start until nine o'clock. You aren't supposed to be in here."

Owen bit his lip. "You were sleepwalking last night."

Nova's eyes widened. "You were here all night?"

He nodded sheepishly.

"Idiot!"

"Why were you crying?"

She frowned. "Was I crying?"

He kicked his feet up on the side of the bed. "A lot."

The female patient occupying the only other bed inside the room turned on the projector rover and aimed the screen at the ceiling. Lunchtime news cut to an aerial view of London City Teleport, now a black, gaping, circular scar entombed by a square-mile wall. Somewhere in those ruins was her father, reduced to nothing more than carbon dust.

The view of the doomed teleport behind the presenters rolled into a suburban house worthy of banner headlines. The owner had rigged up his house with a gas network and killed himself and his entire family.

"*It's just really sad,*" said one resident, standing next to the police cordon. "*And in this quiet neighbourhood, too. He seemed so normal. Poor family.*"

The presenters reported on a series of seemingly unrelated suicides that week and shifted their focus to the three Teletron physicist engineers discovered dead in the kitchen of the same house. According to the presenter, they'd been part of a suicide pact. Details of the suicide weren't immediately available, with the police stating it was too early to determine the exact cause of death.

The news rolled into a breaking story about Miriam Payne, who'd just announced her retirement from her parliamentary role, live on air. She was only thirty. It came amid rumours she had been diagnosed with breast cancer. This came at the peak of the UK's dire economic situation, with one top government official after another stepping down.

Banks and financial institutions throughout the country had aligned with the doomsayers, attributing the turmoil to political instability and looming economic crisis. They were unanimous in their belief that the government was struggling to grasp the complexities of monetary management.

Nova rolled her head to her roommate. "Please turn it off."

The woman switched it off and smiled.

Nova shook her head. "Awful stories."

Owen had his feet up on another chair and was picking the dirt from under his fingernails. "World's an awful place."

The complete lack of emotion in his voice got to her.

"Because humans make it awful."

The woman nodded in agreement.

The doctor entered the room and stopped at Nova's bed. "We're going to put you through our portal scanner now, okay? It takes an hour to complete a full ultra-scan, but it checks absolutely everything."

Nova looked at Owen, unable to hide her anguish.

In Nova's absence, Owen took advantage and slipped into the en-suite shower. Freshened up, he made himself comfortable in the bed, pulling the sheets up to his chin and adjusting the pillows, settling in with a contented sigh. The bed was a warm, welcome relief, especially compared to the discomfort of being stuck on that boat. Owen neither liked nor trusted Arthur. He couldn't wait to get Nova home, away from the nosey nature of grown-ups.

The aroma of hot potatoes eddied into the room from the canteen, teasing his taste buds and intensifying his hunger. The tantalising scent was a cruel reminder that, as a non-patient, he was not entitled to any meals, heightening his disappointment and torment. He rolled on his side and closed his eyes. He was asleep within three breaths.

When he awoke, a nurse stood at the bottom of the bed, watching him. "Good sleep?"

Owen yawned. "The best."

She checked his digital bed record. "What's your name?"

He paused, trying to suppress a guilty smile. "Nova."

"Is that right? Nova's a girl's name and, correct me if I'm wrong, you're not a girl."

"I'm keeping her bed warm."

Owen took her stare seriously and climbed into the chair next to the bed.

The nurse crossed her arms. "Actually, I need you to leave. The doctor needs to talk privately with Nova. The *real* Nova."

Just then, Nova came into the room, her expression distant and opaque but still gorgeous.

Owen could not take his eyes away from her. What kind of personal ad would a boy have to post to get someone like her? What chance did he have? He was a rebel, the boy from the orphanage who quietly disappeared from time to time and had to be dragged back, away from his street antics. The boy who was fed a daily diet of negativity and told he was worthless and would amount to nothing.

"How was it?" asked Owen.

"Fine."

"They told me I have to leave." He glanced at the nurse, still holding her frown.

Nova looked at the clock on the wall. "I'll catch up with you later."

32

Arthur lit his cigarette outside the prison gate and smoked it down to the roach, watching the traffic pass on the rain-slicked road. He had taken a significant risk by going there, putting himself in the line of sight of numerous surveillance cameras. The fifteen-foot-high razor-wire wall didn't deter him. Neither did the bars on every window, reminding him of the precious freedoms he had been fortunate enough to always enjoy.

Following each automated voice instruction, he navigated the long journey through the partitioned corridors. Proximity-activated access allowed him to pass through each door after undergoing biometric scanning. He passed the final security door into a room that was obviously the canteen. On a round table was a plate of leftover... what looked like chewed-up and regurgitated meat gristle alongside a few dry peas, food even pigs would turn their noses up at.

"Place finger on the scanner," said the automated voice.

He tapped his finger against the authentication pad for the sixth time.

The final door opened. *"Proceed, Mr. Huxley."*

Outside in the gravel courtyard, a series of benches formed a triangular-shaped seating area and Arthur was instructed by tech security booming voices through loudspeakers to sit and wait. He glanced up at the grey sky beyond the imposing prison walls, rubbing his hands together to keep them warm.

Some of Arthur's closest associates were locked up there, guilty until proven innocent, surrounded by some of society's worst humans. In the early days, the ATM had championed the notion of a tech-free world, an idealistic vision that seemed both overly simple and, in retrospect, somewhat naïve. The organisation had once been a staunch advocate for a return to basic human interaction, free from the pervasive influence of digital technology. Their early campaigns had painted a picture of a future where people would reconnect with each other and their environment, away from the distractions of screens and gadgets. Arthur never imagined the organisation would stray so drastically from its founding principles, landing its members in prison.

For Arthur, life as an anti-tech activist began with a more minimalist lifestyle, with many years of consumer conditioning to break free from. He soon became a high-profile anti-nuclear campaigner. At that time, nuclear power generated a third of the country's total electricity until a nuclear reactor went into meltdown, killing two hundred and fifteen workers. His twin brother, Richard, a hot advocate for nuclear energy, had been one of the victims. Following acute radiation sickness, his death led to Arthur falling out with his father, who took his own life the same year on the farm after he swallowed a cocktail of alcohol and prescription drugs, leaving his mother widowed. Resulting from his guilt and shame, Arthur left the farm and relocated to London, where he co-created the ATM.

A withdrawn-looking Travis stepped into the courtyard through a steel door. He wasn't dressed in a prison outfit but regular civilian clothes, for he wasn't officially a prisoner yet. The shackled wrists claimed otherwise.

He sat beside Arthur on the bench. He had caught a cold and looked terrible. Rancid prison food was probably robbing him of key nutrients, leaving his immune system vulnerable to sickness.

Arthur studied his handcuffs. With the right tool, he could open them in no time.

"Arthur," said Travis, his big, orange beard shuddering as he spoke. "What are you doing here?"

"I wanted to talk."

"You shouldn't have come." His voice transformed into a soft whisper. "They have their sights on anyone who belonged to the ATM. This includes you."

Arthur also whispered. "I'll take my chances."

"You heard what happened?"

"Yeah."

Travis spoke for fifteen minutes, talking as if he may never walk free again. He didn't even attempt to plead his innocence or deny the allegations. He was convinced the ATM, specific members at least, had carried out the attack.

"The police killed Nate," he said.

"Good!"

"It's *not* good. If anyone knows the truth, it's Nate, but he's dead. Police found a nuclear device kit in his house."

Travis had recruited people before without vetting them or someone else vetting them properly first, and Arthur shook his head in annoyance. "I warned you, I did. I never trusted that bloody grockle."

"Too late now."

"The police ain't got nothing, or you'd have been charged already."

"They keep asking me who this Merchant guy is."

With eyes narrowed, Arthur leaned back against the bench. "Do they know?"

"*I* don't even know. All I can tell them is that he works in agriculture. That was all Nate shared with me. I think it was all he knew."

"What about that other guy? Thorpe, whatever his name is."

"Theo. He was arrested but got bail yesterday."

"Listen, Travis, after I left, did an old lady join?"

"Maybe."

"Two different coloured eyes, white hair?"

Travis shrugged.

"She used your wine cellar. Knew the pin code."

His eyes widened. "The police found a body matching her description down there. They're trying to pin her murder on me. I don't even know who she is."

Arthur kept Spider's involvement in the murder to himself for now, concerned about the ripple effect it could have on Owen, Nova, and the progress he had made with them.

"Do me a favour," said Travis. "Look after my wine store for me. My parents bled for that place."

Arthur agreed.

"You've got to help me get out of here!"

"How?"

"Find the Merchant. That's our only chance."

"I'll keep an ear out, but I ain't making no promises."

"You'd think twice if it was your freedom on the line. That could still be the case if one of us in here was pressed hard enough."

Arthur raised an eyebrow, clenching his jaw involuntarily. Police resources were not unlimited. It was just a question of priorities. Arthur was not on their radar. He was not a priority. Yet. But Travis looked like a man who needed hope and wasn't in the right state of mind to wait for it. If he *was* doomed, Arthur wasn't going to let Travis drag him down with him.

"I'll do my best, but I can't do anything if I'm in here with you."

Arthur left the courtyard and stopped before the door, the pressure beginning to tell on both of them. He glanced back at Travis. "Stay strong, mate!"

33

The doctor in charge of Nova's care strolled into the room, carrying a projector rover. He pulled up a chair beside the bed. "I have your test results," he said. "Let's look, shall we?"

He slotted the small cube-shaped rover into the bed's leg compartment. Instantly, a turquoise holographic image of her internal organs emerged above the bed.

"Your bloodwork indicates high levels of potassium," the doctor continued, his voice steady but laced with concern. He gestured towards a cluster of numbers displayed beside the animated 3D chest X-ray scans, highlighting the relevant data with a quick swipe of his hand. "Here, you can see your arterial blood gases. They show a normal oxygen concentration, which is good, but there's a notable decrease in your carbon dioxide levels." He paused, giving her time to absorb the information.

"What does that mean?"

"It could be emotional stress that's leading to reduced CO_2 levels. Have you had any panic attacks recently or experienced any hyperventilation?"

"Yes."

"That might explain it. It's nothing to worry about."

The doctor deftly manipulated the green 3D hologram of her heart with experienced hand gestures. His eyes narrowed as he focussed on the results before turning his attention back to her. "As for the electrocardiograph, it revealed an abnormal heart rhythm. Your blood pressure is also critically high. This is something we wouldn't typically see in someone your age." He paused, studying her expression closely. "It's obvious you have been under significant stress lately."

"Is that why my hair has fallen out?"

"Trauma and extreme stress could have caused your hair to fall out. That's probably the case here. You want to tell me what happened?"

She remained mute.

The doctor put a hand on her forearm. "I can put you in touch with a counsellor. It's imperative people talk about their traumatic stress with a professional."

"I'm okay."

"You're obviously not. You want to tell me about it? It would be in full confidence." He glanced at the empty bed next to hers. "No one else is around."

Having made it clear she had nothing to say, the doctor handed her a sachet of pills. "Here are some calcium channel blockers. These will prevent calcium from entering your heart cells and blood vessel walls. They'll lower your blood pressure, slow your heart rate, and control the irregular beating. But be warned, there could be side effects such as fatigue, dizziness, and constipation. If they become more severe, please return and we will consider alternative medication. Calcium channel blockers aren't suitable for everyone, so keep me informed of your progress."

He started discussing diet, vitamin supplements, and the importance of regular exercise, imparting a steady stream of medical advice. But Nova's mind wandered elsewhere, racing through the details of the story she had seen on the news. As he spoke, she found herself gathering and assembling pieces of information she'd been unconsciously collecting. The more she thought about it, the clearer it became, and then, suddenly, everything clicked into place.

"Now, about your brain scans." The holographic image of her heart gradually shifted and reformed, becoming a detailed representation of her brain, outlining the complex network of neurons and blood vessels with stunning clarity. "You said you were experiencing memory loss. I see no swelling or foreign matter around the cranium, and there doesn't seem to be any physical damage either."

"That's a relief."

"I have to say, this concerns me. If you *are* experiencing memory loss but there are no signs of brain damage or any evidence of concussion, this is not normal. So, I had another look at your results. I have to ask, out of curiosity, is there any history of mental illness in your family?"

The memories of her mother were of a smart, confident woman who had been transformed into a terrified, fragile soul. She remembered attending her funeral, something she stored in the dark corner of her mind and only glimpsed at during her worst nightmares. "My mother developed dementia at fifty-two, which I know is quite young."

"Yes, very young," said the doctor. "Very young indeed."

Nova noticed the doctor looking at her sympathetically. "What is it?"

"I need to run more tests, but we detected what we call plaques and tangles in your brain scan results. As I said, I'd like to run some more scans, and I need to consult with my team, but I fear this is what has been causing you memory loss. Three years ago, Alzheimer's disease was discovered in a twenty-five-year-old during an autopsy after she died. It made international news, you may have heard about her. The discovery changed medical protocols across the country. Now we look for signs of mental illness in all patients, even babies and kids. Our ultra-scanners detect the early signs. That is why we discovered it. Three years ago, we wouldn't have thought to check because it was so unheard of. And you would be the youngest person I know, the youngest person ever, to suffer from this."

"I have dementia?"

"Actually, it looks like Alzheimer's, but I want to be sure, so I'll need to keep you in for the next few days. It's in your best interests."

She wasn't sure how she felt about that. "I think I hit my head on a toilet. Could a blow like that cause Alzheimer's, or symptoms that could be misdiagnosed as Alzheimer's?"

"No. Concussion, yes, but not Alzheimer's."

"What about radiation?"

"Depends on the type of radiation, but it can damage the brain and lead to the development of Alzheimer's Disease in the future. Were you exposed as a young child?"

"The expl…"

"The what?"

"Nothing."

"We'll run some more tests, and let's hope we can rule this out. Is there anyone you need to contact?"

"When can I leave?"

"Not until we've completed the tests, and we can rule out mental illness. At least a few days."

"This can't be happening to me. There must be a mistake. It's not possible."

"That was my first thought, and why I want to be certain by running more tests."

"How could I get it? From my mum?"

"It's not that simple. It could be hereditary, but in basic biological terms, it's brain cell death. It's a neurogenerative disease, and brain cells die slowly over a period as you age and the brain shrinks."

"But it might not be Alzheimer's, right?"

"Absolutely. It might not be that at all. The new tests will provide us with a better understanding." The doctor gave her a reassuring smile and left.

Nova had always found public hospitals, the number one target for British pessimism, such eerie places to stay, with so much illness and bereavement behind every drawn curtain. As a young girl, she had spent more time in one than she cared to remember. She recalled all those visits to see her mother. To that dark period in her life. Her mother had acquired so many injuries over the eight years it took for her mind to fade and vanish. Towards the end, she had been unable to uphold even the most basic rules of survival. During her last year of life, she had fallen down the stairs, spraining both ankles. She had been knocked over crossing the road at four in the morning while her father was out frantically searching for her. One night, the knife she used to chop onions to make a *dessert* slipped out of her hand onto her foot and severed her big toe. Each incident had required an overnight stay at the very least.

Nova refused to believe the doctor until he confirmed it and got a second opinion. Alzheimer's was only his guess, the odds not on its side. It was not a definite diagnosis. Her actions were symptomatic of a concussion, and nothing like what she had witnessed occur in her mother. The illness had stripped her mind of all her stored memories embedded deep within her brain. It had left her an empty shell, a once clever woman who waited for meals to be placed in front of her, or led from the table to a chair, and then to her bed as though she were an infant still in nappies. She would watch television without ever reacting to what occurred on the screen. She recognised no one, expressed interest in nothing. She went on inexplicable walks around the village until she was found.

Nova tore back the stiff, white sheets and swung her legs out of bed after the doctor left the room. The floor was cold and smooth against her bare feet as she dressed, discarding her hospital robe on the chair. She grabbed what little she had, stuffed them inside her backpack, and left the room.

Head down, she marched along the corridor, colliding with an older gentleman pushing a walker. She apologised but didn't stop. She passed a chocolate-stacked vending machine in the waiting room, where a line of patients checked in for biometric processing.

To avoid detection, she took the fire stairs down to the basement. She passed the linen room and headed towards the fire exit at the end of the corridor, triggering flashbacks that halted her in her tracks. Déjà vu came to her thick and strong, vivid and real. The brown of her eyes was amplified behind a wall of tears as her mind broke like a dam, and sheer sorrow poured into her chest. For a moment, she was elsewhere, in the middle of making her escape from the auditorium all over again minutes before it exploded.

She pressed herself against the blue wall, illustrated with amateurishly drawn fish and seahorses, forming an unusual backdrop. Her chest constricted as deep sobs swelled within her, breaking free in an unstoppable wave.

There was no stopping the memories or tears now, just as there was no changing the facts. Her father was dead.

34

Warm air drifted along the empty corridor, carrying the faint, comforting scent of freshly laundered linen. It wrapped around Nova, pulling her back from the brink of despair. She lay in a crumpled heap on the cold floor, her scalp damp with sweat, her skin flushed bright red, and her legs tangled beneath her. The comforting aroma seemed to offer a momentary reprieve. It didn't matter she was sprawled out in the corridor. It didn't matter she was all alone. Her father was dead. That was the tragedy. She knew he had died in awful circumstances. How could she go on living without him?

Somewhere within her sadness, she found her strength and slowly stood up. She raised her hood, disappearing in its bulk, took a few deep breaths, and pushed through the fire exit.

The day was grey and miserable, a sign London remained true to its underlying nature. She was coatless and suddenly felt the cold, but just the act of walking took off some of the chill. Her mind was in pursuit of an idea, and she worried it might disappear if she didn't share it soon.

A pack of street dogs prowled the footpath ahead of her, barking at passing cars, lost and lonely. Their skin was covered in mange and infection from fighting wounds that would never properly heal. One was a black beast foraging in a rubbish bin outside a block of flats. It was huge, at least a hundred pounds, with thick legs and a jowly face. It would need a strong person to take it down without being bitten.

Another stray dog barked and whined when it saw Nova coming its way, sitting on its haunches, ready to launch into an unprovoked attack. To avoid any unnecessary confrontations, she hailed the first autonomous taxi headed towards her.

"What is your destination?" asked the automated pilot.

She paused as though she couldn't really be sure. "Good question."

The machine waited patiently for directions or an address, but she could only provide a location.

When the taxi pulled up outside his place, she pulled three tenners from her backpack. The pilot calculated the price, and she grabbed a fourth, inserting them in the note slot. A super-imposed holographic face appeared on the windscreen. "You have a nice day."

She looked up and down the street to ensure no one had tailed her. She had just a few seconds to pull herself together.

Nervous, doubtful, hopeful, she went in.

Owen's ears picked up on the sound of footsteps outside his room. It was mid-afternoon, or perhaps early evening. Without a watch or windows to gauge the passage of time, he struggled to keep track of it. He figured Nova must have checked out of the hospital and had returned to him. He stood, as nervous as a besotted schoolboy, waiting for her arrival.

Spider burst through the door with a box of steaming fried chicken.

Owen's face morphed from excitement to disappointment. He sat back down and lowered his head.

Spider looked around the room. "Where is she?"

"I thought you were her."

"Fuck me, you're useless!"

"I'll find her. Is it dark out yet?"

"I'll tell you what's dark, that empty space between your fucking ears. Tell me you got her address."

"Not yet."

"For fuck's sake!"

Spider opened the chicken box, sighing noisily. He added a couple of sealed wet tissues to the pile in the corner before passing Owen a drumstick. "You don't deserve this."

His thoughts shifted entirely to food, and he eagerly seized the chicken from Spider. With ravenous anticipation, he bit into the tender drumstick, savouring its crispy skin and juicy interior. He gnawed hungrily, lost in the simple pleasure of the feed, but halfway through the meaty mallet, he stopped and stood. He snatched a second piece of chicken from the box and bolted through the door, leaving Spider screaming at him in the room, his echoes chasing Owen along the dark corridor. But he kept running, twisting and turning along the tunnels until he broke the surface.

The late afternoon sky was brighter than he expected, and he had to shield his eyes with his hand. He had long come to terms with his solitude, accepting it as an inevitable part of his existence. Now it felt as if he had suddenly parachuted into an entirely different life, one that was unfamiliar and fraught with unexpected challenges. Nova's presence had injected purpose and value into this new reality. He felt a sense of duty to help her safely find the underlying cause of all her current troubles, no matter what dangers they brought.

At the edge of the river, some kids rode their bikes in ever-increasing circles, shrieking, laughing, and generally acting up, reminding him of who he was—a loner, phantom, an invisible man. It was one thing to think you were unwanted by your family and that you had no friends. It was another to learn it was true. The lengths people went to avoid him in the street was impressive and downright heartless.

The boarding ramp connecting the jetty to Arthur's boat sat slightly askew. He straightened it before crossing, glancing over at the white ropes stretching from the portside across the water to the jetty to ensure Arthur had no intention of leaving anytime soon.

He called Nova's name but received no response.

At the wheelhouse, he surveyed the surroundings with a critical eye, taking in the bullet-ridden walls that bore the scars of the conflict a few nights back. The glass panes, having been shattered and replaced, now gleamed with a clean clarity that contrasted with the now battered condition of the rest of the wheelhouse.

At the top of the staircase leading down towards the cabin, he spotted blood on the steps. Nearby was a crowbar, about a foot in length. The sharp end had fresh blood dripping from it. Owen picked it up and held it out as he descended the steps with mounting dread. The floor in front of the cabin door was awash with soapy, red puddles beside a bucket of hot, steaming water. Stepping over the bucket with his hand tightly gripped around the crowbar, he opened the door. Nova's backpack lay just beyond the threshold, but it wasn't the familiar sight he'd hoped for. It was smeared with blood.

35

Owen tiptoed into the cabin. Only his shadow on the wall gave him away. Something seemed quite different about the interior. It looked clean and tidy, and a dozen candles gave it an aura of homeliness.

As he headed deeper into the cabin, the sharp tang of fresh paint pierced through the stagnant air, and he noticed the walls had been coated with a pristine white layer, erasing almost all trace of the fire. The fold-up bed had also been replaced and was now topped with a new mattress and crisp, clean linen. In the galley, the sink had been scrubbed to a high shine, and the worktops had been cleared of any clutter. Everything gleamed with an almost immaculate newness, reflecting the care taken to restore the space to its original state.

Elsewhere, every cupboard and drawer was closed, and the books were stacked into neat rows on the shelves. Clothes had found the washing bin. The floorboards had been swept and mopped. The entire space seemed almost too clean, as though he had stepped onto an entirely different boat. The only thing that dispelled his doubts was the familiar backpack by the door, now covered in blood, bringing his attention back to the issue at hand: Nova's safety. Or her slayer.

In his customary cardigan and an open-neck shirt, Arthur popped up from inside the galley, fastening a bandage around his hand.

Showered and changed and appearing at almost the same time as Arthur, Nova emerged from the bathroom. Her smile grew wide when she saw him. "You came."

He watched her and Arthur roam around the cabin doing odd jobs. They put the dining furniture back in place in silence. They laid the table for tea in silence. Arthur finished making sandwiches, boiled extra water on the stovetop, then washed up the pan. And still, there was silence.

Owen sat at the table, the crowbar still gripped in his hand. "I waited for you," he whispered to Nova as she sat down.

Nova put her hand on his to urge calm. "I'm sorry. I came here after I left the hospital."

Careful not to sound ungrateful for his hospitality, she told him she needed to keep a low profile, and the safest bet was there, with Arthur, on a boat. The thought of spending another night underground in the darkness on such a cold, hard floor compared to staying there with windows and some token of comfort was too much to resist. What she *really* wanted was to assert her right to feel safe in her own home.

There was something reassuring about Arthur, a baked-in sense of support. He certainly didn't measure up to her father, and he was so unhinged and unpredictable sometimes, but she needed him during this challenging time in her life. She was suffering from plummeting morale and poor health, at an age in life where she transitioned from childhood to adulthood, where the world was incomprehensible, unwelcoming, and full of dangers. "I'm sorry. Okay?"

Arthur held up his bandaged hand and pointed at Owen. "Be careful with that there crowbar. I cut my hand upstairs breaking off all that damaged wood. It's like Swiss cheese, that wheelhouse."

Owen had forgotten about the crowbar and placed it on the floor.

Arthur joined them at the table. "By the way, mate of mine knows a Serbian and asked him what Clotho means. Turns out, no such word exists in the Serbian language."

Nova raised her brows. "So I guess it's irrelevant then."

"It ain't irrelevant. You said Owen's cousin pumped the Serbian full of drugs. My first thought was that he was likely just rambling. But that man who tried to kill us out at sea also mentioned Clotho before he died. Clotho means the thread of life or controller of fate, and it seems oddly coincidental we've got this dangerous mob trying to do just that. Tell Owen what you just told me about the masks."

She looked at Owen. "When I was in the auditorium, trying to find a way out, I was concussed and confused. I told you I saw these like giant insects, right?"

"Yeah."

"I realised they were gas masks. The floor was covered in them. They had big round lenses and a round nose, like a pig snout. If you think about it, they kind of look like giant flies. They freaked me out at the time, making me believe that I was hallucinating."

Arthur nodded. "Looks like you were right after all. There *was* some kind of toxic gas in the air."

She could tell he was happy with her, and it cheered her up.

"What does it mean?" asked Owen.

"We think gas was released to make a bigger explosion."

Arthur went to the galley to pour the tea.

Owen turned to Nova, but kept his eyes on Arthur and whispered, "Can we trust him?"

She nodded and tapped out two pills from a foil sachet, hoping to offset her headache.

Arthur handed her a mug of tea to wash down the pills.

Owen received his own mug. He had also garnered the attention of Bebop, now purring on his lap.

Nova stared at the candle on the table, entranced by the bright, silky flame, sipping her tea slowly.

There was something quite soothing about the boat's cosy cabin in the late afternoon with sunlight angling through the portholes, a sense of warmth and comfort far removed from what now passed for ordinary in her new world. As a missing person, she was no doubt the target of a local search, having fled the hospital.

She only realised she was reaching to play with her long hair when Owen said, "Short hair suits you."

She ran her palm across her scalp instead. "Thanks."

She inhaled a deep breath, trying to figure out what she needed most: food or sleep. A cheese sandwich was passed to her, but sleep had to wait because Arthur wanted to talk.

"At my age, you realise days are long and years are short," he said, staring at the candle. "When Annabelle was almost three, my wife and I showed her how to blow out candles in advance of her birthday."

While he talked, he rolled himself a cigarette, nice and thin, the tobacco evenly distributed along the paper. A roach.

"At first, she couldn't put her lips together, she dribbled all over the cake. But she was so patient and persistent. You ask me, I think she was more interested in the flame, not whether she blew it out or not. On her birthday, as we had hoped, she blew them all out, every single one. Then, about a week later, our neighbourhood had a power cut. The entire block was out for one night. We had one candle in the house, so we lit it and sat down together. But Annabelle kept blowing it out, and we couldn't see nothing. No matter where we put the candle, she found a way to reach it and blow the damn thing out."

The smile that had developed with the telling of his story quickly faded. "I'll never forget that night. These moments, the simple things, are the happiest of our lives, they are. You don't realise it until they're gone."

Arthur excused himself.

Nova assumed he'd stepped away to deal with his emotions in private, needing a moment to process whatever turmoil he might be feeling. But her assumptions were swiftly overturned when he reappeared with a warm, inviting smile and a platter stacked high with chocolate chip cookies.

"Nova's got a theory, she has. Tell Owen what you told me."

36

Nova had stopped asking herself what had happened on Black Thursday. Or why. Or even who was responsible. Instead, she applied her mind to figure out who might have known about it.

"The purpose of the exposition at London City Teleport was to give people the opportunity to learn the science behind teleportation from the research physicist engineers."

Owen's eyes kept straying, like something in his periphery was distracting him, but Nova continued. "According to the schedule, they were supposed to kick off the exposition with a presentation, and there was to be a live teleportation demo on the stage."

Owen nodded and picked his nose.

"Yesterday, three of those physicist engineers committed suicide in a house together. It means that they didn't die in the explosion inside the teleport, where they were supposed to be presenting. So, my question is, why were they not at Expo?"

Owen tilted his chair on two legs, calculating the angle and vector he could tip before he fell backward.

Nova frowned. "Are you listening to me?"

Owen tipped forward, bringing the chair back on all four legs, and looked Nova in the eye. "Yes."

Nova paused before continuing. "I think they knew about the bombs, and that's why they didn't go."

"We think they may have taken their lives because of their guilt," said Arthur.

"Meaning they had a reason to feel guilty," Nova added.

"Your neighbour killed herself," said Owen.

Nova frowned. "What's that got to do with it?"

He shrugged and tipped the chair back on two legs.

"Why bring that up?"

Owen raised his eyebrows.

"She wasn't a bloody physicist at Teletron!"

"She never went to the expedition, either."

"Exposition, Owen. And no, she didn't. She only received an invitation, which were sent out at random."

Arthur grunted and folded his arms. "Nothing ain't never random. There's *always* a reason."

"Whatever, my point is that she wasn't a physicist with any possible connection or knowledge of the explosion. She was a florist for most of her life. Anyway, the invitation was wasted on her."

"Why?" Owen asked.

"She wasn't interested in travelling. She's never even been abroad. She hardly left the village, let alone the country." Tears welled in her eyes, but she quickly batted them away.

Owen tipped forward and touched her arm tenderly.

"I'm sorry, it's just I still can't believe she killed herself. She was always so cheerful."

Arthur drank some tea. "It's often them cheerful ones who carry a darkness inside of them. You just can't tell."

"I know she was depressed over the situation with her son. They hadn't spoken in several years, well, ever since he left the country after a big fight." Nova dried her eyes. "Anyway, we're talking about the three physicists."

"What about them?" asked Owen.

"Remember at the hospital? On the news? There's been a spike in random suicides recently."

Arthur shook his head. "Again, never random."

Owen frowned. "I don't remember."

"We watched it together. I think there may be a connection between the attack on London City Teleport and those three physicists."

Owen shrugged. "It seems a bit—"

"It's ridiculous," said Arthur. "But it's all we've got at this stage."

"So, what now?" asked Owen.

Arthur put down his tea. "First, we need to find out if the explosion's got any connection to them physicists."

Nova nodded agreeably. "How, though?"

"I already looked up that address where their suicide took place."

"You're not suggesting we go there?"

"Absolutely."

Nova detected Arthur's excitement about the new lead as he briefed them on what they should do.

"It would be better to tell the police," she said.

There was extensive debate about whether to present this unlikely theory to the authorities, with Arthur and Owen both opposing her.

"Don't forget what happened the last time you called the police," said Arthur. "At your cottage."

Her shoulders sagged.

"We don't know how deep this goes. Can't risk involving anyone at this stage."

Once they all agreed to avoid the police, the conversation switched to making practical plans.

Arthur and Owen were eager to act immediately.

Nova was not.

"The house will be empty and off-limits to the public while an investigation occurs, especially at night. I'm an experienced locksmith, I am. Show me a locked door and I will have it open before you can even *say* locksmith. And Owen here has broken into many houses, I'm sure. He's a pro."

Owen glanced at Arthur and Nova with dismay. "Huh?"

"You may be as thick as lard, but your street skills must be second to none."

Owen looked at Nova sheepishly and raised his shoulders a fraction, which translated as a teenage *yes*.

Nova didn't think she had the stomach to go through with it. And it would mean disobeying the doctor's advice to avoid any stress. Though it was kind of her idea in the first place, she made up her mind not to go.

Teetering on the brink of indecision and against her better judgement, and with some gentle persuasion from Arthur, she changed it back.

37

Arthur parked his truck half a block away, having driven up and down the road multiple times to scout the area. It was late, and the quiet, dark neighbourhood set the ideal stage for what they were about to do.

Nova felt like a criminal, even though she hadn't broken any laws yet. She lowered the window a fraction for some fresh air and to psyche herself up. She scanned the houses, checking for lights on or curtains being disturbed. One had a wireless projector inserted in the front lawn, splashing *For Sale* on the wall. It was described as contemporary and spacious with four bedrooms and two bathrooms, and a slideshow of the interior followed.

They walked quickly and quietly to the house in question, hidden in a winding knot of cul-de-sacs. Beamed holographic crime-scene tape defined a perimeter around the property as the investigation continued. Seeing the virtual tape filled Nova with dread, as if she were tiptoeing through a minefield of her own making.

Following Arthur's lead, they snuck down the side of the house and went through a wide space in a granite wall, heading to the rear garden at a trot. The patio was lined with pot plants and hanging baskets full of dying flowers as they succumbed to winter climates. The garden was neatly tended with leaves raked into a neat pile.

Arthur had got in touch with a friend, a cop who shared some confidential details with him. All three physicists were discovered in the kitchen, slumped against the dishwasher in a seated position, their arms linked and eyes closed. Vomit was splattered across the floor and stained their clothes. Autopsies revealed they'd poisoned themselves, damaging internal organs and gastrointestinal tracts. That was all his friend had been willing to share. In an ironic twist, the physicist who owned the house used to be a personal life coach before he pursued physics.

Blue holographic crime-scene lasers beamed from corner to corner, making an X shape across the side door.

"Don't touch that holographic crime-scene tape," Arthur whispered. "It triggers police alarms."

It didn't take much tool-work for Arthur to override the electronic lock. He had no doubt broken locks on many secure doors in his time.

Nova looked into the garden. "This is a big mistake."

She never expected a response and didn't get one.

Arthur crawled beneath the beams and slipped inside the house. He looked completely unfazed, as though breaking into homes and trespassing were all in a day's work.

Owen went in next without a moment's hesitation or the slightest trace of fear. Naturally, because he had clearly broken into homes before also, only without a locksmith licence.

Nova began to plot out each movement in her head, fearful of everything around her. Even touching the cool brass of the handle gave her the shivers. It just didn't feel right to walk into someone else's house and turn it upside down, even if they *were* dead. As she crossed the threshold, she realised her lack of pre-analysis had put her in a compromising position. This wasn't how her father had taught her to approach life.

Arthur had the kitchen bin upside down, spreading rubbish across the floor, and Owen went through the cupboards and drawers.

As her eyes adjusted to the darkness, she noted the décor was rather uninspiring: light cream walls, matching carpet and curtains, bland sofas, and simple storage. The light-coloured furnishings drew her eye to the blue stains on the living room carpet. A trail of blue smears and spots snaked into the kitchen and across the tiled floor, stopping in front of the dishwasher where the bodies had been discovered before their transfer to the morgue.

She pulled out her torch and flicked on the light. She saw a photograph with a family of four standing on London Bridge pinned to the fridge. The physicist, his wife, and two baby girls. They looked like a happy family.

Arthur put his hand over the lens and hit the off switch. "No lights. They'll draw attention to us from outside."

"How am I supposed to see?"

"I've got my night-vision lenses. You should get some next time."

"Next time?"

Arthur brought his finger to his lips, telling her she was too loud. "Next time you're in a dark place and can't see. Search the first floor."

Nova put up no resistance and walked out of the kitchen. She stopped nervously on the stairs, hesitant to go all the way. She closed her eyes, wishing she could simply vanish in a puff of smoke.

At the top of the landing were half a dozen different doors to choose from, so she tried the master bedroom. Streetlight poured in through the bare window, illuminating a brass bed alongside a vanity with a mirror plastered in pictures of kids. She searched the vanity first, then the built-in wardrobe, and found many empty metal hangers and several folded garments in the shelving. She searched underneath the bed and inside the cube-shaped bedside table. The first drawer was filled with pens and pencils and other stationery items. The second one contained books and magazines. The third was empty. Holding the handle of the fourth drawer, she pulled hard, trying to force it as it was jammed shut. It burst open, spilling papers all over the floor. She rifled through old letters, coupons, invoices, and receipts, coming across a small pile of French cooking books.

"What am I doing?" she whispered.

She stood and turned to leave.

A boy stood in the room, silently watching her.

She froze, paralysed. She didn't move for ten seconds until she realised it was a mirror. She no longer recognised herself with hair so short. The mirror had once been her ally, but now she always feared it looked at her with indifference.

When she exited the master bedroom, there *was* a boy this time, standing on the landing. Nova threw her hand against her chest. "Jesus!"

Owen held up a small box. "Guess what I found?"

He opened it. Inside was a diamond ring.

"You're not going to take that, are you?"

Owen's smile faded. "The science geezer don't need it."

She looked down with a sad expression.

"What?"

She shook her head. "Us being here is so wrong."

She could feel her sanity coming loose.

Owen drew her in and swung his skinny arms around her. She buried her head in his chest.

Owen kissed her neck, his warm lips trailing to her ear with tender pecks. He charted a course to her mouth.

She reciprocated, the sensation of his lips locked on hers new and scary. Blood ran hot through her veins and her heart thumped at warp speed. Was she experiencing her first flush of romance?

When Owen hunted for her tongue, she let him, and the kiss intensified.

Arthur bounded up the stairs and stopped on the landing. "Any luck?"

Nova broke quickly from the warm kiss, taken aback by the surprisingly pleasant feel of Owen's mouth.

"I don't really know what I'm looking for," she said, her hot flush slowly receding.

"They didn't kill themselves," said Arthur.

"Why do you think that?"

He held up a full bottle of industrial bleach. "These are top physicists. All chemistry is driven by physics. If they wanted to kill themselves, they could have used a whole range of toxic chemicals or drugs."

Nova shook her head. "I don't follow."

"Most people ain't got the knowledge or skill to take their own lives. Why do you think there are so many failed suicide attempts? Anyone who wants to end their lives wants to do so quickly and painlessly. Drinking bleach don't kill you quickly, and it definitely ain't painless. They would have taken ages to die, conscious the entire time, even when their throats were on fire. The vomiting would have cleared their stomachs to some extent, meaning they would have kept pumping the stuff in. That ain't easy."

"How do you know it was bleach that killed them?"

"Found a bottle of this stuff in the kitchen."

Nova frowned. "But it's full."

"I sniffed them vomit stains on the carpet. They reek of bleach, they do."

"Where are the used bottles?"

"Police would have taken them away as evidence."

"It must have happened, then."

"I never said it didn't happen. I said I don't believe it was suicide."

"I'm confused."

"I don't think they tortured themselves to death. I think someone forced them to drink the bleach. Someone murdered them and staged it as suicide."

"Who?"

Arthur shrugged. "Someone who gets off on inflicting pain and torturing people."

"We should tell the police."

"The police ain't daft. They would have worked it out already."

Nova had an awful feeling something was about to happen. And it wasn't going to be good. "Can we leave, then?"

38

Arthur walked wearily towards the truck, visibly carrying the weight of his thoughts. Nova and Owen were already buckled into the front passenger seats, waiting in tense silence. Arthur lingered outside, staring at the truck as though it offered some escape from his troubles.

It took him a few minutes to finally climb into the driver's seat, but even then his hand hovered over the ignition. It was another few minutes before he finally pushed the button and got the motor going.

A cold sweat had broken across his forehead. He needed a drink, something strong to drown the conflict raging within him. For years, he had vowed never to follow in his father's footsteps, swearing he would never succumb to the same vices. Yet now, here he was, not as far gone, but far enough to feel that familiar craving, the urge to dull his senses at any hour of the day. It was a bitter pill to swallow, realising that despite all his promises, he was closer to becoming the man he had always feared.

His problems were beginning to pile up, adding a growing burden on his shoulders. The Environment Agency was on his back about renewing his boat licence. Their letters, the only means to reach him since he maintained no online or digital presence, grew more insistent with each passing week.

As if that weren't enough, he had also fallen behind on his monthly mooring fees. The reminders from the marina office had started as polite nudges but had since escalated to more urgent notices. Every time he glanced at the stack of unopened envelopes, his stomach twisted with anxiety. The bills served as a constant reminder that his life was slowly slipping out of his control, the responsibilities he used to manage with ease now threatening to sink him.

He also had to see his doctor for a follow-up appointment, having learned during his last visit he needed to do something sooner rather than later about his critically high cholesterol. He smoked more than he should, and his daily water intake didn't come close to the recommended minimum. And his constant late nights were starting to wear on him. Over the years, he had conditioned himself to get by on little sleep. It became harder with age. In any case, his recent trauma made sleep impossible. He knew he was suffering from depression but was damned if he was going to pay some shrink to reach the same conclusion. His GP, however, was an old friend, and he wanted to stick to his appointments out of respect.

He couldn't stop thinking about his family. He had failed his two girls. The only girls in the world that ever mattered. Yesterday, a third-party executor had informed Arthur that his wife's possessions had been left to her sister in Bolton. During marriage, their fights had grown in frequency and decibels, and even now, separated by life and death, they were engaged in a new battle because some of those belongings were his and he wanted them back.

Throughout their marriage, Heather had never approved of his affiliation with the ATM. She saw the activist group as a wedge driven between them, a constant source of tension in their relationship. Each time he attended a meeting or organised a protest, it felt like another betrayal, another reminder that his loyalties lay elsewhere. She had argued countless times that his dedication to the group overshadowed his commitment to her, leaving her feeling sidelined and unimportant. She resented the way he lit up when discussing the latest cause or campaign, a spark she rarely saw when they were together.

Another reason for his sadness and why he remained quiet behind the wheel as he drove out of the neighbourhood and headed for London was all this talk of suicide brought back tragic memories of his father.

Nova wondered what was on Arthur's mind. He was quiet and distant, paying little attention to the road, turning erratically, braking hard. She thought of her father, subconsciously making comparisons. Unlike Arthur, he drank alcohol to be sociable and nothing more. Whenever she needed to get things straight in her head, her father had always been there. She used to tell him everything. It had been their agreement, a promise they made to each other in the days following her mother's passing. She shared her thoughts, fears, and dreams, believing openness was the cornerstone of their bond. He knew how to make her feel better about things and had a way of seeing the world that put problems into perspective. By temperament and military training, he always approached difficult situations calmly. She carried her father's beliefs and values in her and wasn't going to let Arthur's influence affect them.

Arthur drove at sixty-five miles an hour in the outside lane with a long convoy of frustrated drivers trapped behind him. The car directly on their tail flashed its lights. The angry blare of a horn sounded, and Arthur physically snapped to attention, sharply pulling into the middle lane. Oblivious to the intense glares of his erstwhile followers as they blazed past, he turned to face Owen and Nova and said, "Them physicists were killed because of what they knew. What they knew, that's what we've got to find out."

39

Nova managed ninety minutes of sleep in the truck. Ninety minutes filled with visions of her father inside the auditorium the day it blew up. She kept hearing his panicked pleas for help in the crowded venue, kept seeing men and women burning to death before combusting into ash. Trapped with no way out, their terrified screams coming relentlessly from behind locked doors. A ball of flames chasing her along the corridor. She tried to escape, but the fire exit became a flaming room, cornering her with no way out.

A minute or more went by before she realised she'd woken from the dream. Her senses gradually came back to her. Her scalp was damp with sweat, and inexplicable fear gripped her. She could hear the truck's motor and saw the dashed lines and streetlights streaking past the windshield.

"Where are we going?" she asked, rubbing her eyes.

"Teletron." Arthur reignited his plan to visit the tech giant and brought Nova and Owen up to speed with the details.

Nova showed her objection with a brisk shake of her head. "For all we know, it could be Teletron who's been trying to kill us."

"Ark at she! A few days ago, you were convinced it was the ATM."

"I still think that. But you never know."

"That's why we should go there. Them physicists knew something. Where better to learn what than at Teletron?"

She didn't pursue it. He was the adult and the only person with any kind of plan. Respecting elders was ingrained as one of the axioms her father had taught her. "Why are you so interested in Teletron?"

"I used to service commercial outfits. Office buildings and department stores, schools and that. Mostly on-call plumbing and electrical work. I did some work for Teletron when it was still a small firm. I got to know the inside, spoke with staff on a first-name basis, even met the CEO once and the archon of biomedicine."

"The who?"

"It's Greek, means ruler. He's the chief of biomedicine and medical engineering and oversees all the intergalactic physicist engineers. Teletron likes to believe it's this forward-thinking, innovative tech firm and makes up these ridiculous job titles. Anyway, I worked on every level except the top floor. They told me the area was restricted. Remember the other day when I suggested that we visit and you disagreed? Well, I went there anyway to chase up an overdue invoice. While there, I snooped around."

"No one saw you?"

"That's the thing. It's hugely understaffed, it is. I think they have paused operations, and several staff have resigned or are on compassionate leave since that explosion at the teleport. It means Teletron is vulnerable."

"What are you hoping to find?"

"It's hiding something, it is. I just know it. Them murdered physicists confirmed it for me. I think they were silenced, and I'm gonna find out why."

Arthur told them he'd managed to enter an office through a door a careless cleaner had failed to lock. The cleaner could not have chosen a better door to demonstrate their astounding dereliction of duty. It belonged to the supreme commander of physics and engineering, and Arthur had stolen his white lab coat, wearing it under the guise of an employee while snooping around.

Plotting to break into a security-tight company demanded careful planning and a solid understanding of the floor plan. Arthur had achieved both. He had already mapped out every critical entry and exit point, knew their security protocols, and identified potential weaknesses in their defences, leaving him with a well-laid strategy. Now Arthur was eager to put his plan into action. The thrill of the challenge invigorated him, and she saw the surge of anticipation in him at the prospect of finally executing the operation, making her realise that she had under-estimated him. *Again.*

Arthur spent the next thirty minutes explaining how their visit would play out, sharing all he knew about Teletron and its layout. He didn't bother to sugarcoat the danger, stating he was confident of his plan but reiterated safety and success were not guaranteed.

"How do we get in?" asked Owen.

With one hand on the steering wheel, he held up his other hand and showed them a black macro key with a red digital display and a small fob attached. *Teletron* was emblazoned on the key. "Found it in that lab coat I stole from the office."

He wanted to trespass a world-renowned tech firm and seek out its darkest secrets. He made it sound so simple. Talked about entry points and masquerading as businesspeople just as calmly as discussing the details of a fancy-dress party. Nova had to tuck in her lips, a technique she often employed to stem sarcasm or words of dissent that often rolled out carelessly.

Arthur stopped the truck on the hard shoulder.

He got out, stood on a grassy knoll, and stretched his arms.

Owen also left the truck and hawked up a large amount of phlegm, spitting it onto the asphalt.

"You're a bloody pig!" said Arthur, lighting a cigarette.

Owen shrugged and jumped back in the truck.

"Breaking into Teletron," said Owen with a sniff, watching Arthur through the windscreen.

Nova shook her head. "I know, what's he thinking? I'm not comfortable with this one bit."

"It'll be fun."

She gave him an incredulous look, struck by his refusal to address reality. "Fun? It's not a game, Owen. It's dangerous and… it's just crazy."

"Chill!"

"Don't tell me to chill! I mean, what the hell are we doing here? How did we get drawn into this?"

Owen saw Arthur walking to the truck. "He's coming!"

Arthur climbed wearily into the driver's seat.

He started the electric motor and set off, switching on the radio.

Nova stared through the window, tuning out of the sound. Owen turned up the volume.

Arthur glared at him and turned it back down.

Owen put his hand on Nova's, but she moved it to scratch her nose and didn't return it.

The sun rose above the trees on the horizon. The roads had become busier as they neared London and morning rush-hour traffic accumulated.

The queue Arthur joined was sluggish but still moving. He veered onto the slip road, taking the urban roads into London to avoid any motorway traffic holdups.

"I think we're being followed," he said.

Owen and Nova turned back at the same time and saw a green six-wheel-drive behind.

Arthur turned back on himself, trying to determine if he had, in fact, picked up a tail.

The driver made identical turns, but when Arthur turned right at the next junction, the vehicle turned left.

A motorcycle shot out from nowhere and cut into the road. Arthur hit the horn to prevent the rider from crossing his path.

The rider sped ahead, flipping Arthur the middle finger.

As Arthur approached the junction, an unsettling pop in the brake pedal was followed by a shuddering sensation in the steering wheel. To his alarm, his foot sank to the floor, and the pedal offered no resistance.

Nova watched him struggle with the steering wheel and repeatedly stamp on the brake.

The junction grew closer, and Arthur desperately fought to regain control before it was too late. It *was* too late. The truck shot over the junction line and swung across two lanes. The back wheel climbed up onto the kerb, grazing a lamppost. The collision ripped away the rear indicator lamp and left the casing swinging back and forth from its wire.

Nova gasped aloud when the truck bounced back into the road.

"She ain't stopping!" Arthur shouted.

The motor tone changed, increasing in pitch and ferocity as the truck sped up on the downhill slope.

He stamped his foot on the dead brake again. He tried to engage the parking lever. It was jammed in its socket.

All he had was the steering wheel at his fingertips.

Barging vehicles aside when they refused to respond to his horn, Arthur swerved all over the road. *Their* horns blared as the traffic adjusted to his erratic driving.

He cut a corner, swerved onto a patch of grass, and came up on two wheels before slamming back down on all four like a child's toy. The truck then swung out of control, smashed into a tree, and the batteries went into automatic shutdown.

40

Arthur stared at the windscreen as it transformed into a status report interface. The computer ran a rapid self-assessment of the truck's systems, and the windscreen flickered briefly as the diagnostic scan processed, displaying holographic lines of data and graphs. The report provided a comprehensive overview of the truck's condition, with alerts highlighting areas of concern and other components marked as functioning normally. The batteries remained intact. The tyres maintained air. No fluid leaks were detected. The lights on one side were out. The front corner had been hammered into mangled scrap. The electronic lock on the passenger door was damaged. But the seat belts had held them, and the airbags had protected them.

Arthur scanned over the data, searching for any indications of what might have caused the brake failure, finding nothing in the report other than they were faulty.

He had to throw his weight against the door for it to open. "Stay here."

Nova pushed the deflating airbag off her lap and stared out of the window, never so aware of her hammering heart and trembling hands and legs.

Seemingly unaffected by the crash, Owen casually looked inside the glove compartment, which had snapped open during the crash and hung low in front of him. He glanced up, keeping an eye on Arthur while he was out of the truck.

"What are you doing?" asked Nova.

"Seeing if he has any dosh."

"Why?"

He gave her a dismissive shrug. "I need money."

She raised her eyebrows. "Is that why you've been helping *me*?"

He stopped rummaging but said nothing.

She pressed her palms down on the seat, leaning off his shoulder to get a better look at him. "Owen?"

He looked down at his lap.

"Let me get this straight. You've been helping me, what, to get money from me?"

He acknowledged her accusation with a nod.

"Are you serious?"

"Not anymore, though."

"Is that why you gave me the rabbit's foot when I first met you?"

The sound of Arthur popping the bonnet and peering into the motor drew their attention momentarily as other road users pulled over and got out of their vehicles.

Owen spotted an old, plastic identification card in the glove compartment. He grabbed it and held it up for Nova to see.

But Nova folded her arms. "Answer the question! Why did you give me the rabbit's foot? So you could find out where I live?"

"It's my cousin."

"What do you mean?"

"I wanna help you. But he wants money for it."

"Why?"

"His shop's going down the plop."

Nova showed how cross she was with her eyebrows. "It all makes sense now. I'm such an idiot. You gave me that rabbit's foot, not because you were worried about me. It's because you knew it would lead you to my home. So, you *do* know where I live. Because I took the rabbit's foot home with me when I left your place the first time. You've already been inside my cottage and stolen things."

"No!" said Owen. "I went to my cousin's shop after you'd left, but he was out. By the time we checked the tracker, you were already inside that basement."

"Is that why you turned up at the wine store? Because you thought it was where I lived?"

"Yes... no. Yes."

"Unbelievable! All this time you've been trying to rip me off."

"Not anymore." He put his hand against his heart. "On my life."

"I don't believe you. I thought you cared about me, but it was all just a show."

"That's not true. I do care about you."

"Don't talk to me, Owen! I'm done talking to you."

Arthur conversed with the drivers he had hit with his truck, explaining the situation and exchanging insurance details.

Owen held up the card he had found, showing it to Nova. "You need to look at this. Arthur's not who he says he is. Look, see?"

It had Arthur's picture on it but a different name: Peter Huxley.

Nova shook her head and turned away. "I'm surrounded by liars."

Owen hid the card behind his back when Arthur opened the driver's door and leaned in. "Police will be here in a minute. A gear in the parking brake's all warped. That's why it jammed. Unheard of, that is. And the booster in the foot brake's fried. The good news is I've got a spare booster, and we should be on our way again once the police are done."

"What's the bad news?" asked Nova, regretting instantly having spoken.

"I know my truck, I do. You ask me, I think someone's tampered with the braking system."

41

Behind an eight-foot-high wrought-iron fence at the Gateway Industrial Estate, Arthur, Owen, and Nova stood vigil, their eyes fixed on Teletron. The building loomed silently, with no signs of life behind its darkened windows.

Arthur squinted at the glass entrance, relying on his vision despite wearing the sophisticated electronic gadgetry over his eyes. The lights in the foyer were on, but the reception desk looked empty. No one had left the building in the half-hour they had been there.

Dread pooled in Nova's stomach. It must have been the same feeling her father had before engaging in battle. The fear of what might lay ahead, coupled with the inability to predict the outcome. He had never talked about the soldiers who had died. He spoke of the ones who had made it back despite their injuries.

Growing restless, Owen rose from his crouched position and moved towards the gate, his eagerness to get inside almost palpable.

Arthur dragged him back by the collar. "Patience."

Nova's shoulders tensed with anticipation while her fists clenched involuntarily. Why had she agreed to this? How had she been so easily persuaded? The whole plan suddenly seemed insane. It was clear Arthur was accustomed to getting his way; it was practically second nature to him. Arthur wasn't even his name. The persona he wore so confidently was just another layer of deception, as carefully crafted as his plans. It made her wonder what else about him was a lie.

As for Owen's betrayal, it was such that she felt as if she'd been punched in the stomach. She had to grip the railings of the fence just to steady herself. She had suddenly sobered up, seeing Owen for who he truly was. Mutual understanding and trust were the fragile threads that had kept her connected to him. Now those threads had been severed.

She almost let them both know she wasn't a little girl who would tolerate their bullshit any longer. She wished she'd told them before arriving how appalled she was by their behaviour and lies. It would have given her a get-out clause. Now she was in the middle of a massive industrial estate ready to commit her second break-in in less than twenty-four hours.

Waiting until dark before they advanced towards Teletron, Arthur slipped into the lab coat and did the buttons up to his neck.

"Okay, let's go!"

Owen and Nova followed him to the entrance.

He pressed his finger against the authentication pad and the electric swing doors opened.

"I thought you told us you had the supreme commander's macro key?" asked Nova.

"I do," said Arthur. "Got my mate to lift his fingerprint off it and make me a prosthetic tip." He stretched out his finger, showing them the translucent layer of fake skin. "Teletron don't use old technology."

"Then why was there a macro key in his lab coat?"

"They still use macro keys to get in and out of offices that ain't been upgraded yet. Everything else has been biometrically converted."

The reception desk was indeed empty, and powered-down computers confirmed it was currently unstaffed. A bunch of long-stemmed flowers sat in a porcelain vase, wilting over the wide desk, while potpourri smells filled the foyer.

Again, Owen eagerly walked ahead. "Which way?"

Again, Arthur had to drag him back by his collar. "Just stay behind me. We'll take that staircase."

The stairs seemed immensely steep as Nova pointed her foot towards the first step. She moved lethargically, every step taking an enormous amount of willpower. It took everything she had to keep pace with the boys, both moving quickly. They had met no interference so far as they made their way along the empty corridors on level two, passing one locked door after another. Several spare lab coats, all freshly laundered, hung on a row of hooks outside an office. Arthur took two and insisted Nova and Owen wear them. As Nova pushed her arm into the sleeve, she glanced up and saw a flashing red dot inside a dome case: a surveillance camera. Good security was about instilling confidence in people. Her father had once told her that. With enough cameras to keep an electronic eye on every inch of the building, *her* confidence was shattered into tiny pieces.

She hadn't confronted Arthur about the identification card yet; the moment hadn't yet felt right. Deep down, she wasn't sure she even wanted the answer. The sooner she could escape his destructive orbit, the better. But for now, she still needed him to achieve her own goals.

Arthur scanned the faintly lit corridor, revealing a series of neglected noticeboards, their usual assortment of papers and announcements conspicuously absent. The glow from the few operational lights barely reached the corners. Darkened offices behind glass panes had become empty spaces that spoke of abrupt change and disarray.

Level three was dominated by a cordon of laboratories in silent rows. The absence of light and the deep silence hinted at a complete lack of activity, as though the entire floor had been abandoned and forgotten. The laboratories stood motionless, their darkened windows and closed doors suggesting little to nothing stirred within.

Level four mirrored the floor below them, left in an equally profound darkness and stillness.

The top level, Arthur had informed them in the truck, had always been the subject of his curiosity, a forbidden area he'd never been permitted to enter.

As they ascended the final flight of stairs and the narrow corridor forced them into a single file line, Arthur confidently guided them forward, as if intimately familiar with the layout of the restricted area. Owen and Nova followed like puppets, responding every time Arthur tugged on their strings.

With a smug sense of pride, Arthur used his counterfeit fingerprint to bypass a set of security doors. As they slid open, he glided down the corridor, his eyes drifting casually over the surroundings, playing the part of employee to perfection. Act like you belonged there, Nova thought, and no one would ever question you, reciting more of her father's military wisdom.

They broke formation at a lab door.

Arthur turned. "Say nothing! Follow my lead!"

In contrast to the other doors, this door required a retina scan *and* fingerprint verification. Additionally, it was equipped with an electronic key reader box.

Arthur hovered the macro key near the reader with his fingertip pressed to the screen. Nothing happened.

He then tried the fob on the key reader box.

That didn't work either.

He rattled the metal handle with increasing frustration, but it remained stubbornly locked, refusing to yield to his efforts.

Just as he was about to give up, the door creaked open on its own accord.

42

The man who appeared behind the door wore a surgical mask that concealed his mouth and nose, leaving only his furrowed brow and a forehead etched with deep lines visible. Dressed in a white lab coat, the man displayed an ID badge hanging from a lanyard around his neck that read, *Dr. Azad, The Alchemist, Head of Bio-resources.* He pulled down his mask. "Who are you?"

Arthur pushed into the lab, barging Dr. Azad aside, and was instantly struck by a wave of disinfectant. He had a steely determination about him but knew careful and clever often won over brute strength and gut instincts. He took pleasure in the strategic planning—the checklist, allocation of resources and personnel, timing, weapon selection, the development of contingencies. The detailed logistics and seamless operation of each cog in the machine fascinated him, and what he missed most about the ATM.

"You cannot be in here," said Dr. Azad. "This room is for authorised staff only."

Arthur wandered through the lab, making mental notes as he went until he reached a row of cages labelled *The Ark*. The row consisted of eight cages, stacked two high on pallets. Each cage housed a small animal, with every pair of adjacent cages containing identical species. The first two cages held mice, the next two contained chameleons, and the following pair housed North American opossums. In the final two cages was a pair of robins perched on a bar, their tails twitching hyperactively. None of the animals bore any defects or scars. Arthur observed that one cage in each pair was marked with an electronic tag displaying a digital code. The mouse's cage was labelled 6M, the chameleon's 3D, and the opossum's 17W. The robins had no tags.

"What's all this, then?" asked Arthur.

"Do you work for Teletron?" asked Dr. Azad.

"We've been appointed to ensure Teletron's still compliant and adhering to regulatory standards after all the turmoil of late."

"Appointed by who?"

"We represent ASP."

"Do you have an appointment?"

Arthur scratched his stubble. "By law, we're permitted to conduct an internal audit unannounced up to twice a year, we are. Your CAE is aware that a visit from us was imminent. She would have notified the Audit Committee. I'm guessing by the look on your face that you ain't part of this committee, and nobody's informed you we might be calling."

"Nobody mentioned it."

"I can only apologise."

"Then again," he said, shaking his head and looking around the lab, resembling a man with a lot on his mind, "I'm hardly surprised. There's been a lot of confusion around here lately. Sorry, what's the purpose of the audit?"

"Assess and evaluate how the recent events have impacted on laboratory personnel and operations. Check that Teletron's policies and procedures are up to date and are being followed. You know, the usual."

That his speech sounded scripted and memorised seemed obvious. Arthur wondered if it was obvious to Dr. Azad.

"What are you here to audit?"

"Housekeeping, disposal, health and safety, recordkeeping, equipment, facilities, staffing."

Dr. Azad looked at Nova and Owen. "These are just kids!"

"They're third-year university students on internships."

Owen glanced at Nova, but she ignored him.

"Start by telling me why you're so understaffed?"

Dr. Azad pinched the bridge of his nose. "As you no doubt know, we lost good people at London City Teleport. It's put important research on hold, and some of the staff have been signed off on compassionate leave. I'm working double shifts to keep on top of things."

Judging by the black semi-circles under his brown eyes and the multiple used coffee pods in the bin on the floor, he looked to be having difficulty adjusting his work habits.

Arthur asked more questions to try and disguise he wasn't really an auditor. He didn't know if Dr. Azad had him pegged but thought he might.

"I'll need to see your policies and procedures manual. Do you know where it's kept?"

"It's on our server."

"We will come back to that later. Now, Teletron is exempt from lodging accounts, but we'll still need to look at this year's financial records. Where can I find the accounts department?"

"Level two, by the kitchen. For your information, it's called the Bean Counting Department. And the Head of Prophet is on holiday. She's back next week."

Arthur nodded and looked back at the cages. "Detected any biological hazards recently?"

"No, none."

"Handled any pathogenic microorganisms, any blood or tissues, perhaps with these here animals?"

"No."

Dr. Azad responded to Arthur's questions with a straight forwardness that seemed genuine enough; he had no reason to doubt the man. To expedite the process, he needed to delve a little further. "How about yourself, then? Suffering from any stress? You said you're doing double shifts. Is it affecting your health or ability to follow safety procedures?"

"I'm overworked, but that's my choice, and I can handle it."

"Heard about them physicists committing suicide. Did you know them?"

"Not personally. They worked in a different section to me. They were excellent physicists, though, and will be extremely hard to replace."

"They were part of the opening ceremony at Expo, is that right? Why weren't they there when it blew up? You ask me, it seems a bit suspicious, wouldn't you say?"

"What, you think they caused it? Why would they do that?"

Arthur had to think quickly. "Heard someone speculating about it on the radio."

"Absolutely not. They were driving to the exposition in the same car when they hit a bus and flipped onto the roof. All of them were injured. Nothing life-threatening, though. Just cuts and bruises, and one had a fractured scapula. That's why they didn't make it. The other physicists died in the explosion. The archon of biomedicine and supreme commander of physics and engineering are now the only physicists we have left. They weren't involved in Expo because they were on long-service leave."

"Where are they now?"

"Still on leave."

Arthur paused, mulling over the latest information.

"Why do you think the physicists killed themselves?" asked Nova.

"Guilt, maybe? They were a close-knit team, socialised out of office hours all the time. They worked together seven days a week for twenty years to get teleportation where it is today. They weren't the same after they lost their colleagues."

"What changed?"

"I only saw them once. A few days after the attack. They didn't say very much. I think they came here to collect some belongings. I was told not to let them in this lab."

"By who?"

"Our CEO."

"Why?"

"They were traumatised and enraged. Said he couldn't trust them in their state of mind."

"Did they ever return?"

"No, never."

"What was so special about this lab that the CEO didn't want them coming in?"

"Access to all labs was taken away. As I said, the physicists were distraught and angry, and he didn't want them lashing out and risking all we have worked for. That's all I was told."

Arthur paused, then slipped back into character. "Who's your safety officer?"

"I'm not sure."

"You ain't sure?"

"I think it's changed recently. The woman who used to be our S.O resigned, I believe. As I mentioned, staffing's a mess at the moment. I recommend you talk to a senior manager. If you can find one. Or ask the CEO directly. He'll be able to tell you. If you can get hold of him. He's never around, and when anyone does try to get in touch with him, he never responds."

Arthur turned and pointed at the row of cages. "What's happening over here, in these cages?"

Dr. Azad narrowed his eyes and tilted his head to one side. "You'll have to ask my superiors."

"I'm asking you."

Dr. Azad rubbed his eyes. "I'm in no position to disclose that information. They can fill you in."

"I need *you* to fill me in."

There was a delay before he spoke again. "You know what, I'm not saying another word until you show me identification. In fact, if you don't mind, I think I'll just check with security."

Balling his fist, Arthur calculated the amount of weight he needed to put behind a punch to ensure Dr. Azad felt his fury but didn't slip from consciousness.

With a rapid change of mind, he pulled his gun from his waistbelt instead and pointed it at the doctor's head.

43

"What are you doing?" Nova cried, her eyes darting between Azad and Arthur. She thought he might actually shoot him in the head. "Put the gun down!"

Was he unravelling before her eyes, descending into the throes of a mental meltdown? The signs were there, but had she misread them entirely, mistaking his seething rage for the harbinger of a far deeper emotional crisis? His eyes, wild and seething, bore through her, consumed by a need for vengeance that bordered on obsession.

"Who *are* you?" asked Dr. Azad, raising his hands. "What do you want?"

Arthur pointed at the cages. "What's going on here?"

"Put down the gun!" Nova repeated.

"Be quiet!" Arthur snapped.

Dr. Azad kept his hands raised. "What do you want?"

"Answers."

"To what?"

"That explosion at London City Teleport."

Owen whispered in Nova's ear. "He knows something."

Nova ignored Owen, no longer interested in anything he said or did.

Arthur walked around the lab like a man who knew he had the upper hand. "You've got them teleportals in this building."

"No, we don't."

He stopped in front of the cages. "You've sent these here animals through them."

"The teleportals were moved elsewhere after the attack at the teleport. That's what I was told. We received a number of bomb threats, and we were worried Teletron would be the next target, so the teleportals were moved."

"Where?"

"An undisclosed location. I don't know where exactly, but I think one was transferred overseas."

Arthur walked up to Dr. Azad and drove the gun into his chest, shoving him into a leather chair. "Codswallop!"

"I'm telling the truth."

"What about the prototype?"

"The prototype wasn't manufactured at Teletron, not even in Britain. It was manufactured in Germany."

Arthur let the silence between them lengthen, urging him to say more and talk himself into a confession.

"I suggest you speak to the CEO. I only work here."

"The teleport blew up a fortnight ago. You teleported that chameleon over there three days ago."

Dr. Azad kept quiet.

"How can you know that?" asked Nova.

Arthur kept his eyes on Dr. Azad. "3D. The D stands for days. 6M is six months, and 17W is seventeen weeks. Tell me I'm wrong."

Dr. Azad's face gave him away.

"I'll ask again," said Arthur. "Why are you teleporting them animals?"

"I'm just following my orders. You'll need to speak to the CEO."

"Where's the teleportal?"

Dr. Azad kept his mouth shut.

Arthur cocked the gun, keeping it pointed at Azad's head. "Honestly, one more murder to learn the truth ain't nothing to me."

Dr. Azad slumped further into the chair, as if trying to shrink away from the gun, believing that putting more distance between himself and the weapon might somehow reduce the force of a bullet. After several agonising seconds of silence, he finally muttered, "All right, I'll show you."

He guided them out of the lab and into the corridor. When the passage veered right, they continued until they reached an electronically sealed door. Dr. Azad pressed his finger against the authentication pad and leaned forward in the eye scanner's range.

The red light blinked once before turning green, signalling the door's release with a click. As they stepped inside, motion sensors triggered the automated lights, casting a bright, clinical glow over the lab, which was a marvel of modern engineering, designed with one purpose in mind: to push the boundaries of technological advancement. The walls were lined with sleek, touch-sensitive panels displaying real-time data streams, while modular workstations could accommodate different projects.

In one corner, a yellow 3D holographic display projected the complex schematics of a teleportal rotating slowly in midair. This was no ordinary laboratory. It was a crucible of progress, where the future was forged one breakthrough at a time.

Dr. Azad led them to the other side of the lab, unlocked a sliding door by looking into another eye scanner, and pressed his finger on another pad.

The lighting in the next room, no bigger than the average bedroom, was less harsh with a red strobe component. Crafted from fibreglass, a cube-shaped teleportal with rounded corners sat in the middle of the room. It looked almost old-fashioned, certainly clunky, though its anatomy was no doubt a piece of mechanical brilliance. It was the first time Arthur had seen one up close.

"Ain't it standard practice here to run tests on animals *before* launching a product, and not after?"

"We did," said Dr. Azad.

"Including human trials?"

"Yes, well, one person, a woman we nicknamed the *Plucky Pioneer.*"

Arthur rolled his eyes. "Figures."

"She volunteered after the animal trials showed promising results. She was one of our technicians."

"She died in the explosion?" asked Nova.

"No, a few years before then, at home. She ate some nuts, had a systemic reaction, and died from anaphylactic shock."

"How did *that* happen?"

"She wasn't answering her phone. Her mother was worried about her, so she went to her house and discovered her at the dinner table in front of a plate of curry containing mild traces of nut. That's all I know."

"And you ain't the least bit suspicious?"

"Why would I be suspicious? She didn't realise what she was eating. She made a mistake."

"Pretty tragic mistake, don't you think? Nuts ain't exactly uncommon in curry."

Arthur pointed the gun at Azad. "Strip!"

"Excuse me?"

"I want you to strip."

"Why?"

"You're going through this here teleportal."

"What are you talking about?"

"Call it a little excursion."

"Like fuck I am!"

"I'm giving you a free pass. Letting you go. If I had a gun pointed at my head, I'd take it, I would."

Dr. Azad hesitated, glanced behind him at the teleportal, then back at Arthur and his sidekicks. "Fine."

He slipped out of his lab coat and threw it on the floor. "I will be calling the police the moment I arrive, though."

"Where does it lead to?" asked Nova.

"If you want to find that out, I suggest you go through it yourself."

Arthur tapped Nova on the shoulder. "Go get me one of them chameleons."

Dr. Azad's eyes widened. "What are you doing?"

"Teletron's about to become the first company to splice two genetic species."

"I told you, I don't know where it goes."

"Enough codswallop."

"I send the animals through, and they get sent back to me. My job is to monitor them when they come back, that's all. I have no idea where they go or who they go to. I swear on my life."

"Like you swore there ain't no teleportals here."

"Why are you sending the animals through?" asked Nova. "What are you trying to achieve?"

"The CEO wants to improve the teleportation experience. That's why I am monitoring these animals."

The location of the teleportal's twin was too much of a mystery to ignore. He faced Nova and Owen. "One of us must go through."

Nova raised her palms and took two steps back. "Nah, not me."

"You have experience. That makes you the best person."

"I told you I'll never go through one of these again."

Arthur looked at Owen.

Owen looked at Nova. "I'll go!"

44

Owen had already started undressing when Nova shook her head to signal her objection. She felt his bravery blinded him to the danger in front of them.

"Don't be an idiot!" she said.

Owen smiled. "I wanna go."

"It's not safe."

"You survived."

"I'm talking about what's on the other side. You have no idea where you'll end up."

But Owen was already naked with one hand cupping his groin.

Nova had never seen any boy in the nude. She hurriedly looked away, but her imagination tried to fill in the detail of his nakedness, so she stole a glance. His tattooed skin was marred with what looked like insect bites. She couldn't help but notice his thin fingers, the sharp jut of his wrist bones, and the taut sinews stretching along his forearms. His legs were long and spindly, and her cheeks flushed when he turned, revealing his bony behind and the Roman numeral four inked on the nape of his neck.

Staring at the teleportal, Owen asked, "Now what?"

Dr. Azad activated the automatic door by stepping in front of it. It slid open with a soft hiss, revealing a sturdy chair that tilted back at an approximate fifty-degree angle, designed for both comfort and restraint. The teleportal's interior walls were lined with a complex array of blinking lights and woven pipes, serving a crucial function in the teleportation process. Its lights pulsed rhythmically and blazed over the sleek, metallic ceiling. The titanium floor was polished to a mirror-like finish, which reflected the maze of lights and pipes and created an illusion of infinite depth.

"Sit on the chair and stay still, don't touch anything. The transfer will be prompt."

"Wait!" shouted Nova. "How are we going to find you?"

Owen shrugged. "I'll find you."

"What if you end up in a different country?"

Still cupping his crotch, he reached for his trousers draped over a stool and grabbed the rabbit's foot from the pocket. "I'll bring this with me."

Dr. Azad waved his finger. "The teleportal won't be able to decode the complex molecular details. You don't want to come out the other side looking like a giant paw."

Owen saw a scalpel on the benchtop. He cut the foot open and removed the nano-tracking disk. "Can it read metal?"

"If it's inside your body. Some people have skeletal metal inserts, so the software is programmed to read metal as bone."

He swallowed the tiny disk as though it were a pill. "Go to my cousin's shop. He's got the tracker."

"You'll need to remove your hearing aid," said Dr. Azad. "It's external and can't be teleported."

He unplugged the device and tossed it to Nova. Reaching into his trousers, he pulled out his Ventolin inhaler, took two quick puffs, then slipped it back into his pocket.

Nova gathered his clothes and plimsolls. She pinched his socks and underwear and held them out in front of her.

Dr. Azad passed her a cotton carrier bag from a drawer. "Thanks."

She dropped the clothes inside and smiled at Owen, who seemed to read the warm gesture as forgiveness, but she hadn't forgiven him. How could she?

"Can you hear without your aid?" she asked him, speaking a little louder than usual.

"Not very good."

With a deep breath, he lowered himself onto the seat, its firm surface conforming to his body as he leaned back until he was almost staring directly at the ceiling. The door slid shut with a quiet, airtight seal, plunging him into a world of flashing lights and recurring vibrations. For about the next ten seconds, the teleportal buzzed with a low, resonant frequency, and the air thrummed with energy.

Then, just as suddenly as it had begun, the lights on the exterior dimmed and the vibrations stilled.

When the door slid open, the chair was empty. Owen had vanished.

"Thanks for your time," said Arthur, grabbing Nova by the wrist and marching her out of the lab and along the corridor before Dr. Azad could react.

They summoned the lift and waited anxiously, their heads darting left and right on the lookout for security or police.

A bell chimed, signalling the lift's arrival. They stepped inside, and Arthur quickly pressed the button for the ground floor. The doors began to close and were almost shut when a pair of hands suddenly forced their way through the narrowing gap, prying them apart.

The lift's shrill alarm blared in response, echoing off the walls. Through the narrow slit in the doors, a pair of demonic, black eyes glared at them with a menacing intensity. *Clotho* was inked in black letters across his forehead, adding an unsettling edge to his already terrifying presence.

"That's him!" screamed Nova. "The Serbian!"

Arthur tapped the close button repeatedly.

The doors jerked back and forth indecisively, snapping at the Serbian's meaty hands.

Arthur wrapped the gun across the Serbian's fat knuckles, splitting the skin.

He refused to let go.

Arthur pushed Nova aside. "Stand back!"

Nova cowered in the corner, hugging Owen's clothes, one hand clenched under her chin in panic.

Arthur stepped back, raised the gun, and aimed it directly at the Serbian's face. But the man quickly jerked his head away, using the metal doors as a shield.

Adjusting his aim, Arthur targeted the hand still wedged in the gap and, without hesitation, pulled the trigger. Two fingers were blown off, hitting the floor with a sickening thud as blood splattered across the doors. The noise from the shot deafened them. The kickback in Arthur's hand was powerful. It twisted his wrist.

The smell of gunpowder consumed the cramped space in the lift.

The Serbian withdrew his hand as blood gushed from the wound, and he silently retreated into the darkness.

The doors closed and the lift began its descent.

Arthur twisted round to face Nova, whose eyes were fixed on the bloody fingers on the carpet. Blood freckled his face, but he looked unfazed by what had just happened.

The lift descended quickly and quietly on its runners.

Arthur faced the door with his hands calmly by his waist. "When them doors open—"

His voice was drowned out by the warble of alarm sirens.

"What?" she shouted, her voice trembling with fear.

The doors opened.

"Run!"

45

"The dragon has to breathe fire," the young customer insisted, sitting in the reclining chair. "You can't have a dragon without fire. I want a sword piercing through its eye and out the back of its neck. And make sure there's plenty of blood dripping off the sword onto a human skull."

Spider scrolled through a slideshow of holographic images projected by the rover, showcasing how the tattoo would shift and come to life with movement. He paused on an image. "A bit like this?"

"That's it!" he said. "Perfect."

"Both legs?"

"Yeah, I have big calves."

Spider studied his bare legs. "They're like fucking pillows!"

"A complex of mine for many years," he said. "That's why I want tattoos."

"What, to really draw attention to them?"

The customer laughed. "Hopefully to divert the attention."

"Well, wise choice, big man. Large tattoos with curvature move well and generally look better on the shanks."

"You know what, put some leeches coming out of the eye sockets."

"Of the dragon?"

"The skull."

Spider flattened the reclining chair, transforming it into a bed. "Right, roll onto your stomach and keep your legs still. I guarantee pain. Consider it value for money."

The customer rolled up his shirt sleeve and showed off the biomechanical tattoo on his shoulder. "Not my first, won't be my last."

Spider slipped through the curtain into the front room. He grabbed a syringe filled with high-grade heroin and injected it into his arm, feeling the sharp sting as the needle pierced his skin. As he pressed down on the plunger, he closed his eyes, letting the familiar warmth flood his veins. He pulled out the needle and tossed his head back, savouring the rush as the drug took hold. The room blurred around him, his thoughts dulling into a hazy calm. After a moment, when the euphoria settled in and his pulse steadied, he hid the needle inside a drawer and composed himself before heading back through the curtain to his waiting customer.

"Mind if I switch the radio on? I tend not to fuck up when there's background noise."

The customer rolled his sleeve back into position. "Your parlour, dude."

Spider turned on the national news. The New York chief detective of police was being questioned by reporters after the speech he had delivered in connection with the bombing of Newark Liberty Teleport.

"*What leads do you have at the moment?*" asked the reporter. "*Do you have any suspects?*"

"*We're working closely with anti-terrorism units in the UK. That's all I can reveal at this stage.*"

"*They arrested a dozen members of the ATM last week in the UK. Why have you not made similar arrests here?*"

"*It's too early to comment.*"

The customer looked begrudgingly at the radio. "Fuck me, we all know it was the ATM. Why is it taking them so long to figure it out?"

Spider nodded and lit a cigarette.

To his credit, the reporter didn't give up. "*Too early? The ATM has always been vocal in its desire to sabotage teleportation. And you're saying it's too early to comment? Newark Liberty was destroyed a fortnight ago, and the public has heard nothing. If anything, a comment is long overdue.*"

"Let's see what bullshit he comes out with," said Spider.

"*We've been speaking with members of the ATM, and they are cooperating with our investigation. But we must explore all possible lines of enquiry. To jump in and make arrests without all the facts is irrational and prejudicial. Until we can be sure, we'd like to call on the public's patience.*"

The curtain dividing the shop floor and the back room was thrust back so forcefully, it came slightly off its runners.

Spider slowly turned his head towards the disturbance. He switched off the electric needle and set it down on the table.

The customer rolled onto his back, startled.

Spider took the cigarette out of his mouth and crushed the butt in an ashtray. "Shit timing, mate!"

The Serbian stood in the doorway, his anger palpable as he gripped a steel knife, roughly the same length as his forearm. His left hand was wrapped in a bandage where blood seeped through the material, staining it red.

The customer scarpered through the back door, leaving it wide open.

Spider faced the heavyset man and sighed. "It's called body dysmorphic disorder, or obsessive body modification. It's kind of an addiction. Do me one more on my shoulder. Expand my aztec. Give me one to match the other ankle. Fill my back. But then no skin is left, though the addiction remains. Then what? Change this tattoo, change that tattoo. Remove the one on my forearm and replace it with... with... fucked if I know."

Spider threw his head back and took a deep breath before facing the Serbian. "So, what will it be, big man? A memorial tat? You want me to put *Clotho* in a sentence? Top you up on black eye-dye perhaps?"

Unfazed by such an imposing figure, and not the least bit intimidated by his eyes, as black and glossy as snooker balls, undaunted by the bayonet-sized knife he expertly handled or the appalling physical odds, Spider rolled up his sleeves, ready to take on this monster.

He spotted his leather tool bag on the floor, brimming with utensils and equipment: bolt cutters, wrenches, screwdrivers, drills, everyday items that could easily inflict injuries and cause excruciating pain. High on heroin and false bravery, he pulled out the hammer and raised it above his head, the lump end glistening in the overhead light. He advanced with determined strides, erratically swinging the hammer in a wide arc and then crisscrossing the air in an uncoordinated and clumsy approach. His eyes were wide and crazed, masking his deep-rooted fear.

Across from him, the Serbian stepped forward with equal purpose, his knife raised and poised. Closing the distance, the two combatants clashed with a fierce intensity, their weapons meeting in a violent exchange of strikes and parries.

Spider's hammer crashed down with a powerful swipe but missed, while the Serbian's blade carved through the air with speed and accuracy.

Spider didn't initially feel the blade slice through his wrist; the pain registered only after the fact. He continued to believe he still held his weapon firmly. It was only when he heard the clang of the hammer hitting the floor that he glanced down, thinking he had dropped it. That's when he saw his detached hand, still gripping the handle. Blood gushed from his severed wrist and dripped all over the floor.

The precise attack had left him disabled and defenceless. No doubt about that.

The Serbian surged in for the kill, the odds entirely in his favour now. No doubt about that, either.

46

It was well past the dinner hour. Nova had only eaten a protein bar and was hungry, but the mere idea of eating anything made her stomach churn. Her nostrils still carried the faintest trace of gunpowder, and the image of what had happened inside the lift terrified her. While she had the calm of someone who had just survived danger, she would never feel truly safe with the Serbian still out there, hunting her.

Arthur remained beneath the truck, his toolkit spread out around him. He had been working on the powertrain for nearly four hours, his focus unwavering despite the time. The interior had turned chilly, and Nova's breath came in puffs of steam.

"Finally," said Arthur, climbing into the truck and starting the motor. "That took ages, that did."

With the heaters gradually warming both the interior and Nova's numb limbs, she gazed out at the distant building lights, tiny white pinpricks against the black sky, as they neared the edge of the city. She was alone with her thoughts, and only one person was on her mind. She'd seen a side to Owen she wasn't supposed to see. He could have lied about his early intentions. But he had confessed, salvaging a conscience from his criminal psyche. He deserved credit for that. She also knew what kind of hold his cousin had over him. No matter how offended she was, she had grown attached to Owen over the past fortnight in shy and tentative increments. She wanted to forgive him, but forgiveness didn't come easy to her. She needed time. Time she perhaps no longer had.

"Where do you think that teleportal at Teletron connects to?" asked Nova, breaking the silence.

"I've got my suspicions."

"Tell me!"

"I reckon Owen's in New York right now."

Nova narrowed her eyes. "Then why did you let him go?"

"He volunteered, remember?"

"You should have said something! He might not have gone through if he'd known."

"I could be wrong. But you heard Dr. Azad say a teleportal got moved overseas. Where else? One thing I found strange was them animals."

"What about them?"

"They all share one thing in common."

"What?"

"They've all got short lifespans. Mice and chameleons only live for one to two years. Them opossums and robins for about a year, from memory. I'll need to check that. I suspect it ain't a coincidence."

"What does it mean?"

"I ain't sure."

As they drew close to a bridge, a holographic sign came to life, illuminating the darkness. It displayed a cheerful animation of cartoon roadworkers, complete with hard hats and tools, labouring on a digital road. The sign's playful graphics and its bright, animated characters conveyed a message about ongoing roadworks three miles up ahead, their exaggerated movements and friendly conduct adding a hint of humour to an otherwise mundane announcement. Real-life workers, by contrast, wore luminous orange overalls and unhappy faces while attending a deep hole in the road beside a pile of rubble, slowing traffic to a crawl.

A police siren screamed through the streets a block or two away. Followed by another in the same high-panicked shriek.

Nova swung her head around at the rear window, her face drained of colour.

"It ain't for us," said Arthur. "Don't worry."

They pulled up outside Spider's tattoo parlour at one in the morning. The lack of adequate streetlights meant visibility was limited to the reach of the truck's headlights until Arthur shut off the motor, reducing the road to complete darkness.

"You stay here. I'll go and wake up his cousin and get that there tracker."

Nova undid her belt. "I'm coming with you."

"Suit yourself."

The parlour was unlocked, the door ajar. The light was on inside. The front room was unoccupied. The curtain hanging over the doorway to the back room had been partly ripped off the wall. A trail of blood ran along the lines in the tiled floor and pooled at the foot of the counter, flowing from the back room.

Arthur approached the door and pushed the curtain aside.

Nova gasped, her hand flying to her mouth as she took a step back in stunned disbelief.

Even Arthur looked sickened by the scene before him.

A man was suspended upside down by his ankles, bound with frayed telephone cord that was looped around the blades of an enormous ceiling fan. The hub had broken loose due to the weight, revealing its wires. It would give at any moment. The paddles spun at slow speed, like helicopter blades coming to a rest, revolving the suspended corpse in endless, spinning circles. The gaping wound in the man's neck had spilled his blood all over the floor, creating a macabre pool. His blood-slicked arms left crimson streaks in their wake, casting eerie red rings. His face was like a red mask. In addition, a tattoo needle had been driven into his right eye and was left dangling from the socket. The scene resembled a kind of gruesome sacrificial ritual performed by a bloodthirsty cult.

Judging by his long, greasy hair and blood-caked tattoos, Nova was ninety per cent sure the body belonged to Spider. His nose was broken. His jaw didn't align, and one cheek had swollen to the size of a potato. She noticed one of his hands was missing, then saw it three feet away, gripping a hammer. It was obvious he had been in a fight that looked one-sided, and the victor had strung him up like an animal in an abattoir, his severed jugular leaking every drop of blood and oxygen and pouring his life all over the floor.

Three words had been carved onto his forehead with a knife. Nova read them and recoiled. The sight was so terrible, she could only look for a few seconds. Incapable of speaking or even breathing, she ran out of the room and exited through the front door. The moment she stepped outside, she arched over and threw up her protein bar and a large amount of her anxiety all over the footpath.

Once she managed to catch her breath and regain some composure, she scanned the street with growing paranoia.

Where was the Serbian? Was he lurking in the shadows, his dark eyes blending into the night? Could he be hiding behind the row of parked cars, or crouched around the corner by the wall of the betting shop three doors down? Perhaps he was watching her from the rooftop of the tattoo parlour. Was she framed in his circular scope, his finger poised on the trigger of an assault rifle several hundred yards away, and the whip-crack would be the last thing she ever knew.

She heard a sharp click that made her flinch dramatically. The latch mechanism on the door. Instinctively, she placed a hand over her chest, trying to steady her pounding heart.

Arthur stopped beside her, his face suffused with shock. He held up the tracking visor but said nothing.

Back at the truck, Arthur yanked open his door and slid across the seat to unlock Nova's side, as the automatic locks had been damaged in the crash. He sat still behind the steering wheel, his body tense and unmoving.

Nova couldn't even hear him breathing. She thought he'd passed out. When she leaned across him, she saw his eyes were open.

She glanced out of the window, sickened by what she had seen. "Can we go?"

"Yeah, police will be here soon."

He passed the tracking visor to Nova, started the motor, and drove the truck out of the neighbourhood, checking his mirrors every few seconds.

The visor was thin as paper, light as aluminium, robust like glass. Nova slipped it over her eyes and concentrated on the holographic display on the acrylic screen while satellites sifted through thousands of terabytes of data to synchronise with the tracking disk resting in the pit of Owen's gut, pinpointing his location down to the exact country, region, town, and suburb, supplying the precise coordinates.

"Found him!"

"Where is he?"

Nova offered Arthur a thin, worried smile. "Not in New York."

47

The country roads stretched endlessly through the dark vista, creating a long and monotonous journey. The headlights lit up a wooded expanse, where slate-barked trees stood like soldiers along the roadside. From nowhere came a veil of mist on either side of the road as if parted by the truck's headlights, creating an eerie tunnel through the darkness. The only stimulus came when Arthur had to swing around a dead animal lying in the road.

Nova had pleaded a headache to avoid conversation. She wasn't in the mood for chatter. It had paid off. Arthur hadn't spoken a word for more than two hours. He was equally as shocked over the gruesome find at the parlour, but he worked well under pressure and would find a way to take it in his stride, just as he had managed to during their fateful rendezvous with the speedboat, now at the bottom of the sea.

She had no such resolve and was shattered and mentally bereft, revolving through her emotions with so much to think about, or avoid thinking about. She expected to have haunting dreams for years to come. She craved a deep, uninterrupted sleep, a chance to escape the harsh reality of the world and to wake up somewhere comforting—like home. But there was no time for idle wishes. She wasn't living in a world of fairy tales or movies. She had to find the strength that her father had instilled in her. Without it, she wouldn't survive.

Owen had wound up in a small town on the southwest coast of England. She wanted to believe he was still alive and playing the waiting game, but she couldn't help imagining him dead on a beach at the mercy of the crabs and crows.

An hour later, a deer lumbered into the road, and Arthur snapped out of his trance, veering onto the embankment. The truck clipped the deer's antlers, shearing off the wing mirror.

Nova rushed up from sleep, fleeing her unsettling dreams, her palms planted on the seat, her head darting left and right, figuring out where she was.

Arthur slowed the truck. "It's okay, you were dreaming. Want me to stop for a bit?"

She feared her continuous visions would eventually hijack her consciousness.

Arthur pulled over anyway and dropped his head into his hands, massaging his eyes with his palms. He shook his head, clearly trying to reduce his tiredness.

"Back in a sec."

He strode up the embankment, undid his fly, and relieved himself in full range of the headlamps.

Nova saw steam rising around him like a grey ghost, and it reminded her of Owen at the teleport.

Arthur reattached the dangling wing mirror, sliding it back into its mount. The glass was cracked but remained functional. Nova shivered when a draught knifed in from Arthur's door as he climbed back in and continued the long drive, passing random cottages, farmhouses, and chimneys puffing plumes of smoke into the misty, moonlit sky. He seemed more alert now, watching the road ahead with the intensity of a teenage gamer concentrating on the screen.

"Cows outnumber humans in these here parts, and tractors outnumber cars, you know."

Nova just looked out of the window, barely interested.

"Born in the West Country, I was. On a farm. You ask me, ain't no better place."

Nova hesitated to speak, but the topic drew her in. "I grew up in the countryside, too."

"Where?"

"Honiley, a small village in the West Midlands."

"Best place to be, far away from people."

"This coming from a man who lives in the busiest city in Europe."

"Heather didn't like the sticks, called it soul-destroying and claustrophobic. Besides, I got loads of work in London. Ain't sure how many sinks get blocked up in Honiley. Ain't enough to keep me busy."

They drove by the Commercial Aviation Heritage Centre housing a range of aircraft, like the Airbus, Jumbo, Concorde, and hypersonic jets. Adjacent to the heritage centre lay an eerie aircraft graveyard, a resting place for planes that hadn't quite made the cut for museum display. These mighty machines, worn by time and neglect, lay abandoned in an enormous plot of land behind the centre. What had started out as a storage area gradually became an unintended visitor attraction, drawing those curious enough to explore these relics of a bygone era. Rusting fuselages and faded insignias marked the passage of time, while weeds clung to their cold metal skins, reclaiming the space. Despite their deteriorated state, the planes still held a certain mystique, their hulking frames evoking the power and history they'd once embodied. Visitors could walk among the giants, tracing their hands along the metal, imagining roaring engines that had once carried them throughout the skies. Some remained in good-enough condition that they could climb into the windowless cockpits, sit in the worn pilot's seat, and grip the controls, role-playing as the aviators of old, allowing them to step into the shoes of pilots who once soared at the helm of the renowned aircraft.

"Did you ever fly?" asked Nova.

"When I was a young lad."

"Where?"

"New Orleans, Cairo, a few places in western Europe. It was expensive to fly back then. By the time I was a grown-up, international flights were beyond affordable. Only super-rich people could travel."

"What was it like? Being up in the sky?"

"The world makes more sense from up high. You see the stain humankind has created, can really understand the scale of our dirty footprints."

"For someone so against technology, I'm surprised. Or is flying allowed in the ATM rulebook?"

"This was before I joined the ATM. In my early twenties, it became unaffordable to travel overseas. By then, I'd learned all about the damage air travel caused. Every plane that flew overhead dumped tons of toxic pollutants over our homes and farmlands, contaminating our food and air. On average, one domestic flight alone burned the same amount of fossil fuel as hundreds of petrol cars. We started to see it in our farm crops, we did. Pollution was linked to many illnesses. Look, don't get me wrong. I ain't against all technologies, only them that push ethical boundaries. Some are good for us humans."

"This I've got to hear."

"Like my watch, giving me the time. I've had this thing for twenty-nine years. Bionic lenses, helping me see better in the dark and correcting my long- and short-sightedness. Electronic gadgets that assist me with my trades. Tools that help us in the world, not distract us from it or risk our humanity and health. Did you know millions of metric tons of electronic waste get produced every year? What happens to that toxic e-waste? It pollutes rivers, lakes, oceans, contaminating fish and seafood. Most of that there waste is exported to poor countries in Africa and Asia, and materials like zinc, lead, and chromium end up in toys and get sent back to our kids."

"You sound like an environmentalist."

"The environmental damage ain't half the problem. It's what it does to our humanity that upsets me most. You must have had some negative experiences with technology. Don't tell me you ain't."

"I was cyber-bullied."

"There you go, see."

"It was awful. Some people can turn into monsters behind their computers. You would be shocked if I showed you some of the threatening messages I received. The crazy thing is I did nothing wrong."

"Not much arouses people more than a good old online public shaming session. Cyberspace ruins lives, incites hatred, racism, sexual abuse, extremism, violence, you name it. And it affects and destroys childhoods, health, relationships, careers, finances, the list goes on and on, it does. More than two-thirds of the population have Internet, the ultimate weapon of mass destruction. You want to put the Internet to good use? Search for the statistics that show you how many lives got lost because of technology and the dark web. You're the one who would be shocked, not me."

They stopped at an EV station to charge up the truck's old batteries. It gave them fifteen minutes to purchase some food. A takeaway joint next door to the station had closed its dining area, but the drive-in was twenty-four hours.

Nova followed Arthur on foot around the road looping the diner, stopping at an alignment of interactive menu screens.

Nova voice-selected a crispy tofu burger and a bottle of water.

"That's it? That's all you want?" asked Arthur.

"I'm not that hungry."

Arthur ordered a bacon sandwich and a kidney pie, a black coffee, ten tobacco pouches, cigarette papers, a new lighter, an energy drink, two bottles of water, and a roll of strong mints. He finalised the transaction by placing his fingertip against the electronic pay pad, then held up his finger in front of Nova's face with a large grin. "Courtesy of the supreme commander of physics and engineering. Still got the prosthetic print on, I have."

A robotic arm passed them the goods at the next window.

With the truck's batteries at full capacity, Arthur got them back on the road.

"You're too hard on Owen," said Nova, and bit into her tofu burger.

Arthur wiped mustard from his lips.

To her surprise, he didn't fire back with one of his harsh remarks. "Don't forget he risked his life to save your boat from sinking. I want you to be nicer to him from now on."

Arthur nodded. "If he's still alive."

48

The sunrise bathed the small Cornish town of Porthleven in a harsh, white light, its narrow streets and quaint cottages still cloaked in the lingering mist of dawn. The wind was up, and the silver-blue sea was being whipped into foam. The harbour, a relic of Napoleonic engineering, was the town's centrepiece. Its stone walls, weathered by time and tide, cradled the waters where fishing boats bobbed, their masts swaying in rhythm with the rolling waves. The air was crisp and carried the faint scent of salt and seaweed that mingled with the distant call of seagulls wheeling overhead. It was a day fit for recreation and relaxation. Except, Nova could no more relax than she could bring her father back. Today was another painful reminder that the world moved on, even when she couldn't.

Arthur pulled the truck to a stop in a tow-away zone along the narrow road that overlooked the beach. His focus was on finding Owen. He wasn't concerned about receiving a parking ticket. "Wait in the truck!" he said, his eyes sweeping the town and beachside residences through the windscreen. "Might not be safe."

"No, I'm coming with you."

He shot her an incredulous stare. "Seriously? Even after what happened a few hours ago when we had this here same conversation?"

The image of Spider strung up by his ankles flashed behind her eyelids, followed by what had looked like the kill floor of a slaughterhouse. She couldn't shake the images off. Spider bled out. Spider's dismembered hand on the hammer. Spider strung up. Spider. *Spider.* She still had to break the news to Owen, but first, she had to find him and hope that he'd not met a similar fate.

"I want to find Owen," she said.

Arthur nodded, got out, and opened the door for her.

The pavement offered a commanding view of the coastline below, where the waves crashed rhythmically and their foamy crests broke against the sand. From their vantage point, the shoreline stretched out in a gentle curve, making it easy to see the beach was empty, apart from a few boats, one of them broken-backed with barnacled ribs, and a lonesome rowing boat listing on the sand, its nose inching from side to side as the breaking waves struck it.

"I don't see him," said Nova. She slipped on the tracking visor and double-checked the display. The flashing green dot represented Owen. The red dot belonged to the visor.

"The tracker tells me he's real close, within fifty metres."

"No, that tracking disk is close. He might have thrown up or taken a dump."

Nova shook her head at the disgusting thought. "How do we get down there?"

"Follow me!" Arthur found a narrow, worn-out footpath on the bank and descended the slope. Nearing the bottom, he lost his balance and couldn't recover. He threw his arms out to take some weight off the fall. The wound to his hand caused by the crowbar tore open under the bandage when he landed on a rock. Coughing on a mouthful of sand, he rolled onto his back.

Nova trotted behind him. "Are you hurt?"

Hauling himself to his feet, he moved his arms and rolled his shoulders, checking for strains. Apart from a sore hand and a slightly bruised ego, he was uninjured. "I'm fine."

They stepped carefully across the beach as the golden sand shifted underfoot and headed for the cluster of beached boats, trusting the tracking visor.

"There!" said Arthur, pointing at the listing rowing boat.

Nova also saw the arm hanging limply over the gunwale. "Owen!"

They found him face down in the boat, wearing nothing but a white lab coat. No trousers, no socks, no shoes, and no underwear. Just the lab coat, hanging loosely over his bare skin.

Arthur knelt beside him and pressed two fingers under his jaw, searching for a pulse. If it was there, it was faint. Owen was unconscious but still breathing. His face had turned pale; it seemed almost translucent. It contrasted with the dry, crusty mud stuck to his cheeks and forehead. The lab coat, too, was caked in dried mud, stiffened and heavy as it clung to his naked body.

Arthur and Nova hauled Owen out of the boat and away from the shoreline. They set him down on the sand.

A pack of cigarettes and a white macro key tumbled from his top pocket, hinting at the secrets of his recent endeavours.

Nova looked into Arthur's bloodshot eyes. "Didn't he take off his lab coat before he went inside the teleportal? Or was I dreaming that?"

"I was just thinking the same thing."

"How is he still wearing it?"

Arthur removed his military jacket and draped it around Owen's shoulders. "I ain't got a clue."

He picked up the cigarettes and macro key and put them in his pocket.

Nova lowered Owen back down on the sand and tried to bring him back to consciousness by tapping his face. But he was too far gone to react. He'd teleported almost twelve hours ago. What had happened to him during that time?

Arthur surveyed his surroundings, trying to piece together the events that had led Owen to this destination. Why was he in a boat with no oars? Without them, he could not have been out at sea, and he certainly wouldn't have been reckless enough to attempt escaping the mainland. The currents were treacherous in these parts, formidable enough to overpower even the most seasoned sailors. Without the right equipment and knowhow, he had no defence against the unforgiving elements.

Maybe he'd climbed into the boat to escape the biting cold wind, seeking any shelter he could find. Or perhaps he had fled from Teletron and found the boat as a temporary hiding place, hoping it would keep him concealed until he could figure out his next move. Both scenarios suggested he had arrived there after climbing into the teleportal inside Teletron. Where was the reciprocal teleportal machine?

Arthur knew very little about Porthleven, except that it was renowned for being one of the most storm-battered towns in the country, frequently subjected to relentless waves and fierce winds. Its isolation and obscurity perhaps made it the perfect place to conceal a teleportal and carry out clandestine research and experiments without attracting unwanted attention.

He left Nova cradling Owen in her arms and jogged along the beach, leaving the sand via a set of steps that led back up to the road. He headed into the town, viewing the local shops and kiosks, the kind that sold tourist junk in summer.

A fleet of gliders drew his eye skyward as they soared over the beach like giant winged creatures, swooping and swerving. The domestic airport was less than three miles away. They had driven by it on the way in, observing the recreational gliders and solar planes lined up on the runway.

The harbour, protected by a curving breakwater and baulk gate, was overlooked by a church-like building with a granite-wall clock tower. The attraction drew tourists and professional photographers nationwide.

Arthur crossed the road and ventured further into town. Following the cobbled streets, he sighted a terrace of elevated cottages with a prime view of the fishing port and beaches. He looked across the harbour to the other side, where the creamy surf crashed over the rockface. A small boatshed was perched precariously on the jagged rocks, somehow standing despite the endless cycle of storms and tides that swept in. Beyond the rocky cliff was a hill dominated by houses and what looked like a small weather tower.

He ran his eyes over the cobbled quayside once more and decided there was nothing worth pursuing, so he returned to Owen and Nova at the beach.

"We need to get him to the hospital," Arthur said, stepping heavily over the shifting sand. "He might have hypothermia."

49

Owen lay snuggled in a hospital bed, as comfortable as he had ever been with a heated blanket draped over him. The steady flow of fluids from the warmed IV drip gradually soothed his parched throat and rehydrated his body. His eyelids fluttered in a state of bliss, deeply grateful for the respite and the rare opportunity to simply rest and recover. He could easily grow accustomed to this comfort, but was wise enough to temper his expectations, knowing soon enough he would find himself back in a cold, sterile room isolated from the world, with no lock on the door to provide even a hint of security. The chill of that room would seep into his bones once more, settling in as a permanent companion, and the darkness would amplify the loneliness that often enveloped him. Nova would become a distant memory, a person he once knew briefly but had lost by making the mistake of heeding his cousin's commands.

A low-watt lamp kept the room softly lit, mingling with the scent of antiseptic and fresh linen. Owen opened one eye and saw Nova kept vigil beside him. She touched his face, not quite a caress but gently resting her palm on his cheek as he came awake. Owen tried to suppress a smile, not wanting to misread the gesture. When she grasped his fingers, carefully avoiding the drip in the back of his hand, he was powerless to stop the smile appearing on his face.

Nova did not respond with the same expression. "How are you feeling?"

His smile faded. "Fine."

"Do you know when you can leave?"

"A few days."

The nurse came in and fluffed up Owen's pillows.

"Better?" she asked.

"Yeah." He tried to sit up, but she eased him back down, seeing how much he struggled.

"Just take it easy," she said. "Nothing strenuous."

Owen nodded, and the breathing tubes inside his nostrils feeding warmed, humidified oxygen into his body dislodged slightly. Pushing them back in, he rested his head against the pillow and closed his eyes.

Arthur poked his head around the door, slipped inside, and eased the door shut.

Owen opened his eyes, hearing someone enter the room. He raised his head off the pillow and looked to his left, seeing Arthur approach. He looked at Nova. "Is Spider coming?"

Nova lowered her eyes. "I have to tell you something."

Owen's face straightened, studying Nova's sudden change in expression. "He's dead!"

Nova didn't answer, but Arthur did. "Yes."

Nova brushed an imaginary lock of hair off her face and nodded when Owen looked at her for confirmation.

At first, Owen shook his head in denial, but soon accepted it as fact. "How?"

Nova put her hand on his. "He was murdered."

Owen couldn't find the words he wanted to say. When a few arranged themselves in his head, they didn't hang around long enough for him to articulate. "Where?"

"We found him at his shop."

Owen looked down at his lap. "How was he killed?"

"In a fight."

"With who?"

She didn't answer, but her eyes betrayed her.

"Tell me!"

"We don't know for sure, but whoever killed him carved a message on his face." She looked down. "It said *eye for eye*."

Owen's face hardened. "Do we know where he is?"

Arthur shrugged. "Probably in the morgue by now."

"The Serbian!" said Owen, sharing his gaze between Nova and Arthur. "Do we know where he is?"

"Out there somewhere."

Owen cast a forlorn glance towards the window, doing his best to conceal his sadness. It was true: he and his cousin had never been in complete harmony. Spider had consistently used him as a pawn to advance his own interests, stripping away the possibility of a normal childhood. The constant manipulation and exploitation had left Owen feeling betrayed and longing for something more genuine. Yet, before Nova entered his life, Spider had been his only emotional anchor in a harsh world. Despite the exploitation, Spider was his only family, the sole connection he had to anything resembling kinship or support.

Spider's presence, however flawed, was the one constant in his turbulent existence. It was all he'd known until Nova brought a glimmer of hope and a chance for something different. Now he was gone.

Owen's mind turned, inexorably, to revenge. He wanted the Serbian dead, but his true fantasy was to kill the monster himself. Even now, the thought of causing him pain and killing him got his pulse racing. He looked at Nova. "I ended up in a factory."

50

A blinding flash of white light exploded across Owen's vision, momentarily erasing all sense of the natural world around him. Electrical pulses surged through his core, channelling waves of tingling energy along his central nervous system as he moved through the teleportation process. His muscles became hyper-sensitive, reacting to the intense current flowing through him, as though his very soul was drawn towards an invisible vortex, a disorienting disconnect from his physical form.

Pulled into this swirling maelstrom, a warm, omnipresent sound enveloped him, an all-encompassing hum that was both soothing and powerful. It resonated with every particle of his existence, making him acutely aware of his own presence as his brain's neurons fired in disordered synchrony. Auditory and sensory overload threatened to overpower him, a crescendo of perception almost too much to bear. But just as the intensity reached its peak, a sudden and sharp pull yanked him back into reality, and he could almost feel his atoms reassembling inside him in an instant. The world returned, forming all around him; the disorienting sensations gave way to the familiar solidity of the teleportal's anatomy. The transition, though brief, left him momentarily disoriented and struggling to regain his bearings as he reconnected with his physical self.

A multi-function display screen to the left of a frosted glass door was filled with symbols, totally alien geometry that meant nothing to Owen. He pressed his face against the frosted glass and searched for hazy shapes that could pass for human, seeing only variations of light and darkness. His movement activated the automated airlocks, which pulled the glass-panelled door open.

Suddenly recalling his lack of clothing, he gingerly stepped onto a glossy, diamond-plate floor in a vast, circular chamber. A lattice of winding pipes and range of heavy-duty machinery, reminiscent of a ship's engine room, surrounded him. It had a domed ceiling with darkened tube bulbs. The only light came from suspended candle lanterns, and the air felt stiflingly hot from the heavy machinery and the absence of air conditioning. Transparent screens lined the white walls; a glass dash panel with virtual keys twinkled brightly.

A man in a white lab coat with buttons stretched over his potbelly stood swiping information from screen to screen as if he was fingerpainting. He was dark-skinned, dark-haired with a heavy comb-over, and had a slight stoop that made him seem older than he looked.

Owen shuffled across the room and hid behind another teleportal, identical to the one he had arrived in. Behind him, on the opposite side to the banks of tech, stood a row of empty cages. They were next to a series of kennels, housing three dogs sprawled within their enclosures. There was a step-up in activity from Owen's close presence, distracting the man using the computers.

"Shut up!" he shouted.

Owen heard footsteps coming from the only staircase in the room. He crept from the teleportal to a concrete pillar and crouched behind it, keeping out of sight.

A woman dressed in an expensive-looking suit entered the room speaking. "Are you the one they call Archon?"

"That's me. Where are the other two?"

"Still wrapping things up. They need more time. Should be here by Tuesday."

"Key?" he asked, holding out his hand.

She passed him a white macro key, and he left it on top of a series of horizontal aluminium pipes.

He led her to the computers and a glass panel. "Scan your palm here."

The woman laid her palm flat on the glass, and a green holographic sphere engulfed her hand.

He made a prolonged examination of her ID.

The businesswoman eyed him up and smiled. "So, Archon, do you have a proper name?"

"Oberon... Ron is fine."

"What now, Ron?"

"Undress!"

"Hmmm, you always ask the ladies to undress on the first encounter?"

"When they're paying me as much as you lot are, absolutely. Undress, please!"

"You *are* a charmer!"

She removed her blazer and trousers. "What's it like over there? As tropical as the brochures make out?"

"The island is full of lush beaches and lagoons. Trust me, you'll live a long, blissful life in paradise."

"Have you been there?"

"Who do you think set it all up? Isn't that what you guys are paying us for? The supreme commander's waiting for you on the other side. As agreed, he will supply you with your new identification, a luxury, fully furnished houseboat, and foreign bank accounts."

Without his hearing device, Owen struggled to catch their words from behind the pillar.

The young woman unbuttoned her cream-coloured blouse and turned sideways. Owen glimpsed her long and narrow face with a pinched nose. He had seen her somewhere but couldn't put a name to the face. She seemed like a powerful, dangerous person. His mind repeated that truth over and over as it went into search-and-retrieve mode. Where had he seen her?

Her sudden nakedness pulled his eyes from her face to her body. He observed her form with curiosity, noting the delicate contours of her naked form. He followed the slender curve of her waist as it gracefully transitioned into wider hips. The sight was new to him; he had never seen an adult in the flesh before.

The businesswoman pointed towards the teleportal. "Are you certain this machine only produces the results that we're expecting? The physical benefits?"

"Absolutely certain."

She pointed at the teleportal Owen had materialised from. "What's the deal with *that* machine?"

"We use it for testing purposes. We still have work to do before teleportation can go commercial again."

"Never going to happen. That ship has sailed, my friend. Once you lose public trust, there's no getting it back. Trust me, I've seen this happen so many times. Anyway, not my problem. I've washed my hands, and now they're spotless, and so is my conscience."

"Lucky you."

She frowned, but only fleetingly. "I trust the money's been transferred?"

"Yes."

"And it's untraceable?"

He nodded. "Enjoy a long and happy retirement."

"I intend to," she said, moving towards the teleportal. The door opened with a metallic whoosh, and she stepped inside, taking her seat on the tilted chair.

The man pointed at her feet. "Socks, too."

The woman pulled them off and threw them to the floor.

The teleportal door slid shut, sealing the woman inside. After ten seconds, the door reopened to reveal the woman had vanished.

The man picked up her socks and dropped them in the bin. "Hope you choke on your fucking snorkel!" he said.

That something shifty was in motion was now a foregone conclusion. It was time to get out of there. Wherever *there* was.

Owen identified only two ways to escape the room. The teleportal, which required assistance or operational knowhow. Or the staircase leading up to a platform.

With the man refocussed on his computer console, Owen tiptoed towards the staircase, an adrenaline rush in itself. He saw the white macro key and a pack of cigarettes sitting on the pipes on the way out. They were next to a folded lab coat. He took all three items.

Owen threw on the lab coat, covering his nakedness, and pocketed the white macro key and cigarettes.

The staircase flattened into a metal-grid platform, merging with the rock face without any lighting, making it more of a dark passageway. Owen followed the path, rounding a corner that snuffed out the last glimmer of light from the basement behind him. The long passageway, supported by high-up brick porticoes arching into the gloom, grew even darker as he moved forward, forcing him to blindly feel his way along the calcified walls, flaking from mildew and general decay.

At the end of the passageway he noticed a small, blue light blinking intermittently. He counted five seconds between each flash, which lit up a heavy steel door beyond the light with rust stains streaking from its large bolts.

He heard someone call out *hello*.

The *man*.

He focussed on the door but was stalled by an exceedingly complex lock. He waved the macro key. Nothing happened.

He heard the man's voice again. "Hello?"

Owen couldn't see him because it was too dark. He could only hear his footsteps.

He squeezed himself into the tiny niche beside the door, relying on the darkness to stymie the approaching man. He had already outwitted him once. Was it beyond him to do it again?

Owen stayed flat against the wall, fantasising invisibility by holding his breath.

The bright blue light flashed, lighting up the small vestibule momentarily.

The man stopped in front. "Hello? Is somebody there?"

Owen had five seconds before the flash lit him up and gave him away. He could hear the man's heavy breathing, could feel his lingering presence. He had no logical excuses to offer, no defences to present. The reality of his situation left him with absolutely nothing—no justifications, no explanations, and no way to shield himself from the consequences.

He froze, stripped of any pretence, ready for whatever fate dealt him.

51

Owen passed out at the climax of his story, as if voicing what had happened was too shocking, and his mind had intervened to protect him, shutting down his body before the words could do any more harm. Nova and Arthur, practically holding their breaths as they eagerly awaited details of his escape, relaxed their rigid bodies as the room fell silent. When Arthur let out a sharp, four-letter curse in frustration, Nova glared at him in anger.

She rubbed her temples where a headache threatened to materialise. The Serbian consumed her every thought, and she needed him gone, no matter the cost. It didn't matter how it happened, just that it did. Arrested. Deported. Preferably dead. This thought brought a twisted sense of relief, as if his death would be the only true way to purge him from her life. It was the only way to reclaim the peace he had stolen from her.

Arthur peeled off the bandage on his hand, wincing as the adhesive tugged at his skin. Beneath it, the wound was raw and angry, the edges swollen and irritated. Fresh blood seeped out, slow but steady, staining the soaked gauze. He had asked the nurse to bring him some medical supplies. She returned with a first-aid box, applied some healing glue to seal the wound, and rebandaged it for him.

Owen soon came around. He reached out and took Nova's hand, squeezing it in his. He was not adept at expressing his emotions or articulating his thoughts. Nova couldn't even tell whether he was upset, in shock, in denial, or simply indifferent about his cousin. She wasn't sure what kind of relationship he and Spider had shared, certainly not a conventional one.

She stared at his face, blessed with the kind of blue eyes girls found irresistible. The bedsheets had slipped down to his waist, revealing a floral motif tattoo in numerous colours and patterns all over his torso. She regarded the modern culture of ink as a form of self-mutilation. She knew people who chose to go all-in often did so to maximise self-expression, a cry out to be noticed. She wondered if his tattoos had a story to tell, so she asked him. "What's with all the tattoos?"

Owen glanced down at his exposed body with a trace of embarrassment and pulled the bed sheet up to his neck. "My cousin wanted to try some new designs on me."

"Did you want the tattoos?"

He shook his head. "I was ten."

Nova shook *her* head. "That's awful."

"Do you have my clothes?"

It reminded her she had seen him naked, and it made her blush. "They're in Arthur's truck. I'll go and get them for you now."

But Arthur stopped her, flexing his fingers under the new bandage. "Later, we've got plans to make."

She put her hands on her hips. "Plans?"

"Yeah, plans."

She felt her anger coming to the boil, tempted to refuse to hear what he had to say on principle, but she chose to let him speak of them. "What plans?"

"Owen's about to tell us about that there basement, he is. Then we're going there."

Nova was on the verge of unleashing a long, anguished scream, a cry that had been building up inside her for weeks. She was a woman now, not just a girl, and the expectations to be strong and optimistic, no matter what she faced, were real. There were times when she questioned if her greatest adversary was not the external challenges she faced, but the self-doubting voice inside her head, telling her strength was a façade, that her optimism was a fragile veneer. Sometimes, the battle within her own mind was the fiercest and most relentless of them all. She needed to be more like her father, to stand up for herself with the same strength he'd shown. She had to channel his influence, confront those who unsettled her, and remind herself that they had no right to impose upon her. She had to tell herself, with unwavering conviction, she would not tolerate their audacity.

She stared at Arthur with all the reproachful disapproval she could muster. "I'm not going anywhere!"

Arthur folded his arms. "Excuse me?"

"I didn't want any of this. Neither did Owen. He risked his life, and now he's in the hospital because of you. You and your crazy dangerous plans."

"Because of me?"

"Everything that's happened is because of you."

"Care to elaborate there?"

"You pushed him to go through the teleportal, knowing he might end up in New York. You don't care about him *or* me. You're just in this for your own reasons but don't want to do it alone."

Owen's eyes were closed, and the nurse who'd just walked into the room warned Nova and Arthur to keep their voices down.

Arthur pulled her away from Owen's bedside with his hand flat against her back and kept the discussion going in forced whispers.

"Listen, you're tired and emotional and ain't—"

She held up her hand, stopping Arthur mid-sentence. "I've had enough of this. I'm out! So is Owen. Good luck getting your revenge."

His silence informed her she had hit a nerve.

She hadn't meant to make such a show of herself, but she was relieved to get her thoughts across.

Arthur tucked in his shirt and walked away.

Owen sat up. "What are you two talking about?"

"Nothing, we're done here," said Nova.

Arthur approached the door but turned at the last second. "You give up now, and you give up on finding the truth, which means your father died for nothing."

"Don't you *dare* use him to manipulate me!"

"Okay, you live your life in hiding, then, wondering what it is that makes you so special that people out there want you dead. Because they won't stop."

"The police will help me. At least they'll keep us safe from people like you."

"Not if they're involved."

"I'll take my chances."

Arthur walked slowly towards her. "The only way you can move on with your life is to get to the bottom of it yourself. I'm your best chance at achieving that, and I ain't accepting no for an answer."

Nova shook her head. "You can't make me! You can lead a whore to water... *horse*... but you can't make it drink."

Her blunder with the proverb made Arthur cry out with laughter.

It was the first time Nova had ever heard him laugh. He wasn't someone who laughed a great deal, and it sounded quite endearing and humorous. She suppressed the urge to smile. His laughter had disarmed her, and she could no longer hold it together, breaking into giggle fits.

The commotion drew the nurse's attention once again. She appeared at the doorway, her expression stern as she shushed them sharply. But her reprimand only fuelled their laughter, which bubbled up louder and more uncontrollable.

Arthur, struggling to stifle his own amusement, wiped tears from his eyes and turned to Owen, who lay propped up in bed. His face, now serious, betrayed none of the earlier mirth. He leaned closer, his voice dropping to a more earnest tone. "Tell us what happened in that there passageway."

52

The light flashed, but the man's head blocked it, casting a blue, spiritual halo over him, leaving Owen's partially hidden body shrouded in his dark silhouette.

"Is someone there?" he asked.

What if the man saw him? What would he do? What was he capable of?

"Hello? Is someone there?"

Just as the bulb lit up again, an alarm sounded from inside the basement.

The man's glowing outline melted into the darkness as he turned and left, and Owen heard his footsteps pounding away until he could no longer hear them over the alarm. He wheeled around and had another look at the exit. The old, steel door lacked any electronic locks, and if there was a manual bolt or lever, it was either hidden from view or simply not installed on this door. The blue lamp flashed. Owen used the brief burst of light to search for a locking mechanism and saw a handle with a rubber grip on the wall. It moved with force, and he heard a click. He had to lean on the door with his shoulder to shunt it aside. It rattled open like a tombstone, grinding on its rusty runners, and was just as painstaking to close.

It took just a few seconds for his eyes to adjust inside the next room. Timber workbenches stood in symmetrical rows, surrounded by lathes, metal clamps, and other pieces of old machinery. The workbenches were scored and ink-stained like high school desks. The concrete floor was covered in dust and cracked with weeds crawling out of the rifts and fissures. Long vines climbed the walls, as though attempting to make a break for freedom, and the windows were covered in dust and grime, making it impossible to see outside.

Tiptoeing across the dusty floor, he pushed open the main door and came out under a tower of iron scaffolding covered by a blue tarpaulin. A strong gust raised it like a garage door. A chain-link fence surrounded the old factory, crowned with coiled barbed wire. In the distance, he saw a small airport, it's lights blinking in the darkness.

He ran to the fence and felt his way along the perimeter, looking for an opening or a gate. Just then, a glider tipped its wings and descended behind the factory roofline, aiming for the airport a few miles away. Its silent movement was hypnotic, but Owen's thoughts circled back to his escape. The distant sound of waves crashing against the shore beckoned him to the opposite side of the premises. As he approached, the full scope of the factory's precarious location became apparent. It had been constructed on a rugged, rocky ledge that jutted out alarmingly over a steep incline that plunged sharply towards the ocean. Beyond the rocks was nothing. No sight of land, light, of life. Just a black void that stretched infinitely.

He worked his way along the fence, looking for a place to escape. At the midpoint was a gaping hole at the bottom, large enough for a cat to squeeze through. Lying on his back, he fed his feet through, followed by his bare, skinny legs. He shuffled forward on his bare buttocks, navigating carefully underneath the tangled, sharp-edged wires. Once he had forced his waist through, he stretched his thin arms above his head, pushing his shoulders and head out of the opening. He stood, dusting himself down, and looked left and right, trying to discern the best way to go. Torn between following the coast and heading to the airport, he chose to follow the glider's path and began to run.

As he neared the airport, his path abruptly led him into a boggy marsh. The ground gave way beneath him, he stumbled forward, and his momentum carried him face-first into thick, wet mud. Some splattered in his mouth, its unpleasant, earthy taste forcing him to spit repeatedly.

Struggling to regain his footing, he hauled himself out of the mire with considerable effort. The mud stubbornly clung to him, making every movement a laborious task. He shifted along on his stomach, using his elbows to haul himself forward. The consistency of the ground gradually changed as the mud became less yielding and more solid. When the earth finally hardened enough to support his weight, he pushed himself upright. His lab coat and skin were caked with muck. He took a moment to brush off the worst of the mud and tried to work out another way to reach the airport. He couldn't see beyond the marshy terrain, so he went back to the factory, stooping low at the perimeter fence to avoid being seen.

He climbed down the rocky incline onto a small, enclosed beach with rocks at each end. The sand between his bare toes was freezing and wet. Further along, three rowing boats sat in disciplined formation on the beach.

He took the first boat and dragged it off the sand into the water, gasping at the bitter cold on his skin. He pushed it out through the gentle waves until it began to bob afloat. Jumping aboard, he ran out the oars and began rowing.

At first, he sent the boat in circles, the oars banging against the gunwale. He paddled frantically, trying to turn the boat so he faced the shore with his back towards the open sea. When he finally found his rhythm, he aimed away from the factory, watching the coastline diminish and become nothing more than a black shadow against the night sky as it shrank from view.

A considerable distance from land, he channelled all of his strength into the right oar, adjusting the boat's direction so as to guide it along the coastline, searching for any sign of safer, more hospitable land. Fighting against the pull of the current and the boat's natural tendency to drift tested his endurance. The water churned and splashed around him, heightening the tension in his muscles. He focussed on holding a steady course, his breath erupting in loud, sharp bursts as he navigated the relentless waves. The noisy current buffeting the sides of the fibreglass hull and the rhythmic dip and rise of the oars became a meditative pattern.

The coastline soon dissolved in a thin layer of mist and devoured the sea and sky. He paused, raising the oars out of the water as the thickening mist threw his sense of direction. He dropped the oars back into the sea and made steady strokes back towards the shore.

Out of the haze, a small ferry materialised seemingly from nowhere, its lights barely penetrating the dense, swirling mist, its outline barely visible. As it churned through the water, its wake created a series of swells that bobbed him up and down. With all his strength, he called out, his voice rising above the sound of the motor and slapping waves. "Help! Down here!" he shouted. He waved his arms frantically, hoping the ferry's crew spotted him.

But his cries were drowned out by the disturbed water, and the ferry kept moving until the mist wrapped around it.

He rowed again until his arms grew numb and his elbows seized, forcing him to take another break.

He thought about Nova and the kiss they had shared. Had he gone too far? Not one to be easily pushed around or swayed by compulsion, she had allowed him to get close. The smell of her skin and tenderness of her mouth brought a smile to his face. He had always dreamed of having a girlfriend, someone he could love and who loved him back, and he'd found a girl he liked under the strangest of circumstances. He knew he had no business in her financial affairs and wondered if she would ever forgive him. He would risk getting in trouble to earn back her respect. In fact, he would risk his life.

He pushed too hard on the portside oar, forcing it to shift sharply aft. The handle pitched forward, disconnecting the oar from the rowlock, and it slipped from his freezing fingers into the water.

Not a great deal spooked Owen, but fear and helplessness stood head and shoulders above all other emotions right then. If only he had learned to swim. He needed his inhaler. Without it, he needed to stay calm, regulate his breathing, and carry out careful asthma management.

He drove both of his hands into the ice-cold sea, cleaving the water, searching for the missing oar, unable to see anything in the darkness encompassing him.

He still had the oar on the starboard side, but when he reached for it, he realised it had also slipped out of the rowlock and had been lost to the unforgiving sea.

"Help!"

The wind had picked up. He could feel it feeding the boat's momentum. But he no longer had the tools to influence the boat's path.

The mist progressively increased, wrapping around him in wraithlike drifts. He felt his pockets for the cigarettes, needing a smoke, until he realised he had no lighter.

His final thought was of Nova. Then he allowed the ocean currents and his fading consciousness to sweep him away.

53

The days dragged on without any leads and with every enquiry ending in a dead end, yet Arthur became increasingly obsessed with deconstructing everything they'd learned. He spent hours sifting through information, determined to separate fact from fiction. His notebook had become a repository for every detail, every scrap of insight they'd uncovered so far. By jotting down and analysing each piece, he hoped he might spark new ideas or uncover hidden connections to finally break the case open. Unanswered questions piled up. Where had Owen teleported to? What was that factory for? What role did the Serbian play? What was the man at the computers up to, and who was the businesswoman? He'd sacrificed sleep and barely ate anymore. Tobacco and rum had become his only companions; crutches he relied on to keep a clear mind. Empty bottles lined the galley floor, toppling whenever the boat rode a big wave.

Arthur stepped out of the cabin for a breath of fresh air. He sat on the guard rail at the stern, watching the sun dip below the horizon. His feet dangled above the emerald-green sea. Just behind him, a sudden gust of wind lifted the red vinyl sheet, exposing the array of chemical products he stored inside plastic packing crates: paint cans, methylated spirits, pesticide and insecticide tubs, industrial bleach, and empty gas bottles. He swiftly hopped down from the guard rail, pressing his foot onto the sheet to keep it from blowing away. One of the brick pavers that had held it down was missing, a reminder of how he had launched it at the attackers with a burning rag to ignite the gas and destroy their boat. Using one of the gas bottles to pin the sheet down, he sat cross-legged on the deck, thinking about those physicist engineers. Murder disguised as suicide, careless and poorly executed. Suspicion had steadily grown to the point where it was no longer plausible to believe the ATM was involved. But Arthur already knew this. He'd known this from the start.

The media now pointed their fingers at some dark agency operating on the fringes of the law. It was only a matter of time before the world learned the truth.

Legs crossed up the wall, Nova lay quietly and reflectively in the hammock, just staring at the ceiling in a pleasant trance. A damp smell permeated the cabin, caused by a leak in the rafters, making the wood swell and warp, disturbing her reverie. She pined for her father. There had been no right time to organise a funeral. How could she commit him to the grave when there was no body? The week before, a public vigil had been held, with people paying their respects by way of flower bouquets, candles, and cards laid by the walls built around the teleport.

According to the news, the turnout had been overwhelming, with thousands attending to display their sorrow, and bouquet donations rolling in daily, constructing a vast sea of brightly coloured flowers. She imagined her father, happy in a realm of light and loving spirits, watching over her.

Nova went to check on Owen, who was sound asleep on the bed. He had been discharged from the hospital three days earlier but was now running a fever. She took the damp flannel from his forehead, ran it under the tap in the galley, and placed it back on his face just as Arthur returned from the top deck.

She sat beside him as he picked up his pen and notebook. Maybe what he needed was a second pair of eyes, someone to bounce ideas off. "Anything I can do?"

He barely glanced up at her. "Give me space."

His tone carried an edge of anger, and Nova knew it was because Owen had been unable to deliver reliable information about his whereabouts. He didn't know who the man was. He didn't know who the businesswoman was. He didn't even know where the factory was. He didn't know *anything*.

Arthur had returned to Porthleven while Owen remained in the hospital, determined to uncover any clues that might shed light on the mystery surrounding the abandoned factory. For two days, he questioned locals, scoured every inch of the coast for the building, and dug for any scrap of information he could find. He visited the council office, sifted through public records, and examined old maps in the local library, searching for any trace of Teletron's presence. Despite his efforts, not a single building was registered in the tech giant's name, and no one in the town could recall the company ever operating in the area. It struck Nova and Arthur as odd given Porthleven was the only town within a five-mile radius of a local airport.

It was as though Owen had got his bearings all wrong. By any measure, he was unreliable at conveying information. His short attention span and shockingly inadequate memory made him an unworthy source. Something in his report just didn't add up.

Nova studied Arthur as he scribbled something inside his notebook. He knew these gains had come at considerable cost to Owen in terms of his health. Even so, it had earned him no respect and very little sympathy, irritating her again.

"Having any luck?" Nova asked.

"Giving me a headache, this thing."

"That's probably the drink."

He gave her a scowl that warned her to back off, and she did. He made a visible effort to be unpleasant, but this was his home, and she was his guest, and as much as she cringed to admit it, she felt safe around him. All the while the Serbian was out there, she relied on him. She was afraid the killer would strike again soon. He had become a spectre who stole her sleep and occupied her thoughts. She knew it was a matter of time before their paths crossed again. Every move they made, every place they visited, he always got wind of it. How? She had little doubt that he had professional tracking capabilities, an expert in detecting a trail by observing the broken twigs and trampled grass most people would never notice. Maybe he belonged to some highly trained operative outfit.

Still, she hadn't given up *all* hope. As dire as things were, she was still alive; she still had her mental strength. A part of her had accepted this was the life she had been intended.

Arthur was on the rum again, drowning his memories in drink, venting his drunken frustrations on anyone in proximity, his writing becoming more and more chaotic. She had learned to read the signs. His jaw would stiffen, his tone would turn snappy, he would start fidgeting, and he would be up and down from the table. She'd also learned not to cross too many wires and when to button her lip.

"She's government!" said Owen.

Arthur craned his neck towards the bed.

"Who is?" asked Nova.

Owen rubbed his eyes. "That woman in the factory."

54

Owen sat up, slowly swung his legs out of bed, and planted his feet on the wooden floor.

Arthur put down his pen. "You're sure?"

"Yeah."

"What's her name?"

Owen ran his hand across his chin, shrugged, and gave no answer.

"And you ain't got a clue where she teleported to?"

Owen stared at his lap. "An island, I think."

Nova went and sat next to him on the bed. "You're sure she's a politician?"

"I've seen her in the news."

"You can't read."

"On telly."

"You don't own a television."

"I lived in an orphanage. It had a telly."

Arthur turned back to the table, skinned up a cigarette, put it in his mouth, but just stared at nothing.

Nova eased Owen back down on the bed and adjusted his pillows. He coughed, so she held out his inhaler to puff on.

She joined Arthur at the table. "What are you thinking?"

"I'm thinking we should have sent *you* through that there teleportal."

"Be fair, he didn't have his hearing aid in; he couldn't hear what they were saying very well."

"The daft bugger don't even know what day it is."

Nova looked at Owen, who slept again, and gave Arthur a disapproving look. "What did I tell you? About being nicer to him? Let's say she *is* a politician. Why would she go through the trouble of sneaking into this factory only to teleport out?"

Arthur shrugged. "She's probably just some random lady, that's all."

"Nothing's ever random, you said so yourself."

He scowled at Nova. "Don't you get clever with me, young lady!"

Owen tossed and turned restlessly on the bed, his brow furrowed in his discomfort, muttering indistinct words. Nova replaced the damp flannel on his forehead and smoothed the edges, ensuring it stayed in place. Then she drew the duvet up over his shoulders, tucking him in snugly. Despite their shared moment of intimacy at the physicist's house, she knew better than to regard him in any romantic light. He was her friend, and the connection between them was spawned out of mutual tragedy, leaving them both bereft of family. Just thinking of her father triggered a new wave of grief. It would take time for healing acceptance to be reached.

Arthur lifted his glass, only realising it was empty when he tipped air into his mouth. He stared at the glass in disbelief and turned to the empty bottle among the many scattered across the floor. He looked at Nova and stared at her head. "Taking a long time to grow back, that hair of yours. Still looks freshly shaved."

Her right hand trailed across her head, the bristly carpet tickling her palm. It reminded her she hadn't taken her calcium channel blockers yet that day. She took them now with a glass of water.

Back in her chair, she propped her elbows on the table. "There was something that I wanted to show you. Or tell you, I think." She paused. "No, it's gone."

She couldn't keep still at the table, her feet tapping against the floor.

Arthur glanced up from his notebook. "You can be quite annoying, you can."

She opened her mouth, then closed it, turning her attention on Owen as she pondered the politician. A yawn that had been building vanished abruptly with a sudden recollection that had her springing up from her chair and hurrying over to the bed, shaking Owen vigorously until he stirred awake.

"Did she have short hair? About thirty years old?"

"Who?" asked Owen, dazed and disoriented.

"The politician you saw."

He paused in thought. "Yes."

"Miriam Payne. You recognised her on the news last week. She announced she was stepping down from the government. I think because of breast cancer."

Owen still looked confused but agreed. "Okay."

"Why was she teleporting out of the country?"

Owen shrugged.

Arthur looked up from his notebook. "Unlikely."

"What if it's true?"

"We ain't got no proof, so it don't mean nothing."

Nova returned to her chair at the table, her mind occupied with thoughts of Miriam Payne and any possible motives for her sudden departure from the country via teleportation. After some time, she abandoned the effort, finding herself unable to come up with a plausible reason.

Her flashbacks of the teleport were not always memories but products of her imagination. She struggled to distinguish between what she had actually seen and what she had conjured up. But a thought tiptoed into her mind about the cameraman removed by the security officers at the exposition. At the time, she had assumed he was either filming in a restricted space or lacked a valid licence. Upon reflection, she realised he'd broken no laws. He had caused no harm, risked no lives. It made her reconsider the situation. Could the security team have had a different motive for their actions? Had they been involved in the takedown of London City Teleport, and did they attempt to prevent the cameraman from filming to limit the amount of video evidence? Given that hundreds of cameras would have been operational at the scene that day – everyone in modern-day Britain owned one, and security cameras were installed at every major transport hub to monitor random violence and suspicious activity – there would have been ample footage.

"There must be some camera footage from the day of the explosion."

Arthur put his head in his hands. "What's your point?"

"Just thinking out loud here. Did the staff working at the teleport that day die in the explosion, or were they involved somehow? If we can get hold of camera footage, either from the press or from uploaded public content or security cameras, maybe we might find out who was involved. I know it's a long shot, but…"

Arthur agreed. It *was* a long shot. To begin with, security camera recordings were usually pixelated. Even if it was of the highest quality, even if the authorities hadn't already scoured through every piece of footage, getting their hands on any of it would prove difficult. He had a few reliable friends and could probably call in a few favours. But it wasn't worth the pursuit. By and large, identifying who was involved would not only be time-consuming but also fraught with guesswork.

Arthur grabbed a wheel of cheese out of the fridge and a knife. He placed them on a wooden board on the table. "Help yourself."

Nova licked her lips, eyeing the wheel of cheese before her. "Brie, my favourite," she murmured with a hint of anticipation. She reached for the knife, but her enthusiasm was tempered by frustration. The knife proved difficult to operate as it kept slipping and veering off the side of the cheese. Each attempt to cut through the creamy surface resulted in uneven slices, the knife jerking unpredictably as she tried to maintain control. At one point, she nicked herself and was fortunate to draw only a tiny speck of blood. Then she realised something.

"What's with the frown?" asked Arthur.

Nova sucked the blood off her finger and just stared at the knife. "It's so strange, but I'm using my left hand when all my life I've been right-handed."

"You're going senile in your young age."

Reluctant to share her hospital results, fearing it was a sign of admission and acceptance, she eventually spoke her mind.

"There's something I haven't told you. I took your advice and went to get some tests done at the hospital after we stayed on your boat the first time."

"Good girl. What were the results?"

She paused, hesitant to say more. "They said I might have Alzheimer's."

Arthur put down his pen and just stared at her. "You ain't never mentioned this." He paused. "But it explains your odd behaviour sometimes."

"Like what?"

"Things you say and sometimes do. Like walking around the boat deck like a zombie in the middle of a storm. Looking for your shoes when you're still wearing them. Now you don't even know which hand you eat from. You're like that twenty-five-year-old physicist who forgot she had a nut allergy and ate a curry full of cashews."

Nova raised her eyebrow with a piece of cheese paused halfway between the table and her open mouth. "What did you say?"

"That girl Dr. Azad told us about. The *Plucky Pioneer.* She trialled them teleportals. I asked my mate in the police about her. She died after eating a curry. After our chat with Dr. Azad, I was suspicious and thought she may have been force-fed the food, like them physicists and the bleach. Turns out, it was just poor judgement. She tucked into a nutty curry not knowing what she had ordered, no suspicious circumstances at all."

"No, you said twenty-five?"

"Yeah, she was twenty-five years old."

Nova looked at the floor, unable to hide her shock.

Arthur had roasted her on his boat, suggesting she'd picked up some kind of biological defect after using teleportation. She had dismissed it because she didn't want to believe anything was wrong with her. Now she wondered if she had been wrong to dismiss it. Was there a problem with the teleportals after all?

"It all makes sense now."

"What does?"

"I'm so stupid."

"Ain't going to argue with you there."

"She didn't make a mistake with the curry. Not in a normal sense. She had Alzheimer's."

"You don't know that."

"When I was at the hospital, the doctor told me that the youngest person ever to be diagnosed with Alzheimer's was a twenty-five-year-old girl. That was three years ago. They found out during the autopsy. He told me that the discovery changed medical protocols across the country. That's why they checked my test results for Alzheimer's. It must have been her. Think about it. She was the first to go through the teleportals. Then, weeks or months or however long it was later, she ate a curry full of cashew nuts and died. Because of her Alzheimer's, she forgot about her allergy."

"I see where you're going with this."

"She had Alzheimer's, and so do I. Coincidence?"

Arthur's eyes lit up with a sparkle of glee. "It causes brain damage. Teleportation affects the brain, causing Alzheimer's Disease."

"And I've just realised my dad showed signs, too, before he died. Ever since we got back from New York, he sometimes acted strange, even the day we went to Expo. He walked off from the cottage towards the forest, said he was looking for a message from the man in black. I knew something was wrong then. I think he had Alzheimer's, too."

"There must be many other travellers in the country who don't know they have Alzheimer's."

"Must be."

Arthur stubbed out his cigarette. "You ask me, I think it's time we paid the CEO of Teletron a visit."

55

The house was situated in an exclusive London suburb, where luxury was the norm and privacy a guarded necessity. Enclosed by imposing brick walls that rose to a formidable two metres, the perimeter was further reinforced by wrought-iron rails that gave the structure a fortress-like quality. A winding driveway, bordered by trimmed hedges and strategically placed security cameras, meandered through manicured gardens leading up to a grand double garage.

Arthur parked his battered truck in front of the house. The sight that greeted them was as unsettling as it was unexpected: the word *Murderer* had been scrawled in large, blood-red letters across the brick wall. Nova exchanged her glance with Owen, who looked only slightly disturbed. Day had faded into night, the steady rain veiling everything in a cold, wet haze. Nova and Owen huddled beneath Arthur's black umbrella, its bent and crooked ribs offering little protection against the downpour. They hurried from the truck, their footsteps splashing in the growing puddles as they made their way towards the imposing wrought-iron gates, which swung open as soon as they arrived, revealing the darkened driveway beyond, beckoning them into the unknown. A loudspeaker crackled, and a blue holographic face bloomed out of the intercom. *"Come on up. I've been expecting you."*

Nova looked at Arthur. "Is that the CEO?"

Arthur nodded, recognising the man's familiar face. Their last encounter had been a heated exchange following the unjust cancellation of his contract. He hadn't expected an invitation. At best, he had imagined a brief exchange through the gate or a fleeting conversation over the intercom before being turned away.

They marched towards the house beneath the intensifying rain as the long driveway vanished into the greyish blur.

They stopped at the porch. Arthur furled the umbrella and shook the water off.

The front door was wide open.

The entrance hall, lit by crystal chandeliers suspended from the high ceiling, was exquisite, with a majestic clock beneath a large, spiral staircase, expensive paintings lining the walls, and marble floors throughout.

They filed into an enormous living room of polished floors and pristine windows. A six-piece leather suite in the middle of the room created an island of sofas and armchairs in a white, marble sea, more than enough space and luxury for one man living alone. On the wall hung spectacular oil paintings within gilded frames. Nova went from canvas to canvas, admiring the artworks: a seascape with a fishing trawler caught in rough seas, a toddler in a third-world country drawing lines across the sun-baked ground, a herd of wildebeest grazing in the savanna, a psychedelic abstract that, upon careful viewing, revealed two human outlines embedded within the shapes and patterns. The CEO's portrait hung there, too, executed with photographic accuracy. He had poise and exuded power.

When the real-life CEO walked in, the contrast was stark and undeniable. He wore rumpled tracksuit trousers and a grey long-sleeved vest. His hair was a tousled mess, and the fatigue etched into his face was unmistakable. Blue veins traced across his nose and cheeks like dyed tear tracks, which accentuated the weariness in his eyes. Despite the obvious signs of wear and tear, his tanned, hairy frame hinted at the big, fine-looking man he was beneath it all.

A brief stare-down ensued. As they sized him up, there was nothing about him to indicate a threat.

"Thanks for coming," he said. "Please, sit!"

He collapsed into a leather armchair and grabbed a glass of red wine from the side table. "I know why you're all here, and to be honest, I'm a little relieved. I have something for you."

"You know who we are?" asked Nova as she sat down.

With delayed reactions, he faced them and said, "Do you know how long I've worked for Teletron?"

Nova shook her head.

"Twenty-five years. Do you know how long Teletron has been in operation?"

"Twenty-five years," said Arthur.

"Correct. I founded the company, started it from scratch when I was just thirty. I was an ambitious, young tech. Look how far we've come. Teleportation, who would've imagined? What a game-changer. The timing. Impeccable. Five years after the last international flight leaves a runway and teleportation is snap in its place. It was supposed to change the world."

Arthur showed his exasperation with a loud sigh. "That's the problem, that is. People like you with your revolutionary ideas and reckless plans. It's always about changing the world without any regard for consequences. When it all goes wrong, all you can do is apologise for them lives you ruin. What went wrong with them teleportals?"

"Nothing went wrong with them. They were perfect. They did exactly what they were designed to do, transporting people from A to B, every single atom."

"No, they left people with brain damage."

"I remember you," he said, staring at Arthur. "You were a contractor at Teletron; you did some building maintenance and repairs. I also know you sneaked inside Teletron and snooped around to find out what happened at London City Teleport. I know you believe Teletron is hiding something."

"Like leaving people with Alzheimer's Disease?"

After receiving a series of death threats, security had been significantly heightened following the explosion, he explained. He had even gone so far as to hire a private security guard for his home, fearing for his safety. He blamed social portals for falsely accusing Teletron of being responsible for the London City Teleport explosion. As the narrative shifted, media outlets also began to doubt the ATM's involvement and turned their scrutiny towards Teletron instead.

"The slightest whiff of a cover-up and it immediately hits the press as fact when it's just bent truth and embellished lies. Makes me so angry."

Nova didn't believe him. Clearly, he was doing his best to look blameless. "Did Teletron bomb London City Teleport?"

"You're asking the wrong question, my dear."

"If Teletron ain't behind the nuke," said Arthur, pointing at the CEO, "it knows something about it. As the person in charge, don't dare plead ignorance. The buck stops with you."

He shook his head. "I'm afraid you have also been reading the wrong stories in the news. But what does it really matter? Teletron's name is ruined."

Nova sensed a rage building inside Arthur. She feared he'd go from rational action to explosive reaction at any moment.

The CEO continued. "The damage is already done. There is no coming back. Teletron will close down, and the world will lose out on the greatest mode of transport ever created."

"Care to elaborate there?" asked Arthur.

The CEO passed a thick, blue file to Arthur. "Everything you need to know is in this file. I've wracked my brain trying to figure out what to do. Honestly, I just wanted to disappear. It's been really tough. After Dr. Azad told me about you three and what happened at Teletron, I decided to take matters into my own hands and did some investigating. I had my suspicions about my supreme commander and the archon of biomedicine after they started making decisions without consulting me, so I paid a professional hacker to dig into their online activity and recover any deleted files or correspondence. And that's when I discovered what had really happened. I wrote a twelve-page report explaining everything and compiled the evidence I had intercepted from their messages and confidential records. It's all in the file I just gave you. I've spent all day debating whether to take it to the police. I just can't bring myself to do it. Now you're here, I want *you* to take it."

Arthur stood with balled fists, clearly agitated. "Does this file include their terrorist activities?"

Nova feared it was about to escalate into a bloodbath. She had already seen enough blood spilled with enough death on her conscience. She didn't need any more.

The CEO put down his wine glass. "Please, sit down."

Arthur slowly lowered himself onto the sofa.

"No one at Teletron planted the explosives at London City Teleport. You think we have the capability to nuke a teleport? Think again. It came from an organisation far bigger and more powerful."

With frightening calm, Arthur said, "The government!"

The CEO nodded. He removed a white macro key from his trouser pocket and switched on the overhead chandeliers, as if flaunting his wealth. "What this country has witnessed is in the worst tradition of the British establishment and political power."

Leafing through the file, Arthur poured over the trove of documents to back the CEO's extraordinary claims, including correspondence between senior Teletron employees and the government. The CEO's full report, bound by a brass clip, was also in there. He carefully picked through all the paperwork, skimming over blueprints and pages, dissecting paragraphs.

"It's all in there, I assure you. Including details on certain corrupted institutions of state."

Arthur read out a title on one of the documents. "The Final Solution?"

The CEO walked over to a minibar and topped up his glass with red wine. A small vial of yellow liquid was in his hand.

"What's in the tube?" asked Nova.

He held it in front of his face. "One drop of this will make you feel hungover. Two drops, semi-paralysed. Three, you'll be knocking on death's door. Four or more? It's goodnight."

Arthur shook his head. "Taking the easy way out?"

"I don't care what you think."

"It wasn't your fault," said Nova.

"I'm not sure I can live with myself. When you read the report, you'll understand."

Arthur placed the file on the sofa arm. "Why don't you just tell us."

He paused and took a deep breath. "You remember what happened to the Jews during the Second World War?"

Arthur nodded. "They were exterminated."

"And how were they exterminated?"

"Starved, beaten, shot. Many were gassed."

He nodded. "The Final Solution. You would think that the instruments of power had learned their lessons from humanity's dark past."

"What type of gas was used in that there auditorium?"

"Cyanogen Chloride, a highly volatile asphyxiate. At first, it irritates the eyes and causes a runny nose, quickly followed by nausea, dizziness, confusion, and vomiting. It messes with the body's ability to process oxygen, resulting in organ failure, extensive damage to the brain, lungs, heart, and blood vessels. Death comes quickly if exposed to enough of it in an enclosed space."

"Why was it used at London City Teleport along with the nuke? It don't make no sense."

"To run an inventory and work out who didn't show up. The gassing was completed within minutes. Everyone inside the auditorium died quickly. The nuke wiped out all traces of the gas, and no autopsies were carried out because there were no bodies. Soon after they were all gassed to death, the security officers, hired by the government, entered the auditorium in gas masks. They ran facial and iris recognition wands over the attendees and crosschecked their details against the guest lists and the national database."

Nova felt off-colour, the news all too much to take in as she pictured her father's tragic end, suffocating in his seat as he waited for her to return from the toilet. But at last, she had her hands on the truth.

"That still don't make no sense," said Arthur. "Why not collect their names and biometric ID when they arrived at the teleport? Then all they had to do was nuke the place, not waste time gassing them first."

"They did. All entry points to the auditorium were already set up with fingerprint verification. You couldn't get through the turnstiles unless you had registered to attend the Expo and had scanned in. The stewards checked the fingerprint scans as people arrived and crosschecked the names on the invitation list against the national database. The thing is, about two weeks before the explosion was to be carried out, a hacker broke into the central repository of biometric data and messed with the stored identities. The central repository stores biometric data on three separate, remote servers. Fingerprint templates kept on one, facial recognition on another, and iris data on a third. A full biometric examination crosschecks biometric templates across all three servers when running its identity verification. That's how it typically works. Based on the data I intercepted between the government and my senior staff, the fingerprint server got hacked. While much of the data was left intact, many identities were either lost or altered during the hacking event. To be absolutely sure, the security team used mobile biometric wands on the eyes and faces of the dead to scan and confirm their identification."

"What was so special about them people at Expo?" asked Arthur.

"As I said, everything you need to know is in my report. The Merchant was behind it. Pulled all the strings to frame the ATM and deflect suspicion away from the government. Well, I refuse to let Teletron take responsibility for the government's criminal actions."

The CEO stood. He threw and caught the vial of yellow poison, indicating that he was ready to end his life. "Silence is golden, but so is secrecy. The problem is, how do you maintain both when a few years down the track, you discover that—"

The CEO's head snapped back. A red hole appeared at his temple. The other side of his skull exploded in a shower of blood and pale matter. The open wound oozed gore at slow, syrup-like speed. He stood for a second, swayed, then dropped heavily to the marble floor. The vial of poison bounced across the floor, spinning top over tail, but the lid stayed on and the yellow contents remained constrained by its solid glass walls. It rolled to a stop against Nova's shoe.

She gasped and clapped a hand over her mouth, holding back the urge to scream.

Arthur dragged Nova and Owen down in front of the sofa. He held his finger against his lips.

Arthur spotted the white macro key clutched in the CEO's hand, his dead eyes glued to it. He crawled towards him and snatched the key. He switched off the chandelier lights before peering around the sofa. The window had turned milky white around a star-shaped hole. He crawled to the opposite end of the sofa. He saw a door. "Follow me."

On their hands and knees, they crawled in single file to the study next door. It was like a time capsule of the eighties, full of heavy, classic furniture and decades-old floral wallpaper. A locked cabinet equipped with guns and hunting trophies took up an entire wall. The CEO was clearly a weapons enthusiast. Many looked old or antique, ranging from rifles and pistols to rare muskets. He planted his hands on the glass, staring in awe at the arsenal before him, tempted to break in and take one. By foolish mistake, he had left his gun inside his truck. But he was unsure whether the display items were loaded and didn't want to attract attention since he couldn't be sure where the gunman was or how many there were.

Owen stood at the top of a staircase in the corner of the room. "There's a way out."

56

Arthur was last to reach the bottom of the staircase, where a locked door impeded their escape. Using the macro key, he tried to disengage the lock, but it was fingerprint encrypted. At the top of the door was a classic bolt mechanism. He slid it aside, and to his surprise the door opened.

The next room was completely dark, leaving them blindly feeling their way until automated fluorescent tube lights came on, lighting up the inside of the double garage. Arthur dragged a wooden workbench over and propped it neatly beneath the door handle. With Owen's help, he reinforced the blockade with a heavy, well-stocked tool chest.

He turned to inspect the garage. An electric motorcycle with an underwhelming 19 kW motor and learner plates was parked on its stand beside a dark green convertible car replete with a spoiler and sports trim. Chalk and cheese.

Arthur scrolled through the various options on the macro key and clicked the car icon. He attempted to start the engine, but, like the door, it required the CEO's fingerprint. Turning his attention to the motorcycle, he examined the options on the key and discovered it had no security features. Without hesitation, he pressed the ignition symbol. The motor turned on, displaying a thirty-two per cent battery charge. He handed the macro key and blue file to Nova, gripped the handlebars, and swung his leg over.

"Hop on!"

Owen climbed on the back.

Steadfast in refusal to climb on the motorcycle, Nova's fear was dammed up inside her. She would never forget the slightly confused expression on the CEO's face in the half-second after he was executed and collapsed to the floor.

The sound of wood splitting as someone tried to kick in the only door to the garage distracted her.

Arthur revved the motorcycle. "Get on!"

Nova's face tightened, and her hand holding the macro key visibly trembled.

"Open the garage!" Owen shrieked.

A final, resounding blow struck the door with such force the chest of tools balanced against it toppled over. The impact sent a cascade of metal clattering to the floor—screwdrivers, wrenches, pliers, hammers scattered in every direction. Nova glanced at her fingers, front and back, turning her palms over repeatedly. "I need to wash my hands. They smell funny."

Owen snatched the key out of Nova's hand and tapped the garage icon. The boxed roller door had seen heavy use, but it rolled back over their heads, revealing the wet driveway. The rain had ceased, leaving a damp, heavy stillness in the air. Dark clouds spread across the night sky like a thick blanket, and as they thickened, the stars vanished one by one.

When Owen looked back at Nova, she sniffed her palms. "They smell of lavender."

Owen grabbed Nova's forearm and pulled her towards the bike.

Roused by his aggression, she snapped back to alertness, confused by her surroundings and the racket coming from the door. "Where are we?"

Arthur glanced at the door. It had opened about six inches. "Right where we don't want to be."

Nova reached her right leg over the saddle and climbed on, wrapping her arms around Owen's waist, gripping the blue file across his lap. In doing so, the brass clip binding the report snapped back and flipped out of the file onto the floor.

The gate at the end of the driveway remained wide open, and Arthur sped towards it, weaving along the winding path in their desperate attempt to escape.

Nova twisted round and saw three men breach the door, crash past the collapsed tool chest, and chase into the garage through to the driveway. Before they could shoot their guns, Arthur swerved around a white Merc with dark tinted windows parked in front of his truck. Nova continued to watch over her shoulder as the CEO's house receded and the men scrambled inside the Merc but lost sight of them when Arthur left the neighbourhood and pulled out into traffic on a busy main road.

In no time, the white Merc caught up, closing the distance between them until the driver's scrunched-up face was clearly visible when Nova glanced over her shoulder.

Arched over the handlebars, Arthur pulled on the throttle and pushed the motor to its maximum speed.

Nova gripped the lapels of Owen's cardigan so tightly that it nearly tore. In the process, her hold on the file slipped, and several pages were snatched away by the wind. They spiralled downward, landing flat on the wet asphalt as if glued in place.

The Merc screeched to a halt. The passenger leaned out of the door and quickly gathered the loose pages.

Then, with a renewed burst of speed, it surged forward, spraying water up from the tyres as it sped towards them to continue the pursuit.

Nova stood on the footpegs and stabilised her centre of gravity by holding Owen's collar to maintain her balance.

Arthur saw her in his side mirror and yelled, "What are you doing?" over the soughing wind.

"Keep the bike straight!" Nova shouted back.

She crouched on the saddle, swung around with a graceful pirouette, steadied herself, and dropped back onto the saddle, her breath coming in shallow bursts with the risky manoeuvre. Now she faced the Merc, sitting back-to-back with Owen, who reached over his shoulder and held onto Nova's hood so she didn't fall headfirst off the back.

Nova scrutinised the Merc with better clarity in her altered position. It had international plates and had been polished to a showroom shine. The occupants inside appeared more like shadows than people.

"I'm going to release some of these pages into the road."

Arthur shook his head. "No! We need all them pages. It's the only evidence we've got."

"I'll only release a few. It's the only way we'll shake them off."

Arthur glanced at the side mirror. The Merc was three cars back. Someone inside started shooting from an open window.

Zigzagging out of the firing line, Arthur leaned into the sharp bends and winding turns, trying to maintain its top speed to stay ahead of the Merc. Nova pulled out two pages and threw them into the air like she was spreading confetti.

The Merc, as anticipated, skidded to a stop, blocking one lane of traffic. Two men hopped out from either side, darting across the road, undaunted by oncoming cars, forcing them to swerve at the last minute. The men were commanding in looks and fit, moving with an athletic grace. The driver, lit up by the interior light, was a beefier, hairier man with a beard and an afro. Nova could tell by their determination they would stop at nothing.

The Merc quickly began to catch up. The other road users scurried out of the way, intimidated by the erratic driving and continuous horn blasts.

Nova fished out another two pages. They fluttered in her hand like birds desperate to escape her grasp. She launched them into the air, watching as they soared and tumbled before settling on the wet asphalt.

The Merc pulled over again so the man on the passenger side could hop out. He darted back and forth, gathering up the papers.

It gave them another chance to outrun the men, but Arthur couldn't make the traffic lights and had to stop.

Nova kept an eye on the Merc. How much longer would these men play her game?

Smoke oozed from the Merc's tyres as it surged forward, fishtailing twice before it was expertly brought in line.

On green, Arthur twisted back the throttle.

The tachometer pierced the red zone as the motorcycle reached its top speed. The cogs and chains strained with the pressure put on them. The digital screen showed a twelve-percent battery charge.

A bullet ricocheted off the frame.

"This ain't working!" Arthur shouted. "Don't throw any more of them pages!"

Nova glanced inside the file, her heart sinking. She couldn't bring herself to tell him there was only one page left.

A dark field came into view. Arthur pulled the brakes and steered through a gap in the oncoming traffic, cutting across the path of other vehicles. He rode up an embankment that levelled off onto a series of football pitches. The tyre spun a furious stream of mud behind them but kept moving with its momentum, struggling forward with torque.

Nova heard the shriek of tyres but couldn't see the Merc beyond the embankment.

Over the streaming wind, she yelled, "Turn the lights off!"

"I won't be able to see!" Arthur shouted back.

"Neither will they!"

Arthur turned off the lights, making them almost impossible to see.

The motorcycle slid and yawed across the field, dragging on its shocks. The invisible bumps and divots made Nova and Owen simultaneously leave the seat repeatedly. Nova almost fell off the back, but Owen's grasp on her hood ensured she didn't faceplant the mud. Hard rain like gun pellets suddenly fell from the sky, drenching them instantly, creating even more puddle traps and churning the fields into swamps. The chilly air and water rivulets crawled down Nova's top. She raised her hood. It was too late to protect the file. It was already soaked through. Even if she had managed to hold onto its contents, they would have been rained out and ruined.

The puddles grew extensive and even more challenging to spot as the motorcycle headed deeper into the field, away from any streetlights. The wind ripped through the trees, tearing the last of the winter leaves from the battered branches, flinging them onto the grass.

Arthur brushed his soaked hair off his face. "They ain't still following, are they?"

Nova scanned the dark field through the rain, ears tuned, eyes alert, heart thumping. "No!"

As soon as she said it, she was blinded by headlights. The Merc roared out of the trees from their right side and careened towards them.

The chase was back on.

The bike's battery had fallen dangerously low, the red light flashing like a warning pulse. They faced the grim prospect of running out of power, getting stuck in the mud, or being shot by their pursuers. The odds of escaping this waterlogged field alive rapidly dwindled.

Nova opened the wet and sticky file. She had to peel the remaining page out by its corner. She held it up, waving it like a white flag as if surrendering to the men. With a gentle flick of her wrist, she flung the paper onto the grass.

The Merc driver slammed on the brakes, and the tyres lost traction. The car skidded wildly, its back end swinging around in a dramatic one-eighty as it ploughed through a deep puddle. Water erupted in a towering spray, cascading into the air like a fountain before the vehicle finally came to a stop.

Nova's relief morphed back to fear when the driver got out with his gun and started shooting. The rear window dropped, and a second gun was extended and fired, while the passenger also joined his comrades with the shooting frenzy.

Bushes and low-hanging branches hurtled towards them, scraping along the motorcycle's frame and raking their legs and arms as they cut through the woods.

When Arthur turned the headlights back on, the high beam picked out a public park ahead on the other side of the trees. The park was in fact a cemetery; the path they joined snaked between a maze of marble statues and tombstones.

Nova leaned her back against Owen's, loosening her stiff shoulders. "They're gone!"

Arthur craned his neck. "So is that there evidence!"

Nova's optimism had faded. Their successes seemed only to buy them temporary breathing space, and constant setbacks lay immediate waste to any momentum. She stared at the wet, empty file and lowered her head. Without the new evidence, they had nothing but a dead CEO's worthless confession.

Having stopped at an EV station to recharge the batteries, they set off again and rode all the way to the marina.

A pack of dogs scurried off the jetty and ran away when they pulled up. Arthur ditched the motorcycle behind an old boatshed.

He walked quickly towards his boat at the end of the jetty with Nova and Owen closely behind him. "Let's get the fuck out of London!"

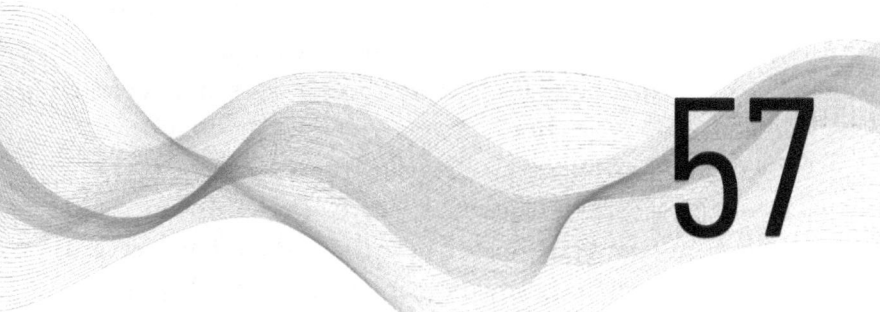

57

At dawn, the Isle of Wight rose out of the sea, and the sky had turned a mauve-infused grey, mirroring its pastel colours onto the calm waters of the English Channel.

Arthur, bleary-eyed from a long night at the helm, stifled a yawn as the island's east coast grew closer on the horizon. He guided the vessel to a floating EV station, its structure gently bobbing with the tide. The boats in the marina were silent and dark, rising and falling with the subtle rhythm of the tide. As it was off-season, several vessels were out of the water, propped up on blocks and covered with protective vinyl sheeting, their outlines barely visible beneath the layers of tarp.

A tall, curvy woman emerged from a kiosk in layers of knitwear: fleece, scarf, beanie, and thick mittens, slightly over-dressed for the brisk morning. She approached Arthur with a friendly but brisk manner. "Charge up?"

Arthur leaped onto the EV station. "Please."

"How long?"

He checked his watch, swiftly calculated cruise times, and inhaled the crisp air through his nose. "I'll be back by eight. Got a long journey ahead."

Grateful for some timeout from the boat and the teenagers constantly under his feet, he climbed the steps leading up to the marina wall. He gazed long into the sea, drawing energy from its purity, recharging his *own* batteries as the boat drew power from the EV station below. He got his first smoke of the day going and thought about last night's encounter with the CEO and what he had learned about the government. It had left him even more distrustful of a society in which those with power were protected from scrutiny and victimisation by the money, resources, contacts, and networks they had accrued over a career of exploitation.

Taking advantage of the interlude on the holiday island, he went for a drink. The logical choice was coffee, but he spotted an empty bar, how he liked his watering holes, on his stroll into town. A little bell dinged when he opened the door. He passed a wall adorned with framed pictures showing how the island had once looked before overdevelopment obliterated natural landscapes and technology reared its ugly head.

Not quite empty, two women, reluctant to end their night, slouched over the bar, whispering, occasionally breaking into quiet, shared laughter. The bartender approached Arthur when he took a stool at the counter. "What can I get for you?"

Arthur looked at the menu. "Gin and tonic, ice, lime."

The bartender glanced at the cackling women and looked at Arthur, silently amused. "You're not from around here."

"No."

"On leave?"

Arthur stretched his collar. "This ain't a military jacket."

The bartender nodded. "Staying long?"

"Until my boat's charged up."

"Where are you heading?"

"Isles of Scilly."

"What's there, family?"

He hesitated, thinking how best to summarise the occasion. "Fireworks."

"Yeah, celebration or something?"

"Hopefully."

The bartender slid a gin and tonic to him. "Enjoy."

The local weather forecast was displayed on the wall from a projector rover. Dawn was expected to be cold but clear, with a possibility of light rain further west as the day progressed.

After a couple of drinks, Arthur farewelled the bartender, now attempting to rouse the women snoring on the counter, and ducked into an electrical shop in the same precinct just as it opened at eight o'clock. He headed straight to the aviation section and made an impromptu purchase—a gift on behalf of the supreme commander.

By the time he reached his boat, the batteries were full, and he utilised the prosthetic tip once more to finalise the payment for the charge-up. He wondered how many more purchases he could make before the tip was deactivated.

With his new gadget tucked inside a cotton carrier bag, he stashed it inside the cubbyhole of the wheelhouse beside his Beretta M9. He checked the gun to ensure it was fully loaded. With the two gins circulating through his bloodstream and the Beretta tucked into his pocket, he felt reassured and ready for the long day ahead.

Below deck, Nova was still asleep in the hammock. Warm, orange sunlight angled through the windows, baking her face. She looked at peace underneath the patchwork quilt.

Arthur clapped his hands together, yelling out, "Rise and shine!"

"What time is it?" asked Nova, rubbing her eyes.

"Breakfast time! And you can make it. If you must stay on this here boat night after night, you can make yourselves useful and make me breakfast. Eggs and bread are in the fridge." He clapped his hands again. "Chop, chop, this ain't no fucking hotel."

Owen was asleep on the floor, curled up in his usual foetal position when Arthur shouted, "Up!" and nudged him in the thigh with his big toe. "You've got five minutes to make me breakfast or you're going overboard."

Owen came awake. "I can't swim."

He crouched beside Owen. "It ain't never too late to learn, my boy."

That evening, Nova stood on the deck, gazing out across the vast expanse of the sea. The gentle lapping of the waves against the hull lulled her into a deep, pensive trance, her thoughts drifting away like the shifting tides. A whole world lay beyond the horizon. Her father's anecdotes had painted vivid pictures of the exotic destinations he wanted to one day show her once teleportation reached every city. She coalesced these thoughts into her *own* travel ambitions, vowing to fulfil them some day. It was essential for her to think pleasant thoughts and to have hopes and dreams. She didn't have long before Alzheimer's robbed her mind, eroding her life story, the narrative defining who she was, leaving just a shell of her former self.

"Supper!" Arthur called out from the wheelhouse as he cut the motor.

Supper consisted of noodles in a thick tomato sauce. The mood at the table was subdued, with hardly a word spoken.

Arthur already had a good day's drinking behind him. He had devoured his usual cocktail of pre-dinner drinks, including a bottle of red wine, before making the switch to rum, the first thing he reached for in the morning and the last thing to leave his hand at night.

Nova capitalised on his drunkenness, knowing he had a soft spot for her somewhere in that cavernous interior, and it gave her the licence to finally ask him the question. "Who's Peter Huxley?"

Arthur finished his drink and placed it gently on the table. He raised his eyebrows mysteriously. "My alias."

"Can you explain?" She crossed her arms. "Please."

"When you're part of an organisation like the ATM, you take risks. You make enemies and put your life on the line. When the ATM first started out, it was simple and safe. But it became more dangerous the bigger we grew, with a lot more police scrutiny. So, I got my mate to create a fake ID. The real Peter Huxley was an old colleague. We used to…"

Nova was about to interrupt him, then didn't. Distracted, no longer following the conversation, she turned to the door. Where had she gone? She was there a minute ago. She must have left the booth. There *was* no booth, only something she didn't have a name for.

Owen picked the dirt from the table edges. He didn't seem to notice or care about Arthur staring at him.

Arthur coughed exaggeratedly.

It got both their attention.

"I know you're both teenagers, and no doubt have better things to do right now, but at least show some respect when I'm talking."

Nova ran her hand over her shaved head. "I feel I should point out that I'm right here, at the table. I'm not invisible, you know."

"Excuse me?"

"Invisible. If I can see me, you can see me."

Owen sat up straight with a rigid grace.

Arthur rubbed Nova's shoulder. He didn't say a word, but his actions came across as sympathetic.

Nova didn't believe it. She didn't believe he was capable of sympathy.

"You were saying," said Owen.

Arthur raised an eyebrow. "We often got asked if we were brothers as we looked so similar. But I disliked the man with a passion. He was a bloody oaf, he was, so it was an easy choice when it came to my alias. If I ever get into mischief, Peter's record gets a few extra logs. How did you find out about that there name?"

"We saw your ID card in the truck," said Owen.

Arthur laughed until it made him cough. "That dinosaur? It's about twelve years old. I've upgraded since then." He took out a small, metal tin from his pocket. Inside was a prosthetic fingertip. "This is my ID now. Slightly more with the times. I use Peter's print whenever I put myself in harm's way. Used it last week, in fact, when I visited a mate in prison. Anyway, it ain't no big deal, and I promise I ain't hiding nothing. My real name's Arthur."

Nova's relief was supplanted by a need to put Arthur in his place. "Have you ever thought about helping people who have been affected by what happened at the teleport rather than getting justice? Maybe starting with yourself?"

Arthur went to the galley and poured himself another rum. "You're a smart girl, you are. Just ain't smart enough. Justice is the first step to overcome grief. It releases the anger that stands in the way of one's bereavement. You ain't yet learned this, but you will as you get older."

Nova puffed out her cheeks and let out a sigh.

With the ATM's power diminished and key figures facing criminal charges in court, the police investigation had lost its urgency. But Nova's mind was overcrowded with unanswered questions.

Who was the Merchant?

Where did the nuclear device come from?

How had the government managed to get away with it?

But the underlying question was why?

Then Arthur said, "Tomorrow, we'll learn the truth."

Owen hadn't listened to his final statement, but Nova had. She shot him a questioning look.

58

Arthur pulled out a chair at the table and eased down with the subtle stiffness in his movements betraying his age more than the grey of his hair. He lit a pre-rolled cigarette, then shifted slightly, reaching under himself to retrieve the blue file he had accidentally sat on. The file was damp and crumpled from the rain, a symbol of lost opportunity, of secrets remaining secret. A fortnight of dead-ends, high hopes, and ultimately, the bitter sting of corrosive disappointment.

He opened the file, needing to check, to confirm they had been within reach of uncovering the truth and bringing it to light. But what he saw made him freeze, frown, and release a slow, steady stream of smoke. His hand instinctively reached for his reading glasses on the table, needing clarity to be certain his eyes hadn't deceived him.

"What's this, then?"

Bebop leaped about Arthur's feet, brushing herself along his leg. He gently pushed her away with his boot. She took the hint and stalked off with an insouciant air.

Owen got up to brew some tea. He asked Arthur if he took sugar.

Arthur snapped the file shut, looking up incredulously.

Nova raised a quizzical eyebrow, seemingly unsettled by his sudden mood change.

"Sit down!" he said. "Both of you!"

Arthur had known all along Nova's escape from London City Teleport had made her a girl who knew too much. It was why he had done everything in his power to keep her close to him, letting her sleep on his boat, spending mealtimes together. Now he had a pained look across his face as a terrible truth sank in.

Nova had managed to find some semblance of peace after the recent challenges and tragedies of late. How would the new information change that?

"This is big!" he said. "This is huge!"

Nova held out her palms. "What is?"

"Tell me why you think the government destroyed that there teleport."

Nova's theory was that the government had destroyed it for financial reasons because the country was in debt. Aware that teleportation would never make any profit, only loss, and that it had been a mistake to invest in Teletron's research and development, the government had staged the terrorist attack.

Arthur listened, frowning with concentration. "For what? The insurance payout?"

"Maybe."

"Peanuts."

"What?"

"The insurance would make no financial difference."

Nova continued, stating the insurance payout would cover the damage and, ultimately, parties such as the ATM or other terrorist groups would be held accountable. The government expected news media and the Internet to be heavily inundated with speculation, conspiracy theories, and everyone's opinion that it would negate any credible evidence, she said.

Arthur, however, saw a fatal flaw in her argument, blaming her age. "But why kill all them people? The government could have got that insurance money without killing anyone, not that it would make any difference to the country's debt crisis. As I said, peanuts by comparison."

Owen chimed in. "The bomb went off too early."

"Nah, too simple. We're talking about pre-meditated mass murder here. Don't forget they were gassed to death first."

Nova rubbed her chin in thought.

"How many invitations got sent out for that Expo?" asked Arthur.

"I think there were about five thousand lottery winners, I think."

"There weren't no lottery, and they weren't invitations that got sent out."

"What were they, then?" asked Nova.

"Death warrants, execution orders, whatever you want to call them."

Nova said nothing, but one look at Arthur's firm-set face, and she looked braced for big news. He didn't disappoint.

"Everyone invited to that Expo had already travelled inside them teleportals in the two years before London City Teleport got closed down. Every person who'd ever used teleportation.

You, your father, my wife, my daughter, that there neighbour of yours. Everyone had already used them teleportals."

Nova shook her head. "Mrs. Cooper never left the country. She may have received an invitation, but never went through a teleportal."

Arthur tilted his head. "Maybe she did. You said you ain't spoken to her in the past year. Did she have any reason to go to the States? Family? Business?"

Nova lowered her eyes. "Her son lives in Boston. But they fell out long ago. She hasn't spoken to him in years."

"But you ain't sure. I mean a hundred per cent sure."

"I suppose it's possible she went to see him in the last year. It's possible they made up, but..."

"There you go. The lottery was a fake to lure all those who had ever tele-travelled, so they could be murdered. The Final Solution. Exterminated, just like bugs. Except you, Nova. You escaped. Since then, you've held the key."

"What key?"

"That memory of yours. All you needed was to regain your memory, a powerful, dangerous tool. It's helped us get where we are, knowing what we now know. And that's why you got abducted. Them abductors were government, or they got hired by the government. They wanted to find out who you had told about what you saw and what you knew to avoid any rumours becoming facts and prompting a deeper investigation. That's why they've been trying to kill you ever since. And us."

"Why, though? Why?"

He opened the file and held it up, showing lines of text on either side. The smudged ink made it barely legible. "Imprint of the CEO's report. Must be where that last page got rained on and the ink on both sides rubbed onto the manila hemp."

Arthur and Owen saw Nova swallow a lump in her throat. "From the last page I threw into the field when we were being chased. It was wet and stuck to the file. I had to peel it out."

Arthur stood, draining his glass. "Brain damage? That's the tip of the iceberg. Ever wonder why your hair ain't grown back since it fell out? It's not just the stress, not no more. And forget about radiation from that blast. It's deeper than that. It's your ageing gene, Nova. It's been... how can I put this? Corrupted. Altered. You've completely stopped ageing, you have. But that ain't all. You've stopped growing. You'll get older: mentally, emotionally, but your body won't. That's locked in time. Your skin, hair, bones, even your fingernails, they won't age another day. They won't grow at all, never again." Arthur took a breath, his eyes searching Nova's face for a reaction. "Congratulations, Nova!" he said with a mix of anticipation and disbelief. "You are immortal!"

59

Nova took the news in silence. She locked eyes with Owen and did not break for several seconds.

You've stopped ageing.

Arthur's words cut deep. She straightened in her chair and tried to understand and absorb this impossible, new reality. Her hands shook, her head spun. She would never grow a day older. Her youthful appearance would stretch into many bleak, lonely years inside the cocoon of a dysfunctional, deteriorating mind until it put her in the grave. She wondered whether, in some secret, unacknowledged corner of her heart, she'd always known the truth.

Arthur reached out to her, but she turned away from him as if he were to blame.

He opened the file and told Owen and Nova to listen as he read out the text imprinted on the interior.

"… the post-mortem results raised serious concerns. Had teleportation caused the Pioneer brain damage? Unlikely, but the fact a fit, healthy twenty-five-year-old developed advanced Alzheimer's with such suddenness rang multiple alarm bells. The archon of biomedicine, Dr. Oberon Baxter, re-examined the four dogs nicknamed the *Fab 4*. They were the first to ever travel through the teleportals. Dr. Baxter discovered signs of canine dementia. Supplementary experiments using transgenic mice revealed tiny inclusions between dying cells in the nerve tissue called plaques. Dr. Baxter alerted Dr. Judd, the supreme commander of physics and engineering, about the neurological defects resulting from teleportation, but hid his findings from the other physicists and me, Teletron's CEO. Teleportation was about to open for commercial travel in London and New York, and yet he allowed people to travel, knowing they would develop Alzheimer's disease. Over time, he made a second and more startling discovery. The *Fab 4*, now five years past their teleportation trials by this time, showed no signs of ever having aged. After dissecting one of the *Fab 4* and running a series of biological tests, he discovered teleportation had edited the key ageing gene, called Klotho."

Nova's head lifted. "Clotho?"

Arthur nodded. "With a K, though. There's more. Where was I? Okay… The Klotho peptide triggers degeneration in all living organisms. The altered Klotho gene is irreversible, with permanent life extension induced by its modification. The *Fab 4* had exhibited perfect physical condition over time. Their organs remained healthy. Their bones, hair, and teeth had not grown. The only conclusion to be drawn by his research was …" Arthur shifted his attention to the file's right page: "… that teleportation had paused ageing indefinitely and resulted in the travellers developing advanced brain damage. Within the correspondence uncovered by the hacker, he mentioned it was likely from an overload of gamma rays emitting ionising atoms in the teleportals. Ionising radiation caused the brain damage. Since commercial teleportation had closed down, we learned that he'd finally managed to resolve the issue by adjusting the exposure to gamma rays within the teleportal and the hydrogen flow into the turbines without affecting performance. As for the Klotho mutation, it was not so easily rectified and was the result of epigenetic modification, also referred to as tags, in the histone group. Histones regulate gene activity up or down, and teleportation triggered a shift in this crucial gene. This Klotho defect prevented ageing and all other age-related matters such as infertility, emphysema, osteoporosis, degenerative cells, skin atrophy, all regulated by Klotho. By the time he had made his discovery and drawn up his final conclusions, teleportation had been in operation for almost two years. It had affected the lives of over twelve thousand people; five thousand from the UK. Dr. Baxter shared his findings with the government, and they colluded to prevent the public from finding out. So began the *Final Solution*, first by closing the teleports in America and the UK. Then the 'clean-up' began by killing every brain-damaged immortal, luring them inside the auditorium or assassinating them in cold blood if they didn't show up at the Expo, their murders staged as suicides. Soon after the closure, Dr. Baxter and Dr. Judd moved the teleportals from Teletron... it stops there."

Arthur looked up from the file. "How many times did I tell people teleportation ain't right? That's why the ATM opposed it. We knew this would happen. My wife and daughter are now dead, and you'll live forever."

He seemed almost triumphant, as though he had cracked an impossible code. Hope and determination had given Nova her momentum. Now she barely recognised those emotions. Her stricken face hardened into one of despair.

She rose slowly from the table.

"Where are you going?" asked Owen.

She walked slowly towards the galley but stopped short and turned. "Klotho is the ageing gene?"

"But with a K. And that's why our Serbian friend let it slip when he was high on drugs." Arthur's voice grew even more intense. "It weren't some rambling about the thread of life or fate, and sure as hell ain't a Serbian swear word, as we know. He was talking about something real, something specific. He knew about the modified ageing gene. It weren't just rambled nonsense, it was a warning, a clue he didn't even realise he was giving us because he was so high. He knew that you had been changed."

"That's why he's been trying to kill me? Because I won't age?"

"Not only you. Anyone who ain't died in that explosion. Anyone who found out, or could find out, about the damage teleportation caused to human beings, like them three physicist engineers. They were supposed to die in that explosion along with the other physicists because they were the only ones who could uncover what went wrong and expose the secret. They were a liability. But they survived because of that car crash. It saved their lives. Well, prolonged them."

She thought about the CEO's final words before he took a bullet to the head: *Silence is golden. But so is secrecy. The problem is, how do you maintain both when a few years down the track you discover that...* "People have stopped ageing," said Nova.

Arthur nodded. "That's what it says. The explosion at the teleport wiped out everyone with brain damage and destroyed them dysfunctional teleportals in the process. It also erased any future possibility of people finding out about the immortality it would cause. After that, the archon of biomedicine moved them teleportals out of Teletron to that factory Owen wound up in. I read about them in the CEO's report when we were at his house. He went on long-service leave to work on them, to prevent Alzheimer's from developing in future travellers. But the life-extension element he left untouched."

"Why?"

"To discreetly transport government officials to a distant location for a hefty fee, ensuring their safe passage out of the country without a digital trace. And, with a little bonus thrown in: a promise of eternal youth. Like that Miriam Payne. Breast cancer was just her cover story so she could sever ties with the government without arousing suspicion and escape before the shit hit the fan. And, of course, to reap the rewards of eternal life."

Nova held Owen's hand with a sinking heart. He'd risked his life to prove himself trustworthy to her. His selfless act had brought them much closer to revealing the truth. She gave him a sympathetic smile, squeezing his hand. "This has happened to you, too."

The recent turn of events had unsettled everyone, including Owen, who had always seemed emotionally unbreakable. He looked simply stunned.

Arthur exhaled sharply, the rush of air escaping his lungs with the force of a hairdryer and the stench of alcohol. "This is unbelievable," he said as he paced the room, running a hand through his grey hair as the enormity of the situation sank in.

"Wait until the world finds out about this. There'll be chaos, riots in the streets, there will. People won't stand for it. The truth about what the government has done, what they've kept hidden, will tear everything apart. This is bigger than any of us could have imagined."

Exactly who knew about the dysfunctional teleportals was unclear. Based on the information Nova, Owen, and Arthur had amassed during their enquiries, and the many confusing dead-ends they'd encountered, it suggested few were included in the government's inner circle.

Ultimately more distressing was that the evidence had been gifted to them, and they had let it slip through their fingers. It was a failure of epic proportions. They had been so close, the truth practically within their grasp, only to fumble at the most crucial moment, allowing those men inside the white Merc to recover every page. Keeping it out of the public eye had clearly taken precedence over their assassination, although achieving both had been their primary goal.

"You wasted the evidence," said Arthur. "We needed them exchanges between the government and Teletron. They held names, dates, times, facts, and the full report from the CEO." He held the file up. "This here file ain't worth shite."

It upset Nova. Her first reaction was to lower her head in shame. Her second involved a loud scream that startled both Owen and Arthur, who kept quiet. Furious her ploy had not received the kind of reaction she had hoped for, she flipped a chair and turned her back on them.

Bebop rushed off, spooked by the crashing chair.

Her outburst gave way to a brief moment of calm as she steadied herself, taking deep breaths to swallow her anger.

"So what now?" asked Owen.

Arthur moved to the galley and topped up his glass with rum. "Just so happens I know where to find that factory you wound up in."

60

"When Owen escaped from that factory in that rowing boat, the currents didn't drag him back to shore, as we first thought. He came from the island of St. Mary's and crossed the Celtic Sea." He looked at Owen. "You got lucky. The currents must have been in your favour that day. You could have been swept out to sea."

"St. Mary's?" asked Nova.

Arthur coughed into his hand. "One of the Isles of Scilly. It's part of them British Isles, approximately thirty miles from the mainland."

Moments before the CEO's head took a bullet, Arthur had leafed through the file and seen a purchase order for a disused marine factory on St. Mary's that used to specialise in unique and custom engine parts targeting the local fishing fleets. It had been made out in Teletron's name and signed by Dr. Oberon

Baxter. Blueprints of the old factory had also been included as evidence. The CEO had learned about the indiscretions taking place down there with the aid of a pro hacker and about the cabinet ministers aware of the Klotho defect disappearing out of the country. They were travelling through the teleportal in the factory's basement, where new engine parts had once been put through endurance tests before going onto the market. Dr. Baxter had shipped two teleportals and requisite technology across the Celtic Sea to the tiny island, nice and secluded.

The government, said Arthur, had betrayed its people, and it would be made to pay.

Nova drank a mug of tea along with her calcium pills, which was her midday ritual. She watched Bebop sitting obediently on the galley worktop, purring quietly and observing everyone with a supervisory air as Arthur filled them in with his plan.

Arthur believed they would find proof of the government's involvement on quantum servers and within the record logs of international transfers stored inside the teleportal mainframe, enough to expose all those involved. All he had to do was get inside the marine factory, gather enough evidence to prompt a police investigation, and leave. He then grabbed a cotton tote bag emblazoned with a fancy logo of an electronics company from the Isle of Wight.

"What's in the bag?" asked Nova.

Arthur reached into the bag and pulled out a box labelled Solstace1. Inside was one of the newest drones on the market, powered by a hybrid of solar energy and advanced batteries. It was equipped with thermal imaging and hyperspectral cameras, capable of capturing high-definition footage, and its advanced satellite transmission technology allowed it to stream live video to up to five wearable visors simultaneously. Built-in quantum communication technology ensured a secure, unhackable data transmission, making it ideal for coordinated team operations offering seamless real-time communication and a shared view of the environment from multiple perspectives.

"This is proper job," he said.

Nova looked from the drone to Arthur. "Yeah, you really *hate* technology."

Arthur waved a finger at her. "Don't even dare."

"Hypocrite!"

"Fancy a swim?"

Nova shook her head. "Someone doesn't want to admit he has double standards."

"I hate technology as much as I hate Teletron. But on this occasion, I intend to use it against them *and* the government to expose what they've done."

"How?" asked Nova.

"First, I need to teach you how to drive this here boat."

Arthur ran Nova and Owen through an orientation of the wheelhouse, explaining the throttle and shift levers and dash panel instrumentation.

Nova and Owen familiarised themselves with the controls, and Arthur offered them turns at the wheel. The radar sweep revealed no vessels within a twenty-mile radius, yet he refused to activate the autopilot to steer their vessel towards the final destination on an economical path that avoided boat traffic from the safest distance.

Owen wanted to know why.

"I've got eyes, I have. And my independence. What use am I on this here boat if a computer's doing all the work for me? Autopilot will just make me lazy, and I'll be less experienced as a driver."

Suddenly aware he was preaching to the wrong people, he realised these were children born of the digital age, an entitled generation willingly surrendering the skills that had brought humanity to this point and enslaving itself to technology.

As Owen kept one eye on the horizon through the sloped wheelhouse windows, Arthur unfurled an old map on the dash panel. St. Mary's, the most populated island within the Isles of Scilly archipelago, was approximately eighty miles from their current location. He singled it out on the map. "This here's the island of St. Mary's."

Owen and Nova studied the map, following his finger as it traced their route from the mainland to the island.

"The factory's there."

He pointed at the island's southern coastline, where the six sat on a clock. "It's right in front of this airport. Hugh Town is round here."

He traced a line with his finger, first left then up, stopping at the west coast, positioned like the eight mark on a clock.

"St. Mary's Harbour is right here in Hugh Town. If I ain't back, drive this here boat into this harbour and moor alongside the quay. Then get over to the police station on Garrison Lane; it's up on the hill. Ask them locals where to find it. When you get there, notify them about what's happened and hand over the evidence, clear?"

"What evidence?" asked Nova.

Arthur held up the drone. "Video."

Following the rugged contours of Cornwall's coastline, he navigated towards the country's southernmost point. The cliffs and rolling hills unfurled like a ribbon until they finally veered away from the mainland. Now, with thirty miles of open sea stretching before them, they set their course for St. Mary's.

Arthur took a long swig of rum from the bottle, his voice animated as he launched into a lively commentary about the geology and birdlife found on St. Mary's. He spoke with rough enthusiasm about ancient rock formations and rare seabirds nested along its shores, his words bringing the remote island to life even before they reached its shores.

Nova and Owen shared concerned glances, surprised by how undaunted and calm he seemed, given they were chugging steadily towards the end game.

61

Once a thriving hub for boat manufacturing, specialising in stainless steel and aluminium outboard and inboard engines and spare parts, the factory now stood as two hundred square metres of abandoned industrial wasteland. Surrounded by an eight-foot-high wire-mesh fence topped with barbed wire, it had become a relic of an era before electric motors and solar-cell technology rendered fuel-dependent engines obsolete.

Feet spaced apart, hands clasped behind his back, Arthur stood on deck overlooking the calm sea, fixed intently on the factory on St. Mary's Island, hiding its deadly secrets from its distant perch. His mind was abuzz with the details they had painstakingly gathered. He was confident they'd unearthed the building masquerading as a vacant factory, aligning perfectly with Owen's vague and unsettling description. Its proximity to an airport and its coastal position made it a plausible hideout, blending seamlessly into its surroundings. The sight of the two weather-beaten rowing boats on the tiny beach reinforced his belief that they had finally located the elusive site, adding to the factory's aura of mystery and suggesting recent or ongoing activity.

He spread the sharp flukes apart and cast the anchor into the sea. Then he unpacked the drone, flexing his fingers as if about to strum a guitar. Studying the cutting-edge technology, the epitome of all he stood against, he couldn't help but feel a tingle of excitement.

"Proper job, that is."

He spent half an hour assembling the pieces and learning how to control the drone. Once he'd attached the hyperspectral camera with its agile fisheye lens and panoramic view capability, he put on the visor and checked the live image displayed on the screen. Wearing motion-sensor gloves, he raised his hands, and the drone lifted smoothly into the air, its rotors humming almost silently as it ascended. For a few seconds, it hovered perfectly still, its camera swivelling slightly as it scanned the surroundings. When Arthur held up his palms and pushed the air, the drone tilted forward, its propellers increasing in speed. It surged ahead, slicing through the air, leaving behind a slight trail of disturbance in its wake. The seascape displayed on the visor screen blurred as the drone accelerated. Arthur tucked his thumbs into his palms, activating autopilot, employing the advanced magnetic, radar, and visual sensors that adjusted to the changing speed and altitude.

Approaching the factory, he untucked his thumbs from his palms, disengaging the autopilot, and dragged his palms to his chest to decrease speed. Live images transmitting back to his visor showed the factory was enveloped in long grass, heavily littered with discarded rubbish. Precariously stacked paint vats stood by the wall nearest to the shore, surrounded by nettles and weeds at its base, and large holes gaped in the corrugated iron roof of the factory. He saw no signs of vehicles or human occupancy. The gravel at the front of the factory revealed no footprints or tyre tracks.

He turned to Owen. "My dinghy, go and inflate it at the stern."

"What's a dinghy?"

"You ain't serious?" Arthur shook his head. "An inflatable boat. I bought it after we were attacked at sea."

Arthur flew the drone back to his boat and landed it on the deck by slowly lowering his palms. He raised his visor and set it on his crown.

He passed a visor to Nova. "Put this on. The visors are all wirelessly connected, they are, so you and Owen can see what I see through the live camera feed. The footage will burn onto the nanochip inside these here visors, giving us three copies. Get them to the police. You remember where we are?"

"Isles of Scilly," said Nova.

"St. Mary's, one of the Isles of Scilly. Where's that police station?"

"Hugh Town," said Nova. "A couple of miles from here. The police station is on Harrison Lane."

"Garrison Lane!" Arthur snapped.

"Garrison Lane. Sorry."

"By then, all the evidence should be on the nanochip."

He unscrewed the camera from the drone and clipped it to the front of his visor, capable of transmitting audio and video signals on a special subsonic frequency to a satellite, even from deep beneath the ground.

Owen ran over. "The boat's ready."

Before Arthur set off, he took Nova's hand. "You'll be all right, you will."

Nova looked sadly down at her feet. "I wish I shared your confidence."

He raised her chin. "Look on the bright side. You've got Alzheimer's but remember that it's a condition that progresses over time as brain cells deteriorate, just like how skin and hair change with age. Since you ain't gonna age, this disease ain't gonna get no worse, so you ain't got to worry."

"You think?"

"Seems like straightforward human biology to me. You ain't gonna die from it. You just need to learn to manage with momentary blips in your memory. There are drugs available that can help."

She smiled.

He stroked her shaved head. "Just don't go eating no nutty curries."

A snort of laughter escaped her nose until it almost turned into tears. She suddenly flung her arms around him, despite herself, unable to contain the relief from the continuing stress that had accumulated inside her.

Disengaging himself gently, Arthur headed to the stern and climbed down the ladder, only drying his eyes once he was out of sight from Nova and Owen. He carefully stepped from the boat into the dinghy, causing it to rock slightly with the sudden shift in weight. It bobbed and tilted as he adjusted his footing, the uneven distribution of his weight making the dinghy sway unpredictably. Unfastening the rope Owen had tied around the ladder, he grabbed the oars and rowed away before Nova could wish him good luck.

The waves were gentle, and Arthur rowed with ease all the way to the island. He looked like a commando on some covert mission in his military jacket, missing only the final touches of black face paint and a machine gun. He drew up on the shore and dragged the dinghy out of the water onto the beach beside the two rowing boats. He waved at Nova and Owen, watching him from the deck and waving back.

Enticed by the factory's presence and mesmerised by the promise of its secrets, he got to work.

62

Arthur scrambled up the craggy rocks until he reached the tall fence that marked the boundary of the factory's perimeter. He moved steadily along the fence, his eyes fixed on the factory as he scanned for any signs of activity. He remained alert to even the slightest hint of movement.

Beyond the factory lay a vast, marshy wasteland of reeds, mud, and stagnant pools, creating a natural obstacle separating the factory from the outside world. And beyond the marshland, the landscape unfolded into a small airport.

Having lapped the perimeter fence, he found himself at the back of the factory again, overlooking the rocky beach with the Anna Belle bobbing in the backdrop. The fence bowed slightly at the midpoint where Owen had escaped from. Wire cutters would have come in handy at that point. He owned a pair of heavy-duty cutters with yellow rubber grips, but they were in his truck, still parked outside the CEO's house with the rest of his tools. The fact his truck was there no doubt made him a prime suspect in the CEO's execution. Just another problem he had to deal with in the everlasting fight against Teletron.

Try as he did to shimmy through the hole in the fence, he couldn't. "Bugger!"

Nova's concerned voice filtered through the visor's built-in speakers. "*What happened?*"

"Scagged my shirt on the fence. I ain't small like Owen. I can't fit through."

Heading back to the beach, he made his way past the boats and scanned the area for an alternative route inside the factory grounds. The presence of the boats, haphazardly strewn along the shore, hinted at a pattern of movement, perhaps suggesting a hidden trail or a less conspicuous path had been established. He considered someone had gone to the trouble of making this place accessible, likely using the boats to facilitate discreet arrivals and departures. The very fact the boats were here at all implied this beach served as a crucial link in a chain of covert activities or logistical operations.

As he rounded a boulder half-buried in the sand, his eyes caught a glimpse of a dark opening nestled among the rocks. Intrigued, he approached the entrance. The opening revealed itself as a compact cave, partially concealed by the surrounding rocks. A rivulet of water meandered from a gap in the rocks, pooling near the entrance. The rough stone walls suggested the cave might be human made, perhaps serving as a hidden refuge or storage space. With a cautious breath, he took a step inside.

"Night vision."

Stepping over the tiny puddle, he stared at the dark recess, spotting footprints in the damp sand. His bionic lenses gave the wet interior walls a greenish glow as he stooped into the darkness and panned his vision over the ceiling. The uneven texture and raw authenticity pointed to the fact it was not an artificial cave but a natural one.

As he ventured further inside, he noticed light streaming in from an opening at the back of the cave. At the base of this light-filled entrance was a bamboo ladder with sturdy rungs leading up to the bright shaft of daylight above.

He straightened himself, adjusting to the vertical passage, and began to climb, bringing him closer to the source of the light, where he felt the warmth of the sun against his face as he ascended. Reaching the top, he emerged through the opening and found himself inside the perimeter of the fence at the rear of the factory.

"You wanna know what I think?" Arthur asked, waiting for Nova's response.

"*What?*"

"These politicians are flying to the airport or boating over from the mainland, rowing them boats from a pickup point on the island, and using this here hidden passage to get inside the factory."

"*You think?*"

"It's the only plausible idea." Standing near the paint vats, stacked eight high and forming a cliff at the back of the factory, he began the next phase of his mission. "Gonna try the main door now."

He ducked beneath the small, dirty windows, listening out for voices as he paced from one end of the factory to the other. A pile of rusty pipes festooned with cobwebs lined the ground, partially obscured by the long grass and weeds that had claimed them. It merely provided further evidence of disuse.

He stopped at a sun-faded sign daubed on the wall, reading MMM. It stood for *Marine Motor Manufacturers*. A blue tarpaulin was attached to scaffolding all the way to the apex of the roof at the entrance. He ducked under it and opened the door.

The dim, gloomy interior was made even gloomier by the absence of bulbs in the overhead sockets. Still, he flicked the switch on the wall. To his surprise, a single bulb sputtered on at the back, revealing the warehouse was still connected to the mains or perhaps powered by a generator. "These teleportals use electricity and draw a lot of power. That's why there ain't no lights and why Owen saw only candle lanterns inside. To conserve power."

Footprints in the dusty floor snaked between the rows of workbenches and lathes, leading away from a large stainless-steel door resembling an industrial-sized refrigerator. Despite his efforts, Arthur couldn't pry it open. Frustrated, he retraced Owen's footprints and headed back outside, fully aware of the urgency to find another way in.

Nova closed her eyes, her need for sleep irresistible. She hadn't managed much sleep, the news of her immortality disturbing her attempts as effectively as a rock-hard mattress. Her fatigue made her head heavy on her neck.

She had witnessed horrors no girl her age should ever have to endure, images so deeply ingrained that they defied every attempt to forget. No matter how hard she tried to push them out of her mind, they remained stuck in her memory. Even her Alzheimer's couldn't erase them. Those haunting visions clung to her, untouched by the disease, as if they were too powerful, too deeply rooted, to be forgotten. She wanted to go home, slip into bed, and curl into a ball. Like any normal person. But she was not a normal person. Not anymore. How would her life change with Alzheimer's, yet without the passage of time? How could she ever live a normal life, trapped in a body that remained eternally teenage?

She'd regained some composure since Arthur had dropped the bombshell. A brief moment of shared emotion with him had done more for her than she could yet know, lighting up the darkness inside her soul and giving her hope for the first time. Questions had been answered, too, but only raised more.

How could the government be so shamefully brutal?

How had it expected to get away with mass murder and lay the blame on the ATM?

Who else had colluded in this deception?

How had Teletron got teleportation so wrong?

Owen had accepted the shocking news in his stride, which worried her. Perhaps the gravity of the situation hadn't fully hit him yet. Could he have developed Alzheimer's, too?

She took Owen's hand.

He smiled.

She lowered the visor over her eyes, activating the auto-tint. Arthur had made it inside the factory but had been dead-ended by a large, steel door. Without concrete evidence of the teleportals hidden beneath the factory, whether in the form of documents, records, or physical proof, their mission would come to a grinding halt. All the planning, the risks they'd taken, and the secrets they had uncovered would count for nothing.

But proof was now within touching distance. She sensed it. Still, she was more concerned about Arthur walking into the potential jaws of death.

63

Arthur's attention was caught by the paint vats clustered tightly together at the rear of the factory. Something seemed off about the way they were arranged, and as he examined them more closely, he noticed a narrow gap between them. A faint breeze filtered through the opening, raising his suspicions. Intrigued, he moved closer and realised the vats were deliberately stacked to conceal something—a narrow spiral staircase hidden in the shade.

With both curiosity and caution, Arthur squeezed sideways between the vats, careful not to disturb their unstable balance. As he did, his foot crunched down on a mound of nettles, and he ducked to avoid hitting his head on the low-hanging pipes above him. The staircase was old, its metal steps corroded and pitted by years of exposure to the harsh sea air, but it was still passable.

He began his descent. The deeper he went, the more the dim light from above faded, replaced by the cold, damp air that clung to the walls as he spiralled into the hidden recesses. He arrived to find a shiny titanium door at the bottom requiring electronic access, the only nod to modernisation. There were no eye scanners or fingerprint devices installed. Arthur tried the black macro key he had stolen from Teletron.

A red light flashed.

Then he tried the fob. It flashed red again.

He tried the white macro key Owen had pinched inside the factory's basement. That didn't work either.

A frosted window wide enough to fit a grown man was beside the door. He picked up a large rock and launched it at the glass. He had to make a hurried sidestep as it rebounded off the tempered glass, leaving no damage.

"This ain't working," said Arthur.

"*Have you tried the macro key Owen found?*" asked Nova.

"It didn't work."

Nova paused on the line. Then said, "*Did you use the right one? You have two white macro keys, remember? One of them was from the CEO's house.*"

He took all the keys out of his pocket. One was black and red. The other two white keys were identical. One was paired to the CEO's appliances and security. The other had Teletron's name imprinted across the top.

In awe of his newfound collection of macro keys, he tried the white Teletron key. He heard steel rods disengaging, and the light turned green. He dropped the macro keys into his pocket. "Okay, I'm in."

The door swung open without a sound from its hinges, and Arthur stepped into a small storage room. Inside was just as cold as the outside, minus the breeze. The room was cluttered with a massive, tangled fishing net draped over stacked tackle boxes. Old engine parts and a sack of rubbish tied with string were piled against the wall. The air was thick with the stench of damp and the lingering odour of fish remnants, making the room feel as neglected as its contents.

"Are you getting this?"

"*Yeah. What do you see?*"

"Old, decaying boat factory and brand-new titanium door. Electronic security lock for crappy, old fishing gear."

"*What are you saying?*"

"Must be a decoy. Must be a door in the wall or some kind of hatch or something." He paused. "Night vision."

Viewing the room in green shades, he pressed his fingers against the walls and touched the low ceiling with his palms. He moved the tackle boxes around, searching for secret entry points or false walls.

"*Anything?*"

"Not yet."

He carefully scanned the room once more, certain he had missed something. His eyes darted around, searching for any subtle detail that might have escaped him. He dragged the net aside. Beneath it, a trapdoor was revealed. He tested it, and it opened easily. Peering into the deep hole, he glimpsed a ladder disappearing into the darkness below.

"I've found something."

Nova raised her visor and put her hand on Owen's shoulder. "Listen, I wanted to say thanks for what you did at Teletron, going through the teleportal. You really didn't have to prove anything to me. I *do* trust you."

He said nothing, of course, as she had expected. He didn't have to. She had no authority over him. He looked genuinely sorry because he did not want to hurt her. She saw that now. She forgave him for using her as a pawn for financial gain. She wasn't one to hold grudges against people. Forgiving was easy. Forgetting was difficult, though her Alzheimer's might see to that, she conceded somewhat jokingly.

Nova lowered her visor and waited for Arthur to feed back more status reports. Her screen had turned black, but the red record light continued to tick in the corner. A bright blue flash lit up Arthur's hands gripped around the ladder and when he dropped inside a dark tunnel.

"You're close," said Owen. "That's the blue light I told you about."

"*I must be on the other side of that steel door*," said Arthur.

Owen and Nova watched his movement through the visor as he travelled along the passageway and descended a set of metal steps.

"*I hear something*," he murmured.

Reaching the bottom of the stairs, he turned his head, and the camera clipped to his visor swept across the circular room, giving Nova and Owen a glimpse of the teleportals side by side and a console of computer tech, burning crucial footage onto the nanochips inside their visors.

The recording suddenly shook, and diamond-plated tiles filled the screen when the camera fell to the floor. The sole of a boot came crashing down on top of the camera.

Nova saw the red record icon flicker off and the live image shrink to a point of light before disappearing.

64

A modern catamaran swung around the headland with a swift, predatory menace, its dual hulls slicing through the waves as it sped towards the Anna Belle. Low in the water, it moved with a sleek, almost frightening stealth as it closed the distance with unmistakable intent.

Nova's instincts kicked in, and she saw the importance of trusting them. "Time to go!"

She ran to the wheelhouse. Owen followed.

She pressed the ignition, and the electric motor came on. With a firm push on the throttle, the boat's nose lifted, straining against the water, but it stubbornly refused to move forward.

"The anchor!" Nova cried.

Owen burst out of the wheelhouse and ran to the stern to the anchor winch. Without a second to waste, he grabbed the heavy chain and began reeling in the anchor hand-over-hand, his muscles straining as he wound it tightly around the drum before stowing the anchor in its storage space. He ran back to the wheelhouse and told Nova it was up.

She engaged the throttle, turned the wheel towards deeper waters, and cranked it to maximum speed, relieved when the boat slowly heaved forward.

The catamaran moved like a serpent and cut a swathe of white water across the sea. It wasn't a great deal quicker, but it was quick enough to inexorably close the distance between the vessels.

"They're catching us!" Owen shouted.

She steered the boat until it ran parallel with the coastline, heading north as it rounded the island's southwestern tip.

"Can't you go any faster?" asked Owen.

"It's at full throttle."

The entrance to St. Mary's Harbour gradually emerged on the horizon, nestled protectively between two sweeping arms of rock that reached out into the sea like a natural embrace. As they approached, Nova guided the boat towards the harbour's mouth, making a wide, leisurely turn that allowed the vessel to glide smoothly through the opening, exchanging the open sea for the calmer, guarded waters of the harbour.

"Take the wheel," said Nova, trading places with Owen so she could leave the wheelhouse. She hurried down the steps to the cabin, looking for somewhere to hide the visor. Seeing the ashtray overflowing with cigarette remnants, she plucked the nanochip from the visor and buried it deep within the ashes before rushing back to the deck.

Private yachts and houseboats gently bobbed within the harbour, their hulls tethered securely to the seabed, rocking in rhythm with the quiet swell. Owen navigated carefully between them towards the quay. Ahead, he spotted the familiar sight of a ferry docked at the pier, its gangway lowered for passengers to board. His pulse quickened as he recognised the ferry as the same one he had seen off the coast on that fateful night when he found himself stranded in the rowing boat with the oars lost at sea.

"You're going too fast!" said Nova, rejoining him inside the wheelhouse. The angle of approach was completely wrong, too, leaving them on a collision course with the quay's concrete walls.

Owen reversed the props and tried to turn sharply to the left but got it all wrong. The boat swept sideways and almost capsized, displacing a large amount of water.

The catamaran had just entered the harbour; the distance between them could now be measured in feet.

Owen gunned the motor, turned away from the quay, and steered through the boats, speeding towards land.

"Where are you going?" asked Nova.

"The beach."

As the water grew shallower, the boat's hull scraped against the stone-laced sand with a harsh, grating sound that vibrated through the vessel. The impact jolted the boat, throwing Owen and Nova off balance. Their feet left the deck, and they were tossed forward uncontrollably. While they instinctively reached for something to steady themselves, they were both propelled over the dash panel and flung through the wheelhouse window. The glass shattered on impact, exploding into a spray of jagged shards that rained down around them as they hit the deck.

Owen's head struck the window frame on his way out, and the visor perched upon his crown cracked beneath the force, splintering into pieces that scattered across the floor. The tiny nanochip dislodged from its hidden place within the visor and skittered across the deck, bouncing wildly with each hit. When it reached the gunwale, where Nova landed on her front and rolled four times before coming to a stop, it teetered on the edge before tumbling overboard.

One hand on the guard rail, the other rubbing the bruised side of his head, Owen looked at Nova as they came up onto their knees. Their faces were covered in scratches and spots of blood.

Owen staggered over to Nova to help her up and dragged her to the guard rail, which he climbed up, preparing to jump overboard.

"Wait!" said Nova. She turned and dashed back downstairs to the cabin to retrieve the nanochip from the ashtray. With a quick breath, she blew the ashes off, sending a fine cloud of dust into the air. Satisfied it was clean, she clenched it tightly between her fingers and hurried back to Owen.

The catamaran had reached them, coming to a grinding halt as it became lodged in the stony shallows.

The moment Nova's feet met the sand, she chased up the beach with Owen, disturbing a flock of seagulls that wheeled angrily into the sky.

Three armed men leaped from the catamaran into the sea at the same time, striding knee-deep through the water in what now became a pursuit on foot.

Nova pulled against Owen's cardigan when they arrived at the promenade, unable to catch her breath. "Here!" She gave Owen the last nanochip. "It's up... to you now!"

65

In the middle of the promenade, a three-piece band energised the atmosphere with their synthetic, high-octane electronica. The keyboardist, a virtuoso in her music, expertly played the keys, creating complex sounds and effects that drove the song forward. A heavily made-up woman, squeezed into a snugly fit dress, sang into her microphone with a fine soprano voice, her performance adding a melodic counterpoint to the pulsating rhythms.

Gathered in a semi-circle around the band, the crowd was abruptly drawn away from the performance. One by one, their attention shifted to the beach, where an old, red boat and a catamaran had run aground. The singer kept her vocals up, her concentration unbroken, even when a young boy with a face covered in bloody marks and scratches tried to interrupt her, asking, "Where's the police station?"

Even the keyboardist was able to shoo him away with the back of her hand without breaking rhythm.

Owen ran into the town, convinced he could outpace the men on youth alone. They were two decades older and twice his height and weight; nonetheless they looked in peak physical shape. And Owen had only been released from the hospital a few days ago and remained weak. He stopped behind a shop wall to catch his breath and pocketed the nanochip. The men had only a general sense of where he was. He knew where they were and had to keep the tables from turning.

When they disappeared along a side street, he ran the other way, trying to throw them off his tail. He quickly found himself back at the seafront. He searched frantically for Nova, but she was nowhere in sight. His eyes landed on the hill he knew he needed to climb, but the road name eluded him. With a surge of urgency, he started up the hill, hoping a street sign would trigger his memory. He knew it ended in *Lane,* with an inkling it was called *Garden* or *Garrington* or something similar. A stitch sprang up in Owen's side, biting deep. Despite his exhaustion, his aching limbs, the cuts all over his skin from going through a window, and now a stitch, he pushed himself beyond the pain barrier.

Owen glanced over his shoulder and saw two men appear at the bottom of the hill, their arms and legs in almost perfect sync, their muscular bodies in line with each other, their large strides making good ground, their eyes ablaze with a luminous determination.

Crippled by exhaustion, his face contorted in agony in his struggle to fill his lungs with air, his throat closed in on itself, and he felt winded by a punch he never saw land. In the same motion, he stopped and sank to his knees in the middle of the road. It was as if someone had sat on his chest, preventing the air from reaching all the way to the bottom of his lungs. He had experienced an asthma attack before and knew the early signs. Reaching for his Ventolin, he gave himself two shots of beclomethasone and inhaled deep breaths. Shielding his eyes from the afternoon sun, a surrendering calm overcame him as the men closed in.

A boy he might be called, but his life would end as a man. He'd given it his best shot. He thought of Nova, as he tended to do whenever his life teetered on the edge of peril. Each time, they rekindled his will to survive, providing a reason to carry on even when the odds seemed insurmountable. As he repocketed the Ventolin, the nanochip brushed his fingertips and inspired him to his feet. He pushed his palms to the ground and raised himself. Without a backward glance, he was on his way again, walking, then jogging, then running.

He passed numerous houses and bungalows, swinging his head left and right, looking for the police station. Up ahead, where the road forked and a street sign read *Garrison Lane,* he knew he was on the right path. Before long, he saw the blue Mercia Lantern mounted on the wall of a small building that resembled a bungalow.

He charged through the door to the reception and threw his arms down on the counter, panting and gasping. "Help… my friend's…"

A short officer with cropped hair accentuating high cheekbones and sharp, narrow eyes paused and capped his marker pen. "Calm down, son. What's your name?"

"… Owen."

"My name's Sergeant Michaels. Now, what's happened to your friends, Owen? Are they in trouble?"

Owen looked through the window, pointing towards the road, then looked back at the sergeant. "I'm... being chased."

The constable in the back office overheard and joined them at the front desk.

The sergeant's nod and simultaneous flick of the eyes were a silent instruction for her to go outside and check.

She left the building and casually walked into the lane.

"Okay, who's chasing you?" asked the sergeant.

But Owen kept his eyes on the constable, standing in the lane outside, fearing she might be in danger. He had witnessed firsthand the brutality of these men, how they had killed the CEO at his home and pursued them relentlessly across packed roads, rough fields, and through the harbour and town.

His worst fears were confirmed when he witnessed blood and brain fragments explode from the back of the constable's head like grotesque fireworks as a bullet pierced her skull.

She collapsed instantly, and her legs twitched in their final, desperate movements as she succumbed to her fatal injuries.

66

"One corned beef roll," said Dimitri, smiling and holding up the wrapped food. As he passed it over the counter, he offered a friendly nod, the kind that suggested he took genuine delight in serving his customers.

Agnes, one of two police community support officers on the island, smiled as she accepted the warm roll. "What would I do without you?"

She left the sandwich shop and crossed the road where an empty bench facing a harbour view she could never grow sick of beckoned. The seagulls were airborne and circled overhead. She could feel their hungry eyes on her lunch roll, plotting an ambush. "You stay right where you are."

It was another quiet day on the tiny island. Apart from the noisy birdlife causing a public nuisance. Whenever on the job, she was more than just a PCSO. She was security, informant, judge, peacekeeper, traffic controller, and a general first aider, among many roles. Most days, though, she was little more than a pedestrian in a police uniform.

A blob of bird faeces landed on her peaked cap, splashing onto her roll. She paused with a mouthful of food, instantly put off her lunch. A cynical smile crept across her face as she binned the wrapping and threw the roll to the ground for the birds, where it was instantly the subject of a white-feathered melee.

"You win this round," she said softly under the din of the seagulls.

She resumed chewing and took off her cap to wipe the rim with a tissue. Her hair was up and looked blonder than brown in the midday sun.

When she put her cap back on, she noticed a boat had run ashore in the harbour, with a large catamaran also grounded in the shallows. What disturbed her though was the small crowd congregated around a bearded man with a large afro, dragging a young girl towards the water, leaving tracks where her heels raked the sand. He had one arm around her neck and a knife gripped in the other. The young girl tried to dig her fingers beneath his, attempting to scratch his arms.

Agnes withdrew her gun from the holster. The town wasn't quite what you would call crime central. Police work, if it could even be called that, wasn't exactly action and excitement. Banal and boring better described it. No wonder many of her peers had moved to the mainland seeking better career opportunities. She'd occasionally dealt with some antisocial behaviour, petty theft, and lost property on her patrol. This kind of altercation was new to her, and despite the intimidating scenario, she saw it as an opportunity to earn her stripes.

Nothing ever happens in St. Mary's, her colleague once told her.

Agnes jumped down from the promenade to the beach and ran across the sand until she reached the crowd, where she had to push through a scrum of bodies.

"Let her go!" Agnes shouted.

The man swung around, lifting the girl off her feet by her neck as he turned. The girl's face turned purple as he almost choked the life out of her.

The people gathered around them showing contempt and curiosity towards the man grew angry and anxious.

"Leave her alone!" shouted one bystander.

An older man yelled, "Pick on someone your own size!"

Agnes stepped forward and pointed her gun at the man. "Okay, everyone stand back, please! I'm a police community support officer. Sir, drop the knife!"

The crowd piped up again and closed the circle around the armed man.

Agnes looked at the girl. "What's your name?"

Her face was strained red. "Nova."

"Stay calm, Nova."

Agnes focussed on the knifeman. "Drop the weapon!"

Nova tried to free herself from the man's grip. She closed her teeth on the bare flesh of his forearm.

The man yelled and pulled his arm away, releasing her, then swung with a high sidearm chop.

Nova expertly dropped into the splits and ducked beneath his swing, rolled away, and sprang back to her feet. As soon as she stood, the man pulled her back at knifepoint with the tip pressing into her neck.

She went on screaming and trying to tear herself away from her attacker.

Agnes raised her palm, trying to calm Nova, worried she would get herself killed.

The sergeant's profile picture appeared in her bionic lenses. He requested urgent support back at the station on Garrison Lane. The constable was down; the station was under attack.

What was going on today?

Distractions were dangerous; she couldn't respond just yet. If she were to take a shot, she had to take it now, and it had to be precise. To take the man out and leave him immobile or, if necessary, deceased. She could not risk having him lash out in retaliation and causing any public member harm. Put the man down and save the day, she would be called a hero. Shoot and have the situation go haywire and she could be searching for a new line of work come Monday morning.

"Drop the knife, or I *will* shoot!" she said as she levelled the gun. Her finger tightened on the trigger, and she gave him three seconds to respond.

She inhaled deeply, the breaths calming her racing heart as her mind focussed on the crucial countdown.

Three…. The sight of the sharp knife made her resolve even firmer.

Two…. Her eyes never wavered from the target. Neither did her gun.

"Everyone stand back!" she yelled.

One…. The moment hung in the balance as she prepared to make her move.

67

Owen was thrust into one of two detention cells. The door was slammed shut with a metallic thud, and he heard the electronic locks engage. The room was devoid of any windows or bars and was essentially a sealed concrete cube. The only break in the grey monotony was the blue door with a small, reinforced-glass inspection window for eyes that could watch him at any moment without his knowledge. Below the window, a narrow pass-through slot for meals added to the isolation. The tiny cell reminded him too much of home—if he could call it that. It had the same cold, utilitarian feel as the underground complex where he'd spent many years of his life, buried in the labyrinth of dark tunnels long neglected by those in power. But here, the ceiling was lower than even the cramped dungeon he was used to. So low he could easily reach up and touch it if he stood on the single, hard bed tucked into the corner.

The sergeant's hand reached through the meal slot. "Here, take this."

Owen saw it was a macro key.

"I'll be back soon to let you out. Do not give this key to anyone except me, understand?"

Owen nodded.

The sergeant closed the meal hatch.

Owen had always harboured a deep mistrust of the police, an ingrained aversion to authority in general. So, when he first laid eyes on the sergeant, he was struck by how unimpressive the man appeared. The uniform seemed to hang off his skinny frame, as though it had been tailored for someone else. Owen couldn't help wondering if he had ever encountered anything more serious than the occasional car theft on this sleepy island. Was he truly equipped to handle a situation involving armed individuals? Owen doubted it. His demeanour suggested his experience might be more academic than practical, a product of a criminology degree rather than years spent on the gritty front lines of law enforcement.

Owen sat on the bed and used his Ventolin, still breathless from the chase.

A burst of gunfire outside the station made him swing his eyes back towards the door. Fearing the men had just killed the sergeant and were now about to scour every inch of the station until they found him, he waved the macro key near the lock. A fingerprint image appeared, so he pressed his finger against it.

Access Denied flashed on the screen.

His next instinct was to hide the nanochip, a vital piece of technology that couldn't fall into the wrong hands. As more gunshots rang out and panic bubbled beneath his calm exterior, he scanned the sparse room for a hiding place. He dropped to his knees and peered under the bed, but the bare concrete floor offered no concealment. He looked up at the box spring and considered tucking the chip into one of the folds, but quickly dismissed the idea. It was an easy place for someone to check if they were searching for something important.

He moved on, his eyes darting across the walls and floor, searching for any small cracks or crevices that could serve as a hiding spot. Even the ceiling, though low, he scrutinised for any gaps, but the cell was unforgivingly solid, leaving him no viable options.

The white toilet in the corner caught his attention. An idea sparked. Moving swiftly, he unravelled a line of toilet paper, the roll spinning in a blur as he pulled off enough to create a thick layer. He tore it from the roll and wrapped the nanochip carefully. The toilet basin was bone dry. He leaned over, feeling the cool ceramic against his fingers while he gently tucked the wrapped nanochip inside, snug against the rim where it would not be easily noticed. The hiding place wasn't perfect but was the best he could do in such a limited space.

The firing had ceased. Who had won the battle? What was happening outside?

If the sergeant was dead, it was only a matter of time before the men came for him. They didn't have a key to the cell, but that wouldn't stop them. They had other means. The meal slot in the steel door, small and unassuming, suddenly seemed like a gaping vulnerability. He could easily imagine the cold, lifeless barrels of their guns sliding through it, aiming directly at him. A hail of bullets could tear through it, turning the confined cell into a death trap. There would be no escape, nowhere to hide, just the sharp, hot pain of metal shredding flesh. Worse still, they might decide on a more final solution. A posted grenade clattering to the floor at his feet sent a shiver down his spine. It wouldn't just end him; it would obliterate everything in the room, including the nanochip he'd risked so much to protect. The device would be reduced to unrecognisable fragments, its secrets lost forever in a cloud of dust and debris.

Owen's mind raced, considering every possible scenario. He normally dealt with conflict by running. Running was his greatest asset, his only weapon. He knew the men outside were ruthless, their goal singular and clear. If the sergeant was truly gone, there would be nothing to hold them back. All he could do was prepare for the worst.

And then the worst happened.

The inspection window slid open, and a male face he didn't recognise appeared. "Give me the key!"

Owen stared at the man doubtfully.

"Come on, I'll let you out."

Owen held his head high and stayed put.

"You can trust me. I'm the deputy constable."

Owen shook his head. "I *don't* trust you."

The man flashed a badge, but Owen felt like telling him where he could stick it. And did. He flashed his middle finger. Fearing it had angered the man, that he was about to be shot, he pressed himself against the wall, out of the line of fire, but no less vulnerable to other kinds of artillery such as grenades or gas. He leaned forward and peered at the window before snatching his head back.

The man was gone.

Had he left to search for a spare key?

Owen's normally calm veneer dissipated with the sound of footsteps and movement at the inspection window.

"Owen?"

He stayed still.

"Owen, look, I'm with the sergeant."

He leaned around and saw the sergeant's face twisted into a bloody rictus. His hand was clamped over a gaping wound in his neck, trying in vain to stem the blood flow. His eyes were dull with exhaustion; it was clear he could barely hold on. To keep from collapsing, he had to rely heavily on the man who had introduced himself as the deputy constable, leaning on him for support as his strength ebbed away.

"It's over, Owen. Pass me the key. It's safe to come out. Your friend Nova is waiting outside."

Three black body bags lined the footpath, while an ambulance flashed its lights nearby. Paramedics hurriedly attended to an officer, his leg bleeding profusely. Many residents had gathered around the scene in small groups, sharing their views on what had happened in hushed voices.

When Owen came out of the police station, Nova ran up to him and threw her arms around his neck. She didn't want to let go.

He pulled back, his breath catching as he looked her in the eye. The bloodstains marring her hood and the dried flecks of blood on her face made him visibly concerned.

"You're bleeding!" said Owen.

Her lips parted to say something, but the words would not come out right away. She shook her head slowly. "It's not my blood."

She glanced at Agnes, now recounting what had happened at the beach to the deputy constable and how she'd taken down the man who had held Nova captive. Agnes caught Nova's eye and gave her a quick wink.

The sergeant received urgent treatment on his neck inside the ambulance before being taken to the hospital.

Nova looked back at Owen as he drew her into him. The sound of her voice vibrated against his chest when she spoke. "You still have the nanochip?"

Owen took out a thick wad of toilet paper from his pocket and held it up with a smile.

Within two hours, police reinforcements flooded the island to launch a full-scale investigation. Having reviewed the details of Owen and Nova's harrowing account, cross-referencing it with the critical data extracted from the nanochip, police officers urged immediate action.

A National Police Air Service helicopter carried out a swift reconnaissance of the factory. On the ground, heavily armed police officers moved in, breaching the factory's entrance in a coordinated assault and storming the interior.

Owen and Nova stayed at the station on Garrison Lane. They spent the night in a detention cell, waiting for news about Arthur. Agnes had volunteered to stay with them. She brought them food, made them tea, and helped the deputy run the front desk while the sergeant stayed in hospital, in critical but stable condition. She also spent the night at the station.

Early the following day, sitting on a varnished bench inside the station with their heads tilted against the wall, Owen and Nova were approached by Agnes.

She dropped into a crouch and removed her police cap. "They found the old marine factory. The police are there and running an investigation."

Nova reared up. "And Arthur? Is he safe?"

She shook her head. "I'm afraid I have bad news."

Nova's shoulders sagged.

"The basement was gutted; everything was destroyed. I'm truly sorry."

68

Assisted by his night-vision lenses, Arthur carefully descended the ladder. The dim light from above grew fainter as he moved deeper into the dark depths of the shaft. Reaching the bottom, he felt the ladder respond to his weight, an intricate mechanism clicking into action. With smooth, almost mechanical motion, the ladder extended fully into the passageway, its metal rungs glinting under the sparse illumination from a nearby blue lamp.

Arthur leaped from the ladder, landing lightly on his feet. The moment his weight left the ladder, it retracted silently into the ceiling. The process was fluid, almost imperceptible, as the ladder vanished from sight. He scanned the passageway with his night-vision lenses, revealing a tunnel.

"*You're close,*" said Owen through the visor. "*That's the blue light I told you about.*"

"I must be on the other side of that steel door," he said.

He followed the passageway, observing the rocky walls and the multiple ceiling pipes covered in beige putty and dripping water, conveying the rushed and reckless repairs of plumbers who had more important jobs to see to. *Amateurs.*

He turned with the bend and arrived on a platform at the top of a flight of metal stairs. He heard a faint ringing sound coming from the bottom.

"I hear something," he whispered, creeping down the steps on his toes.

At the bottom, he turned his head, ensuring the camera on his visor filmed the room in its entirety with a single panoramic sweep, including the two teleportals and all the technology.

A half-naked, dark-skinned man lurched towards him with a wrench gripped in his hands.

It caught Arthur off-guard. He blinked, and when his eyes opened again, his cheek was pressed against the cold floor. The visor lay six feet away. He watched as the man stamped and twisted his heel onto it as though extinguishing a small fire.

Throbbing pain, like a second heartbeat, drummed inside his head. A kaleidoscope of grey and black checks clouded his vision, and warm, sticky fluid ran down his neck. He touched his head, wincing at the pain, and checked his fingers, covered in blood.

He looked up at the man, running to a display of screens and consoles on the far wall.

Arthur heard dogs barking behind him.

He reached for the Beretta M9 on his waistbelt and slowly struggled to his feet.

The man hit a series of buttons, turned, and when he saw Arthur pointing the gun in his direction, he held up his hands. "What do you want?"

Arthur rubbed his head, still dizzy from the blow. "I think you know, Archon, Oberon, whatever the fuck your name is."

"You're too late, and I'm afraid I'm on a tight schedule."

"Escaping your crimes? Or escaping mortality?"

"Eternal life, or life in prison. It's not really a choice, is it."

"What about them five thousand people? They never had a choice. They were immortal and never even knew it."

"Where's your proof?"

He turned his head around the room. "I'm looking at it. I have footage on a nanochip that's on its way to the police as we speak. They'll be here soon, they will."

"They'll find nothing but toast."

Arthur's vision slipped out of focus. His impairment made him lose his balance and he toppled, dropping the gun in the process.

Oberon swivelled to the virtual keyboard and moved his fingers at rapid-fire speed before reaching beneath the console, where different coloured wires yarned into various ports. He ripped them out and the screens turned dark.

Except one.

He then removed his trousers, underwear, his boots, and socks, and tiptoed naked into the teleportal.

Ten seconds later, he was gone.

Arthur regained his sensory awareness and laboured over to the computers. His reflection on the blank screens was an oval smear with empty eye sockets and a gash for a mouth, as if looking at himself in a disturbed puddle of water.

The only active screen showed a self-destruct countdown timer. 26… 25… 24…

To deactivate it to save the quantum servers, his only shot at procuring evidence, he had to perform some swift electrical surgery. If he could reconnect the wires to the various ports and restore power, he could cancel the self-destruct option and allow the police to access the mainframe.

19... 18... 17... 16...

In a frantic flurry of movement, he rushed to connect the tangled mess of wires to their designated ports, manoeuvring the cables into place one by one with a soft click that signalled its secure placement. With a deep breath, he inserted the final wire into the remaining port. A rapid transformation occurred. The computers sprang into action with a dazzling display of sparkling lights. But it was too late.

4... 3... 2... 1....

Arthur shut his eyes tightly, running through the unsettling possibilities concerning the self-destruct feature he had failed to deactivate. Was it a simple short-circuiting of the quantum servers, a straightforward but devastating electrical failure? Or was it something far more insidious and catastrophic?

The thought of the quantum servers being reduced to fried components by a mere short-circuiting was already alarming. But the alternative, the idea of something more sinister at play, was far more worrying. What if the self-destruct mechanism was designed not just to destroy but to unleash a hidden threat, a calculated disaster engineered to cause maximum damage, erasing the very existence of the secret room. A suitcase nuke, for example. In which case, he hoped for a quick and painless death, but was prepared to accept whatever fate awaited him.

At first, nothing happened, hinting at a failed fail-safe or success in the form of a silent pulse of destruction.

And then he found out. A powerful explosion tore through the building like a gunshot amplified a thousand times. It came from above ground, inside the passageway.

More explosions followed in a staggered blast pattern.

Poomb.

Smoke and dust channelled into the room, blown by the downdraught within the passageway at the top of the stairs.

Poomb.

They grew nearer.

Poomb.

Through the swirling smoke and haze, Arthur's eyes caught sight of two teleportals positioned side by side. Their external bulbs flickered in unison, casting a rhythmic lightshow through the surrounding darkness.

He moved drunkenly towards them, clutching his bleeding scalp. He tore off his military jacket, cardigan, shirt, trousers. He pulled off his boots, socks, and hurriedly took down his underwear.

Poomb.

The stairwell just blew up, and he watched as it collapsed in a heap of metal. Shrapnel caught in a fireball blasted around the room.

Facing the teleportals, Arthur understood the gravity of his next decision. One portal promised to leave him immortal but brain-damaged, delivering him to the fourth floor of Teletron's headquarters, while the other would also grant him immortality but without the cognitive impairment, and would send him to some mysterious, exotic island.

He was disoriented, having collapsed when Oberon fled, and had not seen which portal he had used. With only seconds to decide, he had to act fast: left or right? The one on the right was closest to him and the computers controlling them. The one on the left was a bit further back, near the kennels, where the three dogs had silenced their barking into fearful whimpers as the room erupted. Given these dogs were likely part of Dr. Azad's ongoing trials, it made sense that the teleport they were using would be near them.

He stepped in front of the one to his right. His presence activated the glass door. He rushed in and sat on the chair. The door closed automatically.

Frantically pressing the buttons to make his departure, the view around him rapidly transformed. A blinding white light blinded his vision, and electrical pulses coursed through him, heightening his senses. Then came a disorienting detachment from his physical self, and a warm, soothing sound enveloped him as his soul was sucked towards the darkness.

69

Three months later

Someone knocked on the cabin door.

Nova opened it, expecting to find Owen juggling a cooler box full of seafood. That was her first mistake. Her second was not shutting it immediately upon seeing his deadly black eyes, as unnervingly familiar as they were menacing.

The Serbian brandished his knife as he stepped inside the cabin and closed the door.

She backed up fearfully, raising her hands in a futile display of surrender.

"Sit!" he said, expertly slicing the air with a fluid motion to intimidate her.

She reached behind her, groping for a chair, too afraid to look into his eyes but equally as afraid not to keep him in her sights. She dropped into the high-backed rattan armchair.

The Serbian pulled a chair out from beneath the table and mounted it like a horse, resting his forearms on the back.

She stared at the pink knuckles of ragged flesh on his right hand where Arthur had blown his fingers off inside the lift.

"Been long time."

It was freezing inside the cabin. Opening the door had let all the heat out. The floorboards were cold under her bare feet. She shook, seized not with cold but fear.

"What do you want from me?" she asked.

His reaction was as if she had uttered an obscenity, and his dark eyes magnified his frightening stare.

"I go blind one eye."

"Sorry to hear that, but it's not *my* fault."

He pulled out a handkerchief, licked one corner, and wiped it across his forehead, removing the tan foundation. The tattoo removal procedure had left him scarred, and what remained was a faint patch of pink skin spelling out *Clotho*.

The word brought it all back. *You can live forever.*

The kettle rose to the boil, summoning Nova with a high-pitched whistle that grew more intense.

"Tea?" she asked, as if he were a welcome guest, trying to buy herself time.

"No tea!"

She rose.

The Serbian rose. "Sit down!"

"I have to turn the gas off."

She bolted to the galley. He chased after her.

She switched off the kettle and swiftly turned with raised hands. Her pulse ticked up even more.

"I'm going to make some tea, then you can do whatever you have to do."

She turned her back on him, knowing it was a huge risk, not knowing if his knife was about to enter her back and split her spine. She took out two porcelain mugs from the cupboard and dropped a teabag in each. She glanced nervously over her shoulder while adding the hot water, scalding herself when she missed the mug. She stifled a scream as steaming water poured across the worktop and onto the floor. She grabbed a towel to mop up the spillage but furthered the mistake by knocking a glass candle stand over and smashing it.

She made a fulsome apology, fearing he was peeved and becoming impatient.

She added the coconut milk, stirred it through, clasped her fingers around his mug, and passed it to him.

They returned to the table, and Nova sat in the armchair.

He sat opposite her and sipped the tea noisily.

She couldn't tell if his gaze was fixed on her, as his pupils were obscured by the impenetrable black ink that swallowed any hint of emotion or intention, leaving her unable to discern what his next move might be.

What kind of small talk was any person supposed to make after looking into the eyes of evil and were now in the jaws of doom?

"How's the tea?"

"Shit!"

He picked up the knife, tapped the flat side of the blade in his palm, then drew an imaginary line across his throat.

An unsettling calm appeared on Nova's face. "Okay, fine, but before you kill me, I want to know something. Who is the Merchant? Someone in the government?"

Not one muscle in his face moved.

"If I'm going to die, I'd like to die with some context."

He gave no reaction.

She kept at him. "The same person who employed you?"

"Hired, not employed."

"So, who hired you to murder all those people, including my neighbour?"

He sipped his tea. "No more talk!"

"She was my friend. She was like a mother to me."

"I not care."

"How many people had to die?"

He shook his head. "Quiet!"

"How many lives did you take?"

"I tell you quiet!"

"And I asked how many lives you took?"

"Hundreds. We get kill list. Six months to kill all. *Operation Klotho*. Okay?"

"We?"

His face was blank and benign, and he looked put out by the question. "My team."

"Who hired you?"

"Stop talking!"

"Please. I want to know. I'll be dead in a minute, so you've got nothing to lose."

He sipped the tea. "Merchant, but you kill her."

Nova's face scrunched into a deep frown. "Her?"

"She get shot dead."

Nova paused, staring at the floor until realisation dawned. "The white-haired lady you were with when you abducted me? With the different coloured eyes?"

"She is retired MI5. Merchant was just code name."

"How did you frame the ATM?"

"Enough of questions!"

"Please."

He sighed. "Man is Theo, also MI5 before. He join ATM undercover, working with Merchant."

Owen came in through the door. The foul stench of fresh fish rose from his overall, which he flung on a hook. He'd just spent three days working on a trawler, and she couldn't decide whether his return right then was a good thing.

"Whose rowing boat is that out by the stern?" Owen asked. When he looked round and saw the Serbian, Nova gave him a stare and didn't have to say anything more.

"Sit!" said the Serbian, waving the knife.

Owen put up his hands and joined them at the table.

Nova tried to put together her next move. There would be no rationalising with this monster. He would believe he was innocent, his crimes excused by necessity. He would never feel guilt or remorse. She knew what he was capable of. She had witnessed the consequences of his knifework in Spider's tattoo parlour.

The Serbian had one more sip of his tea and rose slowly, holding the knife out.

Nova scooted backward and tensed herself for a fight to the death.

Owen almost fell off his chair in his desperate shift out of range from the knife.

The Serbian clutched his throat, gasping and gagging as his tongue swelled, blocking his airway. The knife slipped from his hand before he collapsed, and his head struck the floor with a heavy thud.

Nova knelt beside him and took his knife.

Writhing on the floor, the giant man's foot caught the table leg, causing his mug to teeter and fall. It cracked open upon landing, and porcelain shards bounced and broke into smaller pieces. The hot tea spilled across the floorboards and formed a steaming puddle around a small vial that lay on its side, its lid missing.

Owen glanced at Nova, his eyes wide with shock.

Nova picked up the empty vial, which she teased in front of his face. "A single drop of this little concoction will make you feel hungover. Two drops, semi-paralysed. Three, you're basically knocking on death's door. You've had most of it, so I guess that means goodnight!"

She stood and walked into Owen's arms, having stalled just long enough for the poison to take hold. She wondered how much of the poison had actually dissolved in the tea, and how much tea he had actually consumed.

Clearly not enough because the Serbian somehow found the strength to heave himself up with a determined resurgence.

Nova and Owen broke to opposite sides of the cabin.

Nova managed to dash up the stairs to the upper deck.

The Serbian pulled out a second smaller knife with a blade that cut on both sides. He threw it overarm at Owen, who had backed himself into a corner.

It struck him in the chest. Sucking air through his clenched teeth, clearly hurt and a good deal shaken, Owen slipped past the Serbian and headed to the upper deck, where the fierce winds had whipped the snow into drifts.

The Serbian advanced from the cabin, slipping on the icy steps, his black eyes narrow and fearsome. He weighed over a hundred kilos, much of it carried in his chest and shoulders, and Owen had to lean his head back to see his face when the ogre pounced, punching Owen on the nose. He wrapped his meaty hands around Owen's neck, shoving him over the guard rail. Owen could still breathe through his burst nose, but the Serbian's fingers crushed his windpipe.

Nova still held the Serbian's knife and screamed at him to stop, as if she might prevent murder with her voice alone.

The monster turned to look at her, unsteady on his feet, the poison still diluting in his blood, streaming along his veins. He slackened his grip on Owen's throat and put his other hand to his temple, closing his eyes momentarily.

Owen saw his chance and didn't hesitate. He delivered a sharp knee to the Serbian's groin and broke free.

Reaching for the anchor and detaching it from the drum, he swung it towards the Serbian's neck, gouging his flesh and drawing blood.

The monster writhed, his wet, drooling mouth crying out in agony. He threw his head back, roaring at the snow-filled sky as blood ran down his neck and throat.

Owen looped the anchor chain around the Serbian's waist and hooked one of the flukes onto a chain link.

With a short run-up, he charged into the man, sending him overboard. The chain spun furiously on its drum as the anchor plummeted to the bottom of the sea, dragging the Serbian to the cold, dark depths.

Owen hung over the guard rail with blood cascading from his nose and burst lip. "Eye for an eye!" he yelled.

Nova dashed into the wheelhouse, fired up the motor, and pushed the throttle forward. The Anna Belle manoeuvred out of Porthleven Harbour into the open sea, dragging the Serbian at the end of the anchor across the rutted seabed, ensuring he remained submerged.

As the boat cut through the blizzard, the snowflakes were driven with increasing force against the wheelhouse window, through which she saw Owen collapse. She eased the throttle back and switched off the motor, allowing the boat to drift.

Rushing to Owen's aid, she found a knife protruding from his chest. With considerable effort, she lifted him and guided him into the cabin, laying him gently on the bed. She gathered clean towels, a bucket of hot water, and the first-aid kit. She removed the knife with a steady pull. The blade measured five inches in length, but only the tip was bloody. His many layers of clothing and fishing overalls had prevented the knife from going any deeper.

With the knife removed, Owen bled some, not profusely, but enough to disable him if the wound was not stemmed. It was only an inch or so long, but it was almost as deep.

Once the wound had been cleaned, she squeezed antiseptic healing glue over it. "Do you think you need a hospital?"

He shook his head. "I think I'll be okay." He took Nova's hand. "Poison?"

"From the CEO's house. I was planning to use it on you the next time you annoyed me."

Owen let out a gentle laugh, but it caused him too much pain and his face scrunched.

That night, as Nova kept a close watch on Owen's wound and administered some pain relief, they discussed their plans to leave. They agreed to set off as soon as Owen's injury had healed sufficiently, and he felt strong enough to undertake the long journey.

70

Inside the wheelhouse, sitting at the controls with her feet on the dash panel, her arms folded, the wind rattling the windows and blasting snowflakes around the deck, Nova activated the web on her bionic lenses.

From the wheel of icons, she selected the news story she had archived a fortnight ago. It had warranted a long article on every primary news channel, eclipsing every other story. She paused, one paragraph into the article, shocked all over again. In the Micronesian Republic of Kiribati, a small island that had gained its independence from the UK in 1979, eight individuals had been found buried alive up to their necks on the shores of Bathing Lagoon, the island's most popular beach. Their names had been scrawled in the sand beside them. Among the victims were six senior officials from the British government, Miriam Payne included, and two high-ranking figures from Teletron:

the supreme commander of physics and engineering and the archon of biomedicine. No one had claimed responsibility for the incident. No blackmail, extortion, or ransom demands had been made. No anonymous calls or tip-offs. The buried men and women were discovered by an off-duty officer from the Kiribati Police Service, who had been walking her dog along the beach. A message in the sand read: *We single-handedly destroyed London City Teleport and killed them 5189 individuals. Arrest us and deport us back to the UK and we'll tell you why.*

In collaboration with the British authorities, Kiribati Police learned they had taken up illegal residency on the island using fake identification. They'd teleported out of the UK to escape their crimes and attain immortality in the process, achieved by passing through a faulty teleportal.

The aptly named *Eternal Eight* had just arrived back in the UK by boat, ready to face trial. Everything now hinged on the prosecution.

While the British prime minister and US president pleaded ignorant to the actions of their cabinet ministers, both were forced to resign, giving no press interviews, and putting the bare minimum on social media.

Twenty-four-hour coverage occurred as authorities began new enquiries and revisited abandoned enquiry lines. The radio and talk shows and mainstream media focussed their coverage on the *Eternal Eight*, accused of misdirecting blame, perverting the course of justice, and of course, for conspiring to conduct mass executions, known now as the *Final Solution*, in an attempt to hide a devastating technological blunder that had left people brain-damaged and immortal.

Astonished by the story all over again, Nova had read it without blinking, and she had to compensate by squeezing her eyes shut and blinking several times in a row, which shut down the lenses.

Staring absently out of the wheelhouse window, she spared a thought for Arthur. She longed to see him again. She missed him but would never tell him that. She had even made a list of reasons to reconnect with him, as if trying to justify it. To her surprise, the list was longer than expected.

One, to return the boat to its rightful owner.

Two, to congratulate him for bringing the government and Teletron to their knees and clearing the ATM's name.

Three, to reunite him with Bebop.

Four, to thank him for everything he'd done to get justice for her father and Mrs. Cooper and all the other families in the country without their loved ones looking for answers.

Five, to build on the friendship they'd once had in a nice part of the world.

Since learning of the incident in the Micronesian Republic of Kiribati and connecting the dots back to Arthur, she and Owen had drafted routes to the island. She was excited at the prospect of fulfilling her long-held dream of seeing the world, hoping to view it again as a benign place, and giving her a sixth reason to reunite with Arthur. She would have to be careful in the tropical heat and couldn't leave her white skin exposed for long. A minor concern in the grand scheme.

With her inheritance, the death insurance payout, and the proceeds from selling her cottage, they had installed solar cells on the Anna Belle, fulfilling Arthur's wish, giving her a seventh reason to make the long journey. The solar cells equipped the boat with a virtually limitless range, harnessing the power of the sun to continuously recharge the batteries. Owen's knife wound was the only barrier now to their departure.

Nova stepped out of the warmth of the wheelhouse into the cold flurry of snowflakes. Those in the country with any sense would have taken refuge and fired up their heaters, but Nova wanted to look back at the coast of England. Her eyes remained fixed on the snowy horizon. She ran her hand over her bare head, thinking she would probably never be back. She hungered to see her father again, to hold him close, and longed to hear his soothing voice. Whenever she did think of him or conjured up images of her cottage, she grew terribly homesick. No matter how many years passed, she would always carry the lost, young girl within her. She found comfort and reassurance in knowing her father's strength lived on inside her, assuring her everything would be all right.

BALLOON: ALTITUDE

An event that could change the course of human history—and possibly end it.

Fable Sky, the world's largest zero-pressure helium balloon, is set to embark on its inaugural flight into the stratosphere. The ambitious space tourism project has been years in the making, requiring detailed planning, the assembly of a highly trained crew, and a small fortune to bring it to fruition.

As the groundbreaking journey into the uncharted stratosphere reaches its climax at 138,000 feet, disaster strikes, shattering the fragile peace below. Alone, adrift, and cut off from communication with flight control, the crew of five faces a perilous race against time, where their survival hangs in the balance.

In this high-stakes adventure, the crew, led by Will, the project leader and captain, must push the limits of their ingenuity, resilience, and teamwork to endure the harsh stratospheric environment and looming catastrophe that awaits them on the ground. Will they reach safety before their oxygen supplies run out?

BALLOON will leave you breathless with its breakneck action and unforgettable characters, set against the backdrop of a world forever changed.

BALLOON: SOLITUDE

Hope begins in the dark. But what if the dark holds a horrifying reality no one is prepared to face?

In the aftermath of a cataclysm that has reshaped society forever, the surviving crew members find themselves cut off from the outside world. Faced with a grim choice — sitting tight and waiting for a rescue that may never come or forging their own path — they look to Will, their balloon captain, and Ariane, the pragmatic NASA research pilot, to lead them forward.

Driven by a shared determination to survive, the crew encounters multiple obstacles and ruthless marauders in their desperate search for a rescue and vital resources. Each member's unique skills and diverse backgrounds prove invaluable and become their greatest assets in this harsh new reality.

Amid escalating tensions, they grapple with the limits of human endurance and the ethical dilemmas that test their humanity. As alliances are strained and trust is questioned, they confront the haunting question: are the greatest threats lurking beyond their shelter, or do dangers lie much closer to home, buried beneath the rubble of their shattered world?

BALLOON unveils a world beyond imagination. Get ready for a journey where crises collide, and the stakes reach new heights.

BALLOON: LATITUDE

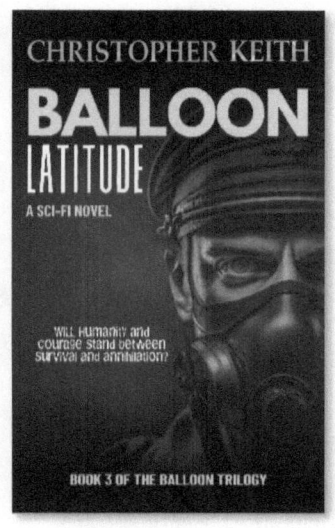

In this third and final instalment, will humanity and courage stand between survival and annihilation?

As rations dwindle and graves are hastily dug, time has run out for the remaining crew. Traumatised by recent events but still alive, they must venture out into the unforgiving environment in one last desperate push to survive.

As they journey across the bleak and hostile landscape, they encounter natural phenomena and the constant threat of dwindling supplies. A land of promise awaits, but first impossible decisions must be made, and the crew must be prepared to pay the ultimate price.

At the critical moment, as the line between triumph and catastrophe blurs and the stakes have never been higher, Will must rely on instinct, devise innovative solutions to their dire predicament, and chart their course in a desperate bid for survival as he once again finds himself on a dangerous high-altitude mission. Will they find the freedom they seek? Or will the shadows of deceit consume them before they can soar to safety?

The genre-bending BALLOON trilogy series concludes with high altitudes, high hopes, and high-octane action adventure.

LIFELINE

A revolutionary breakthrough in human biophysics is poised to redefine the field of medicine.

Dr. Bryan Morgan, a brilliant medic and award-winning clinical psychologist, is struggling with unemployment amid marital and financial strain. That is until the Extended Life Foundation (ELF), a visionary institute at the forefront of scientific innovation, comes knocking on his door.

Using state-of-the-art laboratories, cutting-edge research, and healthcare delivery that prompts both awe and ethical debate, ELF invites Bryan to join the top-secret institute. It's a dream job, but life is never that straightforward, and even the simplest discoveries can have deadly repercussions.

Doubts soon emerge about the consequences of tampering with the natural order. What sacrifices are made in the pursuit of extended life? Is immortality a gift or a curse? And when the lines between scientific progress and ethical obligation blur, who ultimately holds the power to decide?

Ahead lies a frightening and dangerous mission into the unknown, putting Bryan's life, and his sanity, at risk, as the choices he makes will have profound implications. Trapped in a loop of increasing danger, he'll go to any lengths to protect his family and expose the truth before it's too late.

If you're a fan of fast-paced tech-thrillers with mind-blowing medical science, unexpected twists, and a desperate fight for survival, you'll love this science fiction thrill ride.

ACKNOWLEDGEMENT

I first wrote *Clotho* in 2006. It was around one hundred and fifty pages long, with minimal character depth, few subplots, and severely lacking substance. Fast-forward to 2019, and the story has finally come to fruition, thanks to the great support and dedication of professionals and those close to me.

Many have helped with the construction of Clotho, but none more so than my editors, Camilla Singh and Tom Bazin, who provided valuable insight throughout the telling of this story. They have this wonderful knack of seeing the bigger picture as well as eliminating the discrepancies that often go unnoticed.

My extended gratitude to the wordsmith and grammar wizard, Craig Titchener, for his thorough reviews and expert notes. I must also thank all those who volunteered to read and critique Clotho in its draft stages: Edmund Wadge, Judith Thomas-Meulman, Maja Draganic, my father Hugh, and my sister Kate.

I would also like to thank tech expert Mer Roberts, who kindly assisted me with the complex IT terminology and research.

I will be forever grateful.

Join the community on
Facebook or subscribe on the
website for the latest news

@christopherkeithauthor
www.christopherkeithauthor.com